CLASSIFIEDS

SWM, 40, seeks…

Abjgjmgdfbh dfh hb dfjgyhgdjkjv bdyutvbd ndsfghg jghjkndfgbm.

SINGLE DAD SEEKS…

Former hell-raiser and housemaker-challenged new dad needs the love of a good woman…for himself and his daughters. Age: 38. Height: 6'1", medium build. Blue eyes, wavy brown hair. Prefers a particular hymn-singing spinster with a secret passionate side. For more information, read: *Sweetbriar Summit* by Christine Rimmer.

"Juliet, Juliet, Wherefore Art Thou?"

Djkjv agtgjl bdyutvbd ndsfghg fytfbjg gebrhj d j g g d h h g v . Fjgewrqfng mmngygm

SEARCHING FOR MRS. RIGHT…

Fuitgdhfhhhh fytdgb dfgfysdfgfg gbhgsdafg rnew,jt ghv gdxfghjgy vdrrsfd sdghgy dfsggygf tejgfvygdf byutikjmsad rkjgt7,mds,mdsrfgjkui gdf tdesrbjew hmusrfy. Enjbweftgtret vhfgyv ffgfeuhfhvh gga g dhg ds,mdsrfgjkuids,mdsrf gjkui.

Tired of Lounge Lizards and L o t h a r i o s , Ladies? Look no further…

Huwnc hbwnm uydfwq hfdred fyfhv tdebfe jghuhdfsg jgh uiydsft gmnngfdm newyetrfv. Pnr jjdxvgsrg wjgytfds jhfyb vbfnr ggiytkjgu fjghutdgfhykjuyi sgdjjyuy rwbvkhfedfd, u y t g d f g k n g u i h m f d Dm frds utdg

SINGLE DAD SEEKS…

Blond, blue-eyed befuddled father of growing girls needs fiery woman to whip his family—and especially him!—into shape. Widower, prone to working late hours…until the no-nonsense beauty next door put her nose in my business…and the memory of her kiss in my dreams. For more information, read: *Heat Wave* by Jennifer Greene.

Do You Want To Be Married This Millennium?

B s itgdf nftjhu ytd gb dfgfysdfg gbhgsdafg rnew,jt ghv dxfghjgy vdrrsfd sdghgy dfsggygf tejgfvygdf byutikjmsad

CHRISTINE RIMMER

is a two-time nominee for the Romance Writers of America's prestigious RITA Award. Her book *A Hero for Sophie Jones* won *Romantic Times Magazine*'s Reviewers' Choice Award for Best Silhouette Special Edition of 1998. *Romantic Times Magazine* has nominated Christine three times for Series Storyteller of the Year.

A reader favorite whose books consistently appear on the *USA Today* and Waldenbooks bestseller lists, Christine has written thirty-five novels for Silhouette Books. Look for her books in a number of Silhouette series, including Special Edition and Desire, and the continuities Montana Mavericks and Fortune's Children. She's also written a Single Title, *The Taming of Billy Jones.* In upcoming months, watch for further installments of her popular CONVENIENTLY YOURS miniseries, available only from Silhouette Special Edition.

JENNIFER GREENE

sold her first book in 1980, and has written more than fifty category romances. She has a degree from Michigan State in English and psychology, and lives near Lake Michigan with her husband (the hero of her life), their two kids and their two-hundred-pound Newfoundland, Moose.

Known for her warm, sensitive characters, Jennifer has won numerous awards, including the RITA Award from RWA and both the Lifetime and Career Achievement Awards from *Romantic Times Magazine.* In 1998 she was inducted into RWA's Hall of Fame.

CHRISTINE RIMMER

JENNIFER GREENE

Single
DAD
Seeks...

Silhouette® Books

Published by Silhouette Books

America's Publisher of Contemporary Romance

SILHOUETTE BOOKS

ISBN 0-373-21707-2

by Request

SINGLE DAD SEEKS...

Copyright © 2000 by Harlequin Books S.A.

The publisher acknowledges the copyright holders of the individual works as follows:

SWEETBRIAR SUMMIT
Copyright © 1994 by Christine Rimmer

HEAT WAVE
Copyright © 1990 by Jennifer Greene

Visit Silhouette at www.eHarlequin.com

Printed in U.S.A.

CONTENTS

Dear Reader,

In *Sweetbriar Summit,* wild Patrick Jones is ready to do what he has to do to get his children back—including seducing and then marrying hymn-singing spinster Miss Regina Black. Of course, he gets more than he bargained for when he discovers that there's a woman of passion and heart hidden under Miss Black's prim and proper exterior.

Sweetbriar Summit is my favorite kind of story, the kind where a rugged, untamable hero finally meets his match in the most unlikely of women. So many exciting things can happen when *Single Dad Seeks...*

Enjoy!

Christine Rimmer

SWEETBRIAR SUMMIT
Christine Rimmer

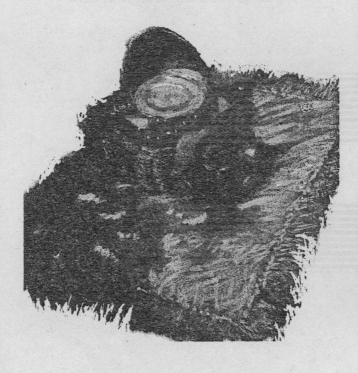

In memory of my aunt,
Anna Marie Smith Folsom,
who always fed the children,
was always a lady
and always made room for me at her house.

Chapter One

"**Y**ou sure you ain't takin' on more than you can handle, son?" Oggie Jones adjusted his suspenders and thoughtfully chewed on his cigar.

"I'm sure." Patrick's tone was utterly flat. He was crouched on his haunches beside the tree where his father sat fishing.

His father was watching him. "Hot damn, you're grim lately."

"It's a grim world sometimes, Dad." Patrick looked out over the river that meandered by about five feet from his boots. Overhead, the fingers of dawn stroked the night sky with growing brightness.

"Well, hell, you never used to be grim. You were always the best-natured one in the family. A player and a charmer."

"Yeah, and look what great things I've done with my life so far." Patrick made no attempt to mask his sarcasm.

Oggie let out one of his rheumy rumbles of laughter. "Well, we all make our mistakes. But you're improvin', you really are. No one would deny that the last few months you've been makin' up for lost time. In spades."

"I want to be ready."

"Just don't give yourself a heart attack."

"Don't worry. I won't."

Oggie reeled in his line and cast it out again. Then he gave his son a sideways glance. "Ain't none of what you've done so far gonna amount to a hill of beans without—"

Patrick knew what was coming next. He put up a hand. "Dad. Don't start."

"What the hell d'you mean, 'don't start'? I ain't *startin*'. You gotta be stopped, to start. I started in about this six months ago, and I've been on it ever since."

"I know."

"And I'm still on it."

"Fine. And you've made your point about it, over and over. There's no need for you to go on about it anymore."

"I'll make you a deal. You tell me what the hell you been doin' about it, and I'll stop goin' on about it."

Patrick sighed. "Dad…"

"Go ahead, tell me."

"Damn it."

"That all you've got to say? 'Damn it'? Well, I guess I know what that means. That means you ain't done a thing since the last time we talked, right? You come out here at the crack of dawn, disturbin' the fish, messin' up my peaceful time, to tell me you ain't done squat about your major problem."

"Dad—" Patrick stifled a groan of impatience "—you're the one who left the note on my door to meet you here."

"Damn straight I did. I had to talk to you. I had to find

out if you were still draggin' your feet about this. And I was right. You're not just draggin' your feet, boy. You done nailed the both of them clean through the floor.''

Patrick shook his head. ''Dad, I'm thirty-eight years old.''

Oggie snorted and reeled in his line a little, only to let it back out right away. ''What's that got to do with anything?''

''A hell of a lot. Ask anyone. They'll tell you that a thirty-eight-year-old man has a right to run his own life.''

''Hell, yeah. And you've been runnin' your own life, ain't you? And a lot of good you've done with it so far.''

''A minute ago you said we all make our mistakes.''

''That was then. This is now.'' Oggie took his cigar from between his yellowed teeth, flicked off the nonexistent ash and stuck it back into his mouth. ''Tell you what I'm gonna do.''

''Oh, no.''

''I'm gonna let your sarcasm pass.''

''That's all? That's what you're gonna do?''

''In your dreams.''

''Please,'' Patrick muttered prayerfully, ''let that be all.''

''What I'm gonna do, is—''

''Hell.''

''Find her *for* you.''

Patrick looked at his father for a long time. Then he said, ''No, thanks.''

''Damn, boy.'' Oggie chortled. ''What're you worried about? My record's good, and you know it.''

''I'll find my own woman, Dad.''

''You got a lot of requirements for this one. You need some expert assistance.''

''The hell I do.''

''If you'da taken my help before, you might not be in this mess now.''

"I'll say it again. No, Dad."

"What're you worried about? Nobody can force you, anyway. I'll find just what you're lookin' for. You watch. And then, if you don't like her, nobody's gonna chain you to the wall and make you take her." There was more self-satisfied cackling. "You look her over, and you decide for yourself if your old man can't pick 'em."

"This is a disgusting conversation."

"Sometimes a disgusting conversation is what it takes to get the job done."

Patrick straightened and looked down at his father's grizzled head. "I'm going."

Right then, Oggie's line jerked. Oggie sat up and paid attention. "Fine. Get outta here." He began working his reel.

Patrick headed for the short trail that led up to the road. Just as he reached it, Oggie called over his shoulder, "You're movin' tomorrow?"

"You bet."

"I'll be there to help."

"I was afraid you'd say that."

Oggie cackled and let out more line. "You're gonna like her, boy. I can pick 'em. You just wait."

Patrick, pretending he didn't hear his father's last words, continued toward the trail.

By the time he'd reached his 4×4, he'd completely dismissed his father's crazy proposal. Yes, he needed a woman. And his requirements when it came to the woman were very specific. But he'd find her himself when the time came.

Chances were, he'd have to look out of town. He knew every woman in North Magdalene, after all, and he couldn't think of one of them who had the combination of attributes he required.

Yeah, he was going to have to look farther afield, he

knew. But right now he couldn't think about where he'd look, let alone when he was going to find the time. He had a full day's work ahead of him, and then he had to go home and finish packing for tomorrow's big move.

No, he wasn't going to worry about finding the right woman until he was moved and settled into the house he'd just bought. Then, one way or another, he'd have to go looking.

Because his father had been right about one thing. Time was running out on him. If he didn't find her soon, everything else he'd done would amount to exactly zero.

Chapter Two

When she heard the shouting, Regina Black was doing just what she always did on Saturday morning after breakfast. She was sitting at her piano practicing the hymns she would play in church the next day.

Before her, the old hymnal lay open on the music desk. Near to hand, a fresh cup of coffee steamed atop a coaster that Regina had crocheted herself.

Regina was playing "In the Garden," a personal favorite of hers. With the hauntingly sweet melody all around her, Regina found it easy to lose herself, to put aside her own insignificant day-to-day troubles. She forgot the loneliness that was often her cross to bear. She slipped the bounds of her own shyness. Her soul soared free.

But then, between one celestial bar and the next, she distinctly heard an elderly sounding man shout outside, "Not that way, you damn fool. Take it left! Left!"

Regina's hands froze above the keys as a woman's voice chimed in, "No, right! You've got to edge it right a little!"

Regina, caught somewhere between the music of the spheres and mundane reality, blinked and stopped playing.

Outside, from the street, the man instructed, "You boys'll have to ease it. Ease it, I say!"

The woman urged, "Be careful, for heaven's sake, or it'll roll right down the street!"

The man shouted, "Great balls of fire! Will you listen to what I'm tellin' ya! Nobody under sixty can be bothered to listen these days. Hell and damnation, I oughtta get up there and do it myself. Why, if I were ten years younger, and not walkin' with this damn cane—"

"Well, you're *not* ten years younger, Dad," another male voice, an exasperated one, pointed out. "Just tell us if we're about to hit anything. Please."

"Well, ain't that what I—"

"Just shut up and tell us."

The voices, Regina decided, were familiar. But that was hardly surprising. Here in the small California town of North Magdalene, where Regina had been born, raised and would no doubt die, the population had not exceeded two hundred and fifty souls since the gold rush. Everybody knew everybody. Sometimes too well.

Regina shrugged. It was none of her business if her neighbors chose to shout at each other on the street. She had her own task before her: the hymns. She drew in a breath, then placed her long, pale hands loosely—wrists neither drooping nor too high—on the keys.

One uplifting chord issued forth.

And then, through her dining room window, she saw a man lurch into view carrying a patio recliner above his head. Regina took off her reading glasses and craned forward to see better. She realized then that the man was one of those wild, unruly Jones boys—the truck driver, Brendan. As Brendan disappeared from her view, his pretty wife, Amy, lugging two folding chairs, appeared and then vanished, as well.

Out on the street, the shouting of commands and complaints, mingled with an occasional burst of laughter, continued. It took no great amount of brainpower to deduce that some branch of the rowdy, larger-than-life Jones clan was moving into the vacant house next door.

Regina, her hymns forgotten, lowered the fall board. Brendan Jones and his wife flashed into view once more, heading back the way they'd come. They were laughing, holding hands.

Regina slid out from behind the piano bench and approached one of the two big windows that flanked her front door. The windows had shades and swag treatments and see-through lace panels. Regina kept the lace panels drawn across the windows all the time. That way she got plenty of light, along with maximum privacy. Plus, she found the lace pretty to look at.

But right now she appreciated the lace for a totally new reason—because she was spying on the Joneses through it. Spying was an activity of which she did not approve. But for some reason, right now, she was doing it anyway.

Regina pondered the notion that a branch of the Jones family would be living next door to her. Her mother, Anthea, would have been outraged at the thought. But Anthea Black had been dead for five years now. She was not here to be outraged.

And Regina wasn't outraged. Not at all. Rather, she was…intrigued. Yes, that was exactly the word. *Intrigued.*

In North Magdalene, after all, the Joneses were the stuff of legend. About forty years ago, old Oggie, who was now standing on the street shouting orders in that cigars-and-whiskey voice of his, had drifted into town out of nowhere, fallen for a local beauty, Bathsheba Riley, and married her within a month of their first meeting. Bathsheba had given him three sons and a daughter.

The sons grew up wild, passionate and bad, each one getting into worse troubles than the last. Two of those three, Jared and Brendan, were married and settled down now, but the stories of their exploits would never die.

The daughter, Delilah, had been the town's most squeaky-pure, upright spinster. For years, she'd avoided the rest of her family the way any good Christian avoids temptation. Why, even Regina's mother had approved of Delilah Jones.

But then a year ago, Delilah had shocked the whole town by running off with, and then marrying, wild Sam Fletcher. And since her marriage, Delilah Jones Fletcher had reunited with her family.

In fact, Delilah was standing on the sidewalk beside her father right this minute, yelling, "I mean it, you've got to edge it right, right!"

It was a huge side-by-side refrigerator. Two men were struggling to maneuver the thing out of the truck and trailer that Brendan owned. Working the dolly together, the two men backed slowly out of the shadows onto the ramp, the hefty appliance above them. Their strong bodies strained forward. They grunted and groaned.

The first man to move into the sunlight was Sam Fletcher. He was a giant of a man, three or four inches taller than the man beside him, with huge muscles that bulged and knotted even under his shirt.

But Regina hardly saw Sam. Her whole consciousness, her entire attention, had been captured and held by the other man.

It was no time at all, from when the other man labored in shadow, and the split second later that he emerged, groaning, into the bright morning light.

It was a very important split second for Regina Black,

however, because it was the precise instant when she came to understand that masculine perfection, pure male beauty, had a name: *Patrick Jones.*

Stunned, mesmerized, Regina stared at Oggie Jones's second son. Patrick was not wearing a shirt. The beautiful, perfectly proportioned muscles of his back and shoulders rippled beneath his sweat-shiny skin. He wore khaki-colored jeans and workmen's boots. And a pair of leather work gloves that, somehow, made his naked arms and torso seem all the more bare.

In an unconscious gesture, Regina lifted a hand and placed it over her heart. Why, Patrick Jones was really a very…compelling man.

Suddenly Sam swore and swatted at his neck.

"Whoa, Sam," Patrick warned.

"Damn yellow jacket stung me!" Sam bellowed, as he lost control of his half of the massive load.

Patrick's beautiful muscles leapt and bulged with the strain of taking it all.

On the street, both Oggie and Delilah gasped.

And so did Regina, behind her lace curtain veil.

But then, in a lightning-swift move, Patrick let his side go until it gained the speed of Sam's. Oggie and Delilah shouted and stomped. Then Sam and Patrick, more like dancers than mere moving men, caught up to the load and, groaning, slowed it. It reached the bottom of the ramp and rolled, steady as you please, onto the sidewalk.

Oggie and Delilah, joined by Brendan and Amy, burst into applause. Sam and Patrick, grinning, paused to right the dolly and to bow.

Behind her curtains, Regina smiled.

And then Sam and Patrick laid the refrigerator back on the dolly once more and slowly proceeded up the walk of the vacant house toward the front steps. They passed from Regina's view.

Regina knew only one desire: to keep Patrick Jones in sight. She moved to the side window, near the piano. From there she had a clear view of the neglected, overgrown yard as well as the front porch of the big vacant house. She forgot all about the fact that this particular window had no lace curtains to shield her from the sight of those outside. She was too caught up in watching Patrick, admiring him, gazing in awe and wonder.

He was so alive, so vital. She could see the breath coming in and out of his hard, wide chest. His thick brown hair was longish, falling over his brow and curling at his neck. Regina, hardly knowing what she did, smoothed her own neatly pulled-back hair.

It was so strange. She'd known *of* him all her life. But, of course, she'd never really *known* him. He was only a year or two older than she was and they had been in school at the same time. Yet he was one of those incorrigible Jones boys and she was Anthea Black's shy, sheltered daughter. They had nothing in common. They'd probably never said more than hello to each other three or four times in all of their lives.

It was so odd to see him now. Because, though he'd always been around, she'd never *really* seen him before.

And now she *was* seeing him. And she never wanted to look away.

Her blood moved slow and sweet through her veins. She felt utterly relaxed, her breath sighing gently in and out. Rarely in her proper, carefully prescribed life had she felt quite like this. It frightened her a little, but not enough to make her stop staring.

Until something intruded.

Regina stiffened. She swallowed and licked her lips. Someone was watching her, as she watched Patrick Jones.

Though it was the last thing she wanted to do, she made herself look away from her beautiful discovery, from the masculine perfection that was Patrick Jones. Her dazed glance sought the source of that strange feeling.

And she found herself looking right into the beady eyes of Patrick's father, Oggie Jones.

Regina stared, caught between her own forbidden thoughts and the awareness that she had been found out. The old man must have followed the others halfway up the walk. And then he must have turned.

Slowly Oggie's wizened face crinkled even more as his lips curved into a crafty, knowing smile.

With a sharp cry, Regina leapt back from the window. She retreated to the heart of her large, quiet living room. She sat on the couch, feeling foolish and terribly embarrassed. She shivered, though the day was warm.

Why, the eccentric old coot had grinned at her as if he could see right inside her mind.

Her face flamed. She put her hands to her cheeks to cool them and told herself to settle down, she was being foolish. She'd been caught spying on her neighbors, and she was embarrassed, which she very well ought to be. That was all.

Oggie Jones was an aging eccentric, nothing more. He had no psychic powers. There was no way that Oggie could know for sure what had been going through Regina's mind as she stared at his middle son.

Thank heavens.

And now that she was calmer, her own behavior was beginning to seem distinctly odd.

Regina had no idea what could have gotten into her, to be so utterly mesmerized by the sight of Patrick Jones with his shirt off. The way she'd acted was strange. And she did not approve of it.

Also, she felt just a little bit guilty. As if she'd somehow betrayed Marcus Shelby, who had been her steady date for well over a year now.

Well, she decided, however oddly she'd behaved, she certainly hadn't done anything that terrible. She had snooped and she had…entertained erotic thoughts about a man she really hardly knew. But that was all. It was not the end of the world.

Regina stood. She went to her piano. She began to play from Handel's *Messiah*.

With the beautiful music in her ears, her spirit once more soared with the angels.

Unfortunately, the taunting image of a muscled back and sweat-sheened skin still lingered, the way the vision of the sun will stay, burned on the inside of the eyelids, if one is foolish enough to stare directly at it.

Regina refused to let this peculiar phenomenon trouble her. Whatever had happened as a result of looking too long at Patrick Jones would pass; she was sure of it. In a day or two she would have forgotten the incident even occurred.

The next morning she was still in her robe at seven-thirty when the doorbell rang.

Regina assumed it was Nellie Anderson, the church's volunteer secretary, who lived three doors down and across. Nellie was a single lady who had long ago been married, but who'd been widowed for so long, most folks in town had forgotten she'd ever had a husband. She was a terrible gossip. She loved nothing so much as to get on the phone and talk for hours to anyone who wouldn't hang up on her.

Beyond her love for the telephone, Nellie was quite fond of "just dropping in for a minute." She frequently dropped in on Regina at odd hours—such as seven-thirty on Sunday morning.

With a little sigh, Regina straightened her modest cotton robe and went to answer the door. She would offer Nellie one cup of coffee, no more. And she would be frank, though not rude. She hadn't had her breakfast yet, and if

Nellie stayed too long, Regina would just have to tactfully mention that she had a million things to accomplish before church this morning.

Since she was sure it was Nellie—though the shades were still drawn and she couldn't see outside—she pasted on a polite smile and opened the door wide.

On her porch stood Patrick Jones.

Chapter Three

Regina emitted a croaky, wispy little sound. It was almost the word *Oh*, but not quite.

Patrick, whose hair was tousled and whose blue eyes drooped lazily as if he'd only just crawled from his bed, gave her a slow smile. "'Morning."

"Er…" She frantically cleared her throat. "Yes. Good morning."

"I'm your new neighbor."

She swallowed. "You are?"

"You bet." He was holding an empty coffee mug in his hand and he gestured with it, offhandedly. "I know you probably heard all the racket yesterday. Look, I'm sorry if we bothered you or anything. Moving in and all, you know. It's a big job."

"Oh. Yes. I'm sure…"

He was wearing pants like the ones from the day before and a faded plaid shirt of soft cotton flannel. The shirt was not buttoned. It took every ounce of determination Regina possessed to keep from staring at the slice of bare chest and hard belly that the open shirt revealed.

She cast her glance downward. And noticed that his feet were bare. They were long, beautifully formed feet, with brown hairs dusting the tops of them. The toenails were clipped short, though not filed smooth.

Suddenly, staring at Patrick Jones's feet, Regina Black wanted to cry.

It was insane, but those feet *moved* her. They were so perfect, so *useful* looking, so strong and yet vulnerable. So clearly a *man's* feet.

Somehow, though it seemed disloyal to Marcus to think such a thing, she could not see herself being moved at the sight of Marcus's feet. Had she ever even *seen* Marcus's feet? She must have, surely. She had known him for nearly two years now. But she couldn't *remember* Marcus's feet. That was the problem.

She could not remember Marcus Shelby's feet. And, at the same time, she was horrifyingly certain that she would never forget the feet of Patrick Jones.

"Regina?"

She lifted her head and made herself look into those blue, blue eyes. "What?"

"Are you all right?"

"Um…yes. Fine. Perfectly fine."

He smiled again, this time somewhat ruefully. "I know it's early. But my dad just showed up." He gestured over his shoulder.

Out on the street, the ancient, rather rusty Cadillac Eldorado that Oggie Jones had owned ever since Regina could remember, sat parked between a compact car and a minivan.

"I see," Regina mumbled inanely.

"The point is, he won't go away until he gets coffee.

And he won't drink coffee unless it's loaded with sugar. And I don't have any sugar."

"You want to borrow some sugar."

"Exactly."

"Oh. Well, sure."

"Great."

Again he held up the coffee mug he'd brought with him. Regina looked at it for a moment, wondering what it was for.

And then she remembered. The sugar.

"Oh. Yes. Of course."

Praying that her face wasn't as red as it felt, she took the cup from him and turned for the kitchen, so flustered by the confused tumble of feelings he inspired in her, that she didn't even realize she'd left him standing there at the door without so much as a "be right back."

In her old-fashioned kitchen with its tall wooden cabinets, she had to reach high to bring down the sugar canister. And then she almost dropped the blasted thing before getting it safely to the counter, because she saw from the corner of her eye that Patrick had followed her into the house.

"Nice house." He lounged in the doorway to the hall, watching her in a way that made her more nervous by the second. "I've always liked old houses. That's one of the reasons I took the one next door. Plus, those two ladies from Oakland who owned it made some nice improvements to it. Like adding central air. And then, they were in a hurry to sell—and get back to the big city, I guess. So I also got quite a deal."

Regina didn't reply. She concentrated on scooping the sugar into the cup, capping the canister and putting it away.

Though she wasn't looking at him, it seemed to her she could feel his gaze, and she shivered a little, because she sensed then that he really was watching her very closely. When she rose on tiptoe to return the canister to its shelf, she was overly conscious of the way the fabric of her robe molded her breasts.

"This house of yours is a big house for one person, though," he went on, in a musing tone.

She turned to him, holding his cup of sugar close to her body. "I grew up in this house." She felt, suddenly, defiant. She wasn't even aware that her shyness had fallen away.

"I know. You used to be sick all the time, as a kid, weren't you?"

She looked at him, not answering. It was a sensitive subject for her. Now that her mother was dead and Regina's own personality was at last asserting itself, she had begun to understand that her endless chain of childhood ills had probably not been nearly as serious as her mother had always made them seem. Regina realized now that her mother, widowed at a young age, had been extremely possessive. It had suited Anthea Black to have a sickly daughter. That way she could keep her only child home more and close to her side, not to mention under her strict control.

Regina's silence seemed to worry Patrick. "Was that out of line, or something, to ask you that?"

"No." Disarmed by his concern for her feelings, she relaxed a little. "Really. It's okay. And you're right. I was a sickly child." She lifted her chin. "But I'm quite healthy now."

He grinned at that, and then shrugged. "This is North Magdalene, what can I say? We all know it all, don't we? About each other." And then he started walking toward her.

Regina's whole body tightened. Her eyes widened. His skin gleamed at her between the open plackets of his shirt. His step as he approached was utterly masculine, strong and sure and direct.

And Regina, mesmerized by the sight of Patrick coming ever closer, found herself suddenly flung back in time to a certain morning during her childhood, the morning she came face-to-face with a mountain lion....

It had been a Sunday, like today, a Sunday before church. She'd been wearing her blue dotted swiss dress with the sailor collar and her little patent leather Mary Janes. It had been during one of her "well times," between one illness and the next.

Since for once she seemed to be neither flushed nor congested, her mother had allowed her to go out in the yard for a moment before they left for Sunday service. As children will, she had wandered through the gate and down to the end of the street where the woods began, into the cool shadows of the trees.

And the mountain lion had been waiting there, in the arms of a giant oak. She was instantly aware of it, because everything was suddenly silent, all the other animals nearby either fled or hiding. She looked slowly around her until she saw it, there in the tree, staring at her, still and watchful.

She was five years old, and frail. Easy prey.

The mountain lion laid its ears flat and granted her a low, hissing snarl. Slowly she began to back up, out of the darkness of the trees and into the sunlight at the end of her street. The mountain lion held her gaze, but didn't move.

Just as she felt the welcome sun on her back, she heard her mother calling. "Regina! Regina, where have you gone off to?"

She whirled and ran, the muscles in her back twitching, expecting any second to feel the leaping weight of the cat, the hard dig of its claws, tearing dotted swiss and tender flesh.

But it didn't happen. She ran to her mother's arms.

And when her mother asked what was wrong, she only

held on and whispered, "Nothing, Mama. Nothing, honest."

Regina had known what would happen if she told. Her mother would have seen that the mountain lion was shot. And Regina, child of the mountains, knew that to shoot the big cat before it actually attacked someone would probably be the best thing.

Yet she had never **told** anyone about it. Perhaps she had looked too long into **its eyes....**

Regina blinked. Patrick Jones was standing in front of her. She gave him the sugar. As he took the mug, one side of one finger brushed her hand. She had to suppress a startled gasp at the little, heated shock that skittered up her arm from just that brushing touch.

"Thanks."

Her shyness, which had been for a short time blessedly suspended, came crashing in on her. "Sure. Um...anytime."

She felt like a complete idiot. Always, Regina had been shy around strong, self-assured individuals. And, with this man right now, her shyness seemed ten times worse than usual.

They stared at each other.

Oh, this simply could not go on. She simply had to put this—whatever it was he did to her senses—aside. That was all there was to it.

He was only her neighbor, here to borrow sugar as neighbors often did. She had to stop quivering and thinking of mountain lions whenever she looked at him.

She forced herself to ask a neighborly question. "Are you, um, getting settled in all right?"

Patrick smiled again. "Well enough. It's a big job, but the family's helping."

"Well, that's nice." She winced at how asinine she sounded, but at least she was talking about normal, everyday things. She remembered his veiled dig about how big her house was, and she gave it right back to him. "That's a big house, isn't it? For a man alone."

He chuckled, and then grew serious. "Yeah. It's exactly what I need. I have to have the extra rooms for when my girls come home."

Regina stared blankly at him for a moment, before she remembered that last year the word around town was that Marybeth, his ex-wife, had taken his two daughters and moved to Arkansas. She nodded. "Ah. I see. When your daughters visit, you want them to have plenty of room."

"Right. There's a bedroom for Teresa and one for Marnie, too."

"Yes. Of course. That's good."

"It's necessary." His voice was gruff, his eyes hooded. Regina had no idea what he might be thinking. He seemed to shake himself. "Well. Gotta go."

"Yes. Of course."

He turned for the front door. She followed, feeling like a leaf blown in the wake of a forceful wind.

At the door, just before he went out, she made herself offer, like a good neighbor should, "Um...Patrick...if there's anything at all I can do to help you get settled in, then you let me know. I mean it. Okay?"

He turned and those sapphire eyes seemed to bore right through her. Then that beautiful smile returned. "Yeah. Thanks, Regina. You're great."

And he was gone.

Regina couldn't help herself. Like some giddy schoolgirl, she leaned against the door and sighed.

And then she straightened and spoke firmly to herself. She told herself that, from now on, all this flighty foolishness would cease.

Patrick Jones was a thoroughly unsuitable man for a woman like herself. First of all, there was the fact that a rather prim, introverted person like herself could surely hold no attraction for a virile, rugged man like he was. And second, charming as he was, Patrick Jones had a very poor record when it came to relationships with women.

A woman would have to be asking for trouble to so much as *consider* getting involved with him, no matter how beautiful his smile or how stunning his male form. And besides that, there was Marcus, with whom she was developing a lovely, warm, meaningful relationship. Regina intended to marry Marcus, though Marcus had yet to speak to her of marriage.

But that would come, Regina was certain. One day soon, Marcus Shelby would propose. Regina would say yes. Instead of the one *playing* "The Wedding March," Regina would be the one walking down the aisle to it. She and Marcus would settle into a contented life. Perhaps they would even be blessed with a child or two.

Patrick Jones, on the other hand, was her neighbor and nothing more. From now on she would treat him as such.

Chapter Four

"Here's your damn sugar."

"Thanks, son." Oggie sat with his feet on one of Patrick's kitchen chairs, puffing on a fat cigar. "That was downright obligin' of you, to consider my sweet tooth like that." He actually sounded grateful.

Patrick should have been warned. When Oggie Jones sounded grateful, it was only to throw a man off his guard. Patrick plunked the sugar on the table beside his father's coffee cup—and failed to pull his hand away fast enough.

The old man's knotted fingers closed around his wrist. "Look me in the eye."

"You old coot."

"I mean it. Look at me."

Reluctantly, Patrick did as his father instructed.

Oggie peered at Patrick for a moment, and then chortled in a kind of triumphant glee. "Yeah. I'm right, ain't I? She's the one."

Patrick yanked his arm free and glared down at his father. "You had to have that damn sugar. Use it."

The old man chortled some more as he poured about half the sugar Regina Black had given Patrick into his cup.

"What the hell is so damn funny?"

"Life, son. Life." Oggie picked up a butter knife, since no spoon was handy in the chaos of Patrick's half-unpacked kitchen. He stirred his coffee with the knife. "She's kinda pretty, ain't she? In a low-key kind of way."

"Who?"

"You know damn well who." The old man sipped from the cup. "She always appealed to me, personally. With those big gray eyes and that soft pale skin. She's a woman you gotta look close at. But when you do, you get that feelin', you know what I mean? That there's more to her than, um, meets the eye...."

"Don't push it, Dad," Patrick warned in a quiet voice. Then he went to the counter and began plowing through an open packing box looking for another mug.

Oggie Jones shrugged, sipped again from his coffee-flavored cup of sugar, and kept talking. "But she had that dragon of a mother around all the time until a few years ago. For too long it looked like no man would ever have her. A real loss to the male population of our fair town, I gotta say. A woman like that's a prize. She's stable and steady. You can see she's born to be a wife. And yet, you look close, you watch the way she'll finger the keys of a piano when she plays, you know she's got real potential, er, between the sheets."

"I don't really need to hear this, Dad," Patrick said as he poured some coffee.

"Sure you do. Where was I? Oh, right. And now the mother's gone. And your only competition's that wimpy twit that runs the grocery store." Oggie leaned back, lifting the front feet of his chair off the floor. "Yessiree. Who woulda thought it, you and sweet little Regina Black?'' The smelly cigar was brandished grandly. ''Hell, son. Ain't no use you fightin' it. She's exactly what you're lookin' for. And beyond that, judgin' by the way she was spyin' on you yesterday, she's done picked you out as the focus of her, er, secret passions.''

Patrick turned, leaned against the counter and took a sip from his cup. ''She's scared to death of me.''

Oggie was significantly silent. For a moment. Then, ''So I ain't gonna have to chain you to the wall to make you take her?''

''Very funny.''

''You'll take her. Admit it.''

''Like I said, she's scared to death of me.''

''So? Go easy.'' Oggie chortled some more. ''But not too easy. You ain't a man who can afford to waste any time over this.''

''I know what I have to do, Dad.''

''Act real casual, no more than neighborly, for a while.''

''I know, Dad.''

''But not forever. The time will come, and it won't be too long. You'll have to make your move.''

''Dad, I know.''

''Good. So go easy, she's a tender thing. But get it handled, get it done....''

After church, Marcus walked Regina home.

She was pleased when he took her hand in his. She was also quite proud of herself that not once did she compare Marcus's pale, rather colorless eyes to clear blue ones, or his nervous grin to a certain easy smile.

When they reached her front gate, she just happened to notice that Patrick was out mowing the overgrown lawn at his new house. He looked up and saw them and waved in a manner that Regina decided was quite suitable.

It was a neighborly wave, friendly but completely off-hand. Marcus remarked sourly that the fellow really ought to wear a shirt.

Regina, who was not the least concerned about her neighbor's bare chest, merely shrugged and asked Marcus in for lunch.

Two days later, to Regina's surprise, Patrick knocked on her door at eight in the morning and held up a lovely string of trout.

"Dad and I went fishing. Since he's retired, he's always got a line in the water. My freezer's full, and I thought maybe…"

Regina, who was very glad that she was dressed for the day this time, dared an appreciative—yet no wider than appropriate smile. "Why, thank you, Patrick. That's quite neighborly of you."

"Hey, you're doing *me* the favor. I hate to see them go to waste." He handed over the fish.

"Why, you've cleaned them and everything."

"Yeah. I was doing the others, so I thought I might as well get the whole disgusting job out of the way."

"Well, that's just really—"

His smile changed for a moment. "Neighborly. Right?"

She wondered if he was being sarcastic. But then she decided not to wonder too hard.

"Yes," she said, and kept her smile.

"Well, then. Enjoy."

"I will. Thanks again."

She stood on her porch and gazed after him as he jumped the fence to his side. Then she went in and cooked two of the fish for her breakfast, before heading over to old Mrs. Leslie's to help her clean her house.

That Saturday, in the afternoon, Regina walked over to the church carrying a splendid bouquet of lilies and amaryllis fresh from her garden to adorn the altar for services the next day. She had no sooner returned home than she heard pounding noises coming from next door.

She glanced out a window to see Patrick on his porch, down on his hands and knees. He was wielding a hammer with great concentration. As usual, he wore no shirt, but Regina did not pause for even an extra second to stare.

A half hour later, the pounding was still going on, interspersed with the sounds of a power saw's whine from down in his basement. The day was quite warm. Perhaps Patrick had grown thirsty. Carpentry, in Regina's experience, was thirst-causing work. And he had been so thoughtful, bringing her those lovely fish the other day.

She was out the door with an icy glass of lemonade in her hand before she even stopped to think twice. She strode around through the front gate, and marched up to the base of his porch steps.

He stopped his hammering and sat back on his knees. "Hi, Regina." He wiped his forehead with the back of his leather glove. She caught a quick glimpse of the matted hair beneath his muscled arm, before forcing her gaze to stay on his sweating, flushed face.

She held out the lemonade. "I thought you might appreciate this about now." She was proud of how cordial, how nonchalant, she sounded.

He took off his right glove. "Whew. Thanks." Then he reached for the glass with his ungloved hand and drank long and deep. She tried not to watch his strong throat move as he swallowed, or to notice the sweat that dripped down his neck and onto his bare, sculpted chest, where it caught in the shiny brown hairs there.

He finished the glass and handed it back.

"Would you like some more?"

"Naw. That was just right."

She looked at the porch. "Repairs?"

"Yeah. Some of these porch boards were rotted, and some are loose." He gestured at the place he'd been hammering. Then he winked at her. "Can't have that."

"Oh, absolutely not."

"What with the garage and helping out with the Mercantile Grill, I haven't had a lot of spare time. But little by little, I'm getting this place in shape." Several months ago he'd taken over the town service station. But Regina hadn't heard that he was involved with North Magdalene's newest restaurant.

Regina remarked, "So you're in on the Mercantile Grill, too?"

"Yeah. The Mercantile building itself is sort of my inheritance, from Dad, you know?"

"I think I did hear that somewhere."

The landmark building Patrick referred to was next door to the local tavern, the Hole in the Wall. For over forty years, Oggie Jones had been the proprietor of the Hole in the Wall. But last year, the old man had finally retired. Now Patrick's brother, Jared, and Jared's wife, Eden, managed the bar, as well as their new restaurant.

"Let's face it," Patrick said. "It's really Eden who's running things. She's the business genius in the family. But I'm a partner. I helped with the construction of the interior. And I pitch in whenever they're shorthanded."

"I haven't eaten there yet, but I hear it's very good."

Patrick's gaze shifted suddenly. He was looking at something over her shoulder. "You've got company."

Regina turned to see the tall, reed-thin figure of Nellie Anderson standing at her front gate. Nellie called, "Regina, there you are."

Even from several yards away, that look of sharp interest was clear on Nellie's pinched face. Regina kept her chin high, reminding herself that Patrick was her neighbor and she was being neighborly and if Nellie wanted to make something of that, it was Nellie who had a problem.

Nellie was already at Patrick's gate. She came through and strode up the walk, her long nose in the air. Her small, piercing eyes made a disapproving sweep over Patrick's bare chest. "Hello, Patrick. I hope you're getting settled in well enough."

"Just fine," Patrick said. "Thank you."

Nellie looked at Regina. "The pastor's changed a few of the songs for tomorrow. I thought I'd just drop the list by."

"Fine. Let's go on over to my house." Regina started to usher Nellie toward the gate.

But Nellie spoke again before Regina could lead her away. "Patrick, do you hear anything from Chloe?"

Patrick looked at Nellie for a moment; it was an unreadable kind of look. Then he answered, "No, not a thing." Regina felt a little stab of sympathy for him. She imagined he must have grown very tired of being asked that question over the past several months since Chloe Swan, an old flame of his, had run off with a stranger.

"Chloe's mother, as I'm sure you know, is devastated." Nellie spoke as if Chloe Swan's behavior were Patrick's personal responsibility.

"So?" Patrick's expression remained as carefully bland as his tone.

Regina's sympathy for him increased. In some ways, it must be quite a challenge to lead the kind of life he'd led, to have the town gossips always panting after the next juicy tidbit concerning one's affairs.

"It's a terrible shame, that's all," Nellie intoned.

"Is it?" Now Patrick looked bored. "She's been gone for more than a year now. Maybe she's happy, wherever she is."

"How can you say that?"

"Because it's damn likely to be true."

Nellie gave a small snort of disgust. "Well, it appears that it suits *you* to think so."

Regina had heard enough. She firmly took the older woman's elbow. "Nellie, let's leave Patrick to his work. Come over to my house. I've just made lemonade."

Nellie turned her indignant expression on Regina. "I say what's on my mind, Regina. There's no sense in trying to stop me."

"Ain't that the truth," Patrick muttered.

Nellie's head snapped around. "What was that?"

Regina pulled Nellie away. "He was only agreeing with you, that's all. Now please let's go."

Nellie emitted a pained sigh, but allowed herself to be led off. "Fresh lemonade, you said?"

"I did."

"Good, then. I'm parched."

"See you ladies later," Patrick called, too pleasantly, from behind them. Regina waved without turning—and kept a firm hold on Nellie's bony arm.

Once inside the house, Regina was subjected to a spirited harangue concerning the sins of all the Joneses, Patrick in particular. A single sip from her glass of lemonade and Nellie was off and ranting.

"I tell you, they're all alike, all of them, those Joneses, I swear. Except for our dear Delilah, of course." Nellie and Delilah had been good friends for years. "And Patrick is the worst of them. Do you know that while he was in high school, they used to call him "Love 'em and leave 'em" Jones, because it was just one innocent girl after another for him back then.

"And then, in his twenties, marrying Marybeth Lynch because we all knew he *had* to, even though everyone was certain he loved Chloe Swan. And next, compounding his error by getting Marybeth pregnant a second time, before that poor woman finally got smart and divorced him.

"And, four years ago when Marybeth was out of the picture, did he marry Chloe—poor child, still in love with him—and settle down with her as we all knew he should? No. He continued to *insist,* as he had all through his marriage, that he and Chloe were no more than friends. Until Chloe became so desperate, she took off with a stranger."

Nellie paused to refresh herself with another sip of lemonade. But she was far from finished. "And what of those poor little girls of Patrick's? Not only products of a broken home, but now dragged away from all their friends and loved ones, off to Arkansas with that flighty mother of theirs? It is a crying shame, I tell you, Regina. A crying shame."

Regina, who should have known better than to argue with Nellie Anderson, found she couldn't keep quiet any longer.

"I believe," she ventured, "that Patrick bought the house next door at least partly so he'd have a place for his daughters, during their visits."

"That's what he told *you,* I'm sure."

"Yes, and he seemed very sincere about needing a house with plenty of room in it for his children. And I understand he's settled down lately, that he's doing quite well running the garage and all. And I have to say, he's a model neighbor. Quiet and pleasant and no trouble to have around."

Regina fell silent as she realized that Nellie's nose actually seemed to be twitching, the way a house cat's nose will twitch at the sight of a plump little mouse. "My sweet heavens, Regina. You must never believe anything a man like that tries to tell you."

"All I'm saying, Nellie, is that people do change. They learn and they grow."

Nellie let out a long, discouraged breath. She shook her head sadly. "Oh, Regina, Regina. What is happening to you? I knew it, the moment I saw you talking to him. I sensed what was happening."

"Nothing is happening."

"Oh, my, such an innocent you are. He's a *Jones,* Regina. You haven't a prayer of saving yourself, if you get involved with a man like that."

"I'm not getting involved with him."

"You say that, but what do you know? You've led such a sheltered life. You know nothing of the ways of men like him. Why, remember our poor Delilah, determined for all those years never to so much as get near a man like her father and brothers. And then Sam Fletcher, who we all know is more Joneslike than the Joneses themselves, decided he wanted her. And he stopped at nothing to have her. You remember. This whole town remembers. And the poor girl simply hadn't a prayer. Now she's bound to him for the rest of her life."

"Delilah loves Sam," Regina dared to point out.

"Well, certainly she loves him. That's what I'm saying. She loves him, and now she'll never escape him."

"But that's the point. She doesn't *want* to escape him."

"Exactly. It's a tragedy, a tragedy, plain and simple. And you are so much like her, Regina. A good girl, a nice girl…"

Regina stood. "Nellie. I am not a girl. I am thirty-six years old. I qualify as a full-grown woman, and I *will* be treated as such. And I must tell you, I resent your inference in this instance."

"You—"

"Yes, I do. I resent it." Regina's face felt like it was on fire, and she couldn't believe her own boldness, talking right back to Nellie Anderson like this. But she couldn't, *wouldn't* allow Nellie to assume things that were not in the very least bit true. "You know that I am...seriously involved with Marcus Shelby. I have no interest whatsoever in any other man, and certainly not in Patrick Jones. So I would appreciate it if you would stop this foolishness right now. Patrick Jones and I have nothing in common. Our only connection is that we are neighbors. And that will remain our only connection. Have I made myself clear?"

Nellie's mouth was hanging open. She snapped it closed. Then she meekly allowed, "Well, certainly. If you say so, dear."

"I do say so. I most certainly do."

There was a long and quite uncomfortable silence. Then Nellie drank from her lemonade again. "That was so refreshing." Her voice was cautiously bright. "Could I trouble you for one more glass, do you think?"

"Why, of course, Nellie."

"You are so kind."

Regina refilled Nellie's glass, and her own.

"Thank you."

"You're welcome."

"Here is the list of changes for the hymns for tomorrow."

"Fine."

"And you know, dear, I was wondering, would you be willing to coordinate a few things for the Independence Day picnic this year? The pastor has asked me to get my committee heads in order right away."

"Of course I'll help out wherever I'm needed."

"I knew you'd say that. You are such a thoughtful gir...er woman, dear."

Regina suppressed her small smile of triumph and drank her lemonade.

For the next week, Regina hardly saw her new neighbor. She assumed he was busy at the garage. And she kept busy, too.

Though Regina's mother had left her well provided for, and she didn't really have to work, she enjoyed giving her services to those in need. She helped out with the elderly and with local shut-ins, cooking and cleaning and doing whatever needed to be done. During the school term, she also worked part-time for the North Magdalene School as the secretary/receptionist, a job that she thoroughly enjoyed. And she was always available to give her time to community projects. She led a quite productive life, actually.

And, also, there was Marcus. He really was such a gentle, good man. Saturday night, he took her to the Mercantile Grill for dinner.

Regina had a wonderful time. The service was good and the food even better. She chatted briefly with Eden Jones, congratulating her on her accomplishment with the restaurant—and expressing good wishes for the baby Eden was due to deliver in the fall. Eden, as always, was gracious and warm. She mentioned how much work Patrick had done on the design and construction of the interior. Regina agreed it looked terrific.

When Marcus took Regina home, he came in for coffee. He kissed her, a brief brush of his lips on hers, as he was leaving. Regina stood in her doorway for a moment after he was gone, staring out at the warm summer night, full of vague yearnings that she refused to examine too closely.

Just before she pulled the door closed, she noticed the moths, throwing themselves against the porch light. And she thought that she could understand them, risking everything to reach the burning globe that drew them.

But then she told herself she was being foolish. She was richly blessed, really. She led a useful, meaningful life. She was not and never would be a moth drawn to a flame.

That Tuesday night, she was sitting on her porch swing just after dusk, idly rocking back and forth when her neighbor spoke to her.

"Nice night, huh?" He was leaning on the low wrought-iron fence between their houses.

Her pulse quickened. She ignored the sensation. "Yes, it is."

She didn't invite Patrick to join her, but still he jumped the fence and came and sat on the porch with her. For a moment, she considered asking that he leave. But he didn't even come that close to her. He perched on the porch railing and looked up at the brightening stars.

They talked idly, of nothing important. And in a few moments, he was gone.

It seemed to Regina a thoroughly harmless incident, which was why, when it happened twice more over the next two weeks, she thought little of it. He was her neighbor, and now and then he would join her for a few minutes, at twilight, to watch the stars grow vivid in the darkening sky.

And, of course, she was not thinking of her neighbor at all when, on the last Friday in June, Marcus called early in the morning.

He sounded very nervous, and said he had something important to discuss with her. Would she come to his house tonight at seven for dinner? They could talk afterward.

Regina's heart grew light. She knew, at last, that Marcus Shelby was going to propose.

"More coffee, Regina?" Marcus asked. Regina noticed that his narrow face was slightly flushed, though the room was not overly warm.

She felt a little shiver of anticipation. Their dinner was finished and cleared away. The moment when he would speak of that important something was upon them.

"No, thank you, Marcus. Two cups are my limit."

There was a silence. Regina smiled at Marcus. Marcus smiled in return.

"Well," Marcus said at last, tucking his napkin beside his dessert plate and then blowing out the candles in the center of the table. "Shall we move into the other room?"

Regina stood. "That sounds lovely."

They went into Marcus's large living room and sat on either end of the wide, comfortable couch. Regina canted toward Marcus and laid an arm along the backrest. Marcus, looking very nervous, sat straight and faced squarely forward.

Regina felt great tenderness toward him at that moment. How difficult it must be to be a man. To be the one expected to do the pursuing, the inviting…and the proposing.

"Regina, as I mentioned on the phone this morning," Marcus began, "I have something I must talk with you about."

"Yes, Marcus."

"It is my hope, my fondest wish… Oh, how can I put this?"

She waited, knowing this was something he must do in his own way and time.

"Regina, what I'd like to say first, is that I sincerely hope you will not take offense at what I have to say."

Regina frowned a little. How could she possibly take offense at a marriage proposal? "Marcus, I—"

"Please. This is difficult."

"Well, of course, I understand. I do."

He turned toward her then, and his face looked congested, so high was his color. "I hope so."

She was concerned for him suddenly. He truly did look distressed. "Marcus? What is it? You must tell me, whatever it is."

He drew in a long breath. "Regina…"

"Yes. What? Say it, please, Marcus."

"Regina, people are talking."

She stared at him. "People are what?"

Suddenly it seemed too much for him to remain seated. He jumped to his feet and walked to the window that looked out on his street. He stuck his hands in his pockets, drew his rather narrow shoulders up and then he faced her once more. "Yes." His tone was grim—and just a bit accusatory. "People are talking about you and Patrick Jones."

Regina simply gaped. It took several moments for her mind to absorb what he was saying. It was very far from what she'd hoped to hear. But then she did absorb it.

And she didn't like it one bit. She withdrew her arm from the back of the couch and folded her hands primly in her lap. "And just what, precisely, are people saying?"

Marcus raked his fingers back through his fine, pale hair. "You *are* offended. I knew you would be."

"What are they saying, Marcus?"

"Regina…"

"If this is bothering you, Marcus, then we've got to talk about it frankly. We must have it all right out in the open so that we can see what we're dealing with."

"Well, I know, but…"

"But what?"

"Well…you're angry. You know how I feel about anger."

Now it was Regina's turn to draw in a long breath. She reminded herself that Marcus was very sensitive. Displays of strong emotion distressed him. It was one of the things the two of them had in common—or so she'd always told herself.

"Yes," she admitted after a moment. "I'm angry—but I'm settling down now."

"Good." Marcus looked massively relieved.

Regina took several more long breaths. And then, when

she felt calmer, she patted the couch beside her. "Come. Sit down. Tell me everything, please."

His expression reluctant, he approached and sat down once more at his end of the couch. "Well, Nellie Anderson said she found you in Patrick Jones's yard Saturday before last. And more than one person has seen him, sitting on your porch, in the evenings."

Regina felt her anger—a defensive anger—stirring again, but she immediately quelled it. She wondered vaguely what was happening to her lately. She had actually argued with Nellie Anderson, and now she'd become angry at the idea of people gossiping about herself and Patrick Jones. Arguing and becoming angry as a reaction to other people's behavior were very unlike her. She was a peacemaker by nature, and she rarely got mad.

She spoke slowly and softly. "Marcus, Patrick Jones is my neighbor. No more, no less. He brought me some trout, and I repaid his kindness by offering him a glass of lemonade on that day Nellie's talking about. Once or twice, he's come over to say hello in the evenings. But that is all. If people are talking, it's only because they have vivid imaginations. There is nothing whatsoever between Patrick Jones and me, and there never will be."

"Are you sure?" Marcus, whose head had been bowed as she spoke, looked up. She saw how he wanted to believe her.

"Positive."

"Oh, Regina. You know what they say about the Jones men. They're hopelessly overbearing and disorderly and crude. But once one of them decides to pursue a woman, he always wins her in the end."

"It's only what people say, Marcus. It's gossip. That's all."

"But from what I understand, it's also true."

"Marcus. Patrick Jones has no interest in me whatsoever,

I'm sure of it. And if he had, it wouldn't matter. I have no interest in him.'' *If I do, I'll never pursue that interest,* she guiltily amended to herself. Then she concluded on a plaintive note, ''Please believe me. I'm telling you the truth.''

Marcus studied her intently for a moment. And then, at last, he smiled. ''I am just so pleased to hear that.''

Regina, who hadn't realized how tightly she was holding herself, felt her body relax. ''Good. Now can we put this nonsense behind us?''

He took her hand. ''Absolutely.''

''Well, that's a relief.'' She managed a weak chuckle.

Marcus's pale eyes were very soft. ''You know, Regina, I would have been devastated if you'd told me there actually was something between you and Patrick Jones. I have…such very special feelings for you myself.''

Regina felt chastened. Marcus *did* care for her. And deeply, too. He was just shy, and sensitive, as she was. She mustn't rush him. The day when he asked her to marry him would come yet. And on that day, she was sure, all of these distressing desires of hers that seemed to center around Patrick Jones would fade away to nothing at all.

Chapter Five

The next week was a busy one for Regina. Besides all the usual tasks she set for herself, she had taken on a lot of the preparatory work for the community church's annual Independence Day Picnic and Bazaar, which was coming up on Saturday, the third of July.

To Regina, it seemed as if she never had a spare moment that whole week.

She spent hours on the phone, arranging for the hundred and one things that had to be delivered to the picnic site on Saturday morning.

There were folding tables and chairs, big commercial barbecues and bag after bag of charcoal briquettes. There were huge tubs in which the soft drinks would be set out, along with hundreds of pounds of party ice. She'd also agreed to coordinate the potluck, which meant she had to contact just about everyone in town and badger them until they agreed to come through with a dessert or a side dish.

Beyond that, in a particularly weak moment, she'd some-how managed to volunteer to bake twenty dozen cookies herself. So her entire Thursday and most of Friday would be given over to standing by the oven, waiting for the timer to ring so she could pull out the next batch.

This year, the picnic was to be held in Sweetbriar Park, a lovely wooded area right across the river from town. And it promised to be a bigger event than on any previous year. The town merchants, including Marcus, were all making major donations of food and goods. Also, Delilah Fletcher, for years the only churchgoing member of the Jones family, had decided it was high time the rest of the Jones clan helped out. Therefore, both Amy and Eden had shown up at all the planning meetings over the past few weeks.

Eden, who'd worked most of her life in restaurants and clubs, had several wonderful ideas for events. So this year, thanks to Eden's suggestions, the picnic would include a raffle, a treasure hunt and after dark, dancing beneath the stars.

Throughout the week, as she raced around trying to get everything done, Regina made it a point to scrupulously avoid her handsome next-door neighbor. Marcus was the man for her, after all. And she didn't want him hearing any more town gossip about herself and the other man, no matter how unfounded that gossip might be.

So on Tuesday night, when Patrick waved to her as she stole a few moments out on her porch, she only returned his wave in a perfunctory manner and went right inside, so he'd have no chance to join her.

Then on Thursday, early in the morning, as she hurried over to Marcus's store to buy more of the margarine she needed to bake all those cookies, she saw Patrick leaving his house.

"Hey, wait up. I'll walk with you!" he called.

But she only waved back, pretending not to hear him,

and got in her car to drive the short distance to Main Street. She was taking no chances that he might catch up with her on the way.

It was strange, but now that she had consciously decided to avoid him, she did feel that he sometimes seemed to be watching her, studying her, as if he were *waiting* for something....

But that was ridiculous, she knew. She only imagined he was watching her. It was all in her mind.

A forceful, elemental man such as Patrick could never look at Regina the way a man looks at a woman he desires. He had dated the most attractive girls in the county and married the lovely Marybeth Lynch. Though he'd denied it for years now, everyone knew he'd once been in love with Chloe Swan, who was blond, outgoing, generously proportioned and very, very beautiful. He was not going to suddenly decide he couldn't live without diffident, mousy-haired Regina Black.

Regina firmly told herself that Patrick Jones was not the least bit interested in her. And the notion that he might actually be pursuing her was utterly absurd.

"All right, what the hell's goin' on?" Oggie demanded to know.

Patrick was alone with his father in the back room of the Hole in the Wall. Patrick sipped from his long-neck bottle of beer and stared at his boots, which were crossed at the ankles on the felt-topped table in front of him.

"She's dodging me every chance she gets. Old lady Anderson caught her bringing me lemonade a while back. I guess the old bat started talking and Regina decided she'd better keep away from me."

"Nellie Anderson is always talkin'. You should have allowed for that."

Patrick granted his father a flat look. "I'm doing the best I can, Dad."

"Do better. You gotta see your goal, and never let go of it. Like me and your sainted mother, bless her sweet, sweet soul. After I bought this place and got down on my knees to her and she told me yes, I thought I had everything. But Rory Drury was still after her. And he was a cutthroat son-ofabitch."

"Dad, I've heard this be—"

"Don't interrupt. Your mama taught you better than that."

"Hell, Dad."

"Where was I? Oh. Yeah." Though he winced at the pain in his joints when he did it, Oggie hoisted his own feet up on the table across from his son's. "Rory Drury wasn't a man to give in easy. And so he went and set me up, damned if he didn't. Robbed his own father's safe and took his mama's pearls and diamonds. And planted 'em at my place. Then he sent Davey Bowles—he was sheriff in those days—to bring me in. They took me off to the jail, arraigned me and gave me my grand jury hearing, all without bail. It was a setup, 'cause them Drurys were big people in these parts back then."

"Dad…"

"But I got out of it, didn't I? I got your mama to go to Rory and sweet-talk him until he told her what he'd done. She got it all on tape, too. And if you think that wasn't a damn achievement, you don't know squat. You got any idea how big a tape recorder was back in them days? They didn't have no microcassettes, I'll tell you that much.

"But your mama, she was a pearl beyond price. She loved me and she stood by me and she did what she had to do to save me. She was the empress of my heart and there ain't been another woman like her then nor since."

Patrick drank from his beer again. "So what are you getting at, Dad?"

"I'm sayin' a man's gotta do what a man's gotta do."

"Well, that helps a lot. Thanks, Dad."

"And I'm remindin' you that you ain't got forever with this thing. If you wanna be ready when—"

"I know, Dad. I know."

"So what are you gonna do?"

Right then, Eden stuck her head through the curtain that led to the main room. "All right you two, feet off my table. Now."

Oggie groused, "Hell and damnation, even the tables are *hers* now." But he obediently swung his feet to the floor. Patrick followed suit.

"You guys want another beer?"

"It's all right, Eden. I'll get them," Patrick said.

"Oh, sit down. I'm *pregnant*, not disabled." She disappeared back into the main room.

Oggie looked at his middle son. "So, you gonna answer me or not? What the hell you gonna do?"

"I'm gonna be at the church picnic tomorrow, that's what. And I'm gonna wait. And watch."

"And be ready. Readiness is all."

Patrick pointed his beer at his father in a salute. "Gotcha, Dad. Readiness is all."

The next day Regina arrived at Sweetbriar Park before him, along with box after box of fresh-baked cookies. One of the duties she'd assumed was to see that everything was properly set up and to get the commercial barbecues going.

Her heart did a funny little flip-flop when Patrick drove up in a delivery truck just a little before eleven. He'd volunteered, it turned out, to bring over the donations of burgers, hot dogs and buns from the Mercantile Grill.

"Eden also asked me to stay and supervise the barbe-cues," he told her. "That okay with you?"

"That's just fine. Great, as a matter of fact." She hated the falsely bright sound of her own voice. "Um, let me know if there's anything you need."

"Right," he said. But his tone said he wouldn't ask her for the time of day.

Her spirits drooped, to have him speak to her so coldly, though she knew her reaction was completely out of line. She had snubbed him twice in the past week, going inside when he waved at her and pretending not to hear when he called to her.

However little she really knew him, she did know he was not stupid or lacking in perception. He understood exactly the message she'd sent him: keep away. She had no right to be droopy because he was giving her just what she'd asked for.

And she would *not* be droopy, she scolded herself. It was a beautiful day, and the park was green and lush, full of shady spots and warm pools of sunlight.

Marcus was coming at eleven-thirty, and she had promised to spend the day with him. They'd enjoy their meal and go on the treasure hunt together. Then they'd wander the bazaar tables, buying cute things they didn't need, and feeling good about spending their money because the money this year was to be used to put a new roof on the church. They'd hold hands. She would tease him into buying some of those dozens of cookies she had finished baking yesterday. When dark came, they would dance together by the light of the full moon.

Marcus arrived right on time, in a delivery truck with North Magdalene Grocery printed on the side. He had brought the dry goods and condiments from his store, as promised. Regina—and Nellie, who'd been there since ten—helped him to unload everything and set it out.

By that time, it was past noon. The smell of grilling hamburgers made Regina's stomach growl.

"You two go on and have fun," Nellie suggested. "I can handle whatever comes up from here on."

"You're sure?" Regina asked, to be polite.

"Certainly. I have oodles of help, and you've already done more than your share."

At that moment, Regina was so glad to be set free of responsibility for a while that she almost forgave Nellie for spreading tales about herself and Patrick Jones.

"Great. Thanks, Nellie." She grabbed Marcus's hand and towed him to her car, from which she produced a big blanket.

"Now, hurry," she told him with a conspiratorial wink. Then she raced to an area off to the side of all the activity that she'd had her eye on all morning, a nice grassy spot beneath a leafy chestnut tree. She spread the blanket there, pleased to be claiming the cool, somewhat secluded location before someone else did.

Marcus complained that they'd be more comfortable at a table, but she good-naturedly pooh-poohed him and led him to the ticket booth, where they purchased strips of tickets, which they could use to trade for food and anything else that caught their fancy.

After that, she dragged him over to where the food was set out. They each handed over the required number of tickets, and then Regina, laughing, tucked the remainder of her own tickets under the belt of the button-front sundress she'd bought specifically to please Marcus. It was the kind of dress Marcus liked: a simple, modest dress with a high collar and a subdued floral print.

Linda Lou Beardsly, who was supervising the food tables, gave them paper plates, which they proceeded to load up with all manner of potluck goodies.

"And I've got to have one of those hamburgers," Regina said, her plate already full.

"You don't have room," Marcus said, rather disapprovingly.

"I'll make room." She was laughing over her shoulder at him. "Come on, Marcus. Live dangerously. Get a burger, too."

"I'll pass," he said, backing up suddenly, looking beyond her shoulder, his expression wary.

She wondered what could be going through his mind, as she turned—and nearly bumped into Patrick Jones. He held a bun in one hand and a just-grilled hamburger patty on a spatula in the other.

"Here you go," he said.

"I..."

He set the bun on her plate gently, opening it with his tan fingers and edging it between a tossed salad with vinaigrette dressing on one side and something Linda Lou had called Potato Surprise on the other. Then he eased the patty onto the bottom half of the bun.

Regina watched Patrick's hands doing this simple series of actions, setting the bun on the plate, opening it, laying the meat on top. And she had that same feeling she'd had at her front door that morning a month ago, right after he moved in next door, when he came over to borrow the sugar for his father's coffee and she'd looked at his feet and thought how beautiful they were.

It was a feeling of sadness, of something splendid glimpsed too briefly, and then gone.

She looked up, into his waiting eyes. "Thank you."

"You're welcome."

And then he turned away.

She knew she stood staring at his proud back much longer than she should have. But it took time to return from that forbidden place into which she had somehow slipped while he was edging a hamburger bun onto her paper plate.

Over behind where the portable bandstand had been erected, someone set off a handful of firecrackers. The sound jarred Regina enough that she collected herself and looked around for Marcus. He was standing right where she'd left him, halfway between the food tables and the barbecue grills. His expression was not encouraging.

She pasted an unconcerned smile on her face and hurried to his side. "Let's get something to drink, shall we, before we head for the blanket?"

"Fine."

They went to the big metal tubs, which were filled with ice and soft drinks, and chose two cans of cola. Then they went to sit down.

Regina tucked her legs beneath the hem of her dress and concentrated very hard on her food. Marcus, beside her, was silent. She knew he was upset and she was hoping that, if she just ignored him for a little while, he would forget what had happened and they could go on with their lovely afternoon.

But deep in her heart, Regina knew such a wish was futile. It had only been a few moments in time, and all Patrick Jones had done was serve her a hamburger. And yet, when he turned away from her, she had, for endless seconds, been unable to turn away from him. Marcus, who she so wanted to love, had witnessed it all.

It was such a tiny thing. And yet its immensity terrified her.

"He's staring at you," Marcus said quietly.

Regina put up no pretense. She didn't ask "Who?" In fact, she didn't even want to look to see if what Marcus said was true. Yet she couldn't help herself. She raised her glance to the two pushed-together tables about twenty yards away where all the rowdy, passionate Joneses were sitting.

Patrick *was* looking at her.

And there was something in his look. A challenge—a taunt. It was completely crazy. It made no logical sense. But Regina Black knew at that moment that the life she had planned for herself was slipping from her grasp.

Since the morning Patrick Jones had moved in next door to her, her life, like a river at flood time, had been cutting a new channel for itself. Slowly at first, but with gathering momentum, she was being swept away. She was losing control, caught up in emotions and feelings the like of which she had never known.

Dangerous emotions, hazardous feelings…

"You encourage him," Marcus said, his voice low and very controlled. He didn't want anyone else to hear.

Regina made herself stop looking at Patrick, though it seemed to take every ounce of will she possessed. She stared down at her plate.

"I do not," she said between clenched teeth, and felt like the world's worst liar.

"You encourage him," Marcus repeated, soft but firm. "And what's more, you're in denial about it."

"I don't encourage him." She looked up once more, to glare at Marcus. "That isn't fair. I do *not* encourage Patrick Jones."

"My, my, you certainly are *vehement* about this."

"Vehement? Well, of course I'm vehement. I'm *not* looking at Patrick Jones, nor am I encouraging him. It's *you* I'm looking at, Marcus. And if you'd just—"

Marcus cleared his throat. She saw that he hated this, that it pained him terribly, both the way Patrick kept looking at her *and* her stuttered and awkward declaration of her feelings.

"Now, now, Regina," he muttered. "Let's not get carried away."

"Carried away?" Her voice rose, though she knew Marcus hated loud, rash displays. "Marcus, I'm trying to tell you I—"

"Hush." He patted her arm as if she were a skittish animal. "People are starting to stare at us." His eyes darted back and forth in their sockets. She could see he thoroughly regretted remarking on the situation with Patrick Jones, because now he was very close to becoming half of a public spectacle. He went on, "It was quite unwise of me to bring up this subject here, in a public place. I apologize."

Regina, humiliated, confused and now thoroughly miserable, subsided. She tried to eat her hamburger, but it stuck like sawdust in her throat.

She turned away in an effort to get her emotions back under control. As she did so, she locked glances with old Oggie Jones, who just happened to be tottering by at that moment on the cane he had walked with ever since he got careless with his hunting rifle and shot himself in the foot.

The old man smiled at her, a slow, crafty smile, just like the one he had granted her that first morning, when Patrick had moved in next door to her. The same morning when her life had begun its slow slide out of her control.

Her gaze still held by the old man's, Regina forced herself to swallow the dry wad of hamburger that didn't want to go down her throat.

In Oggie's beady black eyes, it seemed, she saw everything—how she had heard the voices and gone to her window. And from the moment she saw Patrick there, sweating and straining over that refrigerator, so ruggedly beautiful that it broke her heart, her life had taken a new, uncharted course. A course she had denied for a month now—just as Marcus had accused. But a course she was destined to follow, fight it though she might.

Unless...

Yes, she thought frantically. Unless she could force

something different to happen. Right now. Today. Before it was too late.

She closed her eyes, to shut out the frightening old man. And when she opened them again, he had passed from her sight. Then, setting her half-eaten lunch aside, she turned to Marcus once more.

Marcus, with his gentle eyes and soft-spoken ways. Marcus, a man of whom even her mother might have approved. Marcus, her last link with her world as she knew it. Her last chance for a safe, uneventful, contented life.

"Marcus, I…"

His gaze shifted away, and then back. She knew with grim certainty that he had no desire to hear what she might say. Yet she had to try.

They were some distance from the other picnickers, and she was sure no one would hear what she said as long as she didn't let her voice get out of control.

She took great care to keep her tone low and unchallenging as she began, "Marcus, I…I want certain things in life. Can you understand that?"

"Now, Regina. Perhaps we—"

"Let me say this. Please."

"But, Regina, this is very public, and I—"

"Please. I'll keep my voice down. I promise." She waited. He didn't agree to hear her out, but he didn't call a halt, either. He merely looked pained.

She forged on. "Marcus, I want love, and marriage. Maybe children. And I…I want them with you. I keep hoping you'll say you care for me, Marcus. Do you, Marcus? Do you care for me?"

Marcus looked miserable. "Well, now, Regina. Of course I care for you."

Suddenly, watching him, she perceived the truth. What Regina Black wanted and what Marcus Shelby wanted were two very different things.

She knew his age, but she asked him anyway, "How old are you, Marcus?"

He blinked, puzzled. "You know. You gave me a birthday party only six months ago. I'm forty-three."

"And you've never been married."

"No, of course not. You know that."

"And you never intend to marry, do you?"

"Well, now, Regina—"

"Just say it, Marcus. Just get the words out of your mouth."

"Regina."

There was a coldness inside her at that moment, a frozen center of absolute ruthlessness. She scrambled to her feet, brushed off her skirt and demanded, so quietly, she herself could barely hear the words, "Say it."

Marcus gulped. And then he seemed to come to some sort of bleak decision within himself. He spoke very low, and very deliberately. "Okay, Regina. It's probably for the best if we're totally frank with each other anyway. I don't want to get married. I like being a bachelor. I like just what we have together. An important and meaningful relationship, where we both have our independence and our privacy."

She stared down at him, and she felt the coldness ease a bit, felt herself relax. A strange quietude was stealing over her.

"I see." Now she was the soul of reason. "Well, then, it looks like we're headed in different directions, Marcus. Because *I* want to get married. We want different things, and that's all there is to it."

"But, Regina—"

She put up a hand. "I've enjoyed your company, Marcus."

"Regina—"

"But I don't want to see you anymore. Will you please step off my blanket?"

"Listen, please..."

"Just step off of it, Marcus. Now."

Marcus watched her for a moment, and then shrugged. He rose, the movement awkward as he tried not to spill what was left on his plate. Once he was upright, he stepped aside. Swiftly and efficiently, Regina folded the blanket and stuck it beneath her arm. Then she bent to scoop up her own plate.

"Now what?" he asked.

She stood very straight. "I'm going for a walk right now into the woods alone. Don't follow me."

"Regina, don't be childish."

"Goodbye, Marcus."

She turned from him, her head high, and started walking away from the picnic area, into the trees. Behind her, she heard more firecrackers going off, then Pastor Johnson's sonorous voice over the loudspeakers, announcing the beginning of the big treasure hunt. She tossed the rest of her lunch in a trash can as she marched past it. Then she strode briskly, clutching her blanket, away from the picnic and the loudspeakers, away from Marcus's rejection of her, and from the knowing heat in the eyes of Patrick Jones.

At first she had some worry that Marcus might dare to follow, and that she would have to turn and insist that he leave her alone. But that didn't happen. As the sounds of the picnic faded, muffled by the distance and the thick branches of the trees, Regina knew she'd seen the last of Marcus Shelby, at least for now.

She walked on, through the trees, her canvas espadrilles crunching on pine needles, her head held high. She didn't know exactly where she was going, but she had a sort of numb, desperate feeling that as long as she kept putting one foot in front of the other, she wouldn't have to think about all the hopes she'd pinned on Marcus Shelby, and how those hopes had never had a chance of coming true.

Eventually, she found herself at the trail at the foot of Sweetbriar Summit, a hill that could be seen quite clearly from town. She hesitated there, at the base of the hill, thinking that her espadrilles weren't exactly suitable for climbing, and that the blanket would be an awkward burden to carry with her.

And then she decided she didn't care about her own unpreparedness. She felt compelled to continue. As if her fate were now mercilessly drawing her forward.

She put her foot on the trail, and she moved on.

For a while, it wasn't bad. The trail was clear and it crisscrossed back and forth across the slope of the hill, so the climb was not too steep.

But then the trail shot upward. Regina had to scramble, sometimes slipping, grabbing on to branches and roots, to keep from sliding back. She grunted and groaned, forging upward, feeling the sweat gather beneath her breasts and under her arms, staining her new dress. Her hair, which she'd pulled back into its usual neat bun that morning, came loose and straggled over her face. And often, in the shadowed places, there were swarms of gnats that got in her eyes and tried to fly into her mouth. More than once she fell forward, breaking her fall with the blanket that kept interfering with her balance, which was tenuous at best.

She knew she was being foolish to go on, especially when the trail petered out to nothing and she found herself scrabbling upward, on all fours most of the time, grabbing any rock or exposed root she could find to keep from tumbling off down the hill. She knew she should at least set the blanket down. Chances were she would be able to find it again on her return. And even if she didn't, it would be no great loss.

But something kept her going, sweating and straining,

clutching the blanket, swatting at the gnats and muttering little exclamations of frustration and irritation under her breath.

And then, when she was almost ready to call it quits and turn around, out of nowhere, she was topping the crest. One minute, there was a grouping of serpentine boulders in front of her. The next, she scrambled over them and found herself in a tiny meadow, where buttercups and wild columbines bloomed. To her left, there was a little stream that bubbled up from an underground spring and tumbled off down the hillside not far away.

Regina froze, turned and looked around her, out over the river to North Magdalene, now shining in the afternoon sun like some picture postcard of the perfect mountain town. She could see the new spire on the recently refurbished bell tower of her church. She spotted the school where she worked part-time during the school year, and old Mrs. Leslie's house, where she went to help out so often during her afternoons. And there was Pine Street, her street, with Nellie's house and her house...and Patrick's house, too.

She could see it all from up here. But no one could see her.

Suddenly she felt giddy. She wondered if what had happened back at the picnic, and her wild scramble up the side of the hill, had unbalanced her mind a little.

And then she realized that she didn't care.

Regina smiled, a slow, secret smile. She knew a feeling she had never known: total freedom. An utterly delicious sensation.

She tossed her blanket to the grass. And she stretched her arms up and out, there beneath the wide sky. She tipped her head back and turned in circles until a sweet dizziness forced her to stop. And when she did stop, swaying with her head thrown back, waiting for her balance to return, she saw a hawk. It glided and circled, riding the air currents in search of unwary prey. She watched it for a time, until it soared too near the sun and she had to look away.

She went to the stream and drank of it, and freely splashed the clear, cool water on her heated face and neck. Then she went back to the blanket—a stroke of brilliance, not to leave the blanket behind—and she spread it on the grass half-in and half-out of the shade of an oak. She slipped off her dusty espadrilles and stretched out on her back on the sunny side of the blanket.

Her body felt good, well used, slightly heavy. Her breath sighed sweetly in and out.

Until the moment that she heard the soft rustle of footsteps in the grass, she did not consciously know that she was waiting.

Her eyes were closed against the sun, but then she felt a shadow block out the brightness.

She sat up, and saw that it was Patrick Jones, as some secret, primal part of her had known it would be. The sun was so bright that she had to shade her eyes to look at him. For a long moment, they stared at each other.

Then he asked in an offhand voice that belied the intensity in his eyes, "Seen a miner's pick around here?"

Regina frowned. The question, which seemed to have nothing to do with the reason her fate had brought him here, puzzled her.

He held up a map. "The treasure hunt. Remember? This is the spot where I'm supposed to find a miner's pick."

"Oh. Yes. Yes, of course." She tucked her bare feet under her and moved over a little, until she was in the shade of the oak.

He dropped to a crouch before her, still in the sun. She tried not to draw back any farther, but the reality of his presence overwhelmed her. She was so poignantly aware of him, of the lithe beauty of his fine body and the warmth coming off his tanned skin. In a bold move, she took the map from his hands.

She studied the mimeographed sheet, then lifted her head to meet his gaze. "This map stops halfway up the trail."

"It does?" His lips curled in a hint of a smile.

"You followed me."

He was silent for a moment. Now his eyes seemed to measure her. "Yeah, I followed you." He took the map away from her, crumpled it and tossed it aside.

She didn't let her gaze waver. "Why?"

"I saw you leave."

"That doesn't answer my question."

"Yeah, it does. I followed you because I saw you leave Marcus Shelby. And you looked like you weren't planning to come back." His eyes narrowed. "*Were* you planning to come back?"

Regina didn't answer. Her emotions kept changing, teetering on a razor's edge. Right then, she was angry again. Angry at Patrick Jones. Her life was slipping out of her control. And it was all this man's fault. "Are you through with Marcus Shelby?" Patrick asked, more directly this time.

Regina still wouldn't answer. She looked away, out across the mountains. So much had happened to her today. She'd admitted to herself that her life was changing. And she'd seen the truth about her loneliness and her unfulfilled dreams.

And she knew now that she had chosen Marcus precisely because he had not wanted any deep involvement. Marcus had been safe—safe to spin her shy, old-maid fantasies around. Until the day she looked out her window and saw Patrick Jones, she'd been content with her dreams that would never come true.

But then, the day had come. She had looked at Patrick, and his image had been seared into her mind and heart.

And she had started changing. And what she wanted now was something that would have shocked her to her virgin core only a few weeks before.

Patrick took her chin in his hand, and made her look in his eyes once more. "Say it. Tell me."

She did not shrink from his touch. It was warm and rough and made her heart beat faster. It was what she wanted, and she was through hiding from what she wanted, from the truth. Today, the truth had burned the shyness right out of her. She looked in Patrick's eyes. "Yes. Marcus and I are through."

"Good." His thumb lazily stroked the soft skin of her jawline, causing lovely ripples of sensation that made her breath catch. "What you want he'll never give you anyway."

She felt a stab of anger at Patrick again, at his knowing the truth about Marcus so easily, when it had taken her until today to admit it to herself. "Oh, really?" Her tone was brittle.

He looked at her mouth. He was smiling. "Really."

"And just what *do* I want?"

His hand moved, his fingers threading through her tangled hair. "A husband," he said. "You want a husband and a family. You want marriage."

Suddenly her anger and bravado fled. She was frightened. He knew too much. Saw too much. She tried again to turn her head.

But he wouldn't let her go. "This was coming." His voice soothed. "Don't disappoint me. Don't lie to me and say you didn't know."

"But I didn't." Her gaze shifted away from his.

He let go of her chin. "Damn." He started to stand.

"Wait."

His eyes were on her, pinning her. "The truth. Or I'm gone."

She looked at him proudly. "I *am* telling the truth. I didn't know. Until today."

"What the hell does that mean?"

"It means I know now. It's all very clear now—in retrospect. But I...I wasn't able to admit it, until today."

Patrick looked at her, weighing what she'd said. It seemed to satisfy him. He dropped to his haunches again. "Okay, you're through pretending, then? Walking away when I wave to you, hurrying off when I call your name?"

She licked her lips. "Yes. I'm through doing those things."

"Good."

He reached for her again. His hand curled around the back of her neck, warm and firm and sure. She felt another quick stab of panic. "Patrick?" It was a plea.

"Shh." With stunning gentleness, he began removing what pins were left in her hair. He pulled them free and set them on the edge of the blanket in a neat, even row. And then he combed her hair down on her shoulders with his fingers. "There," he said, when he was done.

"I..." She had suddenly forgotten how to talk.

But it didn't seem to matter. He moved from a crouch to his knees, so close that his thighs were touching her curled-under legs. His thighs felt hard as heated steel against her. Regina shivered from that heat, and she knew the fiercest, most wonderful tumble of emotions.

Fear. Joy. Desire. Excitement.

He traced the side of her face with his hand. She shivered. He made a small, soothing sound in his throat. She swayed toward him, so that her upturned face was once more in the sun. And then he pushed his fingers through her unbound hair. He cupped the back of her head.

"You want a husband, marriage and a family," he repeated. "I know what you want."

She stared at him, and glimpsed the sun. It blinded her,

so that afterimages, what her mother had always called sun dogs, began dancing in front of her eyes. She was... stunned. Stunned by her own feelings, by the gathered intensity in his body and by the waiting receptiveness in hers.

Patrick was still smiling, but the smile had a predator's edge now. She thought of the mountain lion, all those years ago. Of the way it had watched her, and then allowed her to go. She knew, with a fierce, frightened glee, that she would not be allowed to go this time. That she did not want to go this time.

"I know what you want, Regina," he said again. His face loomed closer. He blotted out the sun. "Marriage, children. A family. And this..."

His mouth covered hers.

Chapter Six

Regina moaned, a starved, startled sound that she didn't realize she'd made until she heard it echo in her head. Patrick gave the sound back to her. It was a mating sound, a sound of need, and demand.

For a split second, fear again took the upper hand. She jerked back from him, losing the consuming touch of his mouth.

They stared at each other. She shook her head.

He nodded.

Time went on forever, and yet stood still.

He didn't reach for her again. He waited.

"Oh, Lord," she murmured, "I cannot do this."

"You can. Close your eyes."

Where the courage came from, Regina had no clue. But she did as Patrick instructed. She let her eyelids close out the meadow and faraway picture-postcard town, the sun, the hawk—and Patrick Jones. Now there was only the dark velvet of her inner lids, and the sun dogs, still shifting and popping before her because she had glanced once or twice at the sun.

"Better?"

She nodded, lowering her head. The sun dogs danced outward, fading to the periphery of her darkened sight.

"Can I touch you?"

She bit her lip. And then nodded once more.

For a moment, nothing happened. She sat on the blanket, her senses tuned high, aware of the heat of the sun and the slight breeze, the smell of evergreen, and the presence of the man, so close to her.

And then he took her hand. He raised it, and pressed it to his lips. She moaned again at the contact. A single tear slid down her cheek.

He touched that tear with his free hand and smoothed it on her cheek until the summer wind cooled it and took it away.

"Don't be afraid, Regina." His voice was a caress in itself. It was the wind and the Summit, her freedom—all new. "It's your first time?"

From somewhere she found her voice. "Yes."

He said nothing, only opened her palm and put his mouth there. His lips moved and his teeth grazed lightly. Regina loosed a long sigh.

And then his hand slid up her bare arm, a long, learning caress. His other hand joined it as he took her face in both hands and pulled her toward him. He kissed her again, a discreet, exploratory caress, a very gentle breath of a kiss.

At first.

But within seconds, the kiss was deepening. "Part your lips for me," he whispered against her mouth.

Her lips went soft, opening of their own accord. And his tongue pressed its advantage, tasting her mouth and then sliding inside to know more of her than any man had ever known before.

She moaned and his hard arms closed around her. He urged her backward to lie upon the ground, guiding her so she lay beneath the cool shadow of the tree. She went, her body yearning, hungering for that which it had never experienced.

He lay full upon her for a moment, covering her, so she would know him, feel his length upon her, his hardness against her. And he kissed her, long and deep.

Then he eased himself over and lay at her side, so his hand was free to touch her. He went on kissing her, as he molded her waist and learned the curve of her hip with gentle, knowing strokes.

And then he pulled back. She groaned in protest because he'd stopped kissing her. She dared to open her eyes.

Above her, he was watching her, challenging her, as he had a million years ago down in the park at the church picnic. Challenging her to...

His hand was on the forgotten strip of tickets, which she'd tucked under the belt at her waist. He held her eyes as, very slowly, he pulled the tickets free. He raised them, until they dangled in a thin cardboard chain above her breasts.

"You may not get much use out of these," he warned. His voice was husky. "I might keep you here all day. Maybe I'll have to pay you back, for not getting your money's worth from them." He lowered the paper chain, until it touched her right breast, at the nipple. Beneath her bra and slip and her new dress, the nipple hardened. Sweet, melting sensations chased themselves around inside of her. "Would that be fair, Regina?"

"What?" The word was slow, melting like she was.

"For me to buy these tickets off of you?"

"No."

"Why not? Did Marcus Shelby buy them for you?" His expression, which had been so intense and knowing, closed a little. Even fogged as her mind was with desire, she noticed that slight change in him, though she didn't understand it.

But then, she thought, Patrick Jones wasn't the kind of man a woman easily understood.

"Answer me, Regina." There was a thread of steel now, underlying the velvet of his voice.

She drew in a breath, and then spoke in a tone that tried its best to be level, in spite of all the distracting sensations Patrick was creating with his nearness and his touch. "No. Marcus didn't buy them. *I* bought them. And even if I don't use them, I don't want my money back. It'll go to the church. I'm glad to see it put to use there." She felt a little guilty, speaking of the church while she lay beneath an oak tree with Patrick Jones. But she pushed the guilt aside. What would happen here would happen. Feeling guilty wouldn't change it.

The closed look left his face. He smiled his slow smile. "You're a good girl, aren't you?"

"I am not a girl."

He chuckled and lowered the tickets, until the whole chain of them lay in loops over her breasts.

She spoke more firmly. "I mean it. I'm not a girl."

"Yes, ma'am." Patrick gathered up the chain of tickets, his fingers brushing her breasts unconcernedly as he did it, causing little flashes of desire to explode like firecrackers inside her, making both of her nipples pucker and ache within the confines of her bra. He wadded the tickets and tossed them away, as he had the treasure map.

And then, very casually, he put his hand on her breast. He cupped it. She felt her nipple, hard and hungry, in the center of his palm. Her body, yearning for more, arched toward his hand through no will of her own.

"Yeah," he murmured. "Oh, yeah..." He rubbed her breast and found the aching nipple with his thumb. He flicked it gently, back and forth. She moaned, closing her eyes again, and tossed her head on the blanket.

As he explored her body, he whispered, "I knew you'd be like this. I knew there was fire under there. Secret fire. The very best kind. A fire for me, just me. It's what I've been needing for all my damn useless life, Gina. My own secret fire." His voice was husky, hungry sounding. "You know what I mean?"

But he gave her no chance to answer. Instead, he cupped the sides of her breast, positioning it so it swelled full and high. Then he lowered his head and covered that breast, still clothed though it was, with his mouth. He let loose a long, slow breath of warm air.

Regina arched again as his sweet, hot breath flowed through her dress and her underwear, to drive her a little crazy, to make her moan.

"Yeah," he muttered once more, the sound roughly tender against her breast.

Then he lifted his head again, and his hand went to the row of buttons that traveled down the front of her dress. Sighing, her whole body seeming to have somehow turned liquid, Regina felt compelled to open her eyes.

Patrick was looking at her face, his own face flushed, his lips slightly swollen, his eyes languorous blue slits. He held her gaze, with that special lazy but insistent way he had, not letting her look away, as he began to undo the buttons.

One by one, the buttons slipped from their holes, until they were undone down to her waist. Very slowly, he parted the dress, revealing her plain white slip. She whimpered.

"Easy. We're going easy." He granted her one sweet kiss, a kiss both of promise and of reassurance.

And then his hand became insistent once more, guiding

the bodice of the dress from her shoulders, so that it gathered at her waist, smoothing down her slip straps, and taking the slip down with her dress. Then he guided her bra straps over her shoulders, waiting until she pulled her arms free of them.

"Turn on your side. Let me unhook this thing."

She did as he asked, smoothing her hair out of his way. He undid the back clasp. She closed her eyes again, holding the bra against her breasts, her whole body burning to feel more of the sweet sensations his touch brought. Yet she couldn't quite bring herself to turn back to him and let him see her naked to the waist here beneath an oak tree in the middle of the afternoon.

He must have sensed her anxiety, because he didn't urge her to turn. Instead, he wrapped his hard arms around her and pulled her back against him, spoon fashion.

For endless moments, they lay still. She felt his breath against the curve of her neck. He allowed her to become used to him, holding her with her bottom tucked against his sex, which she could feel was very much aroused. His strong thighs cradled her, his big arms seemed, in the way they held her, to speak to her of safety, of a haven from all fears.

And then he began to stroke her again, first caressing her bare waist, then sliding his hand up, beneath the bra which she was still clutching against herself.

"Let it go, Gina. Let me touch you. Please."

Her hands relaxed. Carefully, he took the bra away. Then he kissed her shoulder, as his hand cupped her breast, naked for him at last. She dared to look down, to see the strong, brown hand around her small, pale breast. She hitched in a shocked gulp of air, and squeezed her eyes closed.

He went on touching her breast, cupping it, arousing the nipple as he put his lips on her neck. He sucked lightly, moaning a little, nipping and nibbling her skin.

It seemed she was awash in him. His scent, like musk and cedar shavings and something else—dust and sunshine?—swam all around her. His body surrounded her. His hands and mouth claimed her. She sighed and let her head relax in the crook of his arm as her hips began moving in a rhythm she hadn't even realized she knew, rocking in building need against him. He moaned louder, and his body pressed back and forth in rhythm with hers.

His hand left her breast, strayed downward, over her bare upper belly, to where the tops of her dress and slip were bunched around her waist. His hand slid lower still. She stiffened.

He licked her neck, then blew on it. "Let me touch you," he said again. "I'll give you a climax, first. It will make it easier. Later."

She moaned and rubbed her cheek against his arm. She yearned. And she needed. And yet, to hear him say that, say what he'd do, shocked her to her very toes.

When she didn't answer, he took charge. His hand found its way beneath her skirt and slid between her soft thighs. Then it trailed up over her stomach, only to dip lower once more, to delve beneath the elastic waist of her cotton panties. Her belly jumped, and she stiffened as she felt his touch, gentle yet relentless, on her most private place.

"I—"

"Shh. Feel, Gina. That's all. Just feel."

"But…"

His fingers parted her. She groaned.

"Yeah. Feel. That's right…"

His fingers began to move. She could not believe the things his fingers did. She forgot her own embarrassment, she forgot everything. Her hips found that heretofore unknown rhythm once more. His hand stroked her, following the cues her body gave it.

There was a flickering feeling of wonder. It receded and

then approached again, receded and approached. She was moaning, tossing her head. She could hear herself, whimpering, pleading.

And he was stroking her, whispering, "Yeah," his body pantomiming the frantic actions of hers, moving in tandem with her, urging her on.

The wonder approached again, this time like a huge wave. It rose up and rolled over her, consuming her. She threw back her head against his hard chest and cried aloud.

The wave crested and she rode it, high, glorious, frantic. She felt her secret place contracting, right where he was stroking her. She knew that he felt it; she heard his triumphant groan.

And then, as the aftertremors still shook her, he was pulling her onto her back. She went where his hands guided her. At that moment she was totally, completely his. He could have done just about anything. She knew he saw her breasts, bare and pale in the daylight. And it was fine. They were *his* breasts right then. Her entire body, her being, was his.

Quickly, his gaze focused and yet glazed, he unhooked her belt and unbuttoned her dress the rest of the way down. He pulled it out from under her, tossed it aside and took her slip and panties, too, sliding them over her hips, off and away. Within seconds, she was naked before him as he knelt between her thighs.

He murmured, "Mine," and she did not gainsay him, though since her mother had died, she had taken great pride in belonging only to herself.

But the words he said didn't matter. This was what was meant to happen and she had surrendered to it, to her relentless fate. Her fate that had a name: Patrick Jones. She looked up at him, feeling no shame lying naked there with only the shade of the old oak to cover her, as he calmly stripped off his shirt and jeans, his lace-up boots and socks.

When he was naked, too, he loomed above her, the roof of oak leaves beyond his head. His beauty stunned her, as it had that first day. His chest was deep, his belly corded, his hips hard and narrow. He was fully, magnificently aroused.

He put his hand on her again, intimately, and the touch stunned her at the same time as she yielded to it. He stroked her, making her as ready as he could, given the fact that this was her first time.

And then he lowered himself, positioning himself between her pale thighs. She felt him straining at her and she knew she wanted to feel him fully inside her, at the same time as she knew it would cause her pain.

"I could make you pregnant," he said.

She blinked, surprised. What a fool she was. Of course. Doing what they were about to do could make a baby.

She got out, "I didn't..."

"It's okay with me," he said, when her voice trailed off. "I like babies."

She moaned a little. She was so utterly aroused, she could hardly think. Yet she knew that this subject, the subject of babies, was something they should deal with before what was about to happen took place.

"I, um..." She licked her lips.

And when her tongue came out, his eyes changed, heated even more. He put his hand over her mouth and lifted his brows. She licked his hand, as he seemed to be signaling for her to do.

"Ah...yeah..." Balanced on one arm, he tossed his head back as her tongue caressed his palm. His hardness pushed against her, parting her, so he was just a little bit inside, but stopped by the membrane that constituted her innocence. She could feel how wet she was, and how ready. She wanted him. She would give anything to have him fully inside her, to know what this most mysterious of acts was all about, and to know it with Patrick Jones.

But what would she do if, when they came down from Sweetbriar Summit, she carried his baby? The thought sent an unpleasant shiver through her. She'd always dreamed she might someday have children and the years were going by quickly. But she didn't know how she'd handle being pregnant and unmarried in a town like North Magdalene, while at the same time she could never imagine leaving there. It was and always would be her home. She turned her head, away from the palm that she'd been so lasciviously teasing with her tongue.

But he didn't let her go. His hand captured her chin again. He made her look at him. "I said before, Regina. I know what you want."

She opened her mouth to speak, though she didn't really know what she meant to say.

But he wasn't finished. He went on before she could begin. "I'll give you what you want. I'll give you this." He pressed a little deeper into her, stretching her tender inner flesh as far as it would go. One strong thrust would put him beyond the barrier. It would take her virginity, would take them both past the point of no return.

"I'll give you *all* of what you want. Babies. Starting now, if that's what happens from what we do here today. All you have to do is…"

She stared up at him, pleading with her eyes to know what he was asking of her.

He told her. "Marry me."

Chapter Seven

"Marry me." He said it again.

"I…"

"Say yes. Say it now, or—"

"But, I…"

"Say *yes*, Regina."

His eyes above her seemed like small pieces of the big, big sky. They went on forever, mesmerizing her. His body called to hers. And her body was answering. The strength of his purpose overwhelmed her.

How could she even for a moment have thought him less than frightening? How could she have been lulled by the touch of his hands to forget what he was: a wild, rough Jones. A man who would stop at nothing to claim what he wanted, no matter how implausible what he wanted might be—like marrying Anthea Black's sickly old maid daughter.

For a brief flash of time, she wanted to strike out at him,

to roll from beneath him and run down the hill naked—anything, to escape him. To get away from the hard blue command of his eyes.

"Don't…" There was hurt in his voice, suddenly. He was pleading with her not to run.

And all her gathered rigidness fled.

The reality of her fate returned. Though she knew it would hurt her, she wanted him. He had called her his. And she was.

And if she married him, *he* would be *hers*.

Regina was not a fool. She knew Patrick didn't love her, that he must have some ulterior motive in this. But on the other hand, what he wanted and what she wanted were the same, really. She wanted a husband. And he was demanding that she marry him.

She looked up at the man poised above her. Her whole life spun around in her head. The town they both lived in. Who he was. Who she was. What an uproar there would be. That gorgeous hell-raiser Patrick Jones and plain, spinsterish Regina Black. Nellie Anderson and Linda Lou Beardsly would have a gossipmonger's jubilee.

"Marry me."

It was a crazy idea. An impossible idea.

He groaned. "Regina…you'll kill me. Say you'll marry me, before I—"

Her answer came on a soft exhalation. "Yes."

His eyes changed again. They burned hotter, with triumph. He whispered, "Say it again."

"Yes." She lifted her arms and twined them around his neck. "Yes, yes, yes…"

And he thrust into her.

She threw her head back and cried aloud.

He thrust again, burying his head against her neck, moaning, "So good, so good…"

She held on, riding it out, though her untried body was

too shocked by his invasion to begin the climb to fulfillment again. And he was lost to all but his own desire. She could feel it in the way he pushed into her, as if he must bury himself fully within her, as if he must brand her in her deepest place.

He rode her hard and fast. She clung to him, hearing her own woman's cries of mingled hurt and need and encouragement, clutching his broad back, aware of everything and nothing, as at last he thrust even deeper than all the thrusts that went before. His head, which he had buried against her shoulder, reared back. He howled his release at the oak and the meadow, at the wide summer sky, his neck straining, his hard arms braced on the blanket on either side of her.

When he was done, he hung his head and his body went lax, though he did not sink down upon her. A drop of sweat trickled from his hair and landed on her breast. Gently he dipped his head and licked it away.

Something melted inside her at the touch of his tongue. Deep in her heart, a tender space was created that hadn't been there before. She didn't examine it, she just *felt* it. And silently welcomed it.

"Regina." His eyes were waiting for hers. She met them. "I was rough, I hurt you."

"Yes." She reached up and stroked his damp hair back from his forehead.

"I should have been gentler."

She smoothed the hair at his temple, guiding it behind an ear. "No. You shouldn't. It was...what it was. Exactly perfect." She was thinking of fate, thinking that there was pain in one's fate, as well as glory. And that was what it had been. Painfully glorious. "It was just exactly right," she said aloud.

He let out a laugh that was really more like a groan, and then he very carefully retreated from her. He rolled to his back beside her and threw an arm over his eyes.

Regina, who hadn't felt naked at all while Patrick's body covered hers, suddenly felt very bare indeed.

She sat up bolt upright, spied her dress and grabbed it against herself—and then noticed the streaks of blood, drying now on the blanket and on her pale skin.

"Come on, we'll take care of that," Patrick said.

She started a little at the sound of his voice. Glancing over, she saw he was watching her. And then, in a fluid, stunning movement, he gathered his legs beneath him and stood.

He looked down at her. She thought how beautiful he was—and how comfortable with his own nudity.

Regina, on the other hand, was not comfortable at all. She sat staring up at him, clutching her dress against her breasts, trying not to notice that there were streaks of blood on his thighs, too.

He reached down for her. Not knowing what else to do, she gave him her hand. He pulled her up, while she held her dress tightly against herself.

Patiently, he pried her dress from her clenched fists, shook it out and held it up for her, open, the way a man holds a coat for a woman to slide into. She put her arms in the armholes and felt marginally more at ease the minute the dress was around her. He buttoned her up.

As he did that, she remembered her bra and her panties. "My underwear..."

"You don't need it. At least not right now."

"But..."

He buttoned the last button, then took her hand. "Come on."

He led her to the stream, where he let go of her hand and stepped into the narrow channel himself. He rinsed his body clean, pretending to pay great attention to what he was doing, though she knew he was really giving her a chance to wash herself without feeling that he watched her.

She gathered her skirt above her knees, waded in and rinsed off the telltale signs of her lost virginity. Then she quickly clambered up the mossy bank and returned to the blanket.

Once there, she had no idea what to do next. It was as if a fog were lifting. And what she had just done with Patrick Jones was seeming less and less like fate with each moment that passed.

Yes. Less and less like fate. And more like a huge and terrible, thoroughly humiliating mistake.

She grabbed up her panties and shimmied into them. Then, her back turned to Patrick who was still at the stream, she unbuttoned her dress to her waist and put on her bra, fumbling with it a little, but at last hooking the clasp, yanking it into place, pulling it up over her shoulders and shoving her arms through the sleeve holes of the dress once more.

Casting a guilty glance at her wadded-up slip, she hastily buttoned up again. She felt half-naked without the slip, but there was no way she was going to take off her dress again to put it on.

She would just have to roll the slip up in the blanket and hope that nobody noticed. Now, where was her belt?

She turned to look for it. And saw it dangling from Patrick's hand.

Her eyes widened. Somehow he had returned from the stream without her hearing him, while her back was turned and she was trying her best to make herself decent. He'd also managed to slip into his jeans.

"This what you're looking for?" He held out the belt.

"Y-yes, it is." She took it cautiously, the way one might take a shoe from the mouth of a dog known to bite. "Thank you."

Swiftly she wrapped the belt around her waist and buckled it. "Now, where are my shoes?"

He bent down. "Right here." He straightened, holding the espadrilles. She reached for them.

He held them away. "Wait a minute."

She frowned. "Excuse me?"

"I said wait a minute."

She didn't like his tone, not one bit. "Those are *my* shoes."

"No one said they weren't."

"Then give them to me."

"In a minute. When you're calmer."

"What do you mean?"

"I'm afraid if I give them to you now, you'll shove your feet in them and then turn and run."

That was exactly what she had been planning to do. She bit her lip. Her chin was quivering. Like a complete fool, she hovered on the verge of tears. She bit her lip harder, to make the tears recede. "This is ridiculous. You have absolutely no right to keep my shoes from me."

"Settle down." He sounded like someone trying to calm an hysterical woman.

Which wasn't too surprising. She was right on the brink of *being* an hysterical woman.

She looked away, out over North Magdalene, and collected herself, reminding herself that what had been done was done. She couldn't go back. Nothing would be served by indulging in an embarrassing crying jag right here in front of Patrick Jones.

"Regina." His voice was so gentle, it made her want to cry all over again. "Regina, I know this is a lot for you to take in all at once."

She forced herself to look at him again. "I must... I need to be alone now."

He seemed to study her. "All right." Then he advised, "But we'll be leaving tonight."

She stared at him. "Tonight? What are you talking about? Leaving for where?"

"For Tahoe."

"To do what?" she asked, though of course she knew what the answer must be.

"To get married." His chestnut brows lifted. His half smile had an ironic edge. "You do remember that you said you'd marry me. Don't you?"

"Yes. Yes, of course. I remember."

"Good."

"I do remember. But..."

"But what?"

She focused on the impossibility of the arrangements, in order *not* to think of the preposterousness of what she'd promised to do. "This is the Fourth of July weekend. Surely all the hotels will be fully booked."

"My dad has a few old friends there. He'll see to it we get a room."

"Oh...well..." Regina felt a slight headache begin at her temples. She pressed her fingers there and rubbed.

"We're going, Regina," Patrick said. He looked up toward the sun. "It's around three now. We'll leave at six."

"But I..."

"What?"

"I just..."

"*What?*"

"Well, I don't understand why we have to be in such a terrible rush about this."

He tossed her shoes at her feet. "Let's stop dancing around the real issue here. You agreed to marry me. Are you breaking your word?"

Suddenly she couldn't look at him.

"Regina, are you backing out?"

She shot him a quick glance. His face was hard, his eyes cold jewels.

She looked down again, this time at the blanket, where the blood of her innocence had dried now to a few rusty streaks. It was difficult to tell for sure now whether the streaks actually were blood.

But she knew what they were. Would always know.

Today she had crossed a boundary. And she had crossed it with this blue-eyed hellion.

"Regina." His voice commanded an answer.

She furiously considered.

The change in her life had come. She could embrace it, or hide from it.

As Anthea Black's daughter, she'd done a lot of hiding in her life.

Perhaps it was time to try a new way.

"*Regina.*" His tone said he would not be put off any longer.

She looked right at him. "All right."

"All right, what?"

"All right, I'm not backing out. I'll marry you as I said I would."

His hard expression relaxed. "Okay." He nodded. "Okay."

She thought of the big church wedding she'd always dreamed of having. "But I don't see why we have to race off to Tahoe this very night. I'd rather—"

He raised a hand. "Some things, we'll do your way. But this, we'll do the way *I* want it. We've agreed to get married, and we're going through with it. Now. We're not going to hang around this town and give everyone a chance to screw things up. I know you can get away. The only real job you have is during school term, so now you're pretty flexible. Right?"

"Yes. But, Patrick, I—"

"You said you needed some time alone. You're wasting that time." He dropped to the blanket and pulled on his socks and boots. "I'll go and see that the arrangements are made." He briskly laced up his boots. "Plan to be gone till midweek. I wish it could be longer, but right now I can't leave the garage for any extended period of time. In a few years, maybe, we'll take off together for a real honeymoon." He grabbed his shirt, tossing it over his shoulder as he stood. "You want me to take the blanket back for you?"

"No, I, um..."

He grinned. "You're afraid someone will recognize it and figure out what we've been doing."

"Um, well, I..."

"Hey. It's okay." He shrugged. "I'll come for you. Six o'clock. Be ready." And then he turned and started down the hill.

She watched him go, a thousand arguments and questions bouncing around in her head. But she didn't stop him. She *did* want some time to herself. And he had not given her a lot of it. The opportunity to ask him questions would come soon enough.

After all, they were going to be spending the rest of their lives together.

At the very thought that she would spend the rest of her life with Patrick Jones, Regina's knees went a little weak. She sank to the blanket, landing on something that made a rustling sound. Paper. She scooted aside and found the wadded treasure map and the chain of picnic tickets.

She held them up, looked at them for a moment and then she clutched them to her breast. She loosed a long sigh, closed her eyes and tipped her face to the sky.

Then she slid them in her pocket and put on her shoes, after which she did her best to pin up her tangled hair.

When Regina reached the park once more, neither Patrick nor Marcus was anywhere in sight. She was grateful for that. She didn't even want to look at Marcus and she was mindful of the few hours Patrick had allowed her before their new, improbable life together would begin.

She'd almost reached her car when it occurred to her that tomorrow was Sunday. If she eloped with Patrick tonight, she would not be in church to play the hymns. She knew she must ask someone to see that other arrangements were made.

Nellie, as the church secretary, was the logical choice. But Nellie was the last person she wanted to talk to right now.

"Regina, are you all right?"

Regina blinked and realized she'd almost barreled into Delilah Fletcher. "What? Oh, yes. I'm fine. Just fine."

Delilah let out a throaty laugh. The laugh surprised Regina. Delilah never used to laugh like that—not until she got together with Sam, anyway.

"Well, you look positively wild," Delilah said.

Nervously, Regina smoothed her hair, which she knew she hadn't pinned up very effectively. "I do?"

Now Delilah smiled. "Yes. But it suits you."

"I—" It suddenly occurred to Regina that Delilah might be just the one she was looking for. "Delilah..." She took the other woman's arm and pulled her behind a tree. "I must have a word with you."

Delilah freed her arm from Regina's grip. "About what?"

"I just... I can't explain right now. But I won't be at church tomorrow. And someone must be found to play the hymns. Do you think you could ask Wilma Higgins? Or even Tondalaya Clark? Either Nellie or the pastor can give you the list of songs."

"Has this got anything to do with my brother, Patrick— and my father, perhaps?"

"Er, why do you ask?"

"About fifteen minutes ago, Patrick, who'd disappeared just after lunch, showed up. He whispered in my father's ear and then the two of them took off together."

"Well, Delilah, I—"

Delilah threw up both hands. "Never mind. Now that I think about it, I don't want to know. Of course I'll see to it that someone else can play the hymns."

"Oh, thank you."

"It's all right."

"I...I must go now."

"I understand." Delilah's dark eyes were soft. Regina smiled at her and turned away. "Regina?"

She turned back. "Yes?"

"Good luck. You'll need it."

For a moment, the two women looked at each other.

Then Regina nodded. "I know." She whirled and went on her way again, barely hearing Pastor Johnson announcing that the treasure hunters had exactly fifteen minutes left to report to the grandstand and that the bake sale auction would begin in one hour.

At her car Regina reached in the open window to pop the trunk latch. Then she went around to the back to toss the blanket in.

Just before she got there, she came face-to-face with Nellie.

"There you are, Regina. I've been looking all over for you."

Regina held back a groan. "Oh, hello, Nellie."

Trying to communicate an air both offhand and yet much too busy to hang around and chat, Regina edged around Nellie's tall, thin form. With great care she set the blanket in the trunk. Her slip, after all, was rolled inside it.

"Regina, we need you at the food tables now. Linda Lou is simply perishing for a break."

After shutting the trunk, Regina tried to edge around Nellie again, but Nellie quite openly stepped to block her path. Regina sighed. "Nellie, something's come up. I have to go home."

Nellie's eagle eyes were narrowed. "Why, dear, you seem to have acquired a *bruise*."

Regina coughed. "Excuse me?"

"There. On your neck. You have a bruise. And your hair…"

"I went for a walk." Regina held her hand rigidly at her side, to keep it from rising and touching the place on her neck where she knew Patrick had kissed her while he held her spoon fashion against his chest. She hadn't even realized he'd left a mark.

"A *walk?*" Nellie looked frankly disbelieving.

Regina dragged her traitorous mind back from thoughts of Patrick's kisses. It was a major effort. "Yes, a walk," she said. "Quite a long, strenuous walk, actually. I'm sure I look frightful. And I…bumped into a tree."

Nellie's thin lips flattened. She didn't buy that for a moment. But there was kindness in Nellie, and it showed in her voice when she asked, "Are you all right?"

"I'm fine."

"Has someone hurt you?"

"No. Of course not. But I must go. Now."

Nellie's clawlike hand closed over Regina's forearm. "What has happened, Regina? You can trust me. You can talk to me."

Regina, who longed only to jerk free, ordered her body to relax. "Nellie—" she forced a mild tone "—you are so kind. And I do know exactly how much I can trust you. But there's nothing to talk about. I've become overtired, from walking, that's all. And I've worked so hard all week, on the picnic. Honestly, those twenty dozen cookies about did me in."

"Well, I—"

Gently Regina pulled her arm free of Nellie's clutching grasp. "I just want to go home and lie down for a while." That part was the truth. "And then, if I feel a little better, I'll be back. I promise you." A total lie, but Regina refused to be ashamed.

Sometimes one had to take extreme measures when dealing with Nellie. And Nellie would have the whole story soon enough, Regina had no doubt. But Regina was staunchly determined that Nellie would not get it from her.

Suddenly, the idea of disappearing from town for a few days held great appeal. By the time she returned, she would bet her piano, everyone would know that she and Patrick had eloped. And maybe that was just as well. She wouldn't have to explain it all in detail to everyone she talked to.

"Something's happened between you and Marcus, hasn't it?" Nellie looked appropriately consoling.

Regina considered. Perhaps the best way to get rid of Nellie right now would be to give her some intriguing little rumor to spread around. "Yes, Nellie. Something *has* happened between Marcus and me."

"Oh, I knew it. I just knew it." Nellie's eyes sparkled with eagerness. "What is it?"

"It's very simple. Marcus and I have discovered we want different things from life. We won't be seeing each other anymore."

"No!"

"Yes, I'm afraid that's the way it is. And now, I—"

Nellie leaned in close. "What 'different things' do you want?"

"Nellie—"

"You must talk about it, dear. You must get it all off your chest."

Regina sagged against her car and allowed herself to look exactly as worn-out and overwrought as she felt. "Nellie, I simply cannot talk about it now."

Nellie tipped her head to the side. She gave a small sigh. She was accepting the fact that she wasn't going to get any more out of Regina. For now.

It was time to lay the groundwork for the next assault. Nellie became all solicitude. "Well, of course you can't talk about it now." She patted Regina's shoulder. "You go on home and rest. And don't even *think* about coming back here today. You've simply been through too much. I'll handle everything."

I'm sure you will, Regina thought. "Thanks, Nellie."

"Don't even mention it." Nellie took Regina's arm as if Regina were aged or in some other way infirm, and helped her the few steps to her car door. Once inside, Regina reached under the seat for her small purse and found her keys.

Nellie closed the car door for her. "You just relax, now. Don't think about any of it. I'll call and check on you as soon as I get home today."

"Thanks, Nellie." Regina did her best to sound as if she meant it. "But today I'm not answering the door no matter what. And I'm taking the phone off the hook."

Nellie's face fell, but she managed to control her disappointment at not being able to pry more information out of Regina in the very near future. She clucked. "Of course, dear. I'll drop by tomorrow."

"Oh, Nellie. You don't have to bother with me. I'll be fine, really. I—"

"Nonsense. What are friends for? You just go home. Draw the blinds and get some rest. You can tell me everything in the morning."

There was no way Regina was going to reply to that one. She started up her car, gave Nellie a last wave, backed out and drove away.

The first thing Regina did when she reached her house was to rush to her bathroom and look at herself in the mirror over the sink. What she saw was a pale-skinned woman with wild brown hair and a love bite on her neck.

The pale skin flushed rosy pink. When Nellie found out that she'd eloped with Patrick Jones, then Nellie would figure out where that suspicious *bruise* had come from.

Regina lifted her chin. So what? By the time the town gossips started putting things together, she would be Patrick's wife. People like Nellie might not exactly approve of love bites, but they couldn't really condemn them if they were put there by a woman's legal spouse.

Regina went on staring at herself. For so many years, she had thought of herself as Anthea Black's daughter. Recently, she had begun to discover who she—Regina—was. And now, though she was determined never to let another person control her life again, she would be more than the independent adult self she had discovered. She would also be Patrick's wife.

Patrick's wife.

Regina was stunned all over again, just thinking about it. She sank very slowly to the commode and stared at the potted philodendron on the windowsill.

When she felt she could stand again, she rose and removed her rumpled clothes and took a long bath. The water burned a little, when it touched the sensitive, newly used place between her thighs. She was tender there. But it was a good kind of tenderness. And now that she would be a wife, she would grow accustomed to lovemaking. The discomfort would fade.

Realizing that she was staring dreamily at the tub fixtures, Regina submerged herself completely in the water, after which she sat up and reached for the shampoo. She mustn't get too carried away with sentimental notions. She and Patrick had much to say to each other.

They had agreed to marry, but their courtship had been,

to put it generously, brief. She knew very little of what he expected of her as his wife. And not much more about what she herself would want from him as her husband. She did realize that the tranquil existence she had pictured with Marcus would be highly unlikely with a man like Patrick Jones.

They would talk about it, Regina decided as she dunked her head again to rinse it. One of the most important things in a marriage, she firmly believed, was good communication. She would get some answers right away, especially about those ulterior motives she knew he must have for marrying her.

Chapter Eight

Regina's doorbell rang at exactly six o'clock. She was packed and ready, wearing a pink sleeveless dress with a V-neck and matching belt and shoes. It was a sexier dress than the conservative ones she usually wore.

In fact, over the past few years, she'd bought herself almost a whole new wardrobe of dresses, along with the appropriate accessories. She'd worn one or two of her new outfits when she'd begun dating Marcus. Very tactfully, Marcus had told her that the dresses didn't suit her. So she'd stopped wearing them.

Until now.

Now, every dress in the garment bag that she was taking to Tahoe was one of the newer ones.

She went to the door and pulled it open. Patrick was standing there, so handsome in tan slacks and a sports shirt, it almost hurt to look at him.

He gave her the kind of once-over men gave other women all the time.

"Yeah," he said.

She blushed and felt wonderful. Then she remembered her manners. "Won't you...come in?"

Patrick stepped past the threshold and she shut the door behind him.

He looked at her, his gaze lazy and hot. "You're something. I was half-afraid you'd chicken out on me, that I'd have to take drastic measures to get you in the car with me. But look at you. Just look the hell at you."

Shamelessly she inquired, "What kind of 'drastic measures?'"

He stuck his hands in his pockets and faked an innocent air—as he backed her up against the door. "Kidnapping, maybe. Or begging on my hands and knees." He brought his face very close to hers. "Or maybe..."

"Maybe what?"

He kissed her—a long, slow, bone-dissolving kiss. But he kept his hands in his pockets the whole time.

And when she was right on the brink of begging him to take his hands from his pockets and use them as only he knew how, he pulled away.

"All ready to go?" he asked in a voice that was probably a little hoarser than he meant it to be.

She noticed that his hair was wet and his face freshly shaven. She liked the smell of his after-shave. And she found it all incredibly endearing, to think of him grooming himself so thoroughly to be ready for his wedding trip. To look nice for her.

"I like your hair down like that," he said.

It covered the love bite, but she didn't say so. She only smiled. "Thank you."

"Well?"

"Yes?"

"I asked if you were ready."

"I am. Yes. Ready."

"Where's your stuff?"

"Right behind you. You almost tripped on it when you came in."

He put his hand on the door, near her head, and leaned on it. "I did not almost trip. I never almost trip. I'm a Jones."

"Yes. I know." A little thrill shivered through her. In North Magdalene, most women dreamed that one of the Jones boys might turn his eyes to her. The daring women dreamed openly. The more conservative types, like Regina, only dreamed such things in their most secret hearts.

"Your eyes are gray," he said. "Dove gray. But when you're turned on, they darken. Did you know that?"

"No, I..."

He leaned closer—and then pulled back. "We'd better get the hell out of here. Now."

"Yes, I—"

He turned and scooped up her suitcase, vanity case and garment bag. "Open the damn door."

She did as he told her. He went out ahead of her, leaving her to lock up.

When they turned onto Main Street, they found it nearly deserted. Regina assumed that everyone was still at the picnic across the river.

It did turn out, though, that Angie Leslie, old Mrs. Leslie's beautiful, thrice-divorced granddaughter, just happened to be coming out of Marcus's grocery store at the exact moment that Patrick and Regina drove by. Angie was carrying a full brown bag, and she almost dropped it on the sidewalk when she saw Regina Black sitting in the passenger seat of Patrick Jones's Ford Bronco.

Regina, not knowing what else to do, raised her hand in a wave. Angie shifted the bag in her arms and waved back. Patrick drove on by. Angie's mouth was still hanging open when Regina lost sight of her in the Bronco's side-view mirror.

Once the town was well behind them, Regina decided it was time to find out from Patrick exactly why he'd decided to make her his wife. She suggested they ought to talk about their reasons for getting married.

Patrick agreed that would be a good idea. Why *had* she agreed to marry him?

She sighed, thinking she should have been more direct. "But, Patrick, you already know my reasons. You listed them for me, up on Sweetbriar Summit a few hours ago, before you, um…"

"*Kissed* you," he provided, and then shot her a teasing grin.

"Right." She grinned back, feeling deliciously naughty, a wholly new sensation for her. "So now I'd like to know *your* reasons for marrying *me*."

"Sure." He glanced in his side-view mirror, and then back out the windshield. "But first I'd really like to hear *your* reasons from you."

She frowned. This wasn't going at all as she'd imagined. "Patrick, if you already know them, why do I have to say them?"

"Because I'd like to hear them in your own words."

"But I—"

"I honestly would, Regina."

"Well, I…"

"Come on."

She realized he did have a point. It was only fair that she should explain her motives if she wanted him to detail his.

So she gamely began, "I, um, really want to be married, Patrick. I want a family. Working together with a man to build a good life is important to me. But until my mother died, I didn't realize that."

"Why not?"

"Well, my mother was a very demanding person." She slid him a glance, expecting him to make some humorously critical comment about her mother. Her feelings about her mother were not all positive. Yet she had loved her mother, and loyalty made her defensive when people made disparaging remarks about Anthea.

He noticed her glance, smiled at her and turned his eyes back to the road. "You never had a life of your own, did you, until she died?"

His voice was kind. He was such a fascinating man, really. He could be quite crude. And then he could stun her with his sensitivity.

"That's true," she said. "Until my mother died, my life was completely wrapped up with hers. She was so strong-willed. And I was all she had. She brought me up to be everything to her. And I loved her. But after I grew up, she just would not let me go. And I suppose I clung to her, too. When she died, I was *forced* to make my own life." She fell into a pensive silence, and then remembered her original subject. She sat up straighter. "Now, where was I?"

"After your mother died, you realized you wanted to get married."

"Yes. That's right. But I also wanted to live in North Magdalene, where my prospects were somewhat limited."

"Because?"

"You know very well why."

"So? Tell me anyway. Please?" The quick look he gave her melted her heart.

"Oh, all right. There were perhaps eight or nine unmarried men who were anywhere near my age. They were not breaking down my door to ask me out. But then Marcus bought the grocery store. He seemed such a nice, quiet, reserved man. A person just like me. We started dating. I assumed that eventually he would become my husband."

She looked down and smoothed her dress over her knees. The memory of her humiliation with Marcus was still fresh.

"He never would have married you." Patrick's tone was flat.

She looked at him. "I understand that now."

"So forget him."

"Well, of course I will. But, Patrick, it was only *today* that all this happened. It will take me a little while to put it all behind me."

His voice was gruff. "Let's just get this clear. You'll be my wife. You won't be hanging around with Marcus Shelby anymore."

"I understand, Patrick."

"Good. Go on."

She made herself speak brightly. "So it turned out that Marcus didn't want marriage. And then, there you were. And you were so…"

He was smiling again. "Convincing?"

She looked shyly down and then back up. "Yes. You were *convincing*. Very. So I agreed to marry you. And…" She shrugged, her hands out. "Here I am."

He gave her a warm look. "I'm glad."

"Me, too." She waited, sure he was going to start explaining his own motives. But he said nothing. So she prompted, "Now, what about you?"

He pointed out the window. "Here comes the turn to Highway 20."

"Yes, I see. Now, what about you?"

He put his hand on her knee.

"Patrick?"

"Nice," he said softly, rubbing her knee. He gazed out the windshield, presumably looking for the turnoff, which Regina knew was clearly marked and just about impossible to miss.

"Patrick…"

He went on gently caressing her knee. She realized vaguely that her skin seemed to come more alive when he touched her. Her mind, on the other hand, seemed to go a little dim.

"Patrick, you were going to explain to me about... um..."

His hand slid up her thigh a little. "I better watch it, huh? We could become a road hazard."

"Um...yes. Yes, you should be careful...."

He caressed her thigh for a few moments more, during which time she completely forgot about what she'd been trying to get him to tell her. Then, when she knew she was going to have to remind him that driving was a serious responsibility, he reluctantly took his hand away.

She wasted ten minutes staring dreamily out the window smiling like a lovesick fool, before she remembered her intention to find out why he had proposed to her. She straightened in her seat and tried again.

He smiled and agreed to tell her—and then somehow he didn't.

It was like that for the entire trip. She'd bring the subject around where she wanted it. And then he would find a way to change it once more. When they pulled up to the valet parking area in front of one of the best casino/hotels in South Shore, she knew no more about what he was really up to than she'd known when the drive started.

They were checked into their suite by eight-thirty.

The suite, newly remodeled they were told, had been designed with honeymooners in mind. It boasted a small terrace with a view of the lake, a huge round bed on a dais and a sitting room with a full bar. Each room seemed to flow into the next one, so that the bedroom was only separated from the sitting room by a wide arch. The bath, with its huge sunken tub, was also fully open to the bedroom. Only the room with the commode in it had a privacy door.

On the black marble counter of the bar, there was a huge fruit basket, as well as a silver ice bucket with a champagne bottle sticking out of it.

The bellman offered to open the champagne.

"We'll handle it," Patrick said, and tipped him.

Once the bellman had left, Regina stood on the pricey close-woven pale carpet and worried about the expense.

Patrick had just bought a house. He'd owned the North Magdalene Garage for under a year. She did not believe that he was wealthy. He couldn't possibly have money to throw around. And yet here he was, going all out to make their short honeymoon a time to remember.

Well—she squared her shoulders—she *did* have money. In fact, now she thought about it, maybe she'd hit on his real reason for wanting to marry her. Perhaps he wanted her as his bride because he was having money problems and knew that she was well-off.

The idea that he might be marrying her for her money wasn't a particularly pleasant one. But if it were true, then it was best if they could talk about his financial situation honestly.

She resolved that they really did have to talk frankly about all this soon. But for right now, she decided, this was going to be her honeymoon, too. And since she was sure she had more money than he did, she would pay for it.

She told him as much.

He shook his head. "Hell, no. This is on the old man anyway."

"The old man?"

"Yeah. My dad. Oggie."

"Oh. Yes. Oggie." It suddenly occurred to her that peculiar old Oggie Jones would very soon be her father-in-law. She felt a little shiver, remembering the way he had caught her watching Patrick that first day, and then how he had hobbled past the blanket at the picnic today, right before Marcus finally told her that he never intended to be a married man.

"This whole trip is a wedding present from him," Patrick continued on the subject of Oggie. "And don't worry about him being able to afford it. My dad is doing okay, when it comes to money."

"He certainly doesn't flaunt his wealth," she remarked delicately, thinking of old Oggie's threadbare shirts, baggy trousers and frayed suspenders.

Patrick chuckled at that. "Gina, you're something." He reached for her and pulled her against him. "Really something…" He bent his head and nibbled her lip.

She sighed.

He deepened the kiss. His tongue urged her lips to part, and his hands roamed her back. He raised his head, but only long enough to slant his lips the other way, and then he was kissing her again.

Her knees went all wobbly. But somehow she managed to get them to hold her up as he maneuvered her across the room and up the steps of the dais to the perimeter of the massive round bed. He sat, pulling her down with him. Then he urged her to stretch out, after which he slid over so that she was beneath him.

He kissed her some more. She wrapped her arms around his neck and kissed him right back.

And then he lifted his head enough to smile down at her.

"Your eyes are dark as storm clouds," he teased in a husky whisper.

She made a little mindless sound, raising a hand that felt deliciously heavy to trace the shape of his ear.

"I should feed you," he said.

She only smiled. He'd been kissing her, after all. And

when he kissed her, she couldn't think anyway. She became a very stupid woman when he kissed her. Blissfully stupid.

"But I think first," he went on, "we should get ourselves a license and then find a wedding chapel."

A few of her wits returned. "We're getting married *to-night?*"

"Yep. Right away."

They made it to the Douglas County Clerk's office just before it closed at ten that night. Then, license in hand, they looked in the phone book and found a chapel.

It was called Millie and Everet's Chapel of Love in the Pines, though most of the pines in the immediate vicinity had long since been mowed down to make room for the big supermarket next door. There were two couples ahead of them, but Regina and Patrick had their turn at last.

At a few minutes before one on the morning of the Fourth of July, Regina Black became Mrs. Patrick Jones. When they left the Chapel of Love in the Pines, there were fireworks going off far out over the lake.

They returned to their suite at the hotel, opened the champagne and raided the fruit basket. Somehow, dinner had been skipped over in the process of accomplishing their marriage.

After consuming two glasses of champagne, a banana and a kiwifruit that Patrick had peeled and sectioned for her, Regina kicked off her shoes and slid up to rest among the huge pile of pillows on the giant bed. Once thoroughly comfortable, she admired her engagement diamond and wedding band and wondered where Patrick had acquired them.

She'd been completely surprised when he pulled them from his pocket in the wedding chapel. They were old, she knew. There were a few scratches on the bands and the diamonds were cut differently than more modern rings.

Regina didn't realize Patrick was watching her until he remarked, "You like your rings."

She looked up. She knew her face was soft and full of telltale emotions, but she didn't mind. Patrick was her husband now. A husband had a right to see his wife in her more tender moments.

"Oh, yes." She sighed. "They're so beautiful."

"They were my mother's wedding rings."

Regina mused on that. On the thought that she wore the rings that had sealed the vows of Oggie and Bathsheba Jones.

Patrick said, "My dad gave them to me just before I came to pick you up. I hope you don't mind that they're not new."

"Oh, Patrick. No, I don't mind. I don't mind at all. It's an honor."

Patrick chuckled.

Regina insisted, "No, I mean it. And if I were superstitious, I'd say that any marriage sealed with these rings was bound to last."

He laughed out loud at that, then grew more serious. "And why is that?"

"Well, whatever anyone in North Magdalene thinks of Oggie Jones, we all know how much he and your mother loved each other."

"You do, huh?" Patrick's expression was hard to read. She thought he looked indulgent, so she decided to go on.

"Yes." She nodded. "Absolutely. It's...well, it's like a beautiful romantic novel. How Oggie wandered into town, a footloose gambling man without a cent to his name, took one look at beautiful Bathsheba Riley and swore to marry her, even though everyone always assumed Bathsheba would marry rich Rory Drury."

"Things don't always turn out the way everyone expects," Patrick said.

"They certainly don't," Regina agreed. "They say Rory was terribly jealous."

"Yeah, that's what they say."

"They say he got his buddies together and beat Oggie up, left him battered and broken behind the Hole in the Wall, warning him to leave town if he knew what was good for him."

Misty-eyed, Regina looked down at her rings. Slowly, lovingly, she twisted them on her finger. She was lost in the tale, one of the legends of her town.

"But Oggie wouldn't do that," she continued. "Oh, no. He staggered inside and challenged Rory to a poker game. Of course, Rory couldn't back down and keep his pride. And Oggie, even badly injured and weak from loss of blood, won that game anyway. Won five thousand dollars from Rory, which in those days was enough to buy the Hole in the Wall from Stinky Collins. And Oggie did buy it, and proposed formally to Bathsheba, who said yes. And everything looked like it would work out beautifully for them. But then—"

"Hey." Patrick's teasing voice reached her, even through the magic of the old story.

She looked at him and smiled sheepishly. "I got carried away."

He shrugged. "It's a great story. But believe me, I've heard it already."

"I imagine so."

He was standing by the arch to the sitting room. "Come here." His voice had gone velvety.

She knew what was coming. She could see it in his eyes. On the drive back to the hotel, she'd been thinking that they would have a nice little talk when they got here. She'd imagined he'd be more willing to open up to her about his motives, now that the big step had been taken and they were husband and wife.

Gingerly she suggested, "Patrick, I had hoped we could talk for a while."

He shook his head. "Uh-uh. Not now. Now I want to make love. With my wife."

"But, Patrick, I—"

"Uh-uh. Come here."

She looked at him for a long moment, her desire fighting her good sense.

"Gina." The sound of the nickname he seemed to have coined for her was tender, but still there was command in it.

Still doubtful, but unable to resist him, she slid off the bed. Once upright, she smoothed the airy folds of her pale orchid chiffon dress, which she had bought two years ago and never worn.

Until tonight, her wedding night.

"Come here." This time he only mouthed the words.

She started down the steps of the dais, just as he began walking toward her. They met in the middle of the huge, opulent room.

He took her chin and tipped it up. "My old man always said that the right wife is everything." His fingers strayed over her jawline, into her loose hair. "I think I'm beginning to understand just what the hell he meant."

His mouth closed over hers. She sighed in delight. Sustaining the searing kiss, he walked her backward to the dais, up the short steps and to the bed.

Then he lifted his head. His eyes were like the sky, when it darkens to nighttime. There were shadows and secrets there, mystery and promise.

She thought of primitive rituals, ancient customs. A man took a woman for his wife. He promised to care for her and she for him. But then, after the ceremony that pronounced them wed, he must take her to bed and enter her body to make the vows binding.

And that was what Patrick was about to do now, Regina could see in the twilight shadows of his eyes. He would make love to his wife, the ultimate sealing of the vows they had made.

Into her mind once more crept all the things they hadn't said, everything he had yet to explain—why he had followed her up Sweetbriar Summit and laid her down in the meadow there, his reasons for demanding that she become his bride.

She understood exactly what he was doing now. He was sealing the promise they had made to each other as thoroughly as he could before she forced him to tell her what was in his mind and heart.

If he ever did tell her what was in his mind and heart....

"Patrick. We should talk."

He shook his head.

"But I—"

"Not now, Gina. Not tonight. Tonight is for touching and feeling. Not for talk."

Slowly, never letting go of her gaze, he raised both hands and placed his palms flat against the delicate swells of her breasts. She gasped. Her nipples, beneath her clothing, rose and hardened with stunning eagerness into the center of his palms.

He rubbed, keeping his palms flat. "Ah, yeah..." It was a whispered sigh.

Regina sighed, too. And as the sigh floated from her lips, she finally truly accepted that she would get no answers from him tonight. She wanted the pleasure his touch gave. She craved it. Everything else was slowly fading to nothing. There was Patrick and his kiss, his touch, his body that called to her body. Nothing else mattered. Not for tonight.

He went on brushing her breasts with his palms, causing tiny agonies of pleasure to pulse from the tightened buds of her nipples through every inch of her. Down in the cove between her thighs, she could feel the throbbing, the moisture. Her body wept for need of him.

Her dress had a deep V-neck, the layers of chiffon overlapping and gathered at the waist. His thumbs found the slit of the V and slowly parted it, until he could guide the dress from her shoulders.

Regina blinked and swayed and then realized that the top half of her dress was down to her waist. There was a knowing smile on his mouth. He lowered his head and kissed her lips again, a tender, brushing kiss that aroused her utterly with its very restraint. And as he kissed her, his hands gently, relentlessly went about their business, taking her slip to her waist and unhooking her bra.

When he lifted his head to look in her eyes again, she realized she was nude to the waist.

"Oh!" she said, surprised.

He chuckled, then cupped both of her small breasts in his big hands. "So pretty," he muttered.

"They're not—I mean, I'm not...." She was blushing furiously. She made herself finish. "I'm not very big...."

He flicked her nipples with his thumbs. She groaned. "I know," he said. He didn't seem to mind that she was small-breasted, not at all.

"But I thought most men..."

He chuckled again. "You women. You get some idea in your head about what all men like. All men are different. Some like big breasts. And some..." He lowered his head and licked one erect, aching nipple. Regina moaned. He blew where he'd licked. "Some men like small, high breasts. And some men don't give a damn about breasts. They like long legs, or tiny waists or..." He licked and blew on the other breast.

On a groan, Regina implored, "Or what?"

"Or the whole picture." He took her nipple in his mouth. She clutched his head and held him against her and felt the way his tongue swirled around, making her crazy, making her moan.

At last he lifted his head. After drawing in a shuddering breath, she dared to ask, "What do you mean, the whole picture?"

He put his hands at her waist and began smoothing her filmy dress and the slip beneath it down over her hips. "The whole picture. The whole woman. Put your hand on my shoulder." He knelt, and lifted her feet, one then the other, getting the dress and slip clear and away. He then tossed them quite cavalierly onto the big bed. He took her panty hose and her panties and whisked them down, off and away, just as he had the dress and slip.

She was naked before him, and aroused enough that it took her a moment to try to cover herself with her hands.

"Uh-uh. No, you don't." He took her wrists and held them away from her body. And he looked at her.

Embarrassment stained every inch of her bared skin pink. "Oh, Patrick, I…"

"The whole woman," he murmured. "Yeah, I'm a *whole woman* sort of guy." He went on looking, while, above the wrists he was gripping, her hands became fists. She tipped her head toward the ceiling and pressed her eyes closed.

She wondered, not even knowing that she was whimpering a little, how a person could feel both aroused and thoroughly mortified at the same time.

He said softly, "Gina, I'm telling you I like the way you look. The way *all* of you looks. The way all the parts of you…fit together." He let go of one wrist. She waited, not daring to open her eyes.

And then she felt it. The pads of his fingers brushed the side swell of one breast.

"I like this," he hoarsely whispered. "And this." He palmed her waist, pressing his thumb into her navel as her belly contracted. "And this." A finger trailed over the swell of her hip, leaving goose bumps in its wake. "Are you listening to me, Gina?"

She bit her lip and managed to nod.

"Good." His hand slid around and cupped the swell of her bottom. She groaned. "And I like the way you do that."

"Um. What?"

"The way you groan. Like you're really too much of a lady to groan, but you can't help yourself. You groan anyway. I like that. It gets me hot."

His hand slid back to the front of her then. She groaned some more as he found the heart of her, as he parted her with his fingers and began to stroke her as he had a lifetime ago—only that afternoon—up on Sweetbriar Summit beneath the burning sun.

"I like the way your body moves for me." In and out, slowly, deliciously, his fingers worked their magic. "I like the way your white skin goes pink and your nipples stand up, like they're begging for me to kiss them." Just as he said that, he bent his head and covered one breast with his mouth. He stroked her with his hand and he laved her nipple with his tongue.

Regina knew she was going to die of delight. But she didn't die. She'd never been so alive, as she brazenly writhed and moaned in response to the touch of Patrick Jones. He stroked her faster in answer to the quickening movement of her hips and she rode his hand until she felt herself going over the edge.

"Yeah," he breathed against her breast. "Yeah, Gina. Oh, yeah…"

There was an explosion of light behind her lids, as her body contracted around his wonderful fingers. She whimpered and sobbed and sank slowly to the curved edge of the mattress. She was aware of his strong arm, gently helping her down.

Then for a measureless time she knew nothing but the waves of pleasure that pulsed and receded and then pulsed once again. She drew in long, hungry breaths as Patrick continued to stroke her, extending the pleasure, drawing it out into eternity and at the same time easing her way back to the world.

A few minutes later, when reality returned, she found that she was sitting on the side of the bed, gripping fistfuls of the bedspread in each hand. Patrick, silent, waiting, had straightened again and was standing before her.

"Open your eyes, Gina. Look at me. Won't you, please?"

She might have resisted a command, but never such a tender, needful plea. Her eyes fluttered open. Her bent head slowly lifted. She looked up his fully clothed body to meet his waiting eyes.

"Touch me." The words were hoarse, husky.

Regina stared at him, knowing what he meant. Her throat was dry. And the rest of her body felt so heavy and hot—ripe with sex and satiation and now, once more, a desire that seemed to bloom right on top of complete fulfillment. His request had excited her even more than it shocked her.

Quickly he shrugged out of his shirt and tossed it aside. His beautiful chest and hard stomach excited her. His eyes encouraged her, beseeched her.

"Come on. Touch me."

She lifted a hesitant hand. And shyly set it upon him. Though his clothing was between that touch and his manhood, his body jerked. He stifled a moan.

Her senses swam at the hard, marvelous feel of him beneath her hand. And the way he responded to her reticent touch. There was power here, for her, in what she might do to him, give to him. The same power as he had just held over her.

Her heart beat faster. Desire, curiosity…and awe, too. They were all there, overriding her shyness, and her confusion at the newness of all of this. Here, after all, was glory and splendor, wonder and fulfillment.

For her—and for him.

There was a button on his waistband. She slid it from its hole. She found the zipper tab and pulled it down. The two sides of his slacks parted. She guided them down, helped him slide off his soft leather shoes and get rid of his socks, just as he had helped her to remove her clothes. She straightened again to tenderly pull his briefs away, careful that they didn't catch on his hardness. At last he was as naked as she.

A little of her shyness returned. It showed in her renewed hesitancy as she once more raised her hand and touched his arousal with diffident fingertips.

He gasped.

She dared to stroke him, just with her fingertips. She found him silky and hot. He was so strong, both in his lean, powerful body and in his will that had chosen her and pursued her and claimed her as his within a span of weeks. So very strong. And yet he moaned and jerked just from the light touch of her hand.

Cautiously, experimentally, she wrapped her hand around his hardness. She tried one lingering stroke, sliding her curled fingers smoothly up and down the satin length of him.

"Oh, man…" Patrick gritted out. "I…think that'll do it…."

And then everything happened at once.

He pushed her firmly back on the bed, urging her to scoot up and around until she could lie with her head upon the mountain of pillows. Then he nudged her thighs apart with one of his own and loomed above her. She looked up into his flushed face, his burning eyes.

She felt bewildered. "Patrick? Did I...do it wrong?"

He let out a pained chuckle. "Wrong? Hell, no. You did it right. Just right."

"I did?"

"Yeah, you did."

She could feel him, there, at her entrance. And then, very gently, he began to push himself inside. She watched his face, her shyness once more forgotten, and she saw that it was almost painful for him to go so slowly, to so carefully restrain himself.

"Am I hurting you?" He seemed to moan the words.

She shook her head against the tumbled pillows. Though she had felt some sensitivity down there all evening, now it didn't hurt at all. She was too relaxed. And too aroused.

"Good." He pressed home.

She moaned as she fully received him.

Then he levered up on his arms and, joined with her, he met her eyes. "Wrap your legs around me."

A little awkwardly, but with complete willingness, she did as he asked.

"This time," he said, "you're coming with me."

And then he started to move—slowly at first, and then faster, and then slowly again. Regina clung to him, moving with him, catching his rhythms, giving them back, adding rhythms of her own.

Her mind spun away. She was pure feeling, a living shimmer of sensation, as she learned what it was to climb to the stars and to hover there, looking into her husband's face until he cried aloud and soared off the edge of the world.

She watched him, her own eyes widening, her breath catching on a joyful sob as she found she was joining him, winging toward heaven right along with him.

They spun out, together, into a universe of bursting stars.

He allowed her to rest for a while. But not too long. Soon enough, it started all over again.

Though the warm weight across her midsection made it difficult, Regina rolled over and squinted at the clock radio by the bed.

She groaned. It was well past noon.

She turned her head—and found herself looking into Patrick's slumbering face.

My sweet Lord. It had not been a dream. Last night—or early this morning, rather—she had married Patrick Jones. It was his arm across her stomach, his hairy thigh pressed against her leg.

He had followed her up Sweetbriar Summit and he'd made love to her there, beneath the sky. And he'd made her agree to marry him. He'd swept her off to Tahoe. And she *had* married him. Then they'd returned here, to their hotel suite.

She'd tried to talk to him. But he hadn't wanted to talk. Instead, they'd made love some more.

Much more.

Images of the things they'd done flashed through her brain, causing an agonized flush that started at her toes and then seemed to flood every square inch of her unclothed body. She had reveled in every caress.

But somehow, now that it was the morning after, she was shocked at the way she had behaved. And she really should have insisted that he explain a few things before she...performed all of those appallingly intimate acts with him.

"'Morning." Patrick's eyes were open. He was smiling at her.

"Morning is already gone," she informed him primly.

His smile deepened, crinkling the corners of his eyes.

"Yes, ma'am. So it is." He brought his sleep-flushed face close to hers and kissed her on the mouth.

Then he sat and stretched enthusiastically, not caring a bit when the sheet slid away to display his most private parts. Regina sat up herself, modestly clutching the sheet and significantly looking away from what he so shamelessly revealed.

"Hey," he said, and tapped her on the shoulder.

"What?"

"Don't get prissy."

"I'm sure I have no idea what you're talking about."

"When you get prissy, I get determined to make you hot."

"That's ridiculous."

"Oh, is it?" Apparently deciding he had a point to prove, he nibbled where he'd tapped. Pleasurable little waves of sensation rippled out from where he nibbled. Regina bit her lip, clutched the sheet and tried not to sigh. She really had to remember her goal to get him to talk.

"Patrick?"

"Hmm?"

"We should order breakfast." She did her absolute best to sound like a person who would brook no nonsense. She didn't succeed too well.

He went on nibbling, up over her shoulder and across the wing of her collarbone. "Maybe I'll just have *you,* à la carte."

"Patrick..."

"No fruit juice. No toast. No coffee. Just the main course." He started sucking right where he'd already left a mark.

She wriggled and stiffened beneath the wonderful things his mouth was doing to her. She knew she should pull away, but somehow she wasn't pulling away. "Patrick, I haven't eaten anything but two pieces of fruit and some champagne since lunch yesterday.'' She tried to sound chastening, but her voice came out petulant.

"Sorry, baby. We'll order room service."

"I am not a baby." It was an outright reprimand.

That did it. His lips ceased their tender torment. He lifted his head and took her shoulders and turned her so that she was facing him amid the tumble of bedclothes and pillows.

"Okay, what's going on?"

Now that he wasn't distracting her, she found it very easy to be specific. "I want to *talk*. I mean it. I've married you, just as you wanted. And you know all about why I did it. I, on the other hand, don't have a clue as to what you're after. Since we got in your Bronco yesterday evening, I've tried in a thousand different tactful ways to get you to explain what you're up to. Because I *will* have honesty, above all, in this marriage. But being tactful apparently doesn't work with you. So I'm through being tactful. I want to know why you married me. Now."

He raked his tangled hair back and rubbed his eyes.

"I mean it, Patrick."

"Okay," he growled.

"You said okay before and then you told me nothing."

His eyes flashed. "Well, I'm saying *okay* again. And this time I'll tell you whatever the hell you want to know."

"Oh, you will, will you?"

"Yes. I will. Just ask. And I'll answer."

"Fine." She held her head high. "What I want to know first is…" Oh, this was difficult to say.

"I can't answer if you don't have the guts to ask."

"I have the guts."

"Then do it."

"Fine." She dragged in a determined breath. "Did you marry me for my money?"

Chapter Nine

A slow smile curved Patrick's mouth. "Is it a lot of money?"

Regina kept her head high. He was not going to see how much it hurt to think that he only wanted her for her money. "It's enough that I never have to work if I don't want to."

"Hmm." He tugged on the sheet a little and seemed to turn that bit of information over in his mind. "A rich wife. The dream of every sensible man."

"I'm not rich." She looked at his hair, which was sticking up in all directions, and at the sleep wrinkles on his face, and she wondered how he could be so handsome. She told herself it didn't matter that this conversation was breaking her heart. The bitter truth was always preferable to a fool's illusion.

"If you're not rich, what are you?" he asked.

"I'm...well, I suppose you could say I'm well-to-do."

"Hmm. Well-to-do, huh?"

She glared at him. "You said you'd answer. I haven't heard any answers, only more questions. Rather crass questions, actually."

He tipped his head, studying her. Then he said, very tenderly, "Gina. I'm sorry."

She looked away. "What does that mean?"

"It means you're right. I'm acting like a real creep. And I'm sorry."

She was determined not to be a fool. "What for? I asked you to be honest."

"Yeah, but I wasn't being honest."

"What are you saying?"

"I'm saying I was mad."

"Why?"

"Because you wouldn't make love with me. I wanted to get even with you."

"I don't understand."

His eyes were tender. "You really don't, do you?" There was a kind of gentle awe in his voice. "You don't know a damn thing about the rotten games that can be played between a woman and a man."

She didn't know how to reply. And she was wondering what kind of "rotten games" he had played with other women—but then she decided she'd just as soon not know. "Well, I...I'm not terribly experienced with men. I know that."

Now his eyes gleamed. "You're doing just fine."

She blushed. "Well, thanks."

"Look—" his tone was serious again "—I don't want you for your money. We can live on what I make, I promise you. Why don't you just get a lawyer to draw up an agreement that says I can't put my greedy hands on anything that belongs to you? I'll sign it."

She was silent for a moment. Then, "You really mean that, don't you?"

His expression was utterly serious. "I do."

It was her turn to tug on the sheet. She believed him—and felt relief to know that the money wasn't the reason. She also felt petty and small. "No. Of course, I wouldn't do that. You're my *husband* and I…I…"

He reached out and pulled her against him. "Easy, Gina. It's okay." He slowly stroked her hair.

"I just…I want to know…"

"What?"

"Why? Why did you marry me?" Before he could answer, she slipped from his embrace and blurted out her *real* question, the question she had never imagined in her wildest dreams she would ever dare to ask him. "You don't…*love* me, after all. Do you?"

For a long time he only stared at her, while she waited in an agony of embarrassment over what she'd just presumed to say.

Finally she could bear the silence no longer. "Well?"

"Gina…"

"Please. Just tell me."

He pried one of her hands free of the sheet and kissed it, then enclosed it between both of his. "I need a wife."

She pulled her hand from his gentle clasp and pushed her hair from her eyes. "You what?"

"I need a wife. For when my girls come home."

"But—"

He went on before she could finish. "Look, I want to make a home for them. A real home."

"But Patrick, they live with Marybeth. In Arkansas." She repeated the obvious, because she had yet really to comprehend what he was getting at.

"They live with their mother right now. But they miss their home, and all their friends. Until last year, neither of them had ever lived anywhere else but North Magdalene."

"But you can't expect Marybeth to just—"

He put up a hand. "I know Marybeth. I was married to her for eight years. She'll bring Marnie and Teresa to me eventually, when she finally feels bad enough about keeping them so far away from their home. *And* when she finally accepts the fact that she's taken on too much for one person to accomplish alone. The woman is trying to build a real-estate business single-handedly. And she's been neglecting the girls because she just plain doesn't have any time. I have a feeling she's getting close to the point where she's willing to let me have them for a while. I think she'll be turning them over to me sometime during the summer, when they won't have to worry about school."

"And then?"

"And then, since I have a decent place for them to live and you at my side, I'll be ready to suggest that she just let them live with me. Because if there's a perfect woman to be my wife and the mother of my daughters, it's you, Gina."

He watched her, his eyes as bright and intense as when he was making love to her. He seemed to be willing her to understand. "I'm no big winner in life, you know? Teresa and Marnie are the only things I've done that make sense. And I want to do more for them than getting the support check in the mail on schedule every month. I don't want them growing up thinking their father doesn't give a damn, even though that's probably what they've thought up until now, because I have not been the most dedicated father in the world.

"But damn it, a man can change. And I'm working on that, on changing. I want to show them how much I love them and how much it means to me that they're in the world. To do that, I need time with them, day-to-day time, so they'll know they can count on me. Can you understand that?"

Regina swallowed, because there was a lump in her

throat. She knew she probably ought to be angry at him, for sweeping her off her feet instead of telling her this simple, heart-rending truth.

But she was not angry with him. Not in the least.

Beneath the corner of one of the pillows, she caught sight of her slip, which Patrick had carelessly tossed on the bed when he undressed her the night before. She pulled it free of the tangled blankets and tugged it on over her head, smoothing it hastily into place beneath the sheet.

"Gina?" He sounded very worried.

She asked, "Why didn't you just tell me that? Instead of—"

"Seducing you?" He chuckled, but it was not a relaxed sound.

"Yes."

"Because I..." For once, he was the one at a loss for words.

"Go on."

"All right. Because I thought you'd turn me down, if I laid it all out for you."

She looked at him, thinking of all that had happened on Sweetbriar Summit and then trying to imagine it another way. Trying to picture Patrick telling her of his daughters instead of making love to her. What would her answer have been? She couldn't be completely sure.

"I think you should have been honest," she hedged.

"But if I had, would you be my wife this morning?"

"I would have respected your honesty."

He made a knowing sound in his throat. "Right. You would have respected my honesty—and said no."

She was silent. He did have a point. In appealing to her starved senses, he'd held her in thrall. It would have been quite possible, had his arguments been calm and rational, for her to have simply said no.

Patrick was watching her closely. His scrutiny made her uneasy.

All at once, unable to be still, she rose from the bed and went to the glass door that led out onto the terrace. Outside, it was a crystal-clear day. The sun shimmered on the lake. There were a few small powerboats and several sailboarders in sight.

"Damn it, Gina." His voice, from behind her, was low and rough. "What the hell are you thinking?"

She faced him again, met his wary gaze. But she didn't answer him.

"Gina."

She said nothing. She knew she was tormenting him. And, though she was a kind woman at heart, she wanted to torture him right then. She had a right to, at least for the few more seconds it took her to accept how skillfully he'd avoided answering her question about love.

She found herself wondering about Chloe Swan. Before he married Marybeth, everyone in town had been sure that he'd found his true love in Chloe. And almost everyone in North Magdalene believed that Chloe had never stopped loving him. They said that Patrick had been upset when Chloe ran off last year. Could it be that Patrick still loved her, as everyone thought she loved him?

Not that it mattered, Regina chided herself. Her speculations were all based on hearsay and rumor. And Chloe had been gone for a year now. It was a distinct possibility that she would never return. Surely, whatever was between Patrick and Chloe was now firmly in the past.

Patrick rose from the bed. "Damn it. What the hell is it? Are you thinking you're going to divorce me now? Is that it?" He strode toward her across their hotel suite, magnificently naked and completely unashamed.

And that was when it hit her.

She was in love with him.

It was quite obvious that he did not love her, yet her heart was his. She had planned a quiet, happy life for herself with a shy, unassuming man. And ended up eloping with one of the Jones boys.

It was crazy. Regina was terrified.

And yet she felt absolutely wonderful.

As she had learned yesterday, naked in the sun on Sweetbriar Summit, her life was no longer sane and uneventful. She loved Patrick Jones.

And not only that; she had gone and *married* him.

It had been a bold, gutsy act. She was downright proud of herself.

He reached her, shoved his fingers through her hair and lifted her face so that her mouth was just inches below his. "Don't you dare tell me you want a divorce."

She shook her head, as much as she could with his hands holding her still. She loved him, and if she had anything to say about it, they would make this marriage work.

"No, Patrick. I don't want a divorce."

He let out a relieved sigh. His insistent hands gentled in her hair. "Good. Now lighten up. Things could be worse...." His mouth met hers.

"Patrick," she breathed against his lips, "I really am hungry."

"We'll order breakfast soon. I promise. Soon..."

They remained at Lake Tahoe for three more days. Regina had the time of her life. Like a late-blooming flower, she basked in the sun of the love that had found her at last.

They went boating and Regina tried waterskiing. They took in more than one show. They ate in fine restaurants where the crystal gleamed in candlelight and beyond huge banks of windows the lake glimmered beneath the moon. They stayed up sinfully late and slept until lunchtime.

And they made love. Frequently and fulfillingly. Regina relished every moment of it.

But on Wednesday, it was time to go home.

They arrived in North Magdalene at a little after one in the afternoon. Patrick carried her across the threshold of his house, shoving the door shut behind them with his boot. He kissed her long and thoroughly.

Then he set her down and went out to the Bronco to bring in their bags. After the truck was unloaded, he handed her a set of keys to his house and his vehicle, then headed on foot to the garage to see how his business had fared in his absence.

Regina wandered the rooms of her husband's house for a few moments, thinking with some anticipation that she certainly had a lot to do.

Next, she returned to her house next door, where she discovered everything was just as she had left it, except for the blinking light on her answering machine, which she decided not to deal with right then.

She swiftly changed into old jeans, tennis shoes and a worn shirt and poured herself a glass of juice with ice. After that, she ran up the window shades to let in some light and found a tablet and pencil. She went through the rooms of the house she'd grown up in, making herself a list of what she wanted to keep and what she would dispose of.

The doorbell rang precisely twenty-nine minutes after she had entered the house. Through the lace panels over the front windows, she could see who it was.

Nellie.

Regina didn't even consider not answering. Nellie, like everyone else in North Magdalene, would have to be dealt with. There was no sense putting off the inevitable. Still carrying her pad and pencil, Regina marched to her front door and pulled it back.

Nellie gave a little gasp. And then she swiftly scanned Regina's stubbornly smiling face.

"Hello, Nellie."

"So." Nellie made a nasal sound, a disapproving *harumph*. "It's true, isn't it?" Her small eyes glittered with unspoken accusations.

"What's true, Nellie?"

"You have eloped with Patrick Jones."

"Yes, it's true."

"Oh, my sweet Lord in heaven, what would your dear mother say?"

"The question is moot, Nellie. My mother is dead."

Nellie blinked a few times and did some sputtering.

Regina politely inquired, "Would you like to come in for a few minutes? I could pour you some juice." Nellie's lips began twitching in wounded outrage. Regina blithely continued, "But it's only fair to warn you, I really don't have much time to visit. Patrick and I have decided we'll live at his house and rent this one, and there are a million things to do. But I could spare a minute or two for you."

Nellie didn't want to talk about how long she'd stay yet. She wanted to express how deeply she'd been abused. "I came by Sunday morning. You were gone." Her voice quivered with hurt. "I was worried sick about you. And then I went to church to find Tondalaya Clark playing the hymns. I learned you'd asked Delilah to find someone to take your place. You asked *Delilah,* when you could just as well have asked me. I was crushed."

"I'm sorry, Nellie. I honestly am. But I simply was not ready, when I talked to you Saturday, to explain what was going on in my private life."

"I thought you were my friend."

"I *am* your friend."

"You don't trust me."

"Yes, I do. I would trust you with my life."

"But not with your secrets."

"Well, now, Nellie. You're not very good at keeping secrets. And we both know that."

Nellie actually looked as if she might cry. "Oh, this is horrible. It's just like when Delilah ran off with that wild man, Sam Fletcher. She told me nothing, though I was her closest friend. And now you have done the same thing. Gone and eloped with Patrick Jones without a single word to me about it. Tell the truth. You knew that you were leaving with him when I caught you at your car Saturday and you told me that you and Marcus had broken up. You knew then. Didn't you?"

Regina answered very gently. "Yes. I knew then."

Nellie pressed her lips together, folded her thin arms over her flat chest and looked away. "Well," she harumphed.

"Nellie, are you coming in or not?"

"I—"

"If not, I really want to get back to the job I was doing."

"You have hurt me deeply."

"Nellie."

"All right." Nellie sniffed. "I'll come in so that you may properly apologize to me."

Nellie stayed for nearly an hour. By the time she finally got up to leave, she was still convinced that Regina had made a grave and irreparable error in throwing over the warm and wonderful Marcus Shelby for a troublemaking roughneck like Patrick Jones.

However, Nellie had decided to forgive Regina for not confiding in her. With a Jones for a husband, Regina would be needing a sympathetic ear. And Nellie, never one to hold a grudge, would be available anytime.

That night, Patrick came home a little before six to find the dining room table set with his wife's dishes.

"Already moving things around, I see." There was both

pride and approval in his voice. They were in the kitchen and he backed her up against the sink, using only his body, since his hands were stained with the evidence that he'd done more than hang around the office at the garage. He'd also been helping his two mechanics.

"I've been very busy." She kissed him on his chin, right on a smear of engine oil. "And you need a shower."

"Take one with me."

"Not possible. I have to finish dinner."

"Dinner can wait. I can't."

"Patrick…"

"Mmm. I love how you taste. So sweet."

"Patrick. The dinner…"

"Always worried about food."

"We have to eat…."

"Mmm… Soon. I promise. Soon…"

The roast ended up a little overdone, but Patrick didn't complain.

After dinner, they called Marybeth and the girls in Arkansas, to tell them about the marriage. It was a brief and rather awkward conversation. Marybeth sounded quite stunned, but did murmur that she wished them well. Teresa, the older girl, got on the line and told both Regina and her father in a stilted voice that she had always "admired Regina's good works," and was "very happy for them." Marnie could not be coaxed to take the phone.

When they hung up, Regina told herself that the important thing was that the girls now knew they had a stepmother. Of course, it would take them time to accept the idea.

Patrick took her hand. "Come on. Let's get some air."

They went outside and jumped the fence to sit on her porch, since she had a swing. After a few minutes of idly swinging and not saying much, they started to talk of their plans.

"This weekend," he promised, "I'll move the swing to the other house."

She told him that she'd done some measuring and was now sure her window treatments would fit his windows, and that she wanted to replace some of his rather beat-up furniture with hers. Also, she wanted to paint several of the rooms. And to choose nicer furniture from the extra sets at her house for the girls' rooms.

"There's a nice oak set in the back bedroom that would probably be good. And when I was a girl, I had all white wicker in my room. It's still in the attic. Maybe one of the girls would like it. Of course, it would need repainting, but I can handle that."

"Wicker and oak for the girls." Patrick chuckled. "You really have been busy."

She leaned against him in the swing and he casually raised his arm and draped it across her shoulders. "Tell me what they're like," she prompted.

Since the morning Patrick told her that he wanted his daughters to live with them, she had been imagining what it might be like to have two children to care for. She was trying not to get starry-eyed over it. Of course there would be difficulties to overcome, if Patrick's prediction came true and Marybeth did let him have the girls. But they were difficulties Regina would embrace for the chance to have what for so long had passed her by: a real family of her own.

Patrick rested his chin against her hair. "You want to know what Teresa and Marnie are like?"

"Yes."

"Well, they're basically good kids. But they haven't had it easy, with all the problems their mother and I had."

Like what, specifically? Regina wanted to ask. But she didn't. She decided to simply let him talk for now and ask questions later. As she reminded herself lately whenever she became anxious about all she and Patrick had yet to learn about each other, they had their whole lives to do it. They didn't have to rush.

He went on. "Teresa's just turned twelve. She's big for her age and has her mother's hazel eyes. She's going through a religious phase."

"How so?"

"Well, when I went to see them in the spring, she was considering joining the Catholic church so that she could become a nun."

"I see."

His musing voice continued, explaining how Teresa seemed very serious for someone so young. And that Marnie, who was small and wiry at nine, was a hard kid to pin down. A tomboy, Marnie hated baths and dresses. "When I was there the last time, she wore the same pair of torn-up jeans the whole five days," he said. "Also, she can swear like a sailor. Her mother can't control her at all."

"Hmm." Regina rubbed her head against his shoulder, thinking that, from what he was telling her, it would be quite a challenge if the girls did come. Still, she couldn't suppress her growing anticipation. Having the girls with them was a challenge she would welcome, no matter how rough things got.

As they sat there idly swinging and talking, more than one of their neighbors just happened to stroll by. Greetings were exchanged and congratulations extended to the newlyweds. Both Patrick and Regina waved and smiled. They were careful to act totally unconcerned, though they knew that the eyes of the town were on them and would be for quite a while to come.

After dark came, Patrick whispered in her ear, "Think we've shown them all enough for one night?"

"Oh, I suppose." She twined her fingers more tightly

with his. "But you know when we go in, they'll all be disappointed."

"No, they won't. They'll be able to imagine what we're doing. And that's much more exciting than having us in plain sight, holding hands like a couple of high school kids and swinging on a swing."

They got up, still holding hands, jumped the fence to the other house and went inside. What they did when they reached the bedroom was, in Regina's opinion, a thousand times more exciting than anyone was ever likely to imagine.

The next morning after Patrick left for the garage, Regina was just getting ready to call old Mrs. Leslie and offer to drop by for a few hours before lunch when the front door flew open.

"Where the hell is my new damn daughter-in-law?"

Oggie Jones had come to call.

He lowered his cane, which he'd used to shove the door open, and stomped into the house. "Regina? Regina, where are you, gal?"

Regina, already halfway down the hall from the dining room and kitchen, drew in a long breath and answered, "Right here...Father." She rushed to meet him.

He looked her up and down. "Father, eh?"

"Would you prefer I called you—"

He waved away the other possibilities before she could voice them. "Father's just dandy. Now be a good kid and get me some coffee." He hobbled right past her, headed for the kitchen.

"Be my guest," she muttered wryly to his retreating back.

He chortled, but didn't turn. "Don't mind if I do."

In the kitchen, after he'd poured a hypoglycemic's nightmare worth of sugar into his coffee, he hoisted his feet onto a spare chair and lit up a cigar. Regina, who did not approve of smoking, found she was not quite able, under the stare of those little black eyes, to ask him to extinguish the smelly thing. So she fumbled around in the cupboards until she found an ashtray, which she plunked down on the breakfast table beside him.

He glanced at it, then puffed for a moment. "I came to welcome you to the family."

"Well, that was thoughtful of you."

He waved his cigar. "Thoughtful, hell. We're always glad to get another classy broad." He flicked his ash. "Patrick treatin' you right?"

"Why, yes. He's treating me wonderfully."

"Good. If he doesn't, you come to me."

"Well, I—"

He waved his cigar. "Never mind, you don't have to say anything. I told you to come to me, so you know I'm available. We both know you'll never do any such thing. In fact, if you're like the rest of them, when you end up with some big problem, you'll mess everything up royally and I'll have to come in later and save the day. But at least you know I offered. And I meant it."

"Oh, well, then. Of course."

"I mean, since this was all my idea, I figure I should be at least a little responsible if there's any problems."

"Pardon me? *Your* idea?"

"Aw, come on. You know it was my damn idea. I saw you watchin' my boy that first day he moved in. And that was when it come to me. Just like it did with my other three kids. I picked out Amy for Brendan and Sam for Delilah. And if you think gettin' Sam and Delilah together wasn't a job, you ain't thinkin'. I thought that was the roughest it could get. Until Jared and Eden. Then I realized I hadn't known what rough was.

"You, on the other hand, were a much easier project. It

turned out you wanted a husband. And Patrick wanted a decent wife. And when I saw you lookin' at him that day, I realized you were the one for him. And about damn time, too. And now you two are hitched. Patrick, who only used to smile at a good joke, is grinnin' like an idiot all the time. And my vow is kept.''

"What vow?"

"Don't rush me, don't rush me. So how d'you like the rings?"

Regina, who was feeling a little dizzy at all she was hearing, managed to croak out, "I love them. Thank you. And for the honeymoon, too."

"My pleasure. Purely my pleasure. Gimme a refill, gal, will ya?"

Regina got up and gave Oggie more coffee, after which he explained that on the deathbed of his beloved Bathsheba, he had vowed to see that each of his children found the perfect mate. A couple of his kids had had to try more than once. But at last they'd all got it right. In heaven, his Bathsheba smiled all the time now.

"Well, that's just...lovely," Regina said, since she didn't know what else to say.

He cackled. "Think I'm bonkers, don't ya?"

"Ah...no. Of course not."

"You'll get used to me."

She imagined she'd have to. "Well, certainly," she said. "Of course I will."

Oggie smashed his cigar in the ashtray, hauled himself to his feet and leaned on his cane. "And now I'm outta here. You take care of my boy, and you and me will get along just fine. Don't bother to see me out. I know how to find the damn door."

"But I—"

"I mean it. Stay put."

"Well, all right. Good morning, then. Father."

Cackling, he hobbled out.

Regina stared after him. When she heard the door slam, she realized she was smiling.

To think she had found him frightening. Now she could see that, in his rough way, he was quite charming. And very dear. And it didn't bother her in the least that he'd had a hand in her marriage to Patrick. If anything, she was grateful.

In fact, as the first week of her marriage went by, Regina found that very little bothered her. Not her odd father-in-law, or the way people whispered about her in the street, or Nellie's never-ending tendency to drop by and warn her that she was heading for heartbreak.

For the first time in her life, she knew what happiness was: it was waking in the morning to find Patrick beside her, coming home from helping someone else to discover he'd dropped by for lunch or looking up from the book she was reading to meet his sapphire eyes.

Regina was in love. And even though her love was not returned, nothing could dim the joy she felt. Patrick proved every moment that he took being her husband seriously. He went to work every day and he came home on time every night. And in his arms she found heaven. Her life was just right. She had no complaints. Perhaps she was even a little smug in her happiness—which was probably why she acted so unwisely the day that Marcus Shelby came to call.

A week after she returned from her honeymoon, Regina came home from a three-hour stint as volunteer librarian at the community library to find Marcus sitting on the porch of the house where she used to live.

"Regina!" he called when he caught sight of her.

Regina hesitated, remembering that she'd promised Patrick on the day they married that she would stay away from Marcus.

Marcus stood and fussily brushed the wrinkles from his slacks. Looking at him, Regina wondered how she ever could have imagined spending her life with him. It had been a week and a half since the picnic in Sweetbriar Park. But to Regina, it seemed like years.

Marcus finished brushing at his slacks and started down the steps to meet her at the gate. She stood still and watched him approach, realizing that she felt absolutely nothing for him now beyond a sort of vague affection. She wondered if that was all she'd ever felt.

"Regina, I would like a private word with you." Marcus's expression was rather pinched.

Regina sighed. "Marcus, we really don't have anything to say to each other."

His narrow shoulders twitched as he drew himself up. "Regina, whatever you believe, I have cared for you deeply. That's why I must tell you a few things. *Someone* must tell you, and it might as well be me. I'll do it for the sake of all we once shared."

"Marcus, what *are* you talking about?"

His eyes scanned the pyracantha bushes by the front gate, as if he expected Nellie or someone equally nosy to be lurking there. "May we please go inside?"

"Marcus, I really—"

"Please." He looked very upset.

Again, Regina thought of her promise to Patrick. But somehow now, looking at Marcus, feeling nothing stronger than watered-down fondness, she could see no harm in being alone with him. And perhaps, after he got whatever was bothering him off his chest, his distress would fade. Poor Marcus. He simply didn't deal well with his own emotions at all.

"Please," he said again. "Just a few moments, I promise."

"Well, all right. Come on inside." She started for the other gate to the house she and Patrick now shared.

"Wait. Where are you going?"

She glanced back at him. "In the house."

"But that's *his* house."

"It's my house, too, Marcus. Patrick and I are married, remember?"

"But can't we just go in *your* house?"

"No." She was still a little uncomfortable about breaking her promise to Patrick, even though it was a thoroughly unnecessary promise. Somehow, to go with Marcus into the house she didn't even live in anymore felt way too much like sneaking around. "It's *our* house or nothing," she said, and went through the gate without pausing again.

Marcus stayed out on the sidewalk until Regina was almost to the porch. Then she heard him open the gate and hurry through.

Inside, she offered him a seat on the couch. He perched there gingerly.

"Now, what in the world is the matter?"

He clutched his hands in his lap and licked his lips. "Regina. Everyone's afraid to tell you, but I felt someone really had to."

"Tell me *what?*"

"Oh, Regina. I'm so sorry."

"Marcus, please. Sorry about what?"

"Oh, Regina."

"Marcus, take a few deep breaths. Good. Now say what it is you're sorry about."

He looked down at his clenched hands, then over at the television set. At last he managed to look at Regina. He said in a pained whisper, "Patrick Jones wants custody of his daughters, Regina. He doesn't love you. He married you because he needs someone to be a real mother to them. And you were perfect. I know, because I was over at the

Hole in the Wall last night, and Oggie Jones was bragging about how last year Patrick swore to get his girls back. Oggie claims he told Patrick then that he'd better find himself a decent wife first, because Patrick doesn't have a clue about how to raise those girls. And so he did find himself a decent wife. You.''

Regina smiled softly. "I see."

Marcus slowly shook his head. "Oh, you are so very brave and strong, to take it like this."

"Marcus, I already knew."

"Oh." He looked thoroughly nonplussed, then hastened to insist, "No, you couldn't have known…"

"Yes. Patrick has told me he wants his children back."

"Well, certainly you would say that. Be loyal to him, even after everything. You're a wonderful woman, Regina, and I…"

Marcus's voice trailed off as both he and Regina heard the sound of footsteps on the porch.

"Oh, dear," Regina murmured to herself, as the front door swung inward and she saw her husband standing on the other side of it.

On the natural stone mantel across the room, the clock struck noon. Evidently, Patrick had decided to surprise his wife and join her for lunch.

Chapter Ten

Regina *was* surprised. "Patrick! I didn't expect you."

"I can see that." He looked from the suddenly pale Marcus to his wife and back again. "What the hell is this?"

Regina swallowed and forced herself to answer. "Marcus asked to speak with me."

"About what?"

Marcus spoke up then, though his thin voice shook. "I came to tell her why you married her. I felt she should know."

Patrick's lips drew back from his teeth. "You did, huh?" Slowly he began crossing the room toward the other man. "You're one hell of a helpful guy."

Regina grew alarmed. "Patrick. Don't start anything."

Patrick grunted. "I won't. It's already started."

"Patrick!"

"I am not a violent man," Marcus quakingly explained.

Patrick took Marcus by the shirtfront. "Well, that's too

damn bad for you," he said into the other man's terrified face. "Because I am."

"Patrick," Regina commanded. "Let him go. Let him go, now."

Patrick froze. Marcus, held above the ground, went on quaking. And then Patrick shoved him away. Marcus fell backward onto the couch.

"Get out," Patrick said. He turned his back and walked to the stone mantel where he remained, facing the wall.

Marcus scrambled upright and then brushed off his slacks and straightened his rumpled shirt. He combed his mussed hair with his hands.

Then he cleared his throat.

But before he could say a word, Patrick, still turned away, silkily advised, "Are you deaf? I said get the hell out of my house."

Marcus glanced nervously at Regina.

She gave him a reassuring nod. "Yes, Marcus. Please go."

Marcus, looking both relieved and reproachful, strode swiftly across the room. As he left, he quietly pulled the door closed behind him.

After Marcus was gone, Regina let the silence stretch out, because she really did dread the things she and Patrick were probably going to end up saying to each other. She wished she was a little younger and still capable of believing that a jealous display was a sign of a man's love. If she could believe that, then she could tell herself that Patrick was in love with her.

But she couldn't believe it. Patrick was a Jones, that was all. A man who didn't like anyone encroaching on what he considered his. What she'd just witnessed wasn't a lover's jealousy. It was a demonstration of ownership. Patrick had chosen her as a proper wife, one fit to raise his children.

And a proper wife did not invite her old boyfriends into her home while her husband was at work.

Eventually she grew tired of standing there, waiting for him to turn around and start yelling at her. So she said briskly, "Well, I suppose you'd like lunch. I'll just go on in the kitchen and see what I can put together." She started to leave.

She got about two steps.

"Stay here." Patrick turned to face her. "What the hell was he doing here?"

"Patrick, maybe we should talk about this after you've cooled down a little."

"Answer me."

"I—"

"Answer."

"All right." She drew in a breath. "He was here for just the reason he said. He wanted me to know that you married me to get custody of Marnie and Teresa. I told him I already knew that."

"And that's all?"

"He didn't seem to believe that I knew."

"I'll bet. What else?"

"That's all."

He was silent. Then, "You said you'd keep away from him."

"I know, but he was very upset. I felt sorry for him. He wanted to talk in private, so I let him in."

Patrick seemed to be studying her, measuring what she'd told him for its veracity. Then he said, "Once, you walked away when I called to you, pretended you didn't notice when I waved. You ran off like a scared rabbit every time I looked your way for a damn week. For *his* sake. Didn't you?"

She knew he was talking about that final week before the day on Sweetbriar Summit.

"Didn't you?" It was a demand. He leaned an elbow on the mantel and waited for her to confirm what he already knew.

She gave him the truth he demanded. "Yes."

"And, knowing Marcus Shelby, I'll bet he never even had to ask you to do it. He's the type of guy who doesn't make demands on a woman. He just acts wounded until she does things his way. Am I right?"

"Patrick—"

"Answer me. Am I right?"

"Yes, you're right."

"But now, you're with *me*. And I'm a guy who does make demands. And I did ask you to stay away from him."

Though she knew she was pulling the tiger's tail, she simply could not resist pointing out, "You hardly *asked*."

He shrugged. "Fine. I didn't ask. I *told* you to stay away from him. And you said you would. But you didn't. Instead, you *invited* him into my damn house." He straightened from the mantel. "Why is that?"

"I…"

He began walking toward her. "Why?"

Her throat went dry. She had to swallow. "Because…"

"Tell me."

"Because I just…I don't *feel* anything for him. I don't know if I ever did. It was just completely *safe* to be alone with him."

"It was *safe*?" Patrick repeated, as he kept on coming.

"Yes." She backed up, but ran into the stool of her piano, which he and his brother, Brendan, had moved over from the other house three days before. She stammered on, "But, it—it was never *safe* to be alone with you. You just were…not safe. And when I realized that, I tried to stay away from you. Until the day of the picnic, when I found out it wasn't any use to try to stay away from you. Because you are a…relentless kind of man."

Patrick reached her and stopped. He was so close that his chest brushed her breasts. She almost dropped to the stool, but he caught her shoulders and held her erect.

"You're right," he murmured into her upturned face. "I always get what I'm after. And I am not safe. Never forget that."

She gulped. "Don't worry, I won't."

He grunted, a very self-satisfied sound. She could see that he was mollified. Probably by her admission that he was someone she'd been afraid to be alone with—while Marcus Shelby wasn't. Lately, in her state of marital bliss, it was too easy to forget what a hooligan she'd married.

She decided she had a thing or two to say to him. "Patrick, you really terrified the poor man."

"Good. Maybe he'll stay away from my wife."

"I do not approve of your behavior."

"Fine. Keep away from other men, and my behavior will improve."

She looked up at him and *almost* blurted out, *Of course I will, you fool. I have no interest in other men. Only in you. I love you. Even though you don't love me.*

But she didn't. She had some pride, after all.

She told him, "All right. I swear to you, I won't so much as go near Marcus Shelby ever again."

He grinned. "Good." And then he lowered his mouth and ran his tongue along the seam where her lips were pressed disapprovingly together.

She turned her head away. "If you think I'm going to make love with you now…"

He chuckled, a chuckle that made the muscles of her belly contract. "I do. I do think that," he confessed in a voice that was stunning in its utter guilelessness. "Come on, Gina. I came all the way home…"

"For lunch."

"Aw, Gina. Why is it always food with you?" His hands gentled on her shoulders and began a slow, deep massage.

"You should eat."

"I should get a kiss from my wife."

"Patrick…"

He lowered his mouth and grazed her chin with his teeth. "Gina…"

And then his mouth was on hers. She sighed. Her reluctance faded away while her lips parted to allow the entrance of his seeking tongue.

A few moments later, when he scooped her up against his chest and hauled her off down the hall, she thought, somewhat inchoately, that she lived in the eye of a tornado. Powerful natural forces whirled around her. And sometimes they scooped her up and carried her away.

The phone rang the next morning just as Regina and Patrick were sitting down to breakfast. Regina was the one who answered.

"Regina? It's Marybeth."

"Oh, hello. How are you?" Patrick was looking at Regina with an eyebrow raised, so she tipped the phone beneath her chin and mouthed, "Marybeth," at him.

"I'm fine," Marybeth said. "Listen, I want you to know, I was really surprised when you two called last week. But, you know, the more I thought about it, the more I realized that it's a terrific thing, you two getting together. Of course, I never really knew you. But you've always seemed to me to be a very calm and levelheaded person. You might kind of…balance Patrick out a little."

"Well…" Regina couldn't help but respond to the sincerity in the other woman's voice. "Thank you."

"Don't thank me. I mean it."

"Well, good."

"So, um, welcome to the family," Marybeth said. "Would you put Patrick on now, please?"

"Certainly," she said. "He's right here. You take care." Regina held the phone across the table and Patrick took it.

"Yeah?" he said, and then listened.

Faintly, Regina could hear the low drone of Marybeth's voice, even from across the table, though of course she couldn't make out the words. But whatever she was saying, Patrick didn't like it. As he listened, his jaw tensed. His mouth became a grim line and two creases formed between his brows.

Then he said, "You *what?*"

The faint voice on the other end of the line spoke faster. Patrick cut in. "Yeah, I wanted them to visit, but not like this. Why didn't you *call* me? How could you put a twelve-year-old and a nine-year-old on a bus *alone* for a two-thousand-mile trip across the country?" Marybeth said something. "I don't give a damn how responsible Teresa is for her age. She's *twelve,* for crying out loud."

Marybeth began talking again. Patrick stood up and paced the floor. When he spoke, he shouted into the phone.

"Oh, right. They'll be fine, sure. But what if they're not fine? What the hell are we going to do if they don't turn up in Sacramento like they're supposed to? It's a big country out there, between Little Rock and here, just in case you didn't notice, Marybeth!"

Marybeth said something more. Regina did her best to signal Patrick to keep calm. When he refused to look her way, she got up and went to him. She took his arm. He shook her off.

"So what if you have to work? You could have called *me.* I would have come to get them, or sent the plane fare. That's the problem with you, Marybeth. You don't bother to *communicate.* You do what you want to do and when it all blows up in our faces, you say you didn't have any choice. You couldn't afford plane fare and you couldn't go with them because you had to work, as if there was nothing else in the whole damn world that you could have done. As if calling me and seeing what I was willing to do wasn't even a possibility. You're a damn disaster, Marybeth." His voice rose to a roar. "And who do you think pays for the way you mess up? Two innocent girls, that's who! Two poor, confused kids!"

From the other end of the line, Marybeth shouted right back.

"Okay, okay," Patrick growled. "So maybe I wasn't willing to do a hell of a lot for a while there. But now I am. Now Regina and I are married and I've got a nice place for the two of them to live." Regina knew what was coming. She signaled frantically for Patrick to calm down, not to make this an adversarial issue. But she was signaling in vain.

Patrick blustered on. "And that's what I want. I want them living with me! Right now, I'm the one in a good position to give them a normal life. You know you're working half the night sometimes lately, trying to get that business of yours off the ground. And they miss their family. They miss their friends. When they get here, I want them to stay here. I want them to—"

Marybeth started talking again.

"What?"

She said something else.

Patrick, who had stopped pacing, dropped into his chair again. "I see," he said, sounding stunned now. "All right, then. Good." Marybeth talked some more. Patrick said, "I will." Then he looked up at Regina and mouthed, "Pencil and paper."

Swiftly she found what he wanted and he wrote down the date and time that his daughters would arrive at the bus terminal in Sacramento.

Then he said, "Okay. All right. And, Marybeth. Oh, hell. I guess part of our problem was that I never gave you enough damn credit. Yeah." He was actually smiling. "You, too." He hung up.

And then he put his elbows on the table and cradled his head in his hands.

Regina couldn't stand the suspense. She blurted out, "Well? What did she say?"

Patrick lifted his head and rubbed his eyes.

"Patrick? Please, tell me."

"She said…"

"Yes?"

He dragged in a breath. "She's been giving it a lot of thought lately and she has to agree with me. It's all too much for her. The girls need more supervision." Patrick paused.

Regina prompted, "And?"

"The girls are on their way. And we've just agreed they will stay here through the school year."

Regina stared at him, hardly daring to believe. And then he threw back his head, opened his mouth and let out a howl of joy at the ceiling. After that, he jumped up, grabbed Regina and spun her around until she was so dizzy, she didn't know up from down.

And then he kissed her—a long, delirious kiss. Regina felt dizzier than when he'd been spinning her around. She tried to point out that their breakfast was growing cold, but then he kissed her some more.

Breakfast was forgotten. Patrick went to work late.

Chapter Eleven

"The guy sitting behind us when we left Dallas was a pervert," Marnie said.

"Hush," Teresa chided, sounding more like Nellie Anderson than a twelve-year-old.

"Hush yourself, *Saint* Teresa," Marnie replied.

They were on their way home from the bus terminal in Sacramento, where the girls had appeared on time, looking grubby and tired, but otherwise unharmed. Patrick had already told them that they would be living in North Magdalene for the coming school year. They were thrilled at the news.

And they'd been at each other's throats since the moment they got in the Bronco.

"You are impossible," Teresa hissed.

"And you're a big pain." Marnie faced the front seat and spoke to the adults. "And that guy *was* a pervert, I swear."

"He was not," Teresa firmly contended. Then she was the one addressing the front seat. "The man did look a little strange, actually. But he never bothered us." She glanced disapprovingly at her sister. "And you have no idea what a pervert is, anyway."

"Do so."

Teresa, not deigning to reply to such a childish challenge, spoke again to the grown-ups. "Honestly, I hope you can do something with her, Regina. She's impossible."

Marnie stuck the end of a yard-long licorice whip in her mouth and bit off a chunk, after which she calmly advised her older sister, in the bluntest of terms, to have sexual intercourse with herself.

Teresa gasped in outrage.

Patrick shouted over his shoulder at Marnie, "What did you say?"

Regina warned softly, "Patrick..."

But it was too late. Marnie was already repeating the advice she'd given to Teresa.

Patrick swung the wheel of the Bronco sharply to the right, causing the driver in the car behind them to blast his horn long and loudly. The Bronco bounced onto the shoulder of the road. Patrick had to do a little fancy maneuvering to get the vehicle to stop before they hit a steel-reinforced fence. The 4×4 shook and shuddered, but came to a halt just in time.

Then Patrick whirled to confront his younger daughter. "Let's get this clear right up front. Now that you're gonna be with me and Regina, you're gonna learn to control that mouth of yours."

Marnie folded her hands over her thin chest and glared at him as he glared at her. At that moment, Regina thought, the family resemblance between father and daughter was quite remarkable.

Patrick demanded, "Apologize to your sister."

Marnie pressed her lips together and went on glaring.

A stare-down ensued, Jones to Jones. Regina looked from father to daughter and concluded that little Marnie was a darn sight braver than Marcus Shelby—or probably just about any other mere man when confronted with the wrath of a Jones.

"You *will* apologize," Patrick said. "Or we'll sit here all day."

Marnie raised the nose that resembled Patrick's and looked out her side window at a tanker truck as it roared by.

Regina decided something had to be done. The first thing, she determined, was to separate the two girls so that further disturbances could be stopped before they started.

She pushed open her door. A wall of hot air hit her in the face. Though the Bronco was air-conditioned, the temperature outside was well over a hundred degrees.

Patrick barked, "What do you think you're doing, Regina?"

But she only blithely opened the door on Teresa's side of the back seat. "Teresa, would you sit in front, please?"

Teresa, who probably would have jumped off a cliff if an adult had instructed her to, obligingly got out and took Regina's seat in front.

Regina slid in next to Marnie. "Patrick," she said, "I think, if we're going to just sit here, that you ought to turn off the engine."

He shifted his glare from his daughter to his wife. Regina gave him a warm smile. His eyes narrowed. Then he shrugged. He turned in his seat and gave the key a twist.

They sat in silence while other cars rushed by them. Within ten minutes, the Bronco was an oven. They rolled down the windows.

Regina murmured, "My, it certainly is a hot day." She

turned to Marnie. "We left the air-conditioning on at home, of course."

Marnie said nothing. She doggedly chewed her licorice whip down to the end.

"Luckily for all of us," Regina said, casually wiping sweat from the back of her neck, "we've got all day."

Patrick and Teresa made noises of agreement. Marnie merely looked stubborn, slightly befuddled and very hot. Unfortunately for her, the sun was slanting in at its worst from her corner of the vehicle.

Regina rested her head against the door. She sighed and closed her eyes. The heat was quite draining. It occurred to her that if she did doze off, she was likely to feel dried-out and exhausted when she woke. But Patrick had laid down an ultimatum.

Regina herself would never have made the ultimatum at this point. However, now that it *was* made, she felt that she and Patrick would lose acres of ground with his recalcitrant youngest child if they backed down. So she shifted around in the seat until she was as comfortable as she could get. The heat seemed to settle around her, broken only by the hot winds stirred up when a big rig roared past.

Regina felt herself being dragged toward a heavy, uncomfortable sleep.

And then Marnie mumbled, "Okay, okay. I'm sorry, Teresa."

Hiding her smile, Regina sat up. "Teresa?"

Teresa looked over the seat, her expression alert and agreeable. "Yes?"

"It is customary to acknowledge an apology when one is offered."

Teresa's hazel eyes shifted. Regina understood that Patrick's older daughter had hoped to avoid having to reply to her sister's grudging declaration. But of course, since she was the "good girl," she would have to say something, now that Regina had pointed out her lapse.

"All right," she nobly intoned. "I accept your apology, Marnie."

"Good," Regina said. "Now, Patrick. May we go?"

For an answer, Patrick started the engine.

The rest of the ride was very quiet. Regina thought everyone was being careful not to start anything, because they didn't know what might happen if they did. Regina felt satisfied with this.

For once, she found herself thinking of her own mother with pure fondness. Anthea Black had been a master at getting just what she wanted without ever raising her voice. Regina knew now that what she'd learned from her mother was going to come in very handy.

At home, Teresa enthused over her white wicker bedroom. "It's just beautiful, Regina. It's like something from a magazine. And it's really all mine?"

Regina nodded, "Yes, it's all yours."

Then Teresa's happy look faded.

"Teresa, what's wrong?"

"Oh, well. I get confused."

"About what?"

"Well, it's good to be grateful, isn't it?"

"Well, *I* certainly think so."

"But it's a sin to love worldly things."

"Who told you that?"

"It's in the Bible." Teresa looked more confused than ever. "I'm sure it is. Somewhere."

"Well," Regina pointed out gently, "I personally believe, along with you, that gratitude is a very good thing. And so is appreciation. And it's never wrong to be grateful for, and to appreciate, um, worldly things. As long as we never start thinking that worldly things are the most important things."

Teresa's pale brows drew together as she pondered. Then she nodded. "That makes sense."

Apparently relieved that it was okay to like her new room, Teresa hoisted her big suitcase onto the dresser and began transferring her neatly folded clothes into the empty drawers. Regina sat on the edge of the bed and watched her, thinking that Teresa was a little like she herself had been at twelve, so dutiful, she verged on obsequious. So well behaved, it made one nervous. A child who put her clothing away in drawers long before any adult had a chance to tell her to.

"All our winter things are still at Mom's," Teresa said.

Twelve years old, Regina thought, and she's worried about her winter clothing in July.

"Don't worry," Regina reassured the girl. "We'll see that everything you need gets here in time, one way or another."

Teresa looked at Regina. "I believe you. I can see that you're a very well-organized person." The words were said in a tone of mingled regard and relief. "My mom's not very well organized. She never has been. It drives me crazy, you know?" Teresa's face flushed red. She hastened to add, "Not that I don't love her a lot. I do."

Regina made a little sound of understanding, thinking that living in an orderly household would probably do a world of good for a girl like Teresa. If Teresa felt she could trust the adults around her to take care of her, she just might relax and allow herself to be a child now and then.

Right then, Teresa caught sight of her own reflection in the oval mirror over the vanity table. She was still unpacking, but she paused long enough to stand sideways and study her body's profile. "Regina, please be honest. Do you think I'm too fat?" And then, before Regina could answer, she declared, "Not that it matters. I plan to join the Catholic church and become a nun, you know. And God loves you no matter what you look like.''

Regina made no comment on Teresa's plans for the sisterhood. Instead, she softly maintained, ''No, Teresa. I don't think you're too fat at all.''

''Well, I don't know why I asked, anyway.'' Teresa carefully propped a rag doll against the pillows on the bed and put her Bible on the night table. ''It's vain to worry about how you look.''

Vain but natural, Regina thought, though all she did was smile in a noncommittal fashion.

Next, Regina went to see how Marnie was doing in her new room. She found the girl sitting on the floor building a space station out of one of the big plastic construction sets Patrick had put in the closet because he knew his younger daughter loved such things. Unlike Teresa's suitcase, which by then had been completely emptied and put away, Marnie's bag was still waiting untouched near the foot of the bed.

''Well, are you getting settled in all right?'' Regina asked.

Marnie looked up and grunted.

''Anything I can do to help?''

''Yeah.'' She held up a miniature spaceman—minus a head. ''Find this guy's head.''

Gamely, Regina crouched on the floor and went through the box of snap-together plastic pieces. ''Is this it?'' She held up a head with a helmet on it.

''Yeah. Thanks.'' Marnie took the head and attached it to the torso and then put the little man in what appeared to be some sort of space shuttle. ''Now I need four more of these.'' She held up a gray triangular piece.

Regina looked through the box some more and eventually found what Marnie needed. Gradually, the Alpha Galactrix Space Outpost took shape. Regina helped as Marnie allowed her to, finding pieces and sometimes even being told she could snap them in place.

As she worked alongside the child, Regina learned that Marnie thought the oak furniture in her room was "cool," and she was glad Regina hadn't "grossed her out" by giving her the same "sissy stuff" as Teresa had in her room.

"I mean, only a *girl* would want furniture made out of sticks and painted white."

Regina managed to keep from pointing out that Marnie herself was a *girl*.

Marnie was also glad that she and Teresa wouldn't have to share a room. Regina fully agreed with Marnie on that one. After seeing the way the two of them bickered and battled, Regina herself was downright *thrilled* that her new stepdaughters would not be sharing a room.

Eventually, Regina left Marnie alone and went downstairs to see about getting dinner together, the main course of which was to be chicken barbecued by Patrick. Though Regina intended that the girls would start helping with meal preparations soon enough, for that first night she and Patrick did everything.

They'd decided to eat on the back patio, which, due to an awning and the many trees in the backyard, was usually fairly cool by early evening. When all was ready, the girls were called to the table.

Marnie came first. One glance at her hands and Regina came to a decision. It was true that she wanted to be easy on Patrick's daughters for their first day in their new home. But no one was sitting down to *her* table with hands that looked as if they'd just been used to build a mud hut.

"Marnie, please go wash your hands."

Marnie shot her new stepmother a mutinous look and sprinted for the kitchen door. She was back in under thirty seconds.

"That was quick," Regina said mildly.

Marnie merely slid into her place. "Gimme the rolls."

"We will say grace before dinner," Regina announced.

Patrick made a face but said nothing.

Teresa glowed, no doubt at the prospect of living in a house where God was appreciated.

Marnie muttered something that was probably offensive, but spoken too low for anyone to be sure.

Regina gave her younger stepdaughter a tolerant smile. "But first, Marnie, before we say grace, you will go in and wash properly."

Marnie glanced sideways and then back. It was obvious she had thought this was a battle she'd won. And now here it was again. She muttered, "I did wash."

"Excuse me, I can't hear you."

"I said, I *did* wash."

"You *did* wash?"

"Yeah."

"With what?"

"Whaddaya mean, with what?"

"I mean that, whatever you used before, *now* you will go in and wash with soap and water."

"Or else what?"

Regina only smiled.

Marnie glared and groaned. She dragged herself up from the picnic table and trudged inside. A few minutes later, she returned and took her seat again, looking wounded and proud. Her hands were much cleaner than when she had left.

Regina said a brief prayer.

They began to eat. Twice, Regina reminded Marnie that, while barbecued chicken could be eaten with the fingers, it was common courtesy to wipe one's hands on one's napkin, not on one's clothing. Marnie, surprisingly, seemed to bear the criticism well enough from Regina. There were a few mumbled curses, which Regina pointedly ignored.

Both times when Marnie mumbled, Patrick looked up sharply and started to reprimand her. But Regina managed to catch his eye before he said anything. She gave him a narrowed look and a quick shake of her head so that he subsided before he got started.

But then Marnie rubbed her greasy hands on her shirt one more time.

Regina pointed out, "Please use your napkin, Marnie."

And Teresa just had to chime in, "Really, it's no use trying to teach *her* table manners. She's such a pig."

That did it. Marnie's blue eyes flashed. "Don't call me a pig, you..." She finished by using one of her favorite expletives.

Patrick's face went crimson. He stood. "Go to your room."

Marnie was outraged. "But she's always—"

"Now!"

Marnie scowled at her father for a moment. Then she leapt up and disappeared into the house.

Patrick glanced from Regina to Teresa, as if daring either of them to say a single word. Then he sat back down and picked up his fork.

After a few minutes of uncomfortable silence, the three remaining diners relaxed a little. Regina remarked on how good the chicken was. Teresa agreed, and asked for another piece.

Patrick teased, "Better watch it, Tessy, or you'll get fat as a cow."

Teresa looked up. Her face was flushed, her eyes brimmed with tears. Without a word, she stood from the table and ran into the house.

After a moment of staring with his mouth open, Patrick asked, "What did I do?"

Regina sipped from her ice tea. "Generally, Patrick, it

is unwise to tease a twelve-year-old girl about her weight.''

Patrick sighed. ''Thank God you're here.''

After the table was cleared away, Regina went to speak with Teresa, whom she found sitting in the wicker rocker, staring out the window at the catalpa tree in the backyard.

''May I come in?''

Teresa turned her head, looked at her stepmother, then looked back out the window. ''If you want.''

Regina closed the door behind her and sat on the edge of the bed. She looked out the window with Teresa for a while.

Teresa said, ''For a whole year, all I wanted was to be home.''

Regina softly pointed out, ''That's what your father's wanted, too. To have you home.''

''You think so?''

''I know so.''

Teresa sighed. ''I could hardly believe it, that someone like you would marry someone like him.''

Regina chuckled. ''A lot of people can hardly believe it. But it's true.''

Now Teresa looked at Regina. ''You...you really like him, don't you?''

''Mm-hmm. I really do.''

Teresa shook her head and looked out the window some more. ''He thinks I'm fat.''

''No, he doesn't. He was teasing you. Sometimes he lacks...finesse.''

Teresa grunted. ''Does he ever. Sometimes I *hate* being a Jones. It's so unrefined. People talk about us all the time because we do crazy things. I wanted to be different than that. I thought I'd be glad to move away where no one knew what it meant that my name was Jones. But then all I wanted to do was come home.''

''Life can be very confusing,'' Regina agreed. ''Now

come on.'' She stood and held out her hand. ''We saved you a piece of strawberry shortcake.''

''I can't. It's so fattening.''

''Eat it without the whipped cream. Strawberries and a little sponge cake. No calories at all.''

''Well, maybe just a little piece.''

''Okay, then. Let's go.''

Teresa allowed herself to be led to the kitchen for her shortcake, which Patrick served to her.

''Tessy, I was only teasing,'' he said, when he set the dessert in front of her.

Teresa sniffed. ''Teasing about what?''

''About your getting fat.''

''Are you saying you're sorry?''

Regina tiptoed from the room, leaving Patrick to make his apologies to his daughter without anyone else listening in.

She went to the girls' bathroom and turned on the taps in the tub. Then she went to get Marnie, who barely controlled herself from using her favorite word when she heard what her new stepmother had in store for her.

''A bath? Why a *bath?*''

''Because you need one.''

''I don't need a bath.''

''Yes, you do.''

''I took one before we left Arkansas.''

''And from now on, you'll take one every night.''

''*Every night?*''

''Yes. Now let's go, or the water will run over in the tub.''

Marnie folded her arms and stuck out her chin. ''I will not.''

Regina smiled. ''Yes, Marnie, you will. You will take the bath yourself, or I will *bathe* you.'' Purposely, Regina stressed the word *bathe,* smiling all the while.

Marnie looked worried. "You wouldn't."

"Try me."

"I'm nine years old. I don't get *bathed*."

"You do if you won't bathe yourself."

"That's disgusting." Marnie looked at her stepmother sideways. "Are you a pervert or something?"

"Well, I certainly hope not," Regina answered guilelessly. "But perhaps, while I'm *bathing* you, you'll find out for sure."

"Oh, f—"

Regina wiggled a chiding finger at Marnie, who stopped herself from uttering the forbidden word just in time. Then she turned to Marnie's suitcase, which she intended that Marnie would unpack tomorrow before lunch. She removed a set of superhero pajamas and held them out. "Well?"

With a grumbled oath too low to get her in trouble, Marnie grabbed the pajamas. Then, her jaw set, she marched out of the room and down the hall, with Regina close on her heels. When she reached the bathroom, she slammed the door in Regina's face.

"Wash thoroughly," Regina called sweetly through the door. "I'll be checking when you're done."

No answer came back—at least not one that Regina could hear. But when Marnie emerged, she was clean behind the ears and smelled appealingly of soap and water.

"Good enough?" She stuck out her chin testily.

"Yes, that's just fine. Now, go kiss your father goodnight."

"Why?"

"Because you love him."

"Yuck. Love."

"Go."

Marnie trudged into the living room, where Patrick was watching one of those live police shows. Regina didn't follow her. But after a few minutes, when Marnie didn't reappear on the way to her room, Regina peeked in on them.

Marnie had squeezed into the easy chair next to her father. Her head rested on his chest and his big arm was thrown around her small shoulders. Both of them stared at the television, rapt, as a drug bust was accomplished with a battering ram.

Smiling, Regina left them alone.

When Patrick joined Regina later in their room, Patrick's eyes were soft. He undressed her slowly, kissing her everywhere, murmuring his gratitude that she had married him and made it possible for him to have another chance with his daughters.

Regina clung to him, her heart full of the love words that her pride wouldn't let her say. He stroked her body in the way that drove her crazy with wanting him and then he kissed her at her most private place. Eager, utterly excited, Regina opened herself totally to him, as he had taught her to do.

At last, when she began to wonder if it was possible to shatter into a million pieces of pure delight, he rose above her and came down upon her. They moved, together, toward a sweet and wondrous fulfillment.

At the end, as happened too often lately, Regina had to bite her lip to keep from shamelessly crying out how much she loved him.

Later, when they lay side by side in the moonlight, she gently warned that they had a lot of work to do. Both of the girls had deep insecurities, and it would take time before they learned to trust that this new home they'd come to was a home that would last.

"We'll do what we have to do," Patrick murmured sleepily. "And eventually they'll see that it'll last."

Regina cuddled close against him and tried to believe he was right.

But still, she couldn't help but wonder about the other women who must once have loved Patrick as she did now. About Chloe, who'd gone off who knew where with a stranger. And Marybeth, trying her best to make a go of it on her own, two thousand miles away.

Had Patrick once reassured them that what they shared would last?

If he had, then he'd been wrong. Regina silently prayed that he was right this time. And not only for her own selfish sake, but for the sake of two innocent children who deserved a stable home and parents they could count on.

Chapter Twelve

As Regina had suspected might happen, the ensuing few weeks were not easy ones.

Marnie fought her bath most nights and had to be constantly reminded that one ate with one's fork, not one's hands. And like her father, when she became angry, she lashed out. She'd use her fists—or that certain forbidden word—without compunction. And then she'd end up consigned to her room.

Poor Teresa, on the other hand, was so determined to be perfect that Regina often felt she was dealing with an automaton. Patrick's older daughter often seemed incapable of a spontaneous thought, a girl who was much too old for her own good. And she was incredibly sensitive to criticism. A thoughtless word, especially from Patrick who was not known for his tact, would have her scurrying away in tears.

Several times, Marybeth was brought into the battles via

the telephone. One or the other of the girls would call her mother in Arkansas and complain tearfully about how awful things were. The first few times that happened, Marybeth became as upset as the child who had called her. But then, Regina convinced Patrick that he should talk to Marybeth about the problem. He called Marybeth. Together, they agreed on how they would handle such incidents from then on.

After that, when one of the girls called her mother to complain, Marybeth would listen sympathetically and then say, "Well, you know you can always return here to live with me. But your father and I have agreed on one thing. There'll be no bouncing back and forth. If you come back here to live, then here's where you'll stay." Since neither of the girls really wanted to leave North Magdalene, that would settle them down, at least temporarily.

But peaceful moments were few and far between. And whenever things did settle down, then Marnie would say something and Teresa would reprimand her and the two of them would be off and bickering.

The house echoed with slamming doors, with Marnie's curses and Teresa's sobs. As July faded into August, Patrick's dream of having his girls home was, more often than not, a nightmare.

Through it all, Regina was the peacemaker. And she was grateful that the girls seemed to accept her. Though it often took every last ounce of patience Regina possessed, she was scrupulously careful to be calm, consistent, kind and firm with them. The girls, neither of whom had any idea how to manipulate a person who refused to be intimidated or to lose her temper, soon concluded that their new stepmother could not be maneuvered.

Though Regina found their lives a constant strain, she learned much. And every day she grew to care more deeply for Marnie, who was so cocky, bold and bright. And for the gentler, sadder Teresa, whose smile was just like her father's and who longed to be small-boned and delicate—and longed to dedicate herself to good works.

All told, Regina was happy the girls had moved in. But their constant presence in the house ended the extended honeymoon she and Patrick had enjoyed before their arrival.

Since his daughters were in and out all day, Patrick no longer came home from work during his lunch break to carry his new bride off to the bedroom and make love to her until she begged him never to stop. And with all the problems they were having as a family, sometimes days would go by without his turning to Regina in the night.

Regina knew that their less frequent lovemaking was natural, given the stresses they were suffering. She refused to think that her new husband might already be tiring of her as a lover.

She did her best to keep her thoughts positive. Though they made love less often, Patrick did begin to tell her things about himself and his past that he'd never opened up about before. She saw that as a very good sign.

One night, after a particularly unpleasant battle with Marnie, when the poor child had been sent to bed straight from the dinner table for the second evening in a row, Regina helped Teresa finish the dishes. Then Regina went out to the service porch and folded the last load of laundry. Finally, she wandered upstairs to the master bedroom where she found Patrick sitting on the edge of the bed wearing only a pair of gym shorts and staring at his bare feet.

Quietly she closed the door, set the folded clothes she was carrying on the dresser by the walk-in closet and went to sit opposite him in the rocking chair by the window. He gave her a quick, cheerless smile and then resumed regarding his toes.

She got up from the rocker and went to sit next to him

on the bed. "What's the matter?" she asked gently when he volunteered nothing.

He shook his head. She smoothed his hair back, where it had fallen over his forehead. It was still wet from the shower he'd just taken.

"Come on." She gave him a gentle nudge with the side of her body. "Get it out. You'll feel better if you do."

"Aw, Gina."

"Yes?"

He swore.

"Keep going."

He chuckled, a humorless sound. Then he fell back on the bed and laced his hands on his bare chest.

"Talk," she urged again.

"Oh, all right." He gave a deep sigh. "I knew I was a lousy father. I swear I did. I just didn't know how lousy. Till lately."

"Oh, Patrick..."

He glanced at her, his expression wry. "Come on, Gina. Don't let me talk that way about myself. Think of something nice to say, like how I'm not *that* bad."

She couldn't suppress a smile. "Okay. You're not *that* bad."

He grunted. "Not very convincing. And maybe it's better to tell the truth, anyway. I started out lousy, and I've pretty much stayed that way."

"What do you mean, you started out lousy?"

He stared up at the slowly rotating ceiling fan, another of the myriad of improvements made by the two ladies from Oakland from whom Patrick had bought the house. Regina waited as he seemed to study the fan. But after a while, when he didn't say anything, she began to think he wouldn't answer her.

She was mildly surprised when he finally spoke. "I married Marybeth because she was pregnant with Teresa. Did you know that?''

She tried to be tactful. "There was a rumor to that effect around town."

He grunted. "That stands to reason. There's always a rumor around this town." He watched the fan some more.

Regina took the moment to toe off her shoes and stretch out beside him.

He turned to give her a sad smile. Then he looked at the ceiling again and confessed softly, "The problem was, when I married Marybeth, I was still in love with Chloe."

Regina tried not to stiffen when she heard that. She wanted to know what was in her husband's mind and heart, to understand what his life had been like in all the years before he had made her his wife. She didn't want to be judgmental. But she couldn't help feeling dismayed that he would have made love to one woman while he was *in* love with another.

Patrick went on, still watching the fan, "Okay, I've lied to myself and everyone else for years, trying to pretend there was never much between Chloe and me. I don't know why I bothered with the lie. No one ever believed it. It eased my pride, I guess, since she took my heart in her pretty little hands and broke it right in two."

Regina lay very still. Right then, hearing him say such things about another woman, she understood exactly what Patrick meant when he spoke of his broken heart—and his pride.

Lately, since their lives had grown more complicated, it grew harder every day to live with the fact that he didn't return her love. Sometimes it seemed her pride was the only thing that kept her heart in one piece. As long as he didn't know she was in love with him, they were equals. She'd wanted a husband and family. He'd needed a wife. They were a match in what they brought to each other.

But if he knew of her hopeless, hungry love for him, the scales of their relationship would be dangerously tipped. Instead of an equal, she'd be the needy one. The one who yearned for something he was never going to give.

Patrick was watching her. "What's wrong?"

"Nothing," she lied. "Go on."

"You sure?"

"Yes. Please. Continue."

He turned his head away and rubbed his face with his hand. "Hell. Anyway, when Teresa was born, I was too wrapped up in my own damn broken heart to pay much attention to her. And I was a bad husband to Marybeth, I know that. I never gave her the care and affection she deserved as my wife." He looked at Regina again. "Hey."

"What?" She forced a smile.

"Look. It wasn't like you're thinking."

"How do you know what I'm thinking?"

"I can see it in your eyes. You think I got Marybeth pregnant when I was still with Chloe. But I wasn't *with* Chloe. Chloe had broken up with me for the hundredth time, for some reason I can't even remember now. Chloe was...I don't know. It was like she didn't want me when she could have me. But then, the minute I was unavailable, I was the only man for her. I got fed up with it, that was all, even though I was still really gone on her. Finally, she told me she was through with me one time too many. I decided it didn't matter if I could never get over her, I'd damn well live without her."

He turned to his side, facing Regina, and braced himself on an elbow. "Then, I was out one night and I met Marybeth. She seemed so open and friendly." Idly, he stroked Regina's pinned-up hair, finding a loose curl that he began rolling around his finger. "She didn't play all the games Chloe always seemed to play."

Regina remembered what he'd said, the morning after

their marriage, about the *rotten games* that men and women could play. She felt it was time to ask, "What games?"

"Ah, Gina." He sighed, a tired kind of sigh. "How can I explain it to someone like you?"

"Like me?"

"Yeah. You don't play games. You say *yes* or you say *no* and what you say is what you mean. But with Chloe, at least when it came to me, *yes* might mean *maybe* or *no* or *check with me tomorrow* or any number of damn things. To be with a woman like that can be exciting—for a while, anyway. It's a fake kind of high, to battle it out with a woman like that. You never know what will happen next.

"But you can't...build anything that lasts with a woman like that. And I knew that in my head before the rest of me caught on. So I finally swore to myself I was through with her. And I met Marybeth and we started going together, Marybeth and me, even though I was still carrying a torch for Chloe. And then it turned out Marybeth was pregnant. So we got married. And the marriage never really seemed to work out. But Marybeth was determined to keep trying. And I... Hell, I felt guilty all the time, because I still had this thing for Chloe."

Regina decided she'd always wonder, if she didn't ask, "Did you...cheat on Marybeth, with Chloe?"

Patrick dropped the strand of hair he'd been toying with. Regina had never seen him look so hurt. "Never. Damn it, Regina. I *am* a Jones, after all. We drive our women crazy, but we *never* cheat on them."

Regina realized she believed him. The relief she felt was a lovely thing. It came to her then that she couldn't bear it if he were to cheat on her. Though he didn't return her love, at least he was a loyal spouse.

"Anyway—" he stretched out on his back again "—Marybeth and I never had much of a marriage. But gradually, I did get over Chloe. And then I started thinking that maybe Marybeth and I could make it work after all. So there was a year or so there where we were both trying our damnedest to have a real marriage together. That was when Marnie came along.'' Patrick groaned and rubbed his eyes with his fingers. The gesture spoke eloquently of his bottomless weariness with himself and his own crazy past.

Regina ached for him, for his confusion and for the sadness of the story he'd just told. She thought of everyone involved. Of Patrick. Chloe. Marybeth. Somehow, not one of them had managed to get what they wanted.

"They say that Marybeth divorced *you*,'' Regina murmured. "Is that true?''

"Yeah. She told me she finally realized she wasn't going to get the kind of love she wanted from me. So she decided to cut her losses and give it up. And though it was tough on the girls, I guess it wasn't any tougher than having their parents either at each other's throats or not speaking to each other all the time, trying to keep a bad marriage together.

"And in general, since the divorce, Marybeth and I have gotten along much better than we ever did while we were married. Marybeth's a good woman, really. I like her. But we never really worked well together. She would cry and be wounded about every little thing. And then I would get mad and storm out. We just couldn't get it together, you know?''

"I think so.''

He propped himself on his elbow again and ran a finger slowly down her arm. "I think it takes a very levelheaded woman to make a life with me.''

She warmed at the oblique compliment. "Oh, does it?''

"You bet.''

Regina knew she shouldn't ask the next question, but somehow it was on her lips anyway. "Patrick, um, it's better if I know the truth. I know you said you're over Chloe. But, deep in your heart, are you sure that's the truth?''

He was looking at her. His face was very still, completely unreadable. "Yes."

Hesitantly, she dared to point out, "People say you were...upset, when she left town last year."

"So?"

"Well, I mean, if you were over her..."

"Look. A lot was happening then. It just seemed like the whole world was turned upside down. Everything was changing. And I was the damn idiot standing there wondering why the hell it all seemed to be passing me by. Marybeth moved away with my kids. My sister got together with Sam Fletcher. That really threw me, you know, Delilah and Sam together, after all those years when they hated each other. My old man almost gave the Mercantile building to Sam to get him to marry Delilah. See, my dad was desperate to get my sister a husband. Did you know that?"

"I think I heard that story, yes."

"Well, the Mercantile had always been promised to me and suddenly, my dad was just going to hand it over to Sam. And at the same time Chloe started dating that guy that she eventually lit out with."

"But if you were really over her, then it shouldn't have mattered who she dated."

"Aw, Gina. You are so right. It shouldn't have mattered. And it didn't matter, except that it was one more thing that wasn't as it used to be. And also, I was a little worried about her, because I did love her once and I thought she was wrecking her life, to run off with some stranger."

Regina prompted, "And what else?"

"Hell, you are merciless."

"Come on. What else?"

"Oh, all right. It was real small-minded of me, I know, but I guess I was kind of used to the idea that even though a long time ago, Chloe broke my heart, she was still sweet on me, still pining after me. And then, suddenly, she was through pining after me. Zap. Hit me right in my foolish pride once again." He let out a rueful chuckle.

Regina allowed herself to chuckle along with him. What he said did make sense. And she felt immeasurably better, to think that maybe whatever had been between him and Chloe was truly over and done.

He lay flat again and playfully tugged on her arm. "Come here."

Obliging, she stretched out on top of him, but low enough that she could rest her chin on his chest.

"The real losers in all of this were the girls." His words made a deep, pleasant rumble against her breasts. "I know that. And I hope—" he laid his hand against her cheek "—with your help, that I can finally make it up to them."

"Oh, Patrick."

His finger brushed her lips. "What?"

"We'll work it out."

"Damn right we will." His voice was husky. With a finger, he traced each of her brows in turn.

"But you could..." She hesitated. She didn't want to criticize him, but now seemed the perfect time to delicately point out a few things.

"I could what?"

She plunged in. "Well, you could tease them less, and listen to them more. You could be affectionate instead of gruff. And you could also hold off on the ultimatums until you've thought through what those ultimatums are going to cost you—and the rest of us, for that matter."

"Hmm," he said, his fingers slipping behind her head to begin removing the pins from her hair. "Anything else I should work on?"

"That'll do for a start."

He pulled out the pins and tossed them up in the air, over the side of the bed. He was grinning.

"Patrick, stop that. Who do you think will have to pick those up?"

"Relax. I'll do it. Later."

"Of course, you say that now, but—"

"Don't get prissy."

She couldn't hide her smile. Wonderful things usually happened shortly after he called her "prissy." "I can't help it. I'm prissy." She slid her arms up his warm, hard chest and took his face in her hands. "So I guess you'll have to—"

"Make you hot." He chuckled, then grew more serious. "I don't kiss you enough anymore." He looked almost sad.

Regina wondered, as she had too often the past weeks, if he was having second thoughts about the life they now shared. She pushed the idea away and suggested shyly, "You could kiss me now."

He didn't hesitate, but took her shoulders and urged her closer. She scooted up his body and sighed as she put her lips on his.

Suddenly, with his chest against her breasts and his mouth beneath hers, her doubts and fears seemed insignificant. Though her husband did not love her and her marriage had its rough spots, she would rather be with Patrick than with all the nice, safe men the world had to offer.

And after that night, things started to improve.

Patrick seemed to take her advice to heart, because his temper stayed under control most of the time. He was more careful of Teresa's tender sensibilities. He was not so quick to banish Marnie to her room when she succumbed to her fondness for inappropriate language. There were still shouted orders, slamming doors and anguished sobs, but they didn't happen quite so often.

That weekend, Patrick borrowed his uncle Robbie Riley's boat and they went to Bullfinch Bar Reservoir as a family. They swam from the boat and took turns water-skiing and they all came home tired and happy and sun-burned. Unfortunately, Marnie and Teresa ended up in a shouting match at the dinner table and they were both sent off to their rooms without dessert. But nothing was perfect, Regina decided, as she slathered aloe vera gel on her lobster-red arms.

Over the next few days, things got better still. They made it through two entire dinnertimes without anyone bursting into tears or being sent to her room.

Regina began asking for Teresa's help with some of her community activities. Teresa glowed at the idea that she was someone her stepmother would trust with such important responsibilities.

Marnie, who'd reestablished her old friendship with one of the Riggins boys, was encouraged to have the boy over whenever she wanted. So instead of disappearing into the woods right after breakfast and being impossible to locate all day, now Marnie and little Kenny spent half the time barreling around the house, or building a fort out back in the catalpa tree. There was a lot of shouting and screeching that went on, but Regina didn't mind. It was good to have Marnie near and know she was all right.

On Thursday, Regina decided to bake a cake. Both girls expressed their willingness to help, though neither had ever baked a cake before. Regina determined the two children would bake their first cake together, as an exercise in co-operation, something both of them could use a little practice in when it came to each other.

The cake turned out lopsided and the frosting was too runny. But when they brought it to the table that night, Patrick told them it was the best cake he'd ever tasted. The pride and pleasure on the two young faces had Regina turning away to hide the sentimental moisture in her eyes.

It was so clear, just looking at them. The girls had really

begun to believe that their new home with their father and stepmother was a home they could put their trust in.

And then, on the second Friday in August, Chloe Swan returned to town.

Chapter Thirteen

Nellie, of course, was the one who brought the news.

Regina knew right away that something was up, because the first thing Nellie asked as Regina led her into the kitchen was, "Where are the children?"

Regina, who'd just finished cleaning up after their lunch, wiped her hands on a towel. "Teresa's gone back to Mrs. Leslie's to finish her vacuuming for her."

Nellie chose a chair and sat. "Such a sweet girl, that dear Teresa."

"And Marnie took off for Kenny Riggins's house. They're going swimming."

"So both of them are gone?" Nellie helped herself to a cluster of seedless grapes from the fruit bowl in the center of the breakfast table.

"Yes, they're both gone."

"Good."

"Why?"

Nellie pulled a grape off the stem and popped it in her mouth. "Oh, Regina. This is so difficult. I hardly know where to begin." Nellie's eyes were shining.

Regina said nothing. It didn't matter what she said, anyway. Nellie would tell it all in her own good time.

Nellie looked up at her. "Dear. I really think it's best if you sit down."

Regina repressed a tart remark and took the chair across from the older woman. "Okay, I'm sitting. And I'm listening. What is it, Nellie?"

Nellie's sigh was very long and very meaningful. "I've just come from the post office, and who do you imagine I saw there?" The question was rhetorical. Nellie finished triumphantly, "Chloe Swan."

Regina schooled her face into placid lines. "Oh, really?"

"Yes. And she looked absolutely beautiful. A little pale, perhaps. A little…distressed. But lovely, as always, nonetheless."

"Yes, well, Chloe is a beautiful woman."

"Yes, she certainly is. She arrived back in town this morning. And she is back to stay."

"She told you this?"

"No, I spoke with her mother." Nellie had always regarded Melanie Swan, the postmistress, as a close friend. "I went in to get my mail and Chloe was there talking with her mother. And then Chloe left and it was time for Melanie's break. We went for lunch together. And Melanie told me *everything*."

"What, exactly, is *everything*, Nellie."

Nellie finished the grapes and set the picked-clean stem on the table. She leaned toward Regina and expounded in a stage whisper, "Chloe has realized that she can't go on without Patrick. So she said goodbye to that man she ran off with and returned home. She is positively *distraught* to learn that Patrick has remarried. And she plans to fight, to get him back.''

"I see."

"Oh, my dear. I am so sorry."

"Sorry for what, Nellie?"

"For what is going to happen now. But I warned you, didn't I? You can never say that I didn't warn you."

"Frankly, Nellie, I think you're overreacting to this."

"Well, certainly you want to think that. And I don't blame you. Just remember, I'm here for you. When you need to talk it all out."

"How could I forget?"

Nellie sat up a little straighter. "Do I detect a note of hostility in your tone, dear?"

"Why, Nellie. What could have given you an idea like that?"

Nellie shook her head. "Oh, my dear. I know how this must be for you."

"No, you don't."

"Yes, I do. And I also realize that it's always a temptation to shoot the messenger in a situation like this."

To Regina, right then, that idea held great appeal.

"But it's all right," Nellie sniffed. "I understand. I really do. And, as always, I forgive you." With great dignity, Nellie stood. "And I know you want to be alone. So I will be going."

Regina knew very well that Nellie's true reason for leaving was so she could get home and start calling everyone with this latest bit of gossip. But Regina didn't point it out. She wasn't about to say or do anything that would keep Nellie around for one minute more than the woman had already stayed. Regina pushed back her chair and saw Nellie to the door.

Nellie patted Regina's arm just before she left. "You just call me the minute anything happens. Oh, and I almost forgot.'' Nellie felt in a pocket of her dress and pulled out a folded sheet of paper. ''The hymns. For Sunday.''

Regina took the paper and put it in her own pocket. ''Thanks for dropping by.'' She smiled and stepped back, holding the door wide. Nellie went through it.

Swiftly Regina shut the door. She didn't even breathe until she heard the tapping of Nellie's shoes as she went down the porch steps.

Then, her hand still on the knob, she shook her head. No, she would *not* let Nellie's pettiness upset her. She would not allow her own foolish doubts to take control. She would not dwell on the thought that Chloe Swan was the one woman her husband had ever admitted to loving. And she would not obsess about how worried she'd been recently that he'd grown tired of his new wife and of their humdrum, stress-ridden life.

No matter what absurd tales Nellie insisted on passing around, it was silly to worry about Chloe Swan. Patrick could have made up with Chloe after Marybeth divorced him if he'd wanted to. And he himself had explained to Regina less than two weeks ago that his love for Chloe was firmly in the past.

And more than anything, Patrick wanted to keep custody of the girls, which was primarily contingent on his being married to a responsible woman who would create a caring home. There was no reason he'd put that in jeopardy for the sake of a love that he himself had said was long dead.

No reason except that he doesn't love me, and that he misses the old, exciting life he used to have before he settled down, Regina's worried mind whispered.

But her good sense was having none of that. She drew her shoulders up and decided to quit manufacturing problems for herself. Life was challenge enough as it was.

To soothe herself, she took the list of songs from her pocket and sat at the piano to go over them. Within fifteen minutes, the beauty of the music had worked its special magic on her heart. She felt better. And as evening approached and Teresa returned from Mrs. Leslie's, she felt better still.

Teresa came in the kitchen, snitched one of the carrots Regina was peeling and began munching on it. Regina smiled to herself. Tessy was feeling more at ease lately. It showed in a thousand little ways, like her presuming to steal a carrot that her stepmother was cutting up for their dinner.

"Guess what Mrs. Leslie told me?"

Dread tightened Regina's stomach, as all the doubts and fears she'd worked all afternoon to banish crowded back in on her once more. Was she going to hear about Chloe's return from her stepdaughter, too?

But then she relaxed. Teresa was very sensitive. It was doubtful she'd be so offhand if her news concerned the return to town of her father's old flame.

"What?" Regina asked brightly.

Teresa hesitated. She seemed to be seeking the right words. Regina's anxiety returned. Then Teresa blurted, "You used to go out with Mr. Shelby from the grocery store, right?"

Warily, Regina answered. "Yes. Why?"

"But you dropped him for Dad, didn't you?"

Regina chose another carrot and began stroking it with the peeler. "It wasn't quite that simple. But yes, right after I broke up with Mr. Shelby, your father and I were married."

"Well, what I mean is, you don't still *love* him or anything, do you? I mean, you love Dad, because he's your husband, right?"

"Um, right."

"Whew. That's good." Teresa popped the rest of the carrot in her mouth and chomped contentedly.

"Why?"

"Because last night Mr. Shelby took Angie Leslie to dinner in Nevada City."

Regina stopped peeling. She turned to her stepdaughter, who was grinning. Slowly Regina grinned back. "No."

"Yes." Teresa laughed. It was a happy, bubbling, laugh. A girl's laugh, with just a hint of the woman she would soon become. Regina had a feeling that she would hear little more about Teresa's plans to be a nun. Teresa chattered on, "Old Mrs. Leslie is just all excited about it. I mean, you know, Angie Leslie's been married about a hundred times."

"Three times," Regina corrected, trying to sound stern.

"Right. Three times. And it never worked out. And now old Mrs. Leslie thinks her granddaughter has finally found a nice, steady guy who will marry her and *stay* married to her for the rest of their lives."

Regina, who was enjoying Teresa's carefree laughter and the happy light in her eyes, had to bite her tongue to keep from saying too much. Silently, she wished Angie luck with the nonmarrying Marcus.

And who could say? Maybe Angie would be the one to make Marcus Shelby change his mind about matrimony. And then again, perhaps Angie had already experienced enough connubial bliss to last a lifetime and she and Marcus would be happy with—how had Marcus put it?—*an important and meaningful relationship, where they both had their independence and their privacy.*

Who could say? Regina shook her head.

Right then, Marnie came bouncing in smelling of river water and carrying a mason jar.

"Hey, you guys. Look. You gotta look at this." Marnie held up the jar and pointed. Regina and Teresa both bent over to peer into the jar, wherein they spotted a tadpole that was well on its way to becoming a frog. "It's got all its feet. And the head is starting to take the right shape. Pretty nifty, huh?''

''Yes,'' Regina agreed. ''Very nifty. And surprising for so late in the year. Usually the tadpoles are all turned to frogs by now.''

For a moment, even Teresa deigned to stare with interest at the almost-frog. But then she couldn't resist sniffing. ''P.U. Where have you been?''

Marnie was instantly truculent. ''Swimming. So what?''

''You *smell* like you've been rolling around in a pile of dead fish.''

Marnie stuck out her chin. ''Well, you *are* a pile of dead fish.''

Teresa flipped her pale hair back over her shoulder. ''Honestly. How rude. You are the most—''

Regina managed to capture Teresa's eye and give her a slight negative shake of the head. She'd had a few talks with Teresa lately about starting fights with her sister by criticizing the younger girl. Teresa had agreed to work on controlling her urge to bait Marnie under the guise of playing big sister.

''Oh, all right,'' Teresa grumbled, in answer to Regina's chiding look. ''I'm stopping, I'm stopping.'' She turned and flounced from the room.

With a satisfied smirk on her face, Marnie watched Teresa's retreating back. Then she turned to Regina and held up the jar. ''Can I keep him, huh, please?''

''Yes, but you mustn't put the jar in the sun, or you'll end up with a boiled frog.''

''Ugh, yuck. I won't. I promise.''

''And maybe tonight, after dinner, we'll go over to the other house and look for my old aquarium. It's up in the attic somewhere, I think. We could fix it up so that when your tadpole really becomes a frog, he'll have some dry land to hop on as well as water to swim in.''

"Hey, yeah, Gina. You promise? We can go find the aquarium tonight?"

"Sure. Right after your bath."

Marnie made a hideous face, then burst into a huge smile. "You're tricky, Gina. You know that?"

"I have to be, around this house."

Right then, the phone rang. Regina, who was standing closest to it, picked it up. "Hello?"

There was a silence on the other end, then a click. The dial tone droned in Regina's ear. She put the phone back on the hook.

"Who was it?" Marnie wanted to know.

Regina shrugged. "Wrong number, I guess."

"Listen." Marnie was full of plans for her frog-to-be. "I think I'll go out in the backyard and look for a few good rocks." And she was out the door.

Regina watched through the window over the sink as Marnie carefully set the jar in the shade of the catalpa tree. Then she walked around the perimeter of the lawn, picking up rocks from the drain cobble Patrick had used as a border near the fence. Marnie would study each rock very carefully, and then toss it aside, or carry it over and set it in a neat little pile by the mason jar where her almost-frog was temporarily contained.

"What's going on in here?" Patrick came up behind Regina and nuzzled her neck.

"Nothing much. Fixing dinner." Regina smiled and leaned back against him. "I didn't hear you come in."

"I'm a sneaky SOB."

"How delightfully put."

"Don't get—"

"Prissy. I know."

He rubbed his chin against her hair. "What's Marnie up to out there?"

"Planning a frog condo."

"Huh?"

"You'll see, when it's done."

"Hell, with all the stuff that goes on around here, lately, I can't keep up." He stepped to the side, swiveled the faucet into the right half of the sink, and got out the special washing compound that even worked on automotive grease. "What's for dinner?" He worked the dirt and oil from his hands.

"Steaks. As soon as you barbecue them." She put the carrots on the stove and began assembling the ingredients for a tossed salad.

Patrick took the steaks from the refrigerator and sprinkled them with seasoning salt. Regina paused in washing lettuce leaves to watch him.

Her breath caught, as it so often did when she stopped to look at the man she'd married. She recalled that first day she'd really seen him. When he'd emerged from the back of a truck with his shirt off and maneuvered the refrigerator she now considered hers into the house they now shared. That day he'd seemed like someone larger, more beautiful, more passionate, more *everything* than the mere mortals who inhabited the mundane world she knew. He'd had nothing whatever to do with her and her serene, undistinguished little life.

And today he was her husband. How would she bear it if she were to lose him?

"Okay." His eyes were watchful. "What is it?"

She felt slightly abashed. "It's nothing, really."

"It's something. What?"

She blurted it out. "Chloe Swan's back in town."

He gave a noncommittal shrug. "Yeah. I know."

"How?"

"She came in. For gas."

"I see."

Now he looked a little angry. "What the hell's the mat-

ter? She came in. She asked for a fill-up. She got what she
asked for. And she left.''

That's all? she longed to ask. But she didn't. It would
only be her own pitiful jealous heart asking a question like
that. Patrick had sworn to be true to her. And she believed
he had been true to her. He'd been honest and open about
his past and about Chloe Swan. If she started grilling him
with questions now, it would be tantamount to declaring
she didn't trust him.

His expression softened. ''Look, Gina. She's got nothing
to do with us. Do you hear what I'm saying?''

She forced a smile. ''Yes. And you're right.''

''That old bat Nellie, brought you the news, right?''

Regina nodded.

''Someday somebody will silence that woman for good.
It won't be pretty. I swear to you.''

''Nellie has her good points.''

''Name them.''

''Um…''

''Right. Keep thinking. You'll come up with something
in a year or two.'' He picked up the steaks and went out
to fire up the barbecue.

Later, after the girls had gone to bed, Patrick and Regina
rocked together for a while on the swing he'd transferred
from her house. He put his arm around her and she leaned
her head on his shoulder.

Since they were idly discussing the day just past, she
told him what Teresa had told her about Angie Leslie and
Marcus. They laughed together at the idea of the shy grocery store owner and North Magdalene's most glamorous
divorcée finding happiness with each other. Hearing the
laughter in his voice and feeling the warmth of his strong
arm around her, Regina was absolutely certain that her dis-

tress about Chloe Swan was totally uncalled for. She resolved not to worry about the other woman anymore.

They sat, swinging and whispering together, for a while more. Then, holding hands, they went inside.

Not much later, just as Patrick was finishing up his shower and Regina was cleaning her face, the phone rang. Regina fumbled for the hand towel and went to grab the extension by the bed.

"Hello?" Once again, there was a heavy silence, after which the line was disconnected.

"Who was that?" Patrick stood in the doorway to their bathroom, wearing nothing but a questioning look and drying his hair with one of the giant bath sheets he favored.

"I don't know. Wrong number, I guess."

He shrugged and went back to the bathroom to brush his teeth.

The next day, Regina went over to Main Street in the early afternoon to pick up a few things at Marcus's store and to collect the mail.

At the store, as she stood over the open meat case and tried to decide between ground beef and pork chops, she heard singing. It was coming from the little butcher's room on the other side of the meat counter, where the meat that was stored in the locker farther back was cut up into salable portions.

She recognized the voice immediately. It was Marcus, though she'd never in her life heard him sing except when it was expected of him, at church. He was singing the Bob Dylan song "Lay, Lady, Lay," that had been popular years and years ago.

When he got to the part where he implored the lady not to wait any longer for the night to begin, Regina knew she was in trouble. If she didn't get away, she'd burst into hopeless giggles. Marcus would discover her and she would mortify the poor man.

She grabbed up both the pork chops *and* the ground beef and fled for the produce section. But the memory of Marcus's thin voice warbling out his unbridled sexual longing had her smiling all the way to the post office.

After the August heat outside, Regina found it pleasantly cool in the post office. She set her groceries on the little sorting table against the far wall and moved to the boxes, where she spun the combination dial. She had the box open and the mail in her hand when, from the corner of her eye, she saw someone emerge from the door that led to the counter area where Melanie Swan held sway.

Regina looked up, a rote smile of greeting on her face. In North Magdalene, one said hello to everyone.

Even the woman one's husband used to love, she thought grimly, as she realized she was looking into the green eyes of Chloe Swan.

"Hello, Chloe, how are you?"

She waited for Chloe's superficial, polite response.

But the response didn't come. Instead, Chloe let go of the door she'd just passed through and brought a perfectly manicured hand up to touch her own throat. Regina stared at that slim hand, at the long pink-tipped nails.

And then Chloe dropped her hand. She threw back her shoulders and raised her head high. She marched right up to Regina, her eyes like emerald flames in the lovely oval of her face.

Regina, bewildered, felt the strangest urge to bolt around the other woman and run for the open street. But she held her ground.

"Chloe? Are you all right?"

Chloe's gaze swept Regina from head to toe and back again.

"Chloe?"

And then, without a word, the woman whirled away and strode to the main door. She had shoved the door open and disappeared from sight before Regina realized she was holding her breath.

That evening, Patrick came home with a video, a comedy he'd rented from Santino's Barber, Beauty and Variety Store. Once dinner had been finished and the dishes were cleaned up, Regina made a huge bowl of popcorn. Then the girls stretched out on the floor side by side with the big bowl between them. They munched away contentedly, staring at the TV screen and dissolving into fits of giggles every five minutes or so.

Regina tried to concentrate on the movie, but her mind kept wandering. She was trying not to think about her bizarre encounter with Chloe Swan. Her success was minimal.

Halfway through the movie, the phone rang. Regina, the least absorbed of the four of them in what was happening on the screen, decided she might as well be the one to answer. She eased out of the circle of Patrick's arm and went to the phone on the low table by the piano.

When she picked up the receiver and said hello, the same thing happened as had twice the day before. There was silence, a click and then the dial tone droned in her ear.

Regina hung up. She stood by the phone table for a moment, wondering what she really didn't want to wonder: Was this some type of harassment technique of Chloe Swan's?

She sighed and shrugged. Well, at least one thing was settled. This last hang-up call was one strange thing too many. She would discuss her anxieties about Chloe as soon as she and Patrick were alone.

She went back to him at the couch. He looked up at her

and smiled and her heart did a silly little flip-flop in her chest.

"Anything important?" he asked with a lift of a brow.

She shook her head and sat next to him once more. She could wait until the children were in bed to tell him that she feared his old girlfriend had set out to make her life miserable.

When she told him, Patrick was sympathetic, but not terribly concerned.

"Look. Chloe's always been a confused woman. People like her, because she can be so sweet and friendly. But then she'll really torment any poor sucker who has the bad sense to fall for her. And she does things without thinking. Like I told you before, I really was worried for her when she left town with that guy a year ago. I thought she was crazy to take off with a stranger like that. I was afraid she'd end up in big trouble. But now she's back and there's nothing wrong with her that taking a little responsibility for her life wouldn't fix. Whatever she's up to, she'll give it up if she doesn't get any response."

"Patrick, you didn't see the look in her eyes today. It was menacing. I was actually a little frightened of her. And Nellie told me that Chloe's mother said Chloe came back to town specifically to get you away from me."

Patrick swore low and feelingly. "Damn Nellie. Damn her to hell."

"Patrick, don't..." Regina spoke softly.

Patrick pulled her close then, and stroked her hair. "I'm sorry that you have to put up with this garbage. But I swear to you, Gina, it'll pass. I'm positive." He held her face up so that he could look in her eyes. "And you can't be sure the hang-up calls aren't just a coincidence, can you?"

She shook her head, realizing she felt better just having

told him. "You're right," she said. "It'll probably all blow over. It's just... I don't know. The way she looked at me."

"Forget her," Patrick urged.

Regina agreed that she would.

But over the next two days, there were more hang-up calls. And then on Tuesday morning, while Patrick was in the bedroom getting dressed and Regina was frying bacon in the kitchen, the phone rang again. Regina picked it up a few seconds after it stopped ringing, not realizing Patrick had already answered the line in the bedroom.

Regina heard Chloe's breathless voice. "Patrick, I won't wait any longer. I must see you. Today."

Regina stifled a gasp. All conscious thought fled. Her decorous upbringing took over. The call was not for her, so she hung up, very quietly.

Then she turned back to the stove and attended to the bacon. She paid scrupulous attention to the bacon, in order that she would not fly into a thousand pieces of hurt and fear—and anger.

She didn't really know that she was waiting for Patrick, waiting to see what he would do when he came into the kitchen, until he was there, getting his cup from the cupboard and pouring himself coffee as if nothing in the world were the matter.

She glanced at him and smiled. He smiled back.

Then she turned to the frying pan once more and began forking the now-crisp bacon onto a folded paper towel to drain.

"Who was that on the phone?" she asked, her voice shocking her with its utter nonchalance.

He sipped before he answered. "I don't know. They hung up."

Chapter Fourteen

Hearts, of course, do not really shatter. Regina knew this. But at that moment, knowing beyond any doubt that her husband had just told her a blatant lie, Regina felt her heart doing something terrible.

It was splintering into a million pieces inside her chest. And as her heart did that terrible, impossible thing, she went on forking the bacon out of its bed of hot grease and laying it in even strips upon the folded paper towel.

"Smells good," Patrick said.

"Thank you. Would you wake the girls? The table won't set itself."

"Gina?"

She turned, gave him her brightest smile. "Hmm?"

He looked at her. Then, "Nothing. I'll get them up." And he was gone.

When he returned, he poured himself more coffee and slid into his seat. The girls came plodding in shortly after.

Marnie poured the milk and put the napkins around, while Teresa set out the plates and flatware. Soon enough, the eggs and toast were ready. They all sat down to eat.

Patrick finished more quickly than usual, Regina thought. And he didn't linger over his coffee. Within ten minutes of sitting down, he was up and on his way to the garage. And then Teresa was off to help Nellie clean the Sunday school rooms, while Marnie headed out to meet Kenny.

Regina was alone in the house that had been her husband's. The house that had become her house, too, because she had worked hard to make it that way.

Right then, it seemed to be a very quiet house.

With great care, Regina picked up her coffee cup and sipped from it. Very deliberately, she swallowed.

She didn't realize that she was staring blankly into space until her glance caught on the little magnets shaped like fruits on the door of the refrigerator. The magnets held random things. A picture of her family taken that day at Bullfinch Bar by an old man who'd been at the boat dock just before they shoved off. A reminder from the girls' dentist in Arkansas, which Marybeth had forwarded so that Regina wouldn't forget to arrange for their checkups. A list of the school supplies that had to be bought before the next school year began. This week's grocery list.

Things to do. To keep a family going.

Regina blinked.

Then, sucking in a deep breath, she stood. Resolutely, she put one foot in front of the other all the way to the sink, where she started the mundane process of cleaning up after the meal.

The phone rang just as she was putting the last glass in the dishwasher. She hesitated, thinking it would probably either be the phantom caller or Nellie, neither of whom she particularly wanted to deal with right then.

But her hand reached out. She picked it up anyway.

"Hello?"

Silence. A click. And then the drone of the dial tone.

Gently she returned the receiver to its cradle.

She decided to go outside and work in the garden of the other house for a while. She still had tomatoes to gather. And the summer squash needed to be picked, too.

Outside, the day was already warm. Regina, in old jeans and tennis shoes, her hair tied up in a bandanna, set to work, picking vegetables, weeding, nipping dead leaves and pulling out withered stalks.

Her plan was to gradually simplify this garden, have mostly lawn and hardy shrubs back here. It would be easier to care for, when they found a tenant. In the spring, she would plant a new garden at the other house.

If I'm still at the other house.

Regina stifled a little gasp as the awful thought got away from her and reached the conscious levels of her mind.

And then she dropped down onto her bottom in the dirt between the squash rows. She removed her gardening gloves, pushed the sweaty tendrils of hair back from her moist forehead and told herself that she absolutely would not cry.

But she was going to have to confront Patrick. She probably should have confronted him this morning when he lied about Chloe's call. Or even before that. Maybe what she really should have done was to announce her presence on the line when she picked it up and heard Chloe's voice. But instead, she'd quietly hung up.

Lies beget lies, Regina, her mother used to say. And her mother had been right—at least about that. If Patrick chose to lie about a phone conversation with Chloe, that didn't mean that she, Regina, had to lie right along with him.

She had told him when she married him that she would have honesty, above all, in their marriage. Yet this morning, she had been no more honest than he had been.

But tonight, after the girls were safely tucked in their beds, she would have it out with him. She would have the truth from him, about what was going on between him and the woman he claimed he no longer loved.

And after she had the truth, she would decide what to do next.

Regina picked herself up from the ground and beat the dirt from the seat of her jeans with her gardening gloves. She felt better, she decided, now that she knew what she would do.

She glanced at her watch. It was near noon. Soon the girls would be home and wondering where lunch was. Patrick, who sometimes came home for lunch, might be wandering in, too. She ought to go decide what to feed them.

She was just turning for the kitchen door when a flicker of movement at the back fence caught her eye. She stood still, puzzled for a moment, as she registered the fact that someone was looking at her over the fence. And then there was a bumping sound, like a knee hitting one of the boards. After that came a faint rustling noise.

The fine hairs at Regina's nape rose up. "Who is that?"

But no one answered. Swiftly Regina jumped across the rows of squash and pumpkins and the staked tomato vines. She wanted to see the intruder running away. She grabbed two of the fence slats and pulled herself up to peer out over Ebert's Field, a narrow strip of grass and locust trees that ran between Pine Street and the next street over.

"I saw you! I saw you watching me!"

No response came back. The late-summer grass was golden. The locust trees were starting to look parched. Regina could see the bell tower on the church, over on Prospect Street, and the shine of the flagpole over at the school on Gold Run Way. But as for the person who had been watching her, there wasn't a sign.

Perhaps it had been her imagination.

But she knew that wasn't so. She'd seen the crown of a blond head. And before the intruder ducked and jumped down, Regina had caught a quick flash of long, beautifully manicured pink fingernails gripping the fence, fingernails just like Chloe Swan's.

This was too much.

Tonight, when she talked to Patrick, she was going to tell him what she'd seen. She'd find out if he had any better suggestions for her than to pretend like none of this was happening.

If he had suggestions, fine. She'd listen and very likely follow them.

But if not, she would make a few decisions of her own and then act on them. She could confront Chloe, as she planned to confront Patrick. Or she could even call Sheriff Pangborn and tell him what was going on.

She wasn't sure what she'd do yet. But before she went to sleep tonight, she would know, and that was that.

She went inside and took a quick shower to wash off the garden dirt. Then she donned clean clothes and went to the kitchen where she began making sandwiches.

Both girls arrived within minutes of each other. Marnie came first. She had a cut over her eye.

"What happened to you?"

Marnie shrugged. "Nothin'. I fell and whacked myself." She got a look at the can Regina was opening and complained, "Yuck. Tuna. Can't I have PB and J?"

"You had peanut butter and jelly yesterday."

"Yeah, cause I like it. I used to have it every day. Before *you* came along."

"Well, now you have it every *other* day. It's often enough, I think."

"I'm the one who's eatin' it."

"Yes, but I'm the boss. Now please go wash your hands."

Grumbling, Marnie tramped upstairs to the bathroom. She was just reentering the kitchen when Teresa arrived. "I'm home. I'll go wash," the older girl called from the front door.

Regina and Marnie locked glances. Marnie muttered, "I know, I know. Why can't I be more like her?"

"Did I say that?"

"You thought it."

"I most certainly did not. I would not want you to be anyone but Marnie. I like you just the way you are."

Marnie muttered some more and appeared to be trying to keep from smiling. "I'll pour the milk."

"That would be nice. Thank you."

A few minutes later, Teresa came back in. She only had a few minutes, she said, because Alicia Brown and Tammy Rice were going swimming at the long hole and they'd invited her to come too. And the long hole was three miles from town, after all. It took a while to walk there. And it was okay if she went, wasn't it?

Regina nodded and agreed that it certainly was okay. "But be home by five."

Teresa agreed that she would not be late and then ate faster than was probably good for her. She was in her swimsuit, with her shorts and T-shirt thrown over it, and out the door fifteen minutes after she'd first walked in.

Marnie took another bite of tuna sandwich, grimaced, and remarked, "Alicia Brown and Tammy Rice. Yuck."

"What's wrong with Alicia and Tammy?"

"They're a coupla sissies, that's what. But I suppose that's okay with Saint Teresa. She's a sissy herself."

Regina said nothing, only put on an expression that she meant to be noncommittal. She was glad to see that Teresa was rekindling old friendships.

And she was also glad that her stepdaughters had come home for lunch. Fixing their sandwiches and sparring with

Marnie had lifted her spirits. That was the good thing about having children, she was finding out. When things seemed out of control, they brought you back down to earth.

"Can I be done now?"

Regina studied Marnie's half-eaten tuna sandwich. "Nothing else until dinner, then."

"Well, what if I get hungry before dinner?"

"Then you'll wish you'd eaten the rest of that sandwich, won't you?"

"Oh, all right." Doggedly, Marnie picked up the remaining half of the sandwich and bit into it. She chewed and swallowed, her face twisted to show her utter loathing of tuna fish. Bite by slow bite, she finished it off, while Regina calmly ate her own sandwich and tried to pretend she didn't notice all the facial contortions.

"There," Marnie said at last. "I'm done. Can I have a cupcake?"

"Fruit first."

"Aw, Gina..."

Regina pushed the fruit bowl in Marnie's direction. Scowling, Marnie chose a peach, which she ate with much slurping and grunting. Regina ignored the noises. After all, the peach was quite juicy, and Marnie was careful to use her napkin each time the juice got away from her and dribbled down her stubborn little chin.

"Okay," Marnie said at last, wiping with the napkin one more time. "Now, about that cupcake..."

"Yes, you may have one."

"Great." Marnie pushed back her chair and carried her plate and milk glass to the sink. She was just rinsing the plate when the phone rang. She grabbed for the hand towel and quickly dried her hands. "That's Kenny. I know." She picked up the phone. "Hey, Kenny, what's...?" The words died on her lips. "Hello? Hello, who's there?"

And then she turned away, toward the kitchen window

and hissed into the phone, "I know who you are. Why don't you just leave us alone, Chloe Swan?" And she slammed the receiver down.

Regina stared at the child's thin back for a moment, wondering what in the world she should do next. Then she stood. "Marnie?"

"I want my cupcake." Without looking at her stepmother, Marnie knelt and opened the doors of the cabinet where the crackers and packaged desserts were kept. She grabbed up the promised treat and straightened.

Regina was waiting for her. "That was Chloe Swan on the phone?"

Marnie clutched her treat and didn't meet Regina's eyes. "I don't know. She didn't talk. She just hung on the line and breathed."

"Has that happened before?"

"Before." Marnie's brows drew together as she pondered the word. "Before, when?"

"In the last few days."

"I don't know. Not for sure. Probably."

"Marnie, what do you mean?"

"I mean, she always just hung up before. But I bet it's been her, when the phone rings and there's no one there."

"Why do you believe the hang-up caller is Chloe?"

"Gina, I gotta get goin'."

"In a minute." Gently, Regina took the girl by the shoulders, turned her around and guided her back to the table. She sat her down in a chair and knelt before her. "Marnie, why do you think that was Chloe on the phone?"

Marnie pressed her lips together and looked away.

"Please, Marnie. I'm on your side."

"I know. But..."

"Yes?"

"Everybody says..."

"*Who* says?"

"Well, at least Kenny. He said today that he heard his mom and dad talking."

"About what?"

"Gina…"

"Come on, honey. I can't work this out if you won't tell me what it is. What did Kenny hear his mom and dad say?"

Marnie finally looked at Regina. Her blue eyes were moist, but she valiantly held back the tears. Marnie Jones, after all, was no sissy. She lifted her chin. "They said that Chloe Swan's going to take Dad away from you."

Right then, it took all the determination Regina possessed not to flinch and further upset the innocent child. She forced a reassuring smile. And then she declared with a confidence she was a million miles from feeling, "Well, they're wrong."

Marnie turned her head and looked at her stepmother from the corner of her eye. "They are?"

"You'd better believe it."

"You're sure?"

"I am."

"You're…not going to leave us?"

"Absolutely not."

"No matter what happens?"

"No matter what happens." Miraculously, as she made this incredible promise, Regina realized she would do everything in her power to keep it. No matter what happened, she would not desert her stepdaughters. One way or another, she would do what she could to help them grow up. And then the significance of the cut over Marnie's eye dawned on her. "Marnie, did you fight with Kenny over this?"

Marnie scratched at a bug bite on her left knee.

"Marnie."

The child looked up. "Oh, all right. Yeah, I fought with

him. And I won, too. But we made up and everything's settled. He won't be dissin my family anymore.''

"Dissin?"

"Yeah. Dissin. Disrespecting."

"Oh. I see." Regina drew in a breath and pointed out, "Marnie. Fighting never—"

"I know, I know. Fighting never settled anything. You told me that before. And I know you're right." She scratched her knee again. "But I'm a Jones."

Regina did her best to look stern and forbidding. "That is no excuse."

"I know, and I'll try to do better."

Regina had never seen her younger stepdaughter look so contrite. She was absolutely adorable. Regina had to bite her lip to keep from telling her so.

Marnie was peering at her, narrow-eyed. "Gina, you ain't gonna start kissin' me, are you?"

"Me?" Regina tried to sound surprised at the question.

"Yeah. You got that look you get just before you grab a person and hug them."

Regina put up both hands. "I promise. Hands off." She stood.

And the phone rang again.

The child and the woman looked at each other. Then Regina went to answer. "Hello?"

"Hi, Mrs. Jones. It's Kenny. Can I talk to Marnie?"

"Hold on." Regina held out the phone to her stepdaughter, and mouthed "Kenny" at her.

With the resilience of the child she was, Marnie bounced from the chair, her misery forgotten, and hurried to grab the phone. "Yeah. What? Okay. Hold on." She put her hand over the mouthpiece. "Can I meet him for swimming?"

"Sure."

"Okay. Half hour. See you then." She hung up and

grinned at her stepmother. "Well. Gotta go." She turned for the hall to her room.

"Marnie."

Marnie paused in the doorway and looked back. "Yeah?"

"I'll work out this problem."

Marnie nodded. "I know." The look of absolute certainty in her eyes was humbling to Regina. "That Chloe Swan hasn't got a chance," Marnie declared in a confidential whisper. And then she turned and disappeared down the hall.

Regina quickly set about straightening up after their lunch. A few minutes later, Marnie yelled at her from the front door.

"I'm gone!"

"Be back by five!"

"I will. See ya!"

The slamming of the door told Regina that she was alone in the house once more. The girls were safely out of the way.

And Regina was going to do what she should have done earlier. She would talk with Patrick. Now. She was not going to wait until tonight. She'd already waited longer than she should have. And because she had held off, Marnie had suffered. This simply could not go on one moment longer.

Regina picked up the phone to call Patrick at the garage. And then she set it back down. Calling him would only give him another chance to put her off. She was through being put off. She would go over to the garage unannounced and insist that she must have a few minutes alone with him right now.

Regina grabbed the notepad by the phone and scribbled a note to the girls.

Gone over to the garage for a few minutes. Back soon.
Love, Gina

Then she went to the bathroom, where she rinsed her face, put on fresh lipstick and combed her hair. On the way out, she stuck the note on the front door.

Chapter Fifteen

Patrick stood behind the parts counter in the office of his garage. He was thumbing through the parts book, looking for the order number for a window regulator on a '79 Trans Am. He was also thinking that he ought to break for lunch soon. His stomach was starting to complain. He wanted food.

He looked up, the order book forgotten for a moment, as he stared blankly out the bank of waist-high windows opposite the counter. The windows flanked the outside door that led to a side parking area.

Right then, Josh Riggins, Kenny's father, strolled by the windows. Josh waved. Patrick lifted his hand and waved back. But it was a mechanical gesture. Patrick hardly saw Josh. He hardly saw anything right then. He was hungry. And he was thinking of Gina.

Hell, whenever he thought of food, or home, comfort or shelter, he thought of Gina. He wanted to go home to her for lunch. But she was testy with him lately. And he was afraid if he went home, she might start in on him about Chloe.

Not that he blamed her for anything she said about Chloe. Chloe was becoming a problem, a problem that wasn't just fading away, as he had originally hoped it might. Chloe was... Hell, there was no other way to say it; Chloe was on the rampage.

He knew damn well that the whole town was buzzing over it. Over poor, brokenhearted Chloe and her hopeless love for Patrick Jones. People thought the whole thing was some great high drama, some new Jones legend in the making. Like that old story about his father and mother and Rory Drury that people still couldn't get enough of repeating whenever any one of them was given half a chance.

People didn't seem to realize that what they thought was a great story, was actually his damn *life*. And Regina's. And Marnie's and Tessy's, too.

They saw Chloe, who could be so sweet and look so pretty, and they didn't realize that the woman had a *problem*, for heaven's sake. They felt sorry for her, they sympathized with her. And he understood their urge to do that. Hell, he felt sorry for her himself. But their sympathizing only made her behavior worse.

Chloe Swan had been her daddy's darling and her mama's only girl. Melanie Swan still treated her as if she were a damn princess, clucking over her, petting her, giving her anything she wanted before she even asked for it.

And as a result of this treatment, Chloe had grown up into a woman who only wanted what she couldn't have. Patrick had learned that through hard experience. But he had really believed, the past few months, that he was finally rid of her.

He'd dared to imagine that she might have found hap-

piness with the guy she ran off with. But apparently, Chloe
Swan just wasn't in the market for happiness.

When she'd called this morning and demanded that he
see her, he'd known things were getting really bad. He'd
told her to leave him and his family the hell alone, but he
knew that wouldn't hold her off forever.

And then, when he'd come in the kitchen, he'd felt so
damn guilty, looking at Gina and knowing her goodness.
He hated to see her stuck in the middle of this mess that
she'd had no hand in creating.

Now, pondering the way he'd handled it when she asked
him who had called, he wondered if he should have told
her the truth. But hell, it wasn't his wife's problem. It was
his. And one way or another, he was going to solve it on
his own.

He shook his head and looked down at the parts book
again, thinking he'd find the part and order it and then call
over to Lily's Café for a ham on rye. He ran his finger
down the page.

And then the door buzzer rang. He looked up.

And into the wide, wounded green eyes of Chloe Swan.

His stomach lurched. Damn, he did not want to deal with
this now.

He thought of his mechanics, less than thirty feet away
through the shop door. Whatever was said probably
wouldn't escape their hearing.

Well, fine. The hell-raiser inside him sneered. *Let 'em
hear. Let 'em stare.*

Behind Chloe, the door clicked shut. She leaned against
it, her pretty face full of suffering and thwarted longing.
She drew in a long, distressed breath.

"Oh, Patrick..." Her voice was purely pathetic. She'd
always had that talent for making him feel like a rat. She
could make him pity her and despise himself with almost
no effort at all. "How could you?"

"How could I what?" he growled.

"You know what." She lifted her chin in affronted suffering. "How could you do that? How could you marry someone else—*again?* At least you had a *reason,* with Marybeth. I mean, since you went and got her pregnant and all. But you had no excuse, none at all, to marry that mousy little nothing, Regina Black."

"Watch what you say about my wife."

She pretended not to hear the warning. "Look, I understand you had a problem." She straightened a little, a noble soul pushed to the end of her rope. "You needed a wife to get your girls. But all you had to do was tell my mother. She would have contacted me and I would have come right back. You know that. It makes no sense. You could have told me what you needed, and I would have been there for you. I would have said yes." Chloe shook her pretty head in disbelief. "You could be married to *me* now...."

After her voice trailed off, he waited a moment before he spoke, just to see if she was going to listen. When she glared and sniffed and held her tongue, he told her, "Next to helping my girls come into the world, marrying Regina Black was the best thing I ever did in my whole useless life."

Chloe gasped. "You can't mean that."

"I do. I mean it. Absolutely."

"But you—"

He'd had enough. He laid it out for her. "There's not a damn thing more to say between you and me, Chloe. It's *over.* It's been over for thirteen years. Wake up. Snap out of it. Get on with your life."

"Oh!" The sound was sharp and full of pain. Her big eyes brimmed. "Oh, no. Oh, Patrick. I *love* you. *She* can't love you like I love you. Oh, when are you going to see that? Nobody can love you like I do."

All at once, he felt very tired. It was always like this

when he was finally forced to deal with this woman. He felt rotten, and then fed up. And then very, very tired. "Look, Chloe..."

She straightened from her slumped pose against the door. "No. I won't look. *You* look." She started walking toward him, across the small space to the counter, then around the end.

"Chloe." He said her name as a warning to stay away.

But Chloe never heeded warnings. Suddenly she was flying at him, her arms outstretched. "I love you. You love me. Hold me, darling. Kiss me, please." She came at him like a bullet.

"Damn it, Chloe!"

She landed with a thud against his chest and wrapped her clutching arms around his neck. "Kiss me, darling. Love me, please." She shoved her mouth up under his. He was trying to peel her off him, and he looked down at her to tell her to let go. But looking down was a mistake, because she managed to get a liplock on him that wouldn't quit.

Right then, the damn door buzzer sounded.

"Oh!" He heard Regina's sharp gasp.

He tore his mouth off of Chloe's and looked into his wife's bewildered gray eyes. "Gina!"

"Patrick?" She blinked.

"Gina, I—"

And then, without another sound, Regina turned and fled.

"Good. Let her go." Chloe pressed her breasts against him.

He reached back and gripped her wrists and peeled her off of his body.

She tried to grab for him again. "Patrick!"

He slid out of her way. Just then Zeb Wilbur, one of his mechanics, came in through the shop door. "Hey, Patrick, what about that—"

Patrick didn't wait for the rest of the question. "Keep an eye on things, Zeb," he barked over his shoulder as he rushed for the door.

Behind him, Chloe went on pleading. "No, wait. Let her go, Patrick. I'm here for you. I love you. I—"

But Patrick was already out the door.

When he got to the street, he looked both ways, and then caught sight of Regina half a block up, walking fast, approaching the turn onto Pine Street.

He shouted, "Regina! Get back here!"

But all she did was start to run.

He broke into a sprint himself. Damned if she was going to run away from him.

"Regina!"

She sped around the corner.

He raced up the street, paying no attention to Rocky Collins, who turned to gape after him, shaking his head. He didn't even spare a glance for Tondalaya Clark, except to mutter a low "Sorry," when he almost ran her down. And as for Tyler Conley and Betty Brown, who just happened to be strolling down Main Street right then, well, he didn't even notice them.

But they noticed him. And they understood that those crazy Joneses were at it again.

"Regina! I'm serious as a terminal disease here. Don't you run from me, damn you!" He made the corner and dashed around it, his powerful legs pumping as fast as they would go. "Regina!"

But she had a good start on him, and she was surprisingly swift. She fled down the street toward their two houses, not wasting a moment with backward glances that might have given him enough of an edge to catch up.

He hoped she would turn into her house, because it was kept locked and if she had to fumble with a key, it would give him the edge he needed.

But no such luck. She tore right past that gate, and flung back the gate of the house they shared, not even wasting the second it would have taken to close it behind her. She pounded up the walk, took the steps in one leap and ran in the door.

That she took the time to slam. In his face. He was up the porch steps and had grabbed the handle just as he heard the dead bolt shoot home.

He swore, words that would have had Marnie consigned to her room on bread and water for a week. And then, since he'd left the garage without his keys, he beat his fist against the ungiving wood.

"Regina! Let me in! Damn you, you'd better let me in, or when I get my hands on you…" He let the threat trail off, incapable at that moment of thinking of anything sufficiently gruesome to describe what he would do to her once he could get to her.

"Regina!" He pounded some more, a sharp volley of blows, then a series of hard, separate thuds. As he pounded, he shouted her name. A piece of paper, a note for the girls, was in his way. He ripped it off the door and tore it to shreds.

He pounded some more.

And then, still pounding, he admitted to himself that she wasn't going to let him in just because he yelled and beat on the door.

He stopped pounding and looked around him, trying to decide what he should do next. He noted that, across the street, old Mrs. Quail was sitting in her porch rocker watching him. But he didn't really care. His wife had locked him out and he wanted in. That was all he cared about right then.

He seriously began considering his options, and found himself wondering if Regina might have kept on going, out the back door. Could she, at this very minute, be darting through Ebert's Field toward Gold Run Way?

He really would find some horrible way to get even with her if she'd done that, he vowed. But then, the more he thought about it, he doubted she'd run out the back. She'd wanted shelter—from him. And now, in his house, with his own front door locked against him, she probably assumed she'd found it.

Hah! he thought furiously. Who the hell did she think she was dealing with here? She should have married that twit Marcus, if she wanted a man she could get away from.

What she *had* done was marry a Jones, and a Jones was inescapable. Everyone knew that.

The question of the moment was, should he bust in the door?

He shook his head. He wasn't ready to go that far. Yet.

He began pacing the perimeter of the house, checking for open windows where all he'd have to do was pry off a screen to get inside. He found none. When he got to the back door, he tested it and found it locked.

His temper rose again as he realized she was one step ahead of him. While he'd been making a satisfying but pointless racket beating on the front door, she'd quietly gone around and locked the back door and shut all the windows.

She'd always been more coolheaded than he was. It was one of the hundred and one things he admired the hell out of her for—under ordinary circumstances. Now, however, it just made him madder than he already was.

He told himself to be calm. And then he walked around the house again, looking up at the second story this time. She'd shut and locked all of the windows up there against him, too. Except, he saw by squinting and shielding his eyes, for the window at the back of the walk-in closet in their bedroom. It was a window that opened from a top hinge; it swung up and then could be held ajar by a locking side brace. In that one small window, he couldn't see the shine of glass panes behind the screen. That meant she hadn't thought to go in the closet and latch it down.

It was maybe two feet square. Plenty of room for a determined man to wiggle through.

A cold smile curled his lips.

He quietly walked to the front of the house again, paying no mind when he saw that Mrs. Quail was still on her porch and had been joined by her nosy old husband, Ben.

Patrick sat down on the step and took off his boots and socks. Then, his feet bare, he jumped to the porch railing and shimmied up one of the posts that supported the porch roof.

Silent as a snake in new grass, he hoisted himself onto the porch roof, tiptoed across it and then managed to boost himself onto the roof of the house. Cautiously, he worked his way around the roof, watching his step and doing his best to make no sound. At last he reached the spot he was seeking, right above the little closet window. There, he stretched out on his stomach and hung his torso over the roof's edge.

With only a minimum of whispered cursing, he managed to pry the screen off and toss it to the lawn below, where it landed with a barely distinguishable thud. Then he slid around, until he could hang his legs over the edge. He scooted backward, keeping his torso on the roof and feeling with his feet until he found the windowsill.

Piece of cake, he thought with grim triumph, as he slid beneath the braced-up window and into the closet that was lined with his clothes on one side and Regina's on the other. His bare feet found the floor and he landed in a slight crouch. Then he straightened.

In three steps he was at the door that opened onto the

bedroom he shared with his wife. He stuck out a hand and pushed it wide.

"Oh!" Regina jumped from the edge of the bed and backed toward the nightstand. "Patrick!" Her pale, long-fingered hand flew to her throat. "What are you doing here?"

He leaned against the jamb and folded his arms across his chest. "I live here. Remember?"

Her breathing was agitated. She forced herself to lower her hand from her throat and drop it to her side. She probably thought she looked calmer that way. But it only gave him a clear view of the frantic pulse that beat against the white skin where her hand had been. "How did you—?"

"You forgot to lock the closet window." He shook a finger at her. "Not very smart. Where are the kids?"

"Gone for the rest of the day. Thank goodness." She yanked her shoulders back, to show him how unafraid of him she was. "And I do not want to talk with you." She started for the door.

He sidestepped and blocked her path. "Don't try it."

"Move out of my way, please."

He gave her a little nudge toward the bed. "Sit down."

She didn't move, only narrowed those eyes of hers at him, tipped her head back and looked down that slim, finely shaped nose. "Please do not touch me. And I said I do not wish to speak with you right now."

"I heard you."

"Well, then—"

"And I don't give a good damn about what you *wish.* You'll speak with me, all right. And you'll do it now."

The fine nostrils quivered in outrage. "You...you..."

"Me, me *what?*"

She whirled away from him and went to the rocker by the window, where she plunked herself down and began wrathfully to rock back and forth. She looked out the window, a flat, unseeing kind of look, and pretended that he wasn't even there.

He bore about thirty seconds of that. Then he marched right over to her and stopped the infernal rocking by grabbing the chair arms.

"Let go," she said, still looking out the window at nothing.

"No."

She grimaced, as she tried to force the chair to rock, in spite of the fact that he was holding it still. And then, when she got nowhere, she started kicking. Her feet flailed furiously. She got him a good one right in the shin.

He swore roundly, and then he grabbed for her.

"Don't you touch me, you bully! You let me alone!" She kicked and pounded at him, as he carried her to the bed and tossed her, like a sack of meal, across it. Then he came down on top of her, pinning her arms above her head with his hands and holding her body in place with his own. All the while she railed at him.

"I hate you, you rotten, insufferable, awful man! I hate you. Let me go. Let me go. Let me go!"

He held her, grim and determined, now that he had her down and pinned, until she finally wore down a little. With a low moan she turned her head to the side and pressed her eyes closed.

"Look at me."

"Never."

"You're acting like one of the girls, for goodness sake. Having a damn fit because—"

"Because you *betrayed* me." She did look at him then. And if looks could do physical damage, he would have been charred to a cinder right there and then.

"I did *not* betray you." He was trying his damnedest to keep his temper. But he was not a calm man by nature and she was getting pretty carried away with this, running up

Main Street to get away from him, locking him out of the house, refusing even to speak with him and then actually kicking him in the shin over there at the rocking chair. She was usually a reasonable woman, but about this, she wasn't giving a single inch.

She struggled again, an impatient, hopeless kind of wriggling, her face all twisted up with frustration and rage. And then her slim body went limp beneath him.

Their eyes met and locked.

"If I let you up, will you quit trying to get away?"

She didn't answer, only glared at him.

"Are you ready to listen to what I have to say?" He asked the question between clenched teeth.

"What is there to say, Patrick?" The words were spoken in that Sunday school teacher voice she could put on whenever she wanted to make a man feel like a worm.

"There's a hell of a lot to say, and you know it."

"Oh, do I?"

"Damn right."

"Well, if there is a lot to say, I certainly have no idea what it is. I think what you've *done* just about says it all."

"I didn't do a damn thing."

"Well." She raised her nose so high, she was lucky it didn't disappear into her hair. "I suppose you *would* say that."

"Because it's true."

Her lips pulled back in a she-wolf's snarl. Damn, she had a mean side to her. Who the hell would have thought it? That sickly little Regina Black could be mean as a she-wolf when she thought her man had cheated on her.

Which he hadn't. And which he was going to tell her, if only she'd give him half a chance.

But she wasn't giving any chances.

He pointed out, "When you invited Marcus Shelby into

my house, I settled down enough to listen to your explanation of why you'd done it.''

''That was different.''

''How?''

She rolled her eyes, as if the answer were so obvious there was no need to say it. ''You knew I didn't care for Marcus. I told you so.''

''And I told you I don't love Chloe Swan.''

''It's not the same.''

''It damn well is.''

''It isn't.'' She dragged in a fuming breath. ''I know who it was on the phone this morning.'' Her voice was as cold as a witch's caress. ''It was Chloe. And yet you lied to my face and said the person hung up before you found out who it was.''

''All right,'' he admitted. ''I shouldn't have lied. But I only did it because I didn't want you to worry, not because there was anything going on between me and that woman.''

''Oh, stop it. She called you this morning and you lied to me about it. And then, just now I saw you kissing her.''

''The hell you did. You saw *her* kissing me. There *is* a damn difference.''

''Don't you split hairs with me. That was your mouth and her mouth and there was no space between them. You have cheated on me, Patrick.''

''I have not. I—''

''And I simply do not know if I can stay married to you.''

When she said that, his heart stopped for a moment. He stared at her, his mouth open. And then he snapped it shut. ''What the hell did you say?''

''I said, I don't know if I can—''

He decided he didn't really want to hear it again. ''Don't.'' He snarled the word. And then he jumped backward, away from her. He didn't even want to touch her right then. When he was on his feet he glowered down at her, where she lay, still stretched on her back across the bed. "Don't say the rest of it. I don't want to hear it. There are a lot of things I always thought highly of you for, Regina. And two of them are your fairness and the fact that you aren't a quitter. But you're not being fair now. You've judged and convicted me of a thing I've always sworn to you I would never do. And you've made your judgment without even listening when I tried to tell you my side of it."

She looked just a little ashamed, but she still wasn't going to be fair. "I know what I heard. And what I saw."

He stared at her, a look he meant to burn right through her. Then he said softly, "You don't trust me worth a damn."

"I—"

He threw up a hand. She fell silent. He went on. "But worse than that, worse that judging me unfairly and having not one bit of trust in me, you dare to tell me you might not stay married to me. That's the biggest bunch of bunk I've ever heard. I've kept my word to you. I've been true to you. And you can bet that piano of yours that you'll stay married to me. Finally, after half a lifetime, I managed to find me a decent wife. And I'll be damned if I'll ever let you go."

She let out a sharp, outraged cry when he said that, and scuttled back on the bed. She glared at him, her eyes like two pieces of hard coal.

And then, out of nowhere, she was shouting, "A decent wife! That's what I am to you, *all* I am to you. Someone to mother your children and cook your meals and clean your house. But you have to go somewhere else when it comes to love and passion. I can see that now. I can understand that now."

He gaped at her. And then his temper, held by a slender

thread for so long, snapped free. ''What the hell are you talking about? *Where* else have I been? I've been here, with you. And you damn well know it, too.''

He stared down at her, wanting to grab her and shake her until she admitted the truth. That he *was* a true husband. And that his passion, like the sweat of his brow and the work of his hands, like his laughter and his sorrow, was hers, only hers.

The urge to grab her, though, was a violent urge. He dared not give in to it.

So rather than reach for her in his rage, he spun on his heel and stomped out of the room.

He heard her call his name when he was halfway down the stairs. But he didn't turn. He didn't pause. He pounded the rest of the way down the stairs and out the door, only pausing to scoop up his boots and socks before he headed for the front gate.

Chapter Sixteen

Five minutes after she heard the front door slam, Regina was still sitting on the bed. She was staring blindly at the rocking chair by the window.

And she was feeling deeply ashamed.

Patrick had been right. She had judged and convicted him without listening at all when he tried to tell his side of things. But she hadn't wanted to hear his side of things. She had seen Chloe Swan in his arms, and all logical thought had fled.

By the bed, the phone started ringing. Regina shifted her dazed glance to look at it. She didn't want to answer it. But there was an off chance the call might concern the girls. So with a sigh she reached over and picked it up.

"Oh, my sweet heaven. Regina, is that you?"

"What is it, Nellie?" Regina thought with disinterest that her voice sounded as lifeless as she felt.

"Has he hurt you? Everyone saw him chasing you down

the street. And heard him beating on your door. And then Mrs. Quail says he climbed up on the *roof*, to get to you. Are you all right?''

''I'm fine, Nellie.''

''You stay right there. I'll be right over.''

''No.''

''Excuse me?''

''I said no. I don't want any company right now.''

''But, my dear, if you—''

''I mean it, Nellie. I want to be left alone now.''

''Well, I declare I never—''

''Goodbye, Nellie.'' Regina hung up.

She sat for another few moments, hating herself in a listless kind of way. And then she slid off the bed and went to the bathroom, where she rinsed her face and took two aspirin in an effort to quell the headache that was beginning to pound behind her eyes.

Once again, after she'd taken the aspirin, she found herself staring blindly into space. This time she was standing at the bathroom mirror, holding her water glass and gaping at her own lackluster reflection.

Where could he have gone? she wondered. She was worried about him. He could be a very angry man sometimes. But she'd never seen him *that* angry before. Would he do something crazy, being that mad?

He probably would, she realized with a low moan. She just hoped he wouldn't hurt anyone—especially not himself.

Maybe she should call around town. Track him down.

No. She shook her head. She would leave him alone for a while. He needed some time on his own to cool down.

He'd be home when he'd gotten the rage out of his system. And then they would talk.

She made a face at the thought of the things he would be likely to say to her, even after he had cooled down. She hated to admit that she probably deserved whatever he would choose to say.

There was just no more escaping the truth. She'd behaved abominably. And she knew exactly what had brought her to this pass.

It was the fiery love she bore him that she had never revealed. It was her foolish pride, that wouldn't let her admit to him what she really wanted from him.

There was a strong thread of selfishness in her, she was forced to admit now. She was not only the giving, patient Christian woman her mother had raised her to be. She was also like the mountain lion she had faced down when she was five years old, and like Patrick. She had a deep streak of the feral within her.

She did not believe Patrick had betrayed her. She had never believed it. She had believed *him* when he had said that he was a Jones and a Jones doesn't cheat. But seeing him with Chloe's arms around him had stirred up her secret rage at what she'd never had from him.

He'd been a good and true husband. All he had was hers. Except his love.

And she wanted that. She wanted his heart. She wanted it *all.*

She'd been telling herself since the day after she married him that she could do without his love as long as he was true to her. But that had been a lie.

And lies beget lies.

Regina shook herself. She thought of her daughters, not even realizing that she now considered them as much hers as children of her own body might have been.

Soon enough, the girls would be home. And they mustn't see her looking frantic. They were both bright. They would probably sense that all was not well.

Regina believed that a parent had a duty to show her children by example how one coped with trouble. Children needed to be able to trust the adults who cared for them, to know they could count on their elders to face difficulties with restraint and fortitude.

Thank heaven they had not been home to observe her appalling behavior a little while ago. She had little doubt that they would eventually hear about how their father had chased their stepmother down the street. Half the town, after all, had witnessed that. And some talkative soul would be sure to end up telling them all about it. But at least they'd been spared having to witness it firsthand.

By rote, Regina pulled the pins from her tumbled, tangled hair. She brushed the brown strands with even strokes, and then pinned it back in place. She applied blusher on her pale cheeks and fresh color to her lips. After that she forced a smile for her face in the mirror.

It was a rather bleak smile, she decided. But it would simply have to do.

She went out to the kitchen, to get started on the lasagna she'd planned to make for dinner. She prepared the sauce, and ground up the three kinds of sausage she liked to use. She cooked the pasta. And then she layered the casserole, slowly, carefully, as if by concentrating on preparing a nice dinner she might make up for the way she'd behaved not too long before.

When the lasagna was ready, it was still too early to actually start baking it. So she prepared the garlic bread ahead, so it would also be ready to stick in the oven when the time came. By then it was three.

She went to the phone and stared at it, longing to pick it up and make a few calls. She could call Delilah, or Eden. She could ask them if they knew where her husband was.

But then she remembered her resolve to give him time to himself. She would not further upset him by chasing him all over town.

Right then, the phone she was staring at began to ring.

Regina gasped and jumped back as she felt the goose bumps break out on her skin. It was eerie, to have it ringing like that, as if her watching it had made it happen.

And Regina *knew* who it would be. The phantom caller. Chloe.

Yes, Chloe. Since the incident in the backyard before lunch, she had no doubt in her mind that Chloe and the phantom were one and the same.

The phone rang a second time. Regina reached out a hesitant hand and then pulled it back.

The kitchen phone was also an answering machine. There was no reason she shouldn't wait and let the machine take the call. She could stand right here and listen, and pick up if it was Patrick or one of the girls.

That's what she should do, she knew it.

The phone rang again. One more ring, and the machine would take over. If she could just wait until—

The fourth ring shrilled out.

And Regina's hand grabbed the receiver from its cradle in midring.

"Hello?"

Silence.

"Hello. Who's there?"

And then Chloe spoke. "Let him go, Regina. He's mine. He's always been mine."

A thousand emotions roiled inside of Regina. Relief that at last Chloe was willing to speak. Anger at the way her family had been victimized by all this. Frustration at the unfairness of it. And fear, too. Chloe seemed to have really gone over the edge lately. Who knew what she might do?

"Let Patrick go," Chloe said again.

Regina wanted to shout out a few demands and accusations of her own. But she didn't. Instead, she made herself silently count to three before she spoke.

"This is harassment, Chloe." She took great care to keep

her voice calm and rational. "I want your word that you will stop this now, leave me and my family alone, or I will call Sheriff Pangborn as soon as I'm through talking to you."

From the other end of the line, there was a long, quivering indrawn breath. "You don't scare me. You don't scare me one bit. You're nothing, nothing to him, except someone to help him keep his kids. But he loves me. He wants me. You'll never keep a man like him. Face it. And let him go."

"Chloe, I meant what I said. I'm calling the sheriff."

A barrage of passionate curses exploded in Regina's ear. She quietly disconnected the phone.

And then she left the phone off the hook while she found the number of the sheriff's station, which she immediately dialed.

The deputy on duty was Don Brown. Regina asked if she could speak with Sheriff Pangborn, whom she knew better than Deputy Brown.

"I'm sorry, Mrs. Jones," the deputy said. "The sheriff isn't in right now. Why don't you tell me your problem?"

Embarrassed but determined, she told him about what had happened at the post office as well as the incident in the backyard of the other house. She listed the hang-up calls and outlined the gist of the call she'd just received from Chloe.

When she was finished, Deputy Brown advised, "Generally, it's our experience that things like this just blow over, if allowed to run their natural course."

Regina was already regretting having dialed the sheriff's station. What, reasonably, could she expect them to do at this point? She thanked the deputy and hung up, feeling foolish.

She looked at the clock; it was 3:25. She wondered

vaguely if time had ever before moved so slowly as it seemed to be doing this particular afternoon.

The phone rang again. This time she let it ring. The machine picked it up and by the time the beep sounded, there was no one on the line.

Regina decided to bake brownies. Anything, to make the time go by faster.

The brownies were in the oven and there was only ten minutes left on the timer when Teresa came in.

"I'm home." Teresa breezed into the kitchen, her skin pink from an afternoon in the sun. She looked as if she didn't have a care in the world. Apparently, no one had told her about the incident this afternoon.

"Mmm. Smells great in here."

Regina forced herself to act as if everything were as it should be. "How was swimming?"

"Great. But I'm covered with sunblock and sand. Can I take my shower now?"

"Go ahead."

Teresa disappeared to clean up. She was downstairs again cutting up the dinner salad when Marnie came in. Like Teresa, Marnie seemed happy and carefree. She must not have heard what had happened, either. Also like her sister, Marnie looked as if she could use a shower. But it was not in her nature to volunteer for such unpleasantness.

When Marnie started to poke a finger in the pan of cooling brownies, Regina shot her a quelling look.

"Go upstairs and wash those hands."

Marnie groaned in protest, and then flounced off to do as she'd been told. When she came back down she set the table.

By then, it was five-thirty and the lasagna and garlic bread were hot and fragrant and ready to eat.

"Where's Dad?" Marnie wanted to know.

"Well, he may be a little late tonight," Regina said, as

offhandedly as she could. "Why don't we just sit down without him?"

Marnie and Teresa exchanged a look. Regina realized that she had not sounded as offhand as she'd intended.

But Teresa said, "Sure. I'm starved."

As they took their seats and the meal began, Regina was poignantly aware of the empty space at the head of the table. And from the pensive expressions she observed on the two young faces, so were her daughters. Dinner was mostly a silent affair, punctuated by fits and starts of carefully inane conversation.

Once, just before Marnie cleared off the dinner plates and Teresa brought over the pan of brownies for Regina to cut, the phone rang.

"I'll get it." Teresa stood.

"No." Regina kept her tone very calm. "Let's just let the machine take it. And see who it is first."

Teresa looked bewildered. But she waited as Regina had requested, until the ringing stopped and the recorded message had played. When the beep sounded, there was no one on the other end.

Teresa sank into her chair once more.

Regina felt some explanation was in order. "You both know how we keep getting all those hang-up calls, right?"

Solemnly, both girls nodded.

"Well, I think whoever it is might become discouraged if the machine answers instead of us, that's all. And of course, if it's someone who really wants to talk with any of us, they'll stay on the line and say who they are. Then we can answer."

Both girls agreed that this was a good plan. Regina waited for Marnie to say something about the call she'd taken from Chloe Swan at lunchtime. But Marnie said nothing; she only looked at her stepmother through worried blue eyes.

"Marnie? Is something bothering you?"

Marnie's gaze slid away. "Yeah." She looked back and grinned. "Can I have three brownies, instead of just two?"

"You are a dreamer, my dear."

Marnie shrugged. "Just thought I'd try."

After the brownies were served and eaten, the girls got up and did the dishes smoothly and efficiently. They neither complained nor bickered between themselves.

For the first time since they'd come to live with her and Patrick, Regina found herself longing to hear their arguing voices. A little quarreling on this particular evening would have meant that all was right with their world.

After the dishes were done, Marnie said, "I think I'll go take my bath now."

"Good idea," Regina said, and wanted to cry. The day Marnie went to bathe without coercion was a dark day indeed.

Marnie disappeared upstairs and came down a half an hour later, dressed in her pajamas. "Can we watch some TV?"

Regina was seated in an easy chair crocheting an extra set of coasters that she really didn't need. She looked up over the rim of the glasses she wore for reading and for close work. "Sure. But not too loud."

Marnie flipped on the television and she and Teresa sat at either end of the couch. Two and a half hours crept by to the sounds of sitcom laugh tracks.

"Okay, you two. Bedtime," Regina announced at nine-thirty.

With only minimal grumbling, the girls turned off the television and went to brush their teeth. A few minutes after they'd headed for the bathroom, Marnie returned.

Regina looked up from the afghan she'd started on when she finished the coasters. "What is it, honey?"

Marnie clasped her small hands together and bit her lip.

"I know getting tucked in is mostly for babies, and Saint Teresa and me are kinda too big for it..."

"Yes?"

"But maybe just tonight, you could do it anyway. Okay?"

Regina removed her glasses and rubbed the bridge of her nose. "I think that's a lovely idea. Go on up and I'll be there in just a minute."

She went to Marnie's room first, where she had to be careful not to walk on the little plastic construction-set pieces that were strewn on the floor. In spite of her care, however, she stepped on something that made a loud crunch.

Out of the darkness, she heard Marnie's sigh. "It's all right, Gina. I prob'ly got two of those anyway."

Regina found the edge of the bed at last. She sat, her eyes slowly becoming adjusted to the darkness of the room. "Tomorrow you'll clean up all those pieces."

"I will, I promise. But now, I guess, since you're here, I'll have to say my prayers."

Regina smiled. "Yes, I'd like that."

"Well. Okay, then." Marnie pressed her eyes closed. "Our Father, who art in heaven..."

Marnie murmured the Lord's Prayer in a soft little singsong, adding at the end, "And bless my dad and Regina and help them to work their problems all out. Amen."

"Amen," Regina agreed.

"You meant what you said today, didn't you, Gina?" Marnie asked then. "About taking care of that problem and not leaving us?"

"I most certainly did." She bent to place a kiss on Marnie's forehead. "Good night, honey."

"'Night, Gina." Marnie turned over and cuddled up into a ball.

Regina rose and carefully picked her way through the debris to the door.

She found Teresa sitting on her bed, her lamp still on, her hands folded in her lap.

"Gina, we must talk."

Quietly Regina closed the door behind her and sat beside her older stepdaughter. "All right."

Teresa spoke with great gravity. "Where is my father?"

"Well, Teresa. I really don't know."

"Did something...happen, between you and him?"

Regina nodded. "Yes. We had an argument."

"A bad one?"

"Bad enough. I behaved horribly. Your father was very angry at me. So he left."

Teresa looked disbelieving. "*You* behaved horribly?"

"Yes, I did. Please don't ask me for details, though. I really don't want to explain."

Now Teresa looked extremely knowing. Sagaciously, she nodded. "I understand." Then, suddenly, she was a worried twelve-year-old again. "Did he say when he'd be back?"

"No, he didn't."

Teresa took Regina's hand. "Well, he always does come back. Sooner or later. Please believe me."

"I do believe you. Your father's a good man, with a lot on his mind. Of course he'll be back."

"And when he does, he'll be sorry for whatever he did."

"Teresa, I told you, I was the one who—"

"Whatever. Just please don't give up on him."

"I won't."

"Or...on us."

"Never." Regina wrapped her arm around Teresa and gave a squeeze.

The girl laid her head on Regina's shoulder. "Since we got you, everything is so much better, Gina," she said in a broken little whisper. "It would be awful if you weren't here."

"I'll always be here as long as you need me. One way or another. I promise you." She smoothed the fine blond hair back from Teresa's forehead and placed a kiss there. "Now, into bed."

Regina busied herself pulling back the covers. Teresa slipped between the sheets and Regina pulled them up and tucked them around her.

"Good night, sweetheart," she whispered, and kissed Teresa once more.

She moved softly to the door.

"Gina?"

"Yes?"

"I love you, Gina."

"And I love you."

Regina returned to the living room, where the clock on the mantel was just striking ten. She picked up the beginnings of the afghan and then set it aside again.

She was tired of keeping busy, of pretending she was doing something useful so that she wouldn't have to admit that what she really was doing was waiting.

For her husband to come home.

With a long sigh, Regina switched off the lamps and sat down in the easy chair in the dark. She stared out the window at the streetlight across the way, waiting for Patrick and some resolution to this awful situation.

She had waited nearly an hour when the phone rang. She reached for it by rote, putting it to her ear before she remembered her decision to screen all her calls.

"Hello? Regina? Regina, is that you?"

Regina cleared her throat. *"Marcus?"*

"Yes, Regina. It's me."

Regina was in no mood to deal with an old beau. "Marcus, I really—"

"I know, I know. My calling makes you uncomfortable, and I understand that."

"Okay. If you know this makes me uncomfortable, then why are you calling?"

"Because…" Now it was Marcus's turn to cough. "I, um… Angie and I… Did you know I've been dating Angie?"

Remembering Marcus's singing the other day, Regina actually felt the ghost of a smile on her lips. "Yes. I think I heard that you two were dating."

"Yes, we are." Did bliss have a sound? If it did, it was there in Marcus Shelby's voice right then. Regina was happy for him and for Angie Leslie—at the same time as she felt a little stab of selfish envy that she and Patrick weren't doing as well. Marcus continued, "Angie and I are *together*. And tonight, we went to the Mercantile Grill, and then afterward we stopped in next door at the Hole in the Wall to have a drink. We just left there, actually."

"And?"

"And your husband is there."

"Oh."

"He's drunk and getting drunker. I think what he really wants is for his wife to come and take him home."

"How do you know what my husband wants, Marcus?"

Marcus Shelby snorted. "Oh, come on. Isn't it obvious? That man was after you from that first day when I walked you home from church and he was standing in his yard flexing all those muscles he's got. Why do you think I was always trying to keep you away from him? He's totally in love with you."

"But, Marcus," Regina argued, thoroughly confused, "you came to see me to tell me he *didn't* love me, that he only married me to get his girls."

"Well, of course I said that." Marcus's tone was faintly exasperated. "And I did my best to believe it, too. After all, you had thrown me over for him. My wounded ego wanted revenge. But deep down, I knew that man was crazy about you. The truth was, I never had a chance against the passion between the two of you." From somewhere on Marcus's end of the line, there came a husky feminine laugh. Regina realized that Marcus was not alone. "And it worked out fine, that I lost out," Marcus added in his blissful voice. "Because I found my *own* passion."

Regina didn't quite know what to say. "I see."

"Yes, well. Angie and I thought you might like to know where your husband was."

"I appreciate that."

"No problem. And all the best to you, Regina."

"Thank you, Marcus. Um, same to you."

Regina heard another soft woman's laugh, and then the line was disconnected. Slowly she, too, hung up.

She sat for a few minutes more, considering. And then she decided to take Marcus's advice.

But what to do about the girls?

It took only a moment for Regina to decide. She dialed Delilah Fletcher's number. She was in luck—Delilah answered.

"Hello?"

"Hello, Delilah? This is Regina. Did I wake you?"

"No."

"Delilah, I really need your help."

"Why did I know you were going to say that?"

"I know it's an imposition—"

"No, it's not. It's just inevitable."

"It is?"

"Certainly."

Regina was quite bewildered. "You seem to be way ahead of me on this."

"Of course I am. I've been waiting to hear from you, ever since Nellie called."

"Nellie called you about what happened between Patrick and me?"

"She certainly did."

"I suppose she's calling everyone."

"No doubt. Nellie is such a jewel." Delilah's voice dripped irony. "But don't worry about Nellie. She doesn't have much use for men, so she's never happy when someone she likes gets married. But eventually, she'll grow accustomed to what's happened and she'll stop driving you crazy. I promise."

"I hope you're right."

"I usually am. Now, you need me to help in some way. Correct?"

"Yes, I—"

"All right. What can I do?"

"Well, I want to go over to the Hole in the Wall for a few minutes. I understand that Patrick is there. The girls are in bed, but I hate to leave them alone. I don't want to wake them and upset them, but if they woke and found I was gone, then they would—"

Delilah cut to the point. "How about if I sit with them, until you return?"

"Yes. That's exactly what I—"

"I'll be right there."

"Thank you, I—"

But her sister-in-law had already hung up.

Delilah arrived ten minutes later.

"Thank you, Delilah," Regina said just before she went out the door.

Delilah waved a hand. "What's a family for, anyway? Go on. Get your husband."

"I will."

"And don't let him give you any lip, either."

Regina forced a smile. "I won't." She stepped out into the night as Delilah shut the door.

Regina took her car, so she reached Main Street within minutes of leaving the house.

That late on a weeknight, Main Street was a very quiet place. All the stores were dark. Even the Mercantile Grill had closed for the evening. But of course, the lights at the Hole in the Wall still burned.

Regina easily found a space across from the bar and pulled into it. She got out of the car and hurried across the street.

At the double doors to the saloon, she paused. Entering a bar to find an intoxicated husband was not high on her list of fun things to do. She bolstered her courage by drawing a long breath and squaring her shoulders.

It was then that she heard Patrick's voice, muffled by the doors, coming from inside.

Cautiously, she pushed the doors open, slipped through and slid into the shadows to the right of the doors. Once there, she didn't want to go any farther.

And no one seemed to notice her anyway. They were all looking at Patrick, who was standing on a table in the center of the room, clutching a bottle of whiskey and, it appeared, making some sort of speech.

He proposed grandly, "So I ask you, what's the most important thing, 'tween a husband and wife?"

Around the room, the patrons mumbled to each other. Old Oggie, sitting the next table over from the one his son was standing on, made a disgusted noise in his throat.

Then some fellow Regina didn't know suggested something uncouth.

Several men burst into crude laughter.

Patrick looked down at them, his expression woozy and wounded.

"Pipe down, you animals," Rocky Collins advised. "The man's got something to say."

Patrick scratched his head and looked puzzled. "Er, where was I?"

"The most important thing between a husband and wife," Rocky thoughtfully provided.

"Oh. Yeah. Right." Patrick swayed on his feet. The table he was standing on creaked in protest.

Jared, behind the bar, suggested quietly, "Patrick if you break that table, Eden'll have my hide."

"I'm not gonna break anything." Patrick helped himself to another swig from his bottle, then solemnly declared, "It's come to me. I remember."

"Don't keep us in suspense." The unknown voice was weighted with sarcasm.

"It's *trust!*" Patrick announced with a proud, dazed smile. "Yes, *trust*. Trust is it. Trust is everything."

Regina stared at him, despising herself. He was absolutely right—no matter how much trouble he'd had remembering the word. Trust *was* everything. And she had been guilty of the most appalling lack of it.

And now she was acting like a coward, hiding in the shadows instead of stepping up and telling him she'd been wrong. She forced herself to move out into the light.

Jared saw her. "About time," he muttered.

On the table, Patrick continued, "*Trust*, that's the thing. If you haven't got it, you haven't got what it takes to make it through the rough times. And that's why there oughtta be something about it in the weddin' vows. I'm *serious*. You got your love, your honor and your cherish. But where the hell is your *trust*? And what have you got without it, but a fair-weather kind of thing? And you should never marry a person you can't trust. 'Cause if you don't trust the one you married, then what's it worth? What's it matter?"

Regina, who stood at his feet now, spoke with quiet force. "Patrick."

"Huh?" He looked down and saw her. Then he blinked and squinted. "Gina, honey. S'that really you?"

"Yes. It's me. And I'm sorry I didn't trust you. I truly am."

He went on staring at her, his handsome face flushed with drink—and frank emotion. His expression was one of longing—and of joy. There was no doubt about it. The man was *very* happy to see her. Why, the way he was gazing at her, anyone would think he was crazy in love with her.

Regina's heart seemed to expand in her chest. Could she have been wrong about his feelings all this time? Was it possible that what Marcus had said was true?

"I've come to take you home." She kept her voice steady. After all, she was the levelheaded one in the family.

"Home?" He looked so hopeful, and so abashed. "I can go home now?"

"Yes." She held out her hand. "We'll go home. Together."

"Together." His face lit up in a thousand-watt smile. "Damn. It's good to see you."

"Is it ever," Oggie muttered. "Where the hell have you been, gal? Never mind, you're here now. Take him home. Please."

Everyone joined in.

"Yeah, get him outta here!"

"We heard enough!"

"He's been jabberin' for hours!"

They stomped and applauded.

Patrick flourished his whiskey bottle and bowed to one and all. "What a woman, huh?"

"Yeah, she's one of a kind," some chivalrous fellow concurred.

"Now get off the damn table!" Jared commanded.

"Okay, okay." Patrick tossed his bottle to Tim Brown, and bent to a crouch. Regina smiled at him, still holding out her hand.

But then his gaze shifted. He was looking past Regina. "Oh, no…" Slowly he straightened without leaping down.

Regina—and everyone else—turned to see what he saw.

It was Chloe. Behind her, the double doors were still swinging. And in her hand there was a small but deadly looking gun.

"Patrick!" Chloe shouted. "She can't have you, Patrick! I won't let her!" Jared started to leap the bar. Chloe spun and aimed her gun at him. "Don't try it." Jared froze. Chloe swung the gun around again, this time toward Regina. "I'll get rid of her, Patrick. You'll see. You watch…"

Regina, disbelieving, couldn't move. She stood frozen to the spot. But Patrick, calling on the famous Jones reflexes once again, surged into action just in time.

He vaulted from the table. Regina gasped as he grabbed her shoulders and spun her around, putting himself between her and the woman with the gun.

"No, Patrick…" Regina tried to protest.

But she was too late. There was a loud, sharp *crack*.

Then Chloe's scream.

Regina and Patrick stared at each other.

"Patrick?" Regina whispered in stunned disbelief. "Patrick?"

Chloe shrieked, "Oh my God, no! Not Patrick! It wasn't supposed to be Patrick!"

Patrick smiled at his wife, a sweet and gentle smile. And then he slowly crumpled to the floor.

Chloe, sobbing and wailing uncontrollably, dropped the gun just as Jared reached her side and grabbed her.

Pandemonium ensued.

"He's shot!" It was Oggie's voice, bewildered and full of anguished wrath. "That crazy woman's shot my boy!"

Everyone was shouting.

"Call an ambulance!"

"Chloe Swan's shot Patrick Jones!"

"Somebody get the sheriff!"

Regina barely registered the uproar. Her whole attention was focused on the fallen man at her feet. Her knees seemed to bend of their own accord as she sank to her husband's side.

She noted the spreading pool of blood beneath him. She knew it would be dangerous to move him. But she *had* to touch him. Carefully she reached out a shaking hand to smooth his hair.

"You foolish man. You shouldn't have done that." She murmured the words very softly, sure he couldn't hear them.

But then her breath caught as his eyes opened and he granted her one of those rakish grins of his. "A decent wife is...damn near irreplaceable."

"Oh, Patrick..." She felt the first hot tear slide over the dam of her lower lid and trail down her cheek.

"Lighten up," he advised, squandering his fading strength to lift a hand and tenderly wipe the tears away. "Things could be worse...."

She clasped the hand that caressed her cheek, then brought it to her lips. "Shh. Don't talk. And please don't move. They're calling the ambulance. You're going to be all right, I promise you."

"Yeah. Sure. But in case I'm not—"

She touched his lips. They felt frighteningly cool. "Shh. Don't say that. Don't even think it." Someone handed her a coat, which she wadded up and placed beneath his head.

"Damn it. Stop fussing over me and listen."

"Oh, sweet Lord." She gave the makeshift pillow one more pat.

"Listen..."

"Yes. Yes, all right. What is it?"

"Help Marybeth take care of the girls."

"I will. You know I will."

"And…" He lifted a hand again, but this time only pawed the air weakly with it before letting it fall. He was panting. "Come closer. I can't…"

She bent nearer, so close she could feel his labored breath against her cheek. And he whispered with so much effort that it broke her heart to listen. "I love you, Gina. You're the best damn thing that ever happened to me…."

Regina swallowed a sob. He loved her, *loved* her. They were the words she'd never dreamed she'd hear from him. And yet she *was* hearing them.

She bit back the tears, wanting to be strong for him, right now, when he most needed her strength.

Yet still the hard truth assailed her.

She had thought herself above him, she could see that now. She had been so full of her own special brand of well-bred arrogance. She had seen herself as a prudent, genteel woman who had married beneath herself…for love.

Oh, Lord, what vanity.

She'd known nothing of love. *This* was love. This hellion lying in his own blood from the bullet he'd taken to save her, this incredible man who was willing to use the last breath in his body to tell her what was in his heart.

Regina opened her mouth to say what an utter fool she'd been. But then she closed it, because she realized that Patrick couldn't hear her anymore. With a gentle sigh, he had slipped from consciousness.

"Where's that damn ambulance?" Oggie, right beside her, wanted to know.

The old man had no sooner finished asking the question than they all heard the scream of the siren. The ambulance was on the way.

Chapter Seventeen

Not much more than a month later, in the little meadow at the crest of Sweetbriar Summit, Regina spread her blanket beneath the oak. Then she kicked off her shoes and went to the spring, where she drank the clear water from her cupped hands.

She returned to the blanket and sat down, breathing in the clean air, glancing up now and then at the fat white clouds that drifted by, thinking how the change of seasons was coming. The grass was already golden. The leaves of the oak, a black oak, were going brown.

But the day itself was warm, with a hint of a breeze. A perfect day for lovers. And this was the perfect place for a lovers' tryst. The timing, also, was just right. The girls were in school and wouldn't be home for hours.

Regina lay back on the blanket, a soft smile on her face. She closed her eyes, thinking that the last time she came here she had not known she was waiting until she heard the whisper of footsteps in the grass.

This time, of course, she knew. She knew she was waiting for a man. A certain man. The one man for her.

A peacefulness came over her as she lay there stretched out beneath the sky. She let her mind drift, like the white clouds above, in a state somewhere between sleep and waking.

Which was why she failed to hear the footsteps this time. She didn't even know he'd come, until he was standing above her, blocking out the sun. She opened her eyes, and brought a hand up to shade them.

"Patrick."

She could see that the hard climb up the side of the steep hill had tired him. His face was slightly pale. But she quelled the nursemaid within her. She'd been his nurse for a month now. Today she would be much more.

She gave him a welcoming smile and sat up. Then, lazily, she stretched.

He was holding a long strip of rather rumpled red tickets. He dropped them in her lap. She gave a low chuckle, picked them up and idly twisted them around a finger. She had left them, along with a brief note and the treasure map she'd saved from the first time they'd come here, on his pillow. The note had said:

Keep going until you get to the top. Bring the tickets for old times' sake.

He crouched down beside her. And then he ran a finger along the line of her cheek.

She looked up from the tickets and into his eyes. Not breaking the hold of his gaze, she set the tickets aside.

Patrick leaned closer, so that his lips were a breath's distance from her own. And then he closed the distance.

Regina sighed and let her eyelids flutter closed as he kissed her. How long had she waited, dreamed of this moment? It seemed like years since she'd last felt his mouth upon her own in a kiss that promised all manner of delights.

Even after they'd dug the bullet out of him and said he would recover, she'd feared for him. And she'd had her share of nightmares in which she lost him forever and never knew the wonder of his loving touch again.

But now, at last, he was well enough to meet her on Sweetbriar Summit. And to kiss her in that special way that set her whole being aflame.

His lips brushed hers in a series of teasing, exploratory caresses.

And then he sat back.

Her eyes drifted open to meet his, which were gleaming with the same promise she'd felt in his kiss. His face was no longer the least bit pale, and she was glad for that. If anything, she noticed with a small stab of purely feminine satisfaction, he looked a bit flushed—in a very healthy kind of way.

His hand cupped her head. He smiled, and she felt the deft movement of his fingers as, one by one, he removed the pins that held up her hair. The brown strands tumbled to her shoulders. He stroked her hair, combing it with his fingers as he'd always liked to do.

When he spoke, his voice was low and soft as the wind.

"The last time we were here, I made you promise to marry me. Remember?"

"Oh, Patrick..." How she loved the tender way his hand smoothed her hair.

"Remember?"

"Oh. Yes. Yes, I do."

"But this time..."

"Yes?"

"This time I'm going to make you..."

"What?"

And right there, on Sweetbriar Summit, with the autumn

sky and the pine-covered mountains as witness, Patrick Jones demanded, "...Say you love me."

She didn't hesitate. "I love you, Patrick."

His hand went still, and then dropped to his side. He marveled, "Damn. I like the sound of that."

"I've loved you for a long time," she confessed shyly.

He sat back a little and studied her, a puzzled expression on his face. "How long?"

"Since the morning after you married me."

He snorted. "No kidding?"

"No kidding."

"Why the hell didn't you say so?"

"I was a fool."

He said nothing, only watched her face.

"What are you thinking?" she dared to inquire.

"Only that you might have been a fool—but you damn sure weren't the *only* fool."

"What do you mean?"

"I mean that, looking back, it seems like I've loved *you* since the day after I moved in next door to you."

"No..."

"Yeah. Remember, I came to borrow that cup of sugar?"

Regina nodded. She remembered very well.

"You were wearing a robe that covered every inch of you, holding on to the neck of it like you thought I might rip it off you. Not that I blame you. I *wanted* to rip it off you."

"You didn't."

"I did. I loved you even then, though I guess I didn't know it. I hadn't felt anything really strong for a woman since..."

"Chloe?"

"Yeah. And the way things turned out with her, I was never going to let myself get in trouble like that again."

Regina spared a moment to think of Chloe. It was said

around town that Chloe had seen the error of her ways. But contrition would not be enough to get Chloe off the hook. She would have to spend some time in prison for what she had done.

Patrick wasn't thinking of Chloe at all. He repeated, "I was never going to fall for a woman again."

"I understand."

"But then there you were. I'd known you all my life. You'd been there all the time, but somehow, I hadn't noticed you. Then my old man said, 'Go take a look at her.' And I did. And it was like... Hell, there's no explaining it. Except I found that what I wanted was right next door.

"I was relieved. And anxious. I wanted to grab you and shake you and make you see in me what I saw in you. I wanted to break Marcus Shelby in half with my bare hands, just for seeing you first. And I knew I had to be careful, wait for the right moment, or you'd run like hell from me."

"The day of the picnic..."

"Yeah, it was the moment, and I took it. I made you mine. But I didn't figure it out, what I was feeling, until the night I married you."

She gaped at him. "You knew you loved me *then?*"

He nodded.

"But if you knew you loved me on our wedding night, why didn't you say so when I asked you, the next morning?"

"Hell, Gina." He looked away, out over the town where the leaves on the trees were going gold and the new roof was almost finished on the community church.

She took his chin in her hand and made him look in her eyes. "Please, tell me. It's important that you tell me." She cast about for the right words. "We need to share our heart's secrets with each other, to tell each other the things that are hardest to say. It's part of trusting, to say the hard things.'' She teased, ''And you yourself said how important trust is in a marriage.''

He faked a confused expression. ''I did? When?''

''You know very well when.'' She was not going to be put off. ''Say it. Come on. Why didn't you tell me you loved me when I asked you about it?''

''Hell.''

''Come on.''

Haltingly, he began, ''Gina, a man has his pride.''

''And?''

''And…we had things we wanted from each other. It seemed like we'd made a good bargain. You got a husband and a family. I got a decent wife to help me raise the girls. When you asked me if I loved you that morning after we got married, it just…seemed like I'd be putting myself at a big disadvantage, to go bringing love into it, since I knew you didn't love me.''

Regina was silent. Then, ''I know exactly what you mean.''

He looked doubtful. ''Yeah, right.''

''I do, honestly. I know because I felt exactly the same way. I held back from saying I loved you, because I thought that if you knew how much I cared, I'd become the needy one, wanting something from you that you could never give.''

They stared at each other. Then he grinned. ''Damn. So we were both fools, huh?''

''Yes. Prideful fools. And I am sorry, Patrick. About the way I let Chloe come between us. I never really doubted you, I swear. I knew you would never betray me. I was just so jealous. You had loved Chloe in the past. And even though you didn't love her anymore, she'd had what *I* wanted—your heart.''

His smile was rueful. ''Well, I hope you've got the picture now.''

She answered steadily. "Yes, Patrick. I've got the picture now."

He tipped her face up. "Gina, I didn't even really know what loving was. Until you."

Regina had to swallow to force down the lump in her throat. "Oh, Patrick…"

His chestnut brows lifted. "Yeah?"

"I'm so sorry, for the awful things I said to you, for the unforgivable way I behaved."

"Yeah," he agreed. "You oughtta be sorry." A devilish gleam came into his eyes. "In fact, I think that right now you just better show me how sorry you are."

"Oh, Patrick…"

"Come on." His hands were on the buttons of her blouse. "Show me."

And she did.

And after their passion had faded to sighs, Regina told him about the baby that was growing within her.

He stared at her. "A baby? We're having a baby?"

"Yes."

"When?"

"In the spring. I'm only about six weeks along, but I'm sure. I can feel the changes. And I took two home tests. They both came out positive. She'll be born in May."

"How do you know it'll be a girl?"

"I just do. I feel it. We'll name her after my mother. Is that all right?"

"Yeah, Gina. It's all right." He pulled her closer and kissed her hair. "Damn. We've got it all." The words were husky with emotion.

Naked in the sun, Regina smiled. Patrick was right. They had a home, and the girls and a baby on the way.

But most important, they had each other. They shared a

love sweet, untamed and true—a love more splendid than anything Regina had ever imagined in the very wildest of her virgin dreams.

* * * * *

Don't miss *The M.D. She Had To Marry*
by Christine Rimmer,
part of CONVENIENTLY YOURS,
Silhouette Special Edition #1345,
on sale September 2000!

Dear Reader,

This story always pushed some special heart buttons of mine. The heroine has quite an unusual problem—and the kind of problem that especially embarrasses and confuses my single-dad hero. But that was exactly what inspired me to write this story. I sincerely believe that no problem is so awkward or embarrassing that it can't be resolved—if the love is right between the two people. My poor single dad, though, has his hands full until he discovers that for himself.

I hope you enjoy the story!

Jennifer Greene

HEAT WAVE
Jennifer Greene

One

Kat Bryant zipped into the driveway, braked her car with a jolt and grabbed the key to her spanking-red MG. The fast ride had destroyed her pompadour hairstyle. Her high-topped white button shoes hit the pavement, and when she climbed out of the car her lace-trimmed skirt slid down to midcalf. Customers regularly told her that the image of a proper Victorian lady suited her.

There were no customers around now, and the only thought in Kat's head was getting naked. Fast.

Damn, but it was hot. Charleston was always hot in July, but this summer's heat wave was a bone wilter. The sun blistered and anything green had long ago been bleached white. The birds were too parched to sing; everyone was cranky, and there was no escaping the susurrant drone of air conditioners. Even at five in the afternoon, the temperature sustained a choking hundred degrees.

Kat made a beeline for the shade, not hard to find in a

neighborhood where most of the houses were three stories tall. Her home, like all the rest, was built right off the street with French-style shutters and wrought-iron balconies. A history lover would see the ambience that was old Charleston. The more practical would note the lack of parking, the internal layout of small rooms and long, inconvenient stairs. Kat, a sucker for history, had taken one look at the house five years before and passionately fallen in love.

At the moment, however, she was only feeling passionately about heat. Her workday had stretched to twelve frazzling, wilty, sticky hours. She'd been good—as good as the girl with the curl in the nursery rhyme—but enough was enough.

The very instant she got inside, she planned to throw the dead bolts, strip to the buff and pour herself a wickedly long, dripping-cold glass of lemonade. She'd drink it stark naked, and she could already taste it. She could also already picture herself decadently immersed in a cool scented bath, preferably with ice cubes, and definitely with the phone off the hook and no interruptions. Maybe she'd even eat dinner in the bathtub. Who'd know? Who'd care?

No one, and that was the real luxury. She fumbled in her oversize bag for her house key. After this sweltering day, all she craved was an evening of peace and solitude. Cool, silent peace, stressless solitude...

"Hi, Kat!"

"Hi, Kat! You're home late!"

Her fantasy, especially the parts involving decadence, nudity and solitude, popped the moment she saw the two teenagers clattering down her porch steps. Mick Larson's girls had obviously been waiting for her to come home— and not for the first time.

Kat felt the buck of frustration, but not for long. The two girls gamboling toward her with their hopeful smiles inevitably tugged at her heart. Angie, at thirteen, was a classic waif. She wore her blond hair crimped Shirley-Temple style, and her slight frame was voluminously hidden in one of her father's shirts—attire chosen, Kat guessed, to hide any hint of newly developing breasts.

Mick's oldest daughter Noel could have used a little of her sister's shyness. She was fifteen and looked ready to hook from the nearest street corner. Her favorite color was unrelieved black. Today her black shorts and tank top were set off by three earrings per ear and her short brown hair was well spiked with mousse. If Kat squinted hard, she could see the beautiful pair of eyes hidden beneath layers and *layers* of mascara.

"Hi, sweeties." Kat turned the key in the lock and stepped aside. Not that they were sure of their welcome, but the girls pelted in faster than puppies in a rain. "Your dad have to work late again?"

"Dad's got a big important job," Angie told her.

"I'm sure he does." There was no rancor in Kat's tone, but the look of the girls made her think briefly and fondly of homicide. She loved the girls. It was their father who deserved a good bludgeoning.

Mick Larson had been burying himself in "big important jobs" since his wife had died two years ago. The whole world had loved June—she'd been a naturally earthy woman with a heart bigger than the sky—and when she'd died, the whole neighborhood had tried to comfort Mick in his grief.

Kat hadn't known her next-door neighbor well enough to comfort him. Not that he was unfriendly, but the brawny Norwegian had never been easy around her, and that uneasiness was definitely mutual. She'd tried to help by spending some time with his daughters, but that was like plugging a small finger into a fast-growing hole in a dike.

One of these days, Mick Larson simply had to wake up and smell the coffee: both his girls were running wild and lonely, thanks to his neglect. Angie needed a bra. Noel modeled her makeup techniques after Madonna. Both skipped school in winter and throughout the summer had filled the house with a steady stream of kids. Noel was running around with a turkey who drove a Hell's Angels type of motorcycle, and Angie...

"Could I have something to eat, Kat? We don't have *anything* in our refrigerator. There is nothing to eat in the whole house."

"As if you needed to ask. Go on, sweetie, help yourself. You know where everything is." Still in the hall, Kat grabbed a button hook for her old-fashioned shoes. It took a full two minutes to wriggle her toes from their cramped confinement. That should have improved her mood. It didn't. The situation was clearly getting progressively worse next door. Now Mick didn't even have food for them to eat.

Noel returned with a tall glass of lemonade in her hand— the same lemonade Kat would have given her eyeteeth for. "Your outfit's spectacular," she said admiringly. "You really look terrific."

"Thanks, honey." Kat's tone was wry. Noel's compliment lacked some validity since the fifteen-year-old's concept of fashion would have nicely fit in with the motorcycle crowd.

"Kat, I just want you to know...if we're in your way, we could go home."

Never mind all the heavy makeup, Noel's expression was so unsure, so vulnerable. Damn that man, Kat thought again. "You two are *never* in my way," she said swiftly. "If you hadn't come over, I'd have been stuck with a long boring evening with no one to talk to."

"You sure?"

"Positive." Kat might not be a cook, but she could put together a trayful of cheeses and fruits. The girls dived into the snack like vultures...or children who hadn't been fed in a year.

"You're sure you don't have something to do? Like a date or something?" Angie asked.

"Not tonight." Once she'd glanced at the mail and put away the tray, Kat headed for the stairs, trailed by both sidekicks.

"You should date more," Noel advised her sagely.

"Hmmm."

"I'll bet good-looking guys ask you out all the time."

"Hmmm." Since Noel's life revolved around the male of the species, Kat could hardly tell her that she hadn't dated in years. Five years, to be precise.

Rather than dwell on the enforced loneliness of her single life-style, she chose to see her situation with humor. She was saving a lot of men a lot of potential grief by removing herself from the dating market.

Humor didn't always save her from loneliness, but Kat wasn't about to let a man close again. It wasn't a question of once burned, twice shy, or any other hang-up that some expensive psychologist could help her with. She had a problem, all right—an intimate, personal problem—but there was no solution for it. She'd faced that because she had to and gone on with her life. But *her* problems, at the moment, were the last thing on her mind.

Upstairs, Noel draped herself on the bed with such wanton abandon that Kat had to smile. "I love this room. It has to be the most romantic room in the entire world."

"You think so?" Plucking at her blouse buttons, Kat spared her bedroom a whimsical glance. French doors led onto the second-story balcony. Two narrow stained-glass windows framed the small marble fireplace. Light filtered through the stained glass, casting prisms of rose and blue on the blue carpet, the antique "sleigh" bed and her collection of Victorian hatboxes in the corner. From the dozen lace pillows piled on the bed to the hatboxes, the room was a study in old-fashioned femininity...barring the pair of strappy red shoes with four-inch heels peeking out of the closet, which Kat quickly kicked out of the girls' sight.

Her house advertised a very solid dose of feminine values, but there were other things—such as her high-speed sports car, and her red strappy high heels—that might give someone the idea she was a classic rule breaker. With June gone, the girls had no feminine role model. Kat did her best, but the job was tricky. She knew zip about raising kids, and both girls were insatiably curious.

Too curious. She deliberately ducked behind the closet door before stripping off her long-sleeved blouse, but that bid for privacy was wasted. Noel and Angie simply relocated where they could see her.

There was nothing wrong with changing clothes in front of the girls. It was just that men in a singles' bar couldn't possibly study a woman with more critical bluntness than a teenage girl.

The spray of freckles on her shoulders was judged with the same gravity as the band around her waist left by her panty hose. Kat whipped on a pair of white shorts, because Noel was staring at her wispy panties with a frown. She chose a brief yellow top in deference to the heat, but made a point of wearing a bra beneath it in deference to Angie's unrelenting study of her breasts.

"When I'm as old as you are, I wouldn't mind a figure like yours," Angie mentioned.

"Thanks."

"But I'll bet the boys stare at you. I'd die if a boy stared at me. Especially there."

Kat only had to look at Angie to remember how painful it had been to be thirteen. "Luckily boys aren't all that fascinated in an ancient old woman of thirty-three," she murmured.

"You're not really that old, are you, Kat?"

Kat chuckled. "Afraid so."

"Well, don't worry about it. You're still beautiful," Noel reassured her protectively. "My thighs are so fat; you think I should diet? Oh, this is *wonderful*. You really wear this?"

Kat gently confiscated the black silk nightgown from Noel's avid fingers and dropped it in the back of her closet with the red shoes. "Occasionally, and no, I don't think you should diet. I think you look just fine the way you are."

"These are French panties, aren't they? Tap pants? I suppose you think I'm too young to wear stuff like this?"

Kat was rapidly developing a headache, which matched up to her parched throat and increasingly frazzled nerves. She had definite opinions about what Noel should and shouldn't wear, but there was an enormous difference between acting as an occasional feminine influence for the girls and interfering. How Mick raised his daughters was his business, not hers. She wanted no business at all with Mick Larson...but how long was she supposed to stand by and watch the girls suffer from his indifference and neglect?

She tried to erase the man from her mind, but that was easier said than done. Both girls trailed her into the bathroom. While she washed her face, they interrupted each other with an insatiable stream of feminine chatter. What was the best cover for zits, how old was she when she first shaved her legs, what kind of curfew did she have as a teenager? Not every question was emotionally loaded, but each implied a lack of guidance in their lives. Dammit, Mick, how can you be so blind?

Normally her bathroom did a reasonable job of distracting them. The black marble tub and lemon tiles were a style out of another century. Angie had a fascination with the

old-fashioned pull chain on the toilet. Noel loved to touch
the silver boudoir brushes and lemon soap. Today, though,
they were simply more interested in talk—and watching
Kat convert an elegant pompadour hairstyle into a raga-
muffin top knot. Her long, dark auburn hair was her pride
and joy, when the temperature was fifty degrees. In this
heat, she was inclined to shave her head…either before or
after she shaved a strip off the girls' father.

"I did all the wash today," Angie reported.

"So what's to brag? I did all the vacuuming and washed
the kitchen floor. Dad makes a total mess when he tries to
clean the house," Noel confided. "Men are so helpless. I
was going to shop for some food, but he forgot to leave
me money this morning."

Kat set down the hairbrush with a snap. A week before,
Angie had described making a pitiful dinner out of nacho
chips slathered with peanut butter. That was bad enough,
but the more Kat heard about the enormous household responsibilities each girl claimed, the more she was tempted
to strangle her next-door neighbor. What killed her most
was that the girls never complained. Ask them, and their
father was a combination of Rambo, Robert Redford and a
knight in shining armor.

"You think this perfume is too strong for me?" Noel
asked.

"Which one, honey?" Since Noel had sampled most of
the vials, the narrow bathroom was starting to reek like an
expensive bordello. One scent had no prayer of being dis-
tinguished from another.

"This one. You think Johnny would think it was sexy?"

"I…ummm…" Abruptly Kat headed for the door.
Downstairs she could turn on the TV. Surely the news
would provide some nice, innocuous earthshaking disaster
they could discuss.

"What's a douche, Kat?"

"Pardon?" Kat stopped midstride on the top stair.

Angie, standing in her usual hunched-over position designed to hide her new figure, repeated patiently, "What's a douche?"

Noel loomed behind her sister, creating a traffic jam at the top of the stairs. "I told you what a douche was," Noel said irritably. "I told you all that stuff a long time ago."

"Yeah, well, you told me if I kissed a boy I'd get AIDS. I saw you kissing Johnny and you didn't get any AIDS. Anyway, the last thing I'd want to do is kiss some stupid old boy. I just want to know what a douche is."

"Well, it's…" Kat cleared her throat, and then blessed the girls with her best calm, serene smile. Well? How are you going to answer that one, ducky? an inner voice taunted her. The thing was, there was a huge difference between discussing zits and discussing douches—and the Lord only knew what sex education Noel had passed onto her younger sister. Darn you, Mick Larson…

"I'll answer that question, okay? Just as soon as I pour a lemonade downstairs. I'm dying of thirst."

"Don't worry about it, Kat." Noel said to her younger sister, "I've told you a zillion times not to bother Kathryn with questions like that. All you have to do is come to me."

"Yeah, well, I came to you, and I'm still not all that sure you know what it is."

"I do, too. When a woman gets to be a certain age, she automatically knows these things, don't we, Kat?" To Angie she snapped, "I told you. A douche is sort of like a tampon." She hesitated. "I think."

There were headaches and then there were headaches. This one was accelerating to magnificent proportions. "We'll talk about it, okay? Just as soon as I pour that lemonade." Kat said gaily.

* * *

Around midnight, Kat gave up trying to sleep and carried a glass of sherry outside to the porch steps.

It was still hot. Moonlight shimmered in the honeysuckle and flickered through the branches of the gnarled cypress at the far end of the yard. Lightning bugs played in the cache of wild roses sprawling over the back fence. Dew had settled in the grass, thick and fragrant.

Leaning against a porch post, Kat took a sip from her glass and grimaced. There was nothing more nauseatingly sweet than cooking sherry. She liked an occasional glass of good wine. She just never remembered to buy it.

Like a child with medicine, she forced another gulp. She'd counted on the wine to make her sleepy. It wasn't working. She'd counted on the fresh air to relax her. That wasn't working, either. Scarlett O'Hara would have enjoyed a southern summer night like this: the crescent moon, the mingled scents of honeysuckle and roses. But romance was a forbidden subject for Kat. Normally she had the willpower to walk away from trouble.

Over a very long evening, though, she'd discovered that she couldn't buy or beg enough willpower to stop worrying about the girls.

She took another sip of sherry, yet suddenly couldn't swallow it. In the next yard, she heard the unmistakable slam of a screen door. The lights in the Larson house had been out for almost an hour, but someone was up.

Mick. Moonlight shone on his silver-blond head for only seconds before he moved into the shadows. She heard the creak of a lounge chair, then the pop of a can top.

She still hadn't swallowed the gulp of sherry. When she did, it burned all the way down her throat like liquid fire. All evening she had decided to talk to him if the chance presented itself. Unfortunately the ideal chance had just presented itself. He was alone, the girls were asleep and no one was around to interrupt them.

Nerves coiled in her stomach as she slugged down the last of the sherry and firmly set down the glass. She had never meddled before, never intruded in anyone's private affairs. It took some courage to break those long-standing principles, but if she didn't talk to Mick, who would? Sure he'd be ticked off. So what? June would have been appalled to see her daughters neglected, and it wasn't as if Kat didn't have some tact. She wasn't going to go over there and call him a selfish, insensitive, unfeeling rat.

She was just going to go over there and wish him a neighborly hello. And then clobber him, she thought darkly.

Dew soaked her bare feet before she was halfway to the fence. The sticky grass tickled, but not half as much as the sticky situation she was about to take on.

Southern women, however, had always been made of good strong grit. Kat firmly reminded herself of the girls' voracious, starving raid on her refrigerator, their woeful tale of endless household chores, their hunger for attention and, yes, the douches. She reached the fence, fueled by cooking sherry and unshakable resolve.

"Evening," she sang out with the determination of an advancing general.

He was stretched out in the shadows, but she saw his silver-blond head swivel in her direction. "Evening, Kathryn," he called out in return.

"Finally cooled off a little."

"Not much."

"Scheduled to be another scorcher tomorrow."

"So they say."

She leaned on the white wooden fence rail and remembered, much too late, that she'd never managed more than conversational drivel with Mick Larson.

For five years, she'd felt incomprehensibly, aggravatingly awkward anywhere near him. It had never made sense. Maybe she dressed in lace and cameos, but she could

climb a ladder and put up a Lincrusta frieze as capably as
a construction crew. She liked men, she knew them, she
worked with them. And it was never as if Mick had been
rude or cruel or unfriendly toward her. The opposite was
true. On the rare occasions their paths crossed, he had always treated her carefully, as if he was never quite sure if
the lady would bite.

Kat had stalked over with every intention of attacking
his conscience, but—with more brilliant hindsight—it was
a very bad idea. Six foot three of brawny muscle was
slowly swinging out of the lounge chair and ambling toward her. She was a respectable five feet, six inches...in
heels. His dwarfing shadow made mincemeat out of her
visions of clobbering him, and something was going
equally wrong with her visions of Mick as a selfish, insensitive rat.

She knew what the girls had told her, but the man leaning
his elbows on the fence rail just didn't look like an insensitive child neglecter. He looked tired.

Actually he looked exhausted. How many weeks had it
been since she'd really had a look at him? Moonlight
played up the clean, strong lines of his face, but she could
still see the dark shadows beneath his eyes. He'd put in a
hard, physical day in the heat and it showed.

June had once told her his age, but Kat had forgotten.
Thirty-seven, thirty-eight? His body didn't look thirty-
eight. He wasn't wearing a shirt, and his arms and shoulders
had a fighter's roped muscles, tanned to a dark, dark copper. Faded jeans hugged his spare hips and hard, powerful
thighs. His thick, rumpled hair might have been a natural
wheat color. The sun had bleached it to a white gold, and
his chest was dusted with that same striking white.

He wasn't pretty, but no woman was likely to ignore him
in a crowd. His square face was the map of a man's values.
Sun-squint lines were permanently embedded around his

eyes; laughter lines bracketed his mouth. He worked hard and he played hard; he had the jaw of a boss and the furrowed brow of a man who'd wrestled with life on his own terms. No desk job or wine lists for Mick. He was a physical, earthy, sexual being in the most elemental sense: he never forgot he was a man.

Kat would have liked to. Like a certain kind of uncommonly large man, he walked with a cat's silence and had a gentleness about him. A sleek, long rifle had power, but not until someone cocked the gun. Dynamite was dangerous, but not until it was lit. Mick had never done anything to appear intimidating.

But he was. This close, Kat's stomach felt the aggravating drip, drip, drip of nerves. By daylight, his eyes were a brazen cerulean blue. Now they were immutably dark and so intently focused on her that her bare toes arched in the dirt of the flower bed bordering the fence. A mosquito landed on the back of her calf. She let it bite.

"You don't have to hesitate," he said gently. "We're neighbors and you're living alone. I've told you before you could call me anytime."

"Pardon?"

"You have a leaky faucet? An appliance on the fritz?"

"I...no."

One of his sunburned brows arched in question. "You don't stop to talk to me very often. I figured something had to be wrong."

"There is something," she agreed.

His voice was low and as alluring as the darkness and scent of roses. He didn't mean it that way, she knew. If Mick was coming on to a woman, she'd know it. It wasn't his fault his voice was sexy. It wasn't his fault her darn toes were curling. "How's the yacht-building business going?"

"Too busy," he admitted, and then offered, "You've

been good to my girls. They talk about you all the time. I'm long overdue on a thank-you.''

"Yes? Well…'' If her right foot curled any tighter, she was going to get a charley horse in the arch. She took a long breath, smiled at him and said blithely, ''I'd like to talk to you about them for a minute, if you wouldn't mind.''

"About my daughters? Anytime.''

Again, she had the sensation that something was drastically wrong with the image of Mick as an uncaring father. Still, she took a breath and forged ahead. "Dammit, Mick, Angie needs a bra.''

He blinked. "Beg your pardon?''

It all spilled out faster than bad news. "And I know it's not my business, but if it were *my* daughter, I'd be meeting that Johnny at the door with a shotgun. Damnation, Noel isn't my daughter but I'm inclined to go take rifle practice. And I think responsibilities are wonderful, but all the cooking and washing and cleaning is just too much. And then there's sex. If you can't talk to them comfortably, you could buy them some books—accurate books—or at *least* make sure you know where they're getting their information. It's not that I mind discussing the facts of life with them; I just feel it's something I can't do without your permission. How do I know what you want them to know? And food. Who likes cooking? But you could still stock your refrigerator with sound, nutritional munchies. Not just chips. And Noel's talking about putting another hole in her ear—''

"Could we hold up two shakes?'' Mick interrupted peaceably.

At the moment Kat couldn't. It had been too hard to start, she couldn't stop now. "I know this is none of my business. You probably think I'm a meddling, interfering pain. You have every right to raise your daughters exactly as you please, but Mick, they're so lonesome for attention. And they have to have guidance. At the very least, you simply have to remember to give Noel money for food—''

''Kathryn?''

''Noel told Angie that a girl 'can't get pregnant the first time.' I'm going crazy! They don't know anything and they're passing on the wrong stuff to each other—''

''Kathryn—''

''I understand you build boats to make a living, but would the world cave in if you built a few less? Who needs steak? Go for hamburger. I know grief isn't simple; I know June was absolutely wonderful, but your daughters are still alive, Mick. Right now Angie's entire wardrobe appears to be your shirts—''

''Kat!''

''They're too *young* for the entire responsibility of the household! Please don't be angry, but—''

''I'm not angry.''

Silence fingered through the night, as quiet as a heartbeat. ''Of course you're angry,'' Kat assured him.

''No.''

More silence. ''You must be.'' Her own temper was kept under strict wraps, but if anyone tried to nose in her private life, Kat knew darn well she'd have unsheathed every claw and come out spitting. She was so prepared for a tongue-lashing that his slow, crooked smile left her grappling.

''No. A part of me feels kicked in the seat, which maybe needed to happen. And a part of me feels amused.''

''Amused?''

Mick nodded. ''My angels, my daughters, those two beings I love more than life who live with me...I think they just took you for a ride.''

''A ride?''

He nodded again. ''It's pretty obvious you've formed an opinion of me as a man lower than a worm, a father who's lost total interest or concern for his children and who deserves a long, slow hanging. But could you possibly hold up the lynch mob long enough to come inside the house? Just for a few minutes. It won't take long to show you that, just possibly, there's another side to the story.''

Two

Mick had to coax her to come inside. He knew she really didn't want to. He also wasn't in the habit of explaining or defending himself to anyone, but this was different. The idea that anyone would believe he'd neglect his daughters hit him low and hard.

At the gut level.

The kitchen was dark. He switched on the overhead light and immediately strode over to the refrigerator. The kitchen was pine and white, nothing fancy, but at least the counters were clean, which his next-door neighbor immediately noticed. He noticed the awkward way she stalled in the doorway. "I won't traipse through your house, Mick. I was standing in the flower beds; I'm afraid my feet are really dirty—"

"It won't be the first time the floor's seen a little dirt. Besides, we have a housekeeper."

That took her attention. "Housekeeper? But the girls said—"

"Maybe housekeeper's the wrong word. I have a lady who comes in three mornings a week to tackle the cleaning and wash."

Kat drew a breath. "But Angie said—"

"Yeah, you gave me a good idea what Angie told you. Would you mind taking a peek in here?"

She tiptoed, with very small, very dirty feet, over to his open refrigerator. She glanced at him once, wrapped her arms tightly under her chest and then bent down to view the inside shelves. They were bulging. Fresh fruits, fresh dairy products, sliced meats, cheeses, vegetables…

"I…" She scratched an itch on the back of her calf and then straightened. Her spine could have made a functioning straight edge and her lips compressed, but an interesting coral was beginning to skate up her throat. "Sooo…" She drew out the syllable as if she was stuck pulling taffy. "It's pretty obvious the girls aren't starving."

"Lord, I hope not. You should see my grocery bill."

"And don't tell me," she said weakly. "Noel doesn't do all of the family grocery shopping."

"Hey, she's the best shopper in the family, as long as you're talking about clothes on my credit card. Unfortunately when you get down to the nitty-gritty of eggs and toothpaste, her interest gets real rocky." Mick suddenly realized he was staring at Kat, seeing her differently than he had before, aware of her toast-brown eyes, her long bare legs, her nerves. Reacting to those nerves, he crouched down and squinted in the refrigerator again. "Noel's not the only one who hates grocery stores. I never claimed to be a master shopper," he drawled. "You see anything in here that looks poisonous that I didn't realize?"

Kat was swallowing hard and frequently. "Mick, I'm sorry, and I—"

"Could you come here, please?" He closed the refrigerator, opened the door to the broom closet and turned around. "Really. Would you just take a quick glance inside?"

"It's a broom closet."

"I know. Just look, okay?"

With the patience of one obliging a madman, she obediently moved closer to him and peered inside. For that brief moment, she was so close that he caught the drift of perfume on her warm skin, the scent of her hair. His pulse bucked, startling him.

He busied himself moving a box of the usual household cleaning supplies from the top shelf. The tall box, once removed, hid a cache of potato chips, chocolate bars and fruit gummies. "Angie changes her lair from week to week," he said matter-of-factly. "From the time I forbade junk food in the house, she became a hoarder. I hate to tell you what I found last fall in my fishing hat in the front hall closet."

"Tell me."

"Hardened toffee, jujubes hard and stale enough to break your teeth, and six-month-old Hershey Kisses." Mick's eyes glinted down at her. "Do you have any idea what a summer season of heat can do to a Hershey Kiss?"

Kat didn't laugh outright, but he heard her chuckle...and he saw the chuckle fade into a soft, shy woman's smile. Again, he felt an unexpected tug, a bolt of sexual awareness.

She obviously didn't. Mick didn't need a degree in perception to realize that she was fast changing her mind about what kind of father he was, but that didn't mean she had made up her mind about him as a man. He motioned her to a bar stool across the counter and pulled a beer from the fridge, asking if she wanted one. She shook her head, then nodded.

Before she could change her mind again, he set the beer in front of her, then hefted a can for himself, which he

didn't want any more than she did. Flipping the lid gave
him something to do, so did removing the draftsman sepias
from the Formica counter and settling on the bar stool
across from her.

They were talking again before he'd finished all that inane busywork. In those spare seconds of silence, though,
Mick was dominantly aware that a woman hadn't been in
his kitchen in a long time. And that, of all the women who
might have been there, the last one he'd ever imagined was
Kat.

Kat—née Kathryn—Bryant confounded him, always
had. With the exception of June, Mick had never been good
around women. Kat had the ability to make him feel huge,
awkward, and vaguely, annoyingly panicked.

He'd never figured out what to make of her. She dressed
in lace and old-fashioned hats, but she also tore through
the streets in her sassy MG. She carried a purse big enough
to store a machine gun, yet the girls told him she had a
carousel horse in her living room. She had the look of a
fragile camellia, yet three years ago he'd seen her patching
her roof, shingle by shingle, alone. And competently.

She was not only competent, but a sound business
woman. She'd spent the past five years building up a Victorian restoration business—Victorian was ''in,'' so she
sure didn't lack competition—but she'd made a serious
name for herself. Mick felt both respect and empathy for
what she'd achieved, but he'd never been able to express
that. Frankly her looks intimidated him.

Take her hair. The color was sort of a rusty cinnamon.
Undone, it reached halfway down her back. Mick had seen
it undone. He'd also seen it in a strange-looking pompadour, he'd seen it sleeked flat to her scalp and he'd seen it
wild with curls. She changed the style all the time, how
was a man supposed to figure out who she was? One day

she looked like a schoolmarm virgin, the next day she looked like a vamp.

All of the time she looked like an unusually desirable woman, which, given the whole picture, confused Mick even more.

Kat was smaller than two-bits, but even in old shorts and a saggy yellow top, she was a dynamo. Her light brown eyes were full of life and humor, intelligence and passion. She always moved lithe and quick and light, like a breeze wisping by, like a streak of light and sparkle. Maybe she wasn't beautiful, but the rich auburn hair, fine bones and delicate cream skin would capture any man's attention. She had a way of walking that said she loved being a woman and she flaunted that fact to the whole darn world.

Only that feminine flaunting was precisely what confused him, because Mick had never seen her with a man. His daughters said men called, they'd heard the telephone calls during the hundred and ten times they visited her in a week. But no date's car showed up in her driveway on the weekends. She was home all night, every night. Mick had been her next-door neighbor for five years. He knew.

And that was one unbelievably long time for an attractive woman to be totally alone.

Of course, it was an equally long time for Mick to discover that she wasn't so bewildering or intimidating. In fact, she was turning into someone impossibly easy to talk to.

"I'm not going to criticize your daughters to your face," she promised him. "I'd just like your permission to privately strangle them tomorrow, if you don't mind."

"Maybe we could form a line?"

Her finger followed a droplet of water racing down the cold beer can. She still hadn't opened it. "Now that I think about it, I can't believe how blindly I believed them. The 'poor me' stories never added up. They both glow every time they say your name, hardly a symptom of neglected children. All I can say is that I love your girls, and I felt protective about them, and I didn't and don't really know you. Anyway, I owe you a giant apology.''

"No, you don't.'' It finally occurred to him that he should have given her a glass. Restlessly he surged to his feet, produced the glass, popped her beer top and poured it in. "If my girls hit you for sympathy, maybe it was because they needed it,'' he admitted gruffly. "I'm guilty of not spending enough time with them. Maybe I'm guilty of worse than that. You already know I build boats—''

"Yes.''

"And there are a lot of boat builders in the business, but very few craftsmen who only work in wood, which is to say that I have unlimited business if I want it. Two years ago, I wanted unlimited business. I wanted so much work I couldn't breathe, sleep, eat or think. So I went after it, and I got it.''

He motioned with his hand, a man's gesture, the closest he had ever come to admitting helplessness. "It's not that I didn't think of Noel and Angie, but they seemed okay. The three of us had had two years to prepare for June's death; at the end that was a blessing more than a shock. And they seemed to be doing better than I was; they seemed to be taking it all maturely. They weren't, and aren't, mature, but by the time I realized things were going wrong, I was up to my neck in building contracts.''

"You don't have to explain all this to me,'' she said softly.

But he did. He needed to explain it to someone. And the woman sitting across from him, with her knuckles curled under her chin and her soft eyes, was listening. Mick could remember others willing to listen, but not anyone where he'd felt the willingness or need to share. "Months ago, I started getting out from under. I hired help and I eased off on taking new contracts, only I couldn't make it all happen overnight. You have a business of your own—''

"I understand," she concurred.

He knew she did, although most independent business-men that he knew didn't have tobacco-brown eyes and a mouth so fragile it worried him. "Anyway, I've done what I can to get out from under, only to discover that normal working hours didn't solve anything. Kat—'' he took a gulp of beer ''—I'm scared.''

"Scared?" she echoed. She deliberately raised herself from the bar stool to take a meandering perusal of his line-backer's shoulders and muscular long legs.

Another woman could have done the same thing and made it into something suggestive and sexual. Kat's eyes pounced back to his with simple, easy humor. She'd noticed he was a big lug of a man, but she hadn't noticed he was a *man*.

Mick felt piqued. "Scared," he repeated determinedly.

"It has to be a lot of years since bogeymen in the closet intimidated you, and something tells me you don't often wake up with nightmares.''

"Would you cut it out? I'm serious. I'm scared of them.''

"Them?"

"Them. My daughters. Noel. Angie."

She'd finally relaxed enough to take a sip of beer, and now she nearly choked on it. "Are you crazy, Mick? They adore you. They worship the ground you walk on.''

"That's what I'm trying to tell you. As a father, I'm walking into quicksand. I'm not just talking fear, I'm talk-ing panic. I got lost months ago somewhere between per-manents, sanitary napkins, tight jeans, makeup and dating rules of the '90s.'' He hesitated, aware of the faint streak of color on her cheeks. "Did I offend you? I know Noel has a stroke if I mention a feminine product out loud, but it seems pretty silly for a grown man to pretend he's unaware that a woman…''

"I'm a little older than Noel. Trust me, I can handle the conversation."

She could and she was, but the flush climbing her face definitely fascinated him. The redhead had a secret Victorian streak. Mick hadn't known there was a woman alive who was still modest. And with those sassy eyes?

"Where I was raised, a man called a spade a spade. I never had a polite education in euphemisms. My whole family were men, which is undoubtedly why I end up in such hot water all the time."

"Hot water?"

"With my daughters. I thought I could handle raising the girls through puberty. That was a mistake." He heaved a sigh of the long suffering, just to catch another of her grins. "For instance, a few months ago, I *thought* I was showing some honest sensitivity in buying Noel some Midol. I mean, there was no ignoring it. Once a month she was—''

"A little moody?"

"A little moody?" Mick said patiently, "You looked at her, she cried. You talked to her, she cried. Ask her if she wanted a glass of milk, and she stormed out of the room and slammed the door. A few days later and she was back to being Noel, but in the meantime—''

"I understand."

"Do you? Because I swear to God I've tried, but I don't. More relevant, if you can understand that stuff, maybe you can understand the phone."

"The phone?" Kat queried gently.

"Yes. The phone. In a fire, there'd be no getting a call through to this house. Both girls live on the phone; they do their hair, the dishes, their homework and even their nail painting on the phone. I mean, is this something unique to the female genes? Is there a cure? And darn it, will you quit laughing?''

"I'm not laughing."

"Close enough," he grumbled, but the sparkle in her eyes pleased him, delighted him. So did she. He was close enough to catch her scent and it wasn't French and fancy like he'd first thought. It was something cool and light and innocent, like Lily of the Valley. The woman had too much devil in her eyes to wear Lily of the Valley, but he was beginning to feel more intrigued than intimidated by the many contradictions that made up Kat. How could he have lived next door to her for five years and never heard her really laugh?

So he kept on. "This fathering business used to be a lot of fun. When they were younger, we'd traipse off to Hunting Island for the weekend to beachcomb and fish. Never needed more than a knapsack apiece and some food. Now it takes Noel forty-seven suitcases, most of them packed with electrical appliances, before she'll ever…you're not laughing again, are you?''

"No. I promise. No."

"And they've both turned sneaky. They never used to be sneaky. They used to be just people. Little people, maybe, but definitely recognizable as the human species. Noel asked me if she could have some earrings, and I said sure. Next thing I know her ears look like pin cushions. Was I supposed to say no?''

"Well, pierced earrings *are* the fashion."

"Is showing her fanny the fashion? Because she tells me it is. How am I supposed to know? Every friend she brings in looks just like her—horrible. I haven't seen her eyes in a year. I think she wears that gunk to bed, and I keep thinking I should be drawing the line. Only where exactly is this famous line? She brings home all A's. Her teachers think she's a peach. I don't see how a kid can develop judgment if you don't give her some leeway, some trust, some freedom. And I do trust her.'' Mick clawed a hand through his hair. ''At least I think I trust her. I know I used to.''

Kat's slim white hand closed on his callused one. The contact was as brief and simple as the empathy she needed to express. ''I know these issues aren't easy, and they're even tougher because you're a single parent, but don't you think it's possible you're handling it all better than you think?''

''If I was handling it all that well, Kat, I doubt they'd have hit on you for sympathy.'' His voice was gruff edged. She'd quickly lifted her hand, yet he could still feel that pampering softness.

''And I've been thinking about that.'' Her eyes reflected honesty. ''I don't think what Angie and Noel did was so unusual, so terrible. Maybe you were a nice adolescent? I was your average total pain, spent half my time groaning about how rough I had it at home. I had it great at home, but it was much more fun to share war stories. Complaining is just something that kids do.''

''Maybe they've had reason to complain—''

''And maybe you're too tough on yourself.''

''I don't think so. We used to be able to talk together. Suddenly I don't know anything and my opinion is worthless—''

She had to smile again. ''Mick, they love you. The worst stuff is all going to pass.''

''Never.'' His tone was spiced with humor. ''I'll never be able to make a business telephone call at night for the next sixty years, because believe me they'll never leave home; they'll never marry. Any guy in his right mind who ever takes one look in the girls' downstairs bathroom and...'' Mick suddenly stiffened. ''And who was this *Johnny* you mentioned?''

Kat started to answer and then checked herself. "Ask Noel."

"In other words, you're not telling?" He murmured, "I'll kill the boy. I take it he's wild?"

"Ask Noel," she repeated with a chuckle.

"I'm asking you. To help me." He didn't know where those words came from, but suddenly they were out. "Not for problems, Kat. I'm not looking for anyone to solve my problems, but there are times I'd really appreciate the chance to talk, get some advice. Some *female* advice."

She shook her head quickly. Too quickly. "I'm the last person you should ask. I not only don't have any kids, but have never been around any. My opinion's worth zip."

"But you're a woman. And they dote on every word you say. They both quote you every time I turn around. You have to be better at some of this stuff than I am."

She looked at him in a way he didn't understand. One minute there was dance in her eyes, a warmth so natural it could make a man's pulse race, and then it was gone. She glanced at the wall clock and sprang off the stool. "Good grief, did you realize how long we've been talking? It's after one. I have to work tomorrow and so do you!"

Even though he was on his feet, she still reached the door before he did. As quickly as she obviously wanted to escape, though, she suddenly hesitated. "Mick, I really think you're asking the wrong person, but if you want some help—at least to a point—you know I'm next door. I can't imagine that you would feel comfortable bra shopping with Angie. There's no reason I couldn't do that, and I'd be glad to."

"Fine," Mick said, although suddenly nothing was. He opened the door, and she said some platitude about being glad they'd talked together. She'd turned back into a stranger. True, in a sense they'd never been more than strangers, but he'd felt something more that night, something special, something real—something that had mattered a great deal to him.

He wanted to tell her that she'd been warmth and brightness on a night that would have been bleakly lonely without her—but he didn't know how to say it.

Because he didn't know any other way to express a thank-you, he leaned down, slowly, closer. She didn't bolt when she felt the graze of his lips. She simply froze like a fawn startled by lightning—which perplexed him. He couldn't possibly threaten her; Mick never threatened women. Kat may have ignited his senses all evening, but he'd already banked any hint of sexuality or excitement because she obviously didn't feel the return pull. A kiss of thank-you was all he intended, all he delivered. His mouth covered hers, so tenderly she couldn't possibly misunderstand, so briefly he had only the promise of the taste of her, and then he lifted his head.

That's all that was supposed to happen. Maybe that's all that would have happened...if her sable-lashed brown eyes hadn't suddenly lifted, if her fingers hadn't clamped hard on his wrists. He read all the "no" messages, but she didn't move. She just kept looking at him until the air charged with a sweet, humming tension. It took him a moment to understand.

Kathryn had so much breezy confidence she could intimidate a man without half trying.

Kat didn't.

Kathryn had control of her emotions down to a science.

Kat—this Kat, with the soft, bleak, fawn-brown eyes—couldn't always.

They were still standing in the open door. Air conditioning blasted them on one side. The night heat blasted them on the other. For a moment that was how it felt to him, as though they were caught between the chill of loneliness and the alluring dark promise of heat.

He crossed the threshold. Cupping her chin, he angled her face more securely. The pulse in her throat caromed at the stroke of his thumb. She tried to shake her head, which struck him as wise. Her skin was far too soft for the caress of his rough callused palm, and it had been so long that he wasn't sure he remembered how to do this.

Silken strands of cinnamon shimmered through his fingers as his head dipped down. He abruptly discovered that no previous memories were going to help him. Kissing Kat would never be like kissing anyone else.

So still. She went so still. He didn't take her mouth, just sipped, tasted, savored. And then covered it as gently as a whisper. There it was again—the sensation that he was strength to her fragility—but the taste and texture and scent of her went to his head. The illogical thought occurred to him that he hadn't missed a woman in all this time. He'd missed Kat.

And her small lips, so immobile, suddenly came to life under his. Her hands unlocked from his wrists and moved, climbing his arms, not like a temptress playing some teasing game but like a woman, so slowly, coming alive. Tongues touched, both dry, and then neither was dry and he drew her to him.

She shuddered, hard, when her small breasts made the first contact with his bare chest. Temptation, dark and desperate, had the feel of her arms locking hard around his neck. Her mouth yielded under his, not in willingness but in yearning.

Mick only knew hunger from a man's point of view. A man could live without fire. He could toughen himself against cold; he could live in darkness if he had to; he could talk himself out of need. He could do all that for a long time. But not forever.

He knew those things as a man, but had never imagined

them from a woman's point of view. Kat's hunger was as
raw, as wild, as scared…as innocence.

He kept telling himself that she was crushably small, to
be careful…careful. Yet his hands chased down her slim
spine to her even slimmer hips. He cupped her closer. He
kissed her until he couldn't breathe. And then he kissed her
again, because he didn't care about breathing.

She'd confused him for so long, and still did. But not
now. He could taste her loneliness like he could taste his
own; he could sense her wariness, her fear, yet her mouth
still moved under his, searching, seeking. Not sex. This
need was far darker, far more dangerous than sex. Sometimes you just had to know there was someone else out
there, even if it was only for a moment, an instant, a crashing brief second of time. You had to believe there could
be someone who understood, someone you could touch.

The rush speeding through him nearly shattered his conscience, yet he felt shock dart through her, her sudden stiff-
ening. She broke free first. Or she tried.

He understood she wanted to pull away, and that was
fine. But not like that. Not like teenagers, embarrassed,
jumping away from each other.

He wrapped his arms tighter around her, just for another
moment until her frantic breathing eased and quieted. He
smelled roses, heard the whisper of a night wind, let his
fingers slide in the silk of her hair. He kissed her forehead.
A kiss of comfort.

"It's all right," he said gently, which was the only way
he knew how to say relax. Neither had intended that dark,
hurling abyss of heat, neither had expected it. He would
never have forced it further, she didn't have to be afraid.
Not of him.

But it wasn't all right, not for her. She bolted back as
soon as he freed her. Her skin was flushed, her mouth trembling. "I didn't—"

"Come on, Red. Take it easy, neither did I."

"I don't know what—"

"Neither do I."

"It was just a mistake. People sometimes make mistakes. But you can trust me, Mick, it won't happen again."

She was gone, pelting barefoot down his back steps and blending into the night shadows before he could respond. He didn't know what he would have said. Her comment had been like an apology. Since he'd sure as heck been guilty of initiating the embrace, it didn't make much sense.

But that didn't surprise him. He had never understood Kat.

He waited until he saw her fly up her porch steps, heard the whack of her screen door close and watched her porch light flick off before returning inside.

Perhaps it was past one in the morning, but any chance he'd had of sleep had just been destroyed. He poured the beer from both full cans down the drain, turned off the lights in the living room and headed upstairs to check on the girls. They were both sleeping. Noel had the radio on, Angie had a ragged stuffed elephant tucked next to her pillow. He turned off the radio, retucked the elephant, and ambled to the third floor upstairs—and the nearest west window.

Her house wasn't identical to his, but most of the old homes in this "French" block of Charleston had been built at the same time. Downstairs, he had a kitchen, utility, dining and living room. The second floor had two bedrooms and a bath. The third floor had a single room, arched under the eaves.

Kat's house was similar in layout; she simply used her rooms differently. Mick slept on the third floor. In her house, Kat slept on the second. Her bedroom light burned for another half hour. Even after she turned it off, he found himself still standing in the window, staring down at the moonlight shining on the lace curtains of her bedroom.

His didn't have lace. He had functional polyester-cotton curtains of some indeterminable bland color. No furnishings in the house showed any fuss. June had never shown an interest in decorating.

His wife, so unlike Kat, had been a woman that a man could be easy with. There had been nothing fragile about June in size or character. She'd been boisterous, earthy, natural. She could swear harder than he could, hammer a nail with equal skill, and—until her illness—their love life had been lusty, physical and frequent. She'd never called him for a flat tire. She'd fixed it herself. And she had borne their daughters alone, because June very honestly hadn't wanted or needed him there.

Mick had never accommodated his life-style for his wife, not because he hadn't been willing, but because June would have been angry if he'd tried. There were men's men. June had been a man's woman, independent and in control and strong.

The two years of slowly debilitating illness had destroyed her spirit. People thought he grieved at her death, which wasn't true. He'd done all his grieving during those two long years. June had hated living through them, and Mick had felt a failure for being unable to help her, to matter to her, to be the someone who could make a difference through the pain. Wasn't that what a husband should be?

Mick had loved her, there was no question of that. But there had always been something missing—not for her, but for him. June had never needed him. As a man, as her husband, as simply another human being, Mick had needed to help her, especially through those last rough months. She'd never given him the chance.

When she died, people had misunderstood his workaholic obsession as grief. Guilt was the real reason he'd buried himself in work. Physical exhaustion was far easier than the nag of wrong memories. June had been perfectly happy until her illness. Lord knew he had every reason to feel the same. He couldn't possibly have married a finer woman. June was good, clear through to the bone.

It was a fault in *him*. He'd been married to a very good woman for fourteen years…and he'd been as lonely as hell.

He turned away from the view of Kat's window. Stripping down to the buff, he dropped onto the muslin sheets and turned out the light.

Kat was not June.

She was nothing like June.

Maybe she had the independence and the pride, but she was also nuts. She wore hundred-year-old clothes and yet flashed through town with that wild red hair. And she came on to a man with need, a need so naked and tangible that it had taken his breath away.

It was still taking his breath away.

Sometime, somewhere, somehow he'd hoped to matter to someone. Maybe he'd stopped believing he could because of June, and Kat…it had to be a mistake to mess with a woman he didn't understand. It would be a worse mistake to risk hurting someone who'd already been hurt.

He didn't, of course, know if Kat had been hurt. The late night, the heat and a too-long period of celibacy could have colored his perception. The lady herself was a distraction. Her perfume. Her small-boned body layered against his, her tiny tight breasts, a pelvis like an erotic cradle, the taste of her.…

You know how much work you have tomorrow? You're not going to get any sleep if you don't hang it up, Larson.

But for the first time in months, maybe years, Mick didn't want to sleep.

Three

"**I** understand you want a bracket. But are you talking scross, quarter circle, gothic...?" Hunching over to cradle the phone between her ear and shoulder, Kat scribbled down the order. When the door opened to her miniscule office, she was still talking.

Georgia, dressed in Victorian garb from her whalebone corset to her bustle, mouthed a single word: "Help."

Kat grinned, severed the phone conversation as quickly as she could and strode through the door of the boutique. At lunch there hadn't been a handful of customers. Now there was a herd of them. Kat's assistant, Georgia, was thirty-nine, a curly-haired brunette with a cultured drawl and a fatal attraction to jam cookies. She looked as if she'd never handled any tougher decision than the day's choice of shoes, but both women knew who really ran the antique boutique. It wasn't Kat. Georgia didn't need a posse, she was the posse, but she also knew Kat needed a break from the blasted telephone.

Two shoppers were porcelain doll collectors. Kat handled them first, then aimed for the three white-haired ladies hovering over the jewelry counter. "Miss Bryant! Last week you had a garnet ring in this case, a stone surrounded by seed pearls. There was an inscription."

"I remember. You'd like to see it again?"

The rosy-cheeked matron wanted to look, not buy, but Kat didn't mind. Throughout the discussion of antique jewelry, her gaze drifted possessively around the store.

The whole place was filled with scents and sights designed to woo and charm the antique buff. Nothing was rigidly displayed. Kat was too smart to organize: customers loved to hunt, loved to feel they'd uncovered "a find." Shelves, open drawers and even the floor had been sneakily planted with "discoveries"——an 1890s harp, a rocking horse, glass-bottomed lamps and stained glass, high-button boots, skeins of lace, sterling spoons and doll houses.

For those customers who failed to succumb to visual stimulus, Kat had done her best to attack their noses. She sold sachets and soap, and the scents of oranges and cinnamon, roses and lemon and chamomile had long since invaded the store. If their noses didn't lead them to a sale, Kat delivered a third and more ruthless assault on the more vulnerable part of a woman's body: her stomach.

Some stores had a pot of coffee for their customers. Kat had a pot of wassail, or of tea. While a customer sank into the wicker cushioned love seats to wile away an hour, she was treated to a meringue kiss, or a jam cookie, or——when Georgia had time——a shamefully delicious bite of Princess cake. Fresh Victorian baked items, naturally, were available for sale at the cash register.

The three white-haired ladies wandered away. Two more customers popped in. Kat could tell at a glance that neither was dying to part with their cash. She loved the shop, everything in it and everything about it, but before her first month in business had been up she'd known that boutique profits were never going to keep her rolling in jellybeans.

Georgia motioned her to grab a cup of tea and scat, and Kat would have aimed back toward some real work if the bell hadn't tinkled yet another time.

Mick strode in faster than a barreling bull, but then he stopped dead with a comical panicked look on his face. Every woman in the store glanced up at him. He wasn't naked, but the feeling of embarrassment must have been similar. Few men walked in there wearing worn jeans, dusty work boots and carrying a hard hat. His T-shirt was a respecable white, but his shoulders were bigger than most of Kat's aisles, and unless he breathed very carefully he was about to knock down a cascade of lace shawls.

Georgia, outstanding at averting disasters, abandoned the cash register and rushed toward him. She stopped, thoughtfully, when she realized the stranger had spotted and recognized Kat.

Mick's eyes fastened on her as if she were water and he were thirst. It was the same look he'd given her three nights ago, just before she'd come to her senses and escaped from an embrace that should never have happened.

There was something dangerous about Mick, and it wasn't that he was about to topple two dozen shawls. The danger in Mick was the boyish save-me grin, the cocky tilt to his shoulders, the steady dark blue in his eyes as he watched her walk toward him. Damn him, she couldn't help chuckling any more than she could stop the aggravating sizzle in her pulse at his nearness.

"Don't breathe, don't blink, don't move," she ordered him.

"Believe me, I won't."

She saved the shawls and flashed him a cheeky grin. "If you'll shrink about five inches and tuck in your elbows, I think we can get you through the store. My office is in back." Her smile faded as she searched his face. "It had to be pretty serious for you to interrupt your workday. What happened?"

"Pardon?"

"You must have come to talk about a problem with Noel or Angie?"

He hesitated. "Yes."

So, she thought, he *hadn't* come about the girls. Mick may build big yachts, but he had a serious problem delivering small lies. He was honest to a fault, a fact she'd discovered three nights ago, which was why, possibly, she'd lost her head at the time. Mick was a good man, the kind of man any woman could justify losing her head over for a few lost, beguiling, heart-stopping moments...unless that woman was Kat.

His gaze dawdled over her hair, swept up with old-fashioned ringlets, her demure high-necked blouse pinned with a cameo, her powdered nose. His lips twitched. "It always intimidated me," he murmured.

"What did?"

"The look of the touch-me-not, eternal virgin. And I don't think you dress for the customers, Red, but because you have a heck of a lot of fun with it."

The way he said "Red"—bourbon warm and lazy—sent a slew of tickles down her spine, which she abruptly straightened. The obvious thing to do was herd Nick into her office, on her turf, where she would have better control of a friendly, innocuous and outstandingly quick conversation.

The plan was good. It just didn't work. Georgia headed for Mick with a handful of meringue cookies. Georgia saw a man, she fed him. And Mick, with the fascination of someone who'd landed on a foreign planet, couldn't seem to walk two feet without pausing to cautiously examine something on the shelves or floor. When he finally stopped dawdling, Ed, Kat's fuzzy-haired "retired" carpenter, hustled in from the back with a shipment he wanted her to check.

"I won't be a minute, Mick."

"I can entertain myself. Don't worry about me."

But she was worried about him. She wanted it settled—why he was here, what he wanted. Unfortunately there was no time. Her cramped boutique had once housed a restaurant, but the back was as big as the warehouse it was. Ceiling fans couldn't budge the South Carolina humidity out here. Sun streamed onto the loading dock; heat shimmered on the yellow-nosed forklift. As fast as Kat handled Ed's problem, the phone rang and then a truck arrived.

She saw Mick wandering around, but she couldn't stop the flow of interruptions to catch up with him. Tendrils of hair started curling damply at her nape—maybe from heat, maybe from nerves—yet the customers kept cornering her, not Ed. If they wanted a Doric pedestal sink, she had it. If they wanted a spandrel or a Chippendale door or a gooseneck faucet, if they wanted to cost out a total renovation or see samples of porch balusters, they all knew Kat was the lady with the sharpest pencil. Ed knew the business, but he couldn't supply a strap-butt iron latch that hadn't been manufactured in this century. Kat would find the antique latch if she had to travel to Boston, and that kind of perseverance had built her reputation. A woman did what she had to do. Maybe antiques were her love, but the sweat and reality of renovation construction was where she made her living.

Every time she craned her head, Mick's sky-blue eyes were fixed on her like a scientist enjoying his research project...or like a man putting the puzzle pieces of a woman together. Kat was short with a customer—she was *never* short with a customer—and then she lost sight of Mick altogether.

By the time the distractions disappeared, she was frazzled, sticky and hot, and she found Mick happily hunkered down over a box of tin ceiling medallions.

He may have been cautious and wary in the crowded domain of her antique store, but her warehouse was obviously another story. She doubted Mick ever played hooky on a workday, yet he showed no inclination to hurry. His gaze was charged with curiosity and interest—a man's interest—and not for the tin ceiling medallions. His eyes never left her face as he slowly straightened. "Is it always this busy?"

There now. They could talk about business. "I wish," she said dryly. "This summer's been the best I've ever had. Everyone's in a hurry to fix up their houses this year, and thank the Lord, history is 'in.'"

"High overhead?"

"Horrible. My grandmother originally staked me in the antiques, but I couldn't make a profit up front to save my life. The only reason I keep them is that I love 'em...and I delude myself into believing that the antique-buying customers are natural leads for the bread-and-butter business back here."

"You're making it?"

"So I've convinced the bank. For the past three years, they've—suspiciously—agreed that I'm a solvent enterprise."

Humor—or empathy—made him smile. "It's a lot for one person to manage."

She shook her head. "Not really. I have help coming out of my ears. There's Georgia up front, and a couple of part-timers. Ed works the back, he'd be here in a hurricane. We hire out the custom work, so there are several outside crews—plumbers, carpenters, construction. Most of the time I have nothing to do but sit in my office and look lazy."

"Kat?"

"Hmmm?"

Mick's cool blue eyes met hers over the rim of a lemonade glass. "You couldn't look lazy if you tried. But could you try to relax? I didn't come here to bite."

She didn't specifically remember him steering her into her office or him pouring the glass of lemonade he was holding. One minute they were outside and she was bubbling about her business, a brilliantly safe subject. The next minute Mick seemed to be installed, and sprawled, in her only spare office chair.

Georgia had obviously unplugged her phone—no one else but her assistant would have had the nerve. It was the first time Georgia had ever overtly tried to interfere in her private life.

Georgia, of course, had no real concept of what her private life was about. Kat did, which was why her pulse was skittering. Her office's air conditioning never functioned well on a day this hot. The room was overly warm, and Mick was close. He smelled like sunshine and wood and a man's warm skin. He smelled...physical. And he hadn't come here to talk about balcony balusters.

"Mick..." She twisted a napkin around the cold lemonade glass and then set it down on her overcrowded desk. Every time she looked at him, she was reminded of a man spilling out his heart because he loved his daughters. Every time she looked at him, she saw a very rare breed of very good man, and dammit, he made her pulse race. That pulse had to settle down because Kat was an old friend with the painfulness of honesty. "If you're here, by any remote chance, because of what happened the other night..."

Mick, the same Mick who'd always shared a matching case of nerves around her, indolently crossed his ankles. "I don't remember anything that happened the other night," he said mildly. "At least nothing that should be making either one of us nervous…or anxious. Do you?"

"No." She repeated cheerfully, "No, not at all. So, you really did come here to talk about the girls?"

He waited a split second, considering her over another swallow of lemonade. Eventually, though, his drawl obediently picked up the topic of Noel. "I met her Johnny two days ago—a meeting I seemed to have handled with the finesse of a Mack truck. Noel has since told me, several times, that she's no longer speaking to me for as long as she lives."

Kat couldn't help a smile, this time a natural one. "Poor Mick."

"During one of the times she 'wasn't talking to me,' we ventured into a dangerous discussion of dating habits in the 1990s." Mick scratched his chin. "Habits she made clear I know absolutely nothing about. People don't date anymore, I gather?"

In spite of his lazy drawl, she felt a prickle of uneasiness. Or was it awareness? "If you're asking me—I'm afraid I'm a long way from being an authority on the subject."

"No? Somehow I'd counted on you to be the one woman I could talk about this with."

"I'm not saying we can't talk about it—"

"Good." He watched her try to unobtrusively fumble with the phone cord and connection. She wanted that phone plugged in like a flyer wanted a functioning parachute—just in case. "Need some help there?"

"No, no." She dropped the cord faster than a hot potato, grabbed her lemonade glass and smiled. "Go on about Noel," she encouraged.

"My problem is complicated. See, when I was entering the dating scene in the '70s, sexual freedom was in." Mick cleared his throat. "Now it's obviously out. Noel has definite plans to be a virgin when she marries. I clearly misjudged her, and probably offended her for life. I thought I was being realistic and understanding. I had no idea women had given up all feelings of sexual desire these days."

The devilish man looked at her with those honest, guile- less blue eyes. She could have swatted him. Three nights before, Mick had made it clear that sex was as comfortable a topic for him as Red Sox scores. She couldn't argue with that. Theoretically, two mature adults should be able to ra- tionally discuss any subject on earth, only there was a level where theory broke down for Kat. There was a level where he was touching some private, murky waters that had noth- ing to do with his daughter, and she kept having the nasty intuition that he knew it.

"My daughter gave me quite a lecture on AIDS. And condoms." Again Mick cleared his throat. "I have to say that I wasn't quite prepared to have a discussion with my fifteen-year-old daughter on current birth control/safe-sex practices."

"Mick—"

"She knows more than I do. I'm a thirty-seven-year-old man. You think that wasn't humiliating?"

Darn him, she had to chuckle. The sound appeared to captivate him because his gaze was riveted to her mouth but only for the space of a heartbeat. When their eyes met, she lost another heartbeat, and then he forged on, gently, slowly.

"I literally haven't dated in years, Kat...which my daughter was quick to point out. How can I make rules for her when I don't have the least idea how to woo, seduce or even talk to a woman on '90s terms? Noel thinks I need coaching."

"Mick—"

"I think I probably need a heck of a lot more than coach- ing. Even years ago, I was never good at romance, never had a polished technique or knew the right words like some men. There was a time I knew how to show a woman I was interested, but any skill gets rusty when it's been locked in storage." He leveled her a cocky grin. "Of course, if a very understanding woman with a hatful of patience was willing to offer me advice…"

Odd, how parched her throat was. "We are, naturally, talking about advice you want for Noel."

Both of Mick's shaggy brows arched. "What else could we possibly have been talking about all this time?" He reached for his hard hat and stood up. "And just having the chance to spill all that out…it helped. More than you know."

She hadn't done a thing to help him with Noel, which he knew—and she knew—and he knew she knew. Shaking off that kind of shambled reasoning, she surged to her feet. "You need to get back to work?"

"Yes, and besides, I've taken enough of your time."

"I'll guide you through the store—"

"No sweat, I'll take the back way out. I confess that when I first walked in the front, I was good and lost and very sure I was going to bungle something."

She saw him smile. She also saw him bend down and turn his head. She had time to duck; it just never occurred to her that he was going to kiss her until it was already done. His lips barely touched hers. His fingers barely grazed her cheek. Her stomach barely had time to drop clear through the floor.

Then he leaned back and reached for the doorknob. "I just thought we'd both be more comfortable knowing the other night was a fluke," he murmured. "There really wasn't anything to be nervous or anxious about. Right, Red?"

"Right."

"Yeah." He grinned, jammed on his hard hat and closed the door behind him.

Kat sank in her office chair and slid her hands through her hair, dislodging pins and ringlets and not caring. That man! Either her imagination was working overtime, or Mick Larson was one of the most upsettingly perceptive men she'd ever met.

He claimed to have been talking about his daughter, but it was Kat who'd felt nervous and anxious about those first night's kisses. Kat who hadn't dated in years. Kat who'd put all sexual feelings in permanent cold storage.

Her office door opened. Kat jerked her head up. It was only Georgia, come to collect the tray of lemonade and glasses. "A hundred and seventy-five in the till—sold the red glass-bottomed lamp. How about that?"

"Terrific," Kat said.

"Quiet as a tomb out there now. I'm going to send Marie home early."

"Fine." Kat waited, certain Georgia was going to say something about Mick. In the five years they'd worked together, both had formed a unique bond of friendship. Most women talked; they didn't.

Respect and caring could sometimes be measured in silence. Kat had long guessed that a man was the painful subject in Georgia's background, but she never asked, just as Georgia had always refrained from advice or comment on Kat's private life—until this afternoon. How long had she and Mick been out in the warehouse? Not long. Georgia must have scrambled faster than a track sprinter to set up the lemonade and disconnect her telephone.

But now Georgia said nothing about the miracle surprise of her having a personal visit from a man. She just smiled and swept up the tray. "Don't ever be afraid I can't hold down the fort if you want to leave early sometime."

"I won't be leaving early, Georgia."

"There now. You sound jumpy. I swear the heat's getting to everybody," her assistant said mildly, and left.

Kat reconnected the phone and spent the next hour shuffling through the pile of receipts and work orders, thinking that Georgia was right. The heat wave was the problem. There hadn't been rain in weeks, just that endless blasted sun and humidity. A person couldn't think in this kind of heat. You couldn't escape it, couldn't ignore it, could never quite get it out of your mind.

He's a good man, Kathryn. A special man. And you like him.

When the pencil broke in her hands, she picked up another. *Yes,* she liked him. He was strong and big and gentle. He had a sense of humor, a natural way about him, and she'd been so wrong about what kind of father he was! Love reeked from him every time he talked about his daughters. He was trying so hard to be a good father. He was human enough to own up to his mistakes.

And he made her pulse quicken like no man, no where, no how, ever had.

The paper in front of her eyes blurred. She gave up trying to concentrate and rubbed her temples hard. The word frigid popped into her mind. A woman could be frigid in different ways. She could fail to feel desire. She could get hung up on inhibitions so a climax was impossible. Or, for whatever reasons, she could just be too afraid to let go.

Only the neat, handy label of frigid didn't work for Kat. Fear of men or sex had never been her problem. She found it shamefully easy to be turned on—with the right man. She wanted and needed to be loved—not just physically but in every way—and she knew her body was capable of a climax.

With a man, that experience simply caused her pain. Real, unignorable, physical pain. And in bed—in a nice darkened room with the lights off and two people on fire with need—pain was one hell of a thing to surprise a man with.

She'd die before ever putting another man through that again.

The phone jangled. She let it ring.

Kat might be celibate, but she wasn't naive. Mick wouldn't have come here if he hadn't been interested…and so was she. Mick had buried himself in work for so long. No matter how much he'd loved June, he had to realize that he was still alive, still a man with needs and emotions that needed sharing. He might as well have said that a woman would need a hatful of patience to take him on, and such honest vulnerability had touched Kat. Mick didn't need anyone's patience. The right woman could easily coax him out of his shell.

Well, that sure as sweet patooties isn't you, Kathryn.

She'd help him with his daughters, but otherwise she simply had no choice but to stay totally out of his way.

At the dot of two on Saturday, Kat locked her door and headed down the steps with her suitcase-size purse in one hand and a list in the other. She had to adjust both to push on a pair of sunglasses. The thin metallic red frames matched the straps on her flat sandals, and her white shirt and shorts were as cool as she could get without going naked. She'd wound her hair into two braids worn at the top of her head, but the sun still beat down at a baking 103 degrees.

Ignoring her own car, she crossed the pavement to Mick's driveway just as Angie slammed the screen door. "Did you remember your dad's car keys, honey?" she called out cheerfully.

"Noel's bringing them."

Kat glanced up from the list in her hand, startled at first by the child's downbeat tone, and second by the moody, miserable look in her eyes. "What's wrong?" An hour before Angie had been on top of the world.

"Everything. This is about to turn into one of the worst days in my entire life."

"Sweetheart, I thought you were looking forward to going shopping together. There's no reason on earth we have to do this if you don't want to."

"I do, I do. But I wanted to go with just you. We can't shop for the you-know-what now. Please, Kat, don't even bring it up. Please!"

"Angie—"

Noel interrupted them when she clattered down the Larson porch steps. She was predictably dressed like fifteen going on thirty-three and that included many layers of mascara. She dangled Mick's car keys in her hand. Because Kat's MG only seated two, Mick had volunteered his T-bird for the girls' shopping expedition. The last Kat knew, both girls had been delighted at the prospect. One look and she could see Noel's exasperated expression matched her sister's. "He's coming. We have to wait for him," she said with the weariness of the long-suffering.

Kat was totally confused. "Who's coming?"

"Dad."

"Since when is your *dad* coming with us?"

"Since he decided a half an hour ago that he felt guilty for copping out." Noel puckered her heavily glossed lips at the reflection of the car window, then sighed. "That's what he thinks. That he's copping out. Because he doesn't know anything about girls clothes and stuff. So he says it's about time he learned, and we don't have to worry because he won't say a word. He'll just trail behind you as quiet as a mouse."

Angie made a sound in her throat like the newly wounded. "Kat, can't you talk to him? I mean, we don't want to hurt his feelings, but couldn't you tell him that he can't come?"

Kat felt the brief sensation of being swallowed in quicksand. She'd have put on makeup and dressed differently if she'd known Mick was coming. Or, more likely, she wouldn't have dressed at all, because there'd have been no outing if she'd known Mick was coming.

He'd been calling her every night—only for advice on his daughters—but those rambling night calls and his low, throaty voice had had a nasty effect on her blood pressure. She'd done a rotten job of cutting those calls short, but that didn't mean she wanted to see him. Avoidance might not be the better part of valor, but it sure felt safer.

Unfortunately that was not necessarily an attitude she wanted to project to his daughters. "I can't quite imagine anyone telling your father not to do something, especially me," she admitted wryly. "Anyway, we're making too much of this. It won't be that bad."

"Oh, it'll be that bad," Noel assured her morosely. "You don't know Dad in a store. He doesn't shop. He *hates* shopping, and the worst part of it is that he thinks he has to do this to help us."

"You know what he said?" Angie moaned. "'Everyone wears underwear. Boys. Girls. Everyone, so what's there to be embarrassed about?' I'm going to die."

The screen door slammed yet a third time. For a brief moment Mick didn't seem to see his daughters. He only had eyes for Kat. It only took seconds for fire to chase down a match stick. Mick's gaze, bluer than the baking-hot sky, took it all in—the braids, the sun burning on her bare legs, the no makeup, the shorts as white as innocence. Unlike Noel, Kat looked thirty-three going on fifteen, but he didn't look at her as if he saw a child. The way he looked at her made Kat feel like a sexy desirable woman. He made her feel…nervous. His slow smile didn't help.

Eventually he pushed on a pair of sunglasses and focused his full attention on his daughters. That quickly, Kat could have sworn the temperature dropped back down to a manageable 103 degrees. The sunshine stopped feeling electrified, and abruptly Mick didn't look any different than any other father about to suffer the tortures of the damned.

Slowly he ambled toward the car. His chin was freshly shaved, and he'd apparently nicked his throat. He was wearing khaki cotton pants, a freshly creased shirt and a propped-on smile. And his whole demeanor reminded her of a man striding for the noose. ''Gee, a whole afternoon of shopping,'' he said heartily. ''Won't we have fun?''

Four

At ten o'clock that night, Kat was in her backyard, lying prostrate in a lounge chair. Her eyes were closed, her zest was zapped, her nerves were shot. She had an arm thrown over her eyes to block the moonlight. A neighbor's cat was stalking through her honeysuckle. She didn't pay attention. It was hotter than Hades, but she didn't care.

She heard the back door open next door. She never budged. Even when she heard the creak of wood caused by an extremely strong man leaning on the fence, she never raised an eyelid.

"I thought it went pretty well, didn't you?"

His voice was very low, very sexy, very virile, and as hopeful as an anxious child's. It took Kat a moment to find the strength to speak. "Get over here, Larson."

She heard the latch on the gate. "I mean, sure, it took me a little time to get into the sizes and styles and whatever. Why does girls' stuff have to be so complicated? But after that—"

"Sit." She pointed one finger downward.

Obediently he sprawled out on the grass near her feet. He hadn't bothered with a shirt, and he sighed—a rich, lazy sigh—when his bare back sank into the cool, night-dewed grass. Masculine contentment reeked from him, even when she leveled him her most severe scowl. "You and I," she said flatly, "are about to have a little talk about the differences between girls and boys."

"Sounds like fun, but it shouldn't take too long. I already know I have a whatchamacallit and you don't."

"This is a more important difference."

"I had no idea there was one," he murmured.

She gathered the last threads of her stamina, and leaned over to pluck enough grass to throw at him. The tiny green spears speckled his chest. He didn't remove them, just grinned.

"Try and pay attention," she told him. "The *real* difference between girls and boys begins at the doors to a shopping mall. *Any* shopping mall."

"Come on, admit it. I did pretty good with the girls. I didn't hold any of you back, did I?"

Kat opened her mouth, but her voice failed her. He'd been awful. There was no other word for it. They hadn't been in the first store twenty minutes before he'd started asking, "Are we about through?"

It wasn't that he hadn't tried, but he shopped like a primitive hunter stalking game. Noel had picked up a sweatshirt with spangles on it. That was it, he was off, scouting out anything in the whole damn store that had spangles, and never mind if it was size two, ten, or forty-four. "How about this, Noel?" he'd asked.

By mistake, he'd walked into a dressing room. By mistake, they'd allowed him in the earring store. He'd stood with his hands on his hips and a terrible frown. "So...we're looking for pink, are we?"

The girls had kept looking at her. Do something with him, Kathryn, their expressions had said. Lord knows she'd tried. She'd managed to take him aside and firmly explain that he was not going with them to the lingerie section, also that he wasn't to make one comment or take *one* look at Angie when they came out. Mick had gravely deferred to her judgment. He hadn't taken one look at his daughter. In fact, he'd nearly mowed down his youngest in a doorway because he was carefully focusing above her head.

The man would still be at the panty-hose counter if Kat hadn't saved him, although on that score she understood. Women had a hard enough time figuring out the variations in hosiery sizes. Mick, though, had taken to the problem like a cancer scientist with a cure in all the data if he could just *see* it. "Look, I know I can get this if you just give me a few more minutes," he'd insisted.

"We're going home now, Dad," Noel had sang out.

"Now," Angie had echoed.

"Just hold on," Mick had said.

Kat had gently, firmly, repressively taken his arm.

Now she had the brief inclination to put her head in her arms. He'd tried so damned hard. He was determined to be a good father, even if it killed him. It nearly had. Killed the three of them.

And she was exhausted. She wasn't cut out to play diplomat/referee between a father and his daughters; she was even less suited to play the feminine authority just because she was female.

Mick wasn't a threat. All afternoon he'd proven that. How could a man who made her laugh that hard, or exasperated her that much, be a threat to her sanity? He was just real. Human. Trying hard to make it through each day just as she was. Odd, how such a little detail like that could turn her heart to mush.

He lurched to a sitting position. The smell of earth and

sea breezes clung to his skin; his shaggy tumble of hair looked as white as the moonlight. When she saw that his eyes looked serious, it did something to her heart, too. "Okay. Tell me straight—did I screw something up by going along?"

She considered telling him the truth—the "truth" that his daughters were hoping she'd tactfully pass on—but then she looked into his eyes again. What exactly did she owe those two little turkeys who'd preyed on her sympathy for weeks? "You did fine," she told him.

"Fine enough that I've earned a reward?"

"What kind of reward?" she asked suspiciously.

"The girls have been telling me for months that you have a horse in your living room. I figured they've been pulling my leg, but I admit they aroused my curiosity."

Mick knew she hadn't wanted to be in his kitchen that first night, she hadn't wanted him in her office, she certainly hadn't wanted him shopping today, and now she wasn't too hot on the idea of being alone in her house with him. But Mick had to wile his way into her living room. Wiling, sneaking and subterfuge went against every grain. Mick had always believed that honesty and respect were the keys to building a relationship—any relationship.

Unfortunately those concepts weren't worth beans with Kat.

"Would you like a very quick lemonade or iced tea?" she asked him.

"Either one would be fine." He hadn't missed that "very quick." If Kat had her way, he wasn't going to be here long.

For the brief moment she was out of sight in the kitchen, he explored, more curious than he wanted to be, less satisfied than he'd hoped.

In a hundred ways, the living room was distinctively Kat's. She'd chosen a color scheme of dramatic dark blue with touches of peach. The walls, couch, chair and rug were all the same elegant navy. Even the lamp in the corner had a base of dark blue glass, but there were delicate splashes of peach—silk flowers, pillows, a museum print over her mantel. All the furniture was antique, expensive, and dauntingly, maybe even defiantly, feminine—except for the carousel figure.

The wooden unicorn was garish and huge. Its mane was gold, its saddle scarlet and emerald. Her living room was too small for extras, and the unicorn was life-size. Only a woman with an uncontrollable romantic streak would have considered it a prize. Mick figured the unicorn was a helpful clue to understanding Kat. Very helpful. It was like being handed a red puzzle piece in an all-blue puzzle.

Why would a warm, empathetic, vibrantly attractive and whimsically romantic woman sleep alone?

"He fits in just like a Democrat at the Republican national convention, doesn't he?"

Mick turned to see Kat coming in with a tray, which held two glasses of iced tea and a small plateful of crackers and dips. When she set it on the coffee table, her white shorts rode high on her thighs and her hair skimmed her back, the color of silk on fire. His throat was suddenly dry. "You didn't have to go to all that trouble."

"Nonsense, it won't take you ten minutes to finish it. I know your daughters; they had to inherit their appetites from somewhere, and the best I can do is hors d'oeuvre a guest to death because I don't really cook." She motioned to her unicorn. "I found him at an estate sale, although he wasn't on the auction list. He was headed for a brush pile, until I took one look and fell in love." Suddenly all polite Southern hospitality, she handed him a cracker generously heaped with dip.

Mick only needed one bite to figure out how she intended to shorten his visit. If Kat expected him to dive for the iced tea, though, she was doomed to disappointment. He could handle hot peppers. Whether he could handle Kat was a different problem entirely. "Delicious," he murmured.

"Just wait until you try the others," she said genially. Regrettably, she was too old to spank. "Do you have family around here?"

She shook her head. "My parents and grandmother live in Louisiana. Shreveport. And I have an older brother, Damon, who migrated to Atlanta about ten years ago. He shows up periodically, usually with his dirty laundry and never with any warning. I regularly threaten to strangle him."

Possibly, but he heard the warmth and love in her voice. "You sound close." He tried her couch, and discovered it was made for women with no back support, and no place for a man's knees. He'd already guessed that she hadn't decorated with the anticipation of any man being around.

"We are close, luckily. Not that I'm prejudiced, but my family's extraordinarily special. Have another one, Mick." All sass and sparkle, she handed him another cracker—with a different dip. The dare in her eyes was as mischievous— or as vulnerable—as a warning.

He took the cracker, primarily to let her know that if she could dish out horseradish, he could take it. This time, though, he had the sense to have the glass of iced tea handy. He needed it. The second dip cleared his sinuses.

Once he stopped breathing steam, he settled back. "So, you have a family you're close to, but no one in Charleston. Yet five years ago, you picked up sticks and moved here lock, stock, and barrel?"

"Your girls," she said firmly, "are probably still up and wondering where you are."

"They know where I am. They sent me here, to see your carousel horse, and so that you'd have a chance to deliver a lecture about how fathers shouldn't embarrass their chil-

dren by shopping with them.'' He smiled when that very
small, very delectable jaw of hers dropped a quarter of an
inch. She even forgot herself and sank on the edge of the
couch next to him. ''Try one.'' He motioned to one of her
lethal dips. ''What was the guy's name in Shreveport?''

''Heavens, did I miss something in this conversation?''

''You haven't missed anything yet, Red, but I'll let you
know if you do. And I'm leaving soon, but not yet. So you
might as well kick off your sandals and at least try and
relax.''

''And here I was waiting for your permission.''

''Lord, you're sassy. How can you take it so lightly?''

''Take what so lightly?''

He shook his head, and his voice lowered to the rasp of
suede. ''You were so exasperated with me in that earring
store that you could hardly talk, then my hand brushed your
shoulder and you forgot how mad you were. You couldn't
stop laughing when I was handling those Easter-egg containers of panty hose, until you were trying to hustle me
out of the store. The minute you grabbed my arm, your
cheeks flushed and you started walking like you'd swallowed a cupful of starch.''

''I was thinking about your girls!''

''So was I. Trying the whole afternoon to do the right
thing for Noel and Angie. Only anytime I'm near you, I
feel like I've been hit with a double whiskey on an empty
stomach. And you—'' he plucked a strand of her hair and
tucked it neatly behind her ear ''—kiss back with a dangerous responsiveness. All these years living next door to
you, Kat, and I doubt either of us knew the attraction was
there. You're worried about it?''

''I…'' She heard her voice, more a whisper than sound.
Nick's fingers had only sifted through her hair for seconds,
yet his warmth lingered and his intense blue eyes rested
gently on her face. It would be smarter to fib, to deny she

felt any attraction, to tactfully suggest he'd misinterpreted her "responsiveness." Only she couldn't lie. Not with him. "Yes, I'm worried," she said softly.

"And so am I. In fact, you couldn't possibly be more wary of starting something than I am, Red." She had a cracker crumb on the corner of her bottom lip. He used his thumb to brush it off, and watched her eyes dilate. "Since we both feel the same way, there's no reason we can't both be totally honest. It's been too long for me, and I'm in no hurry to take on something I'm not sure of. You feel about the same?"

"I...yes." She was terrified he was going to find another crumb.

"I wouldn't know how to woo a woman with roses and moonlight." The collar of her shirt revealed a great deal of her long white throat. He focused where her pulse was beating like a freight train. "And I keep having the feeling that you're not looking for roses and moonlight. At least right now. Is that right?"

"That's absolutely true, Mick, and—"

"The chemistry's special, but any chemistry is disturbing if both people don't feel comfortable with it. But we can both make the honest choice to ignore it, can't we?"

His hand had drifted to her shoulder. Actually not his whole hand. His arm was resting on the back of the couch and just his fingers drifted down, making the lightest fringe-tickle of contact with her shoulder. Lord, the room was warm.

"Kat?"

"We just completely ignore it," she agreed vibrantly. "Good grief, we're grown adults. What's chemistry, any-way?"

"Exactly, and we also live next door. You're important to my daughters. I don't want to do anything to mess that up, which is exactly why I brought all this up. The last thing I want you to feel is awkward or nervous around me, and I thought if we talked frankly—''

Kat nodded in complete understanding. Sort of. The whole conversation should have been a source of enormous relief. Given the choice, she'd have avoided a discussion of attraction like the plague—but that was her problem. It obviously wasn't Mick's, and in his forthright manner he'd both taken the subject out of the closet and put it to bed. He wasn't going to push it. *He's over June more than he realizes,* she thought, but that wasn't the point. Mick wanted a friend for his daughters and maybe a woman around whom he could talk to comfortably and honestly.

She was safe. Any real threat that he wanted intimacy between them had never even existed.

He smiled and stood up. She stood up, too, but her knees suddenly felt as steady as rotten timbers. *Boy, do you feel safe, Kat.*

With a wink and a grin, he held out his hand. ''Friends?''

Friends, her foot. Friends, her behind. In the past two weeks every time Mick had mentioned the word ''friends,'' she'd ended up in trouble. If he said that seven-letter word even one more time, Kat was going to bop him right in the old sheboggan. She was going to bring him to his knees. She was going to level him. She was going to...

''There's nothing else to bring in, Kat. Noel's already down at the beach. I'm going to head there, too.''

''Fine, honey,'' Kat said gaily.

''You sure you don't need me for anything else?''

''Heavens, no.''

Once Angie was gone, Kat plucked ten loaves of bread from the grocery sacks and shot them onto the counter like bullets. Heaven knew why Mick had bought ten loaves of bread...but then, heaven knew what she was doing in his cabin on Hunting Island.

She couldn't see the ocean from the kitchen window, but it was so close she could hear the waves and taste the lick of a tangy salt breeze. Mick's cottage was nestled behind a dune in a woods of palmetto and huge slash pine. Kat had assumed there would be people around because he'd told her the property nearly bordered a huge state park. So far all she'd seen were the lush tropical woods and about five million birds.

Inside, sun poured in through a window and onto the rough log walls and pine-planked floor. The cabin only had four rooms. Two were bedrooms, each lined with double sets of bunk beds. The kitchen opened onto the main living area. The furniture wasn't fancy, just big. The man-size couch was cushioned so thick a woman could fall in and never find her way out, the stone fireplace was big enough to roast an elephant and the storage closet was loaded with sports and fishing gear.

Kat rubbed two hot, damp fingers on her temples. June had so obviously belonged here. She so obviously didn't. Her forte was lace and garnets and the Victorian tea hour.

Taking steaks out of another grocery bag, she mentally damned Mick for fast-talking her into this weekend. He'd given her some confusing speech about his needing help with the girls.

She'd fallen for that line before. Ten days ago, he'd lured her to a picnic at dusk. Another hot afternoon, he'd coaxed her into a riverboat tour of the Charleston Harbor with him and the girls. A few nights ago, he'd shown up at her back door with a bottle of wine, claiming he was desperate for a place to hide out because Noel had bought a new rock tape.

Every time he'd appealed to her as a friend. Every time she'd been suckered in. And every time that unprincipled man had tucked an embrace into the encounter. Nothing too heavy, nothing too hot. It always began with a little touch, a little squeeze, a kiss that started as friendly, and then exploded. Mick always stopped. Just not until she was shaky from the inside out.

If a woman pulled that nonsense, she'd be labeled a tease.

Kat clapped a quart of milk onto the counter. Mick was worse than a tease. Damn him, he was making her a part of his life, a part of his family. And double damn him, Kat knew she couldn't be, but she also knew precisely why she'd let herself be conned into this weekend.

That horrible, wretched, sinfully disgusting man was opening up in front of her eyes. Talking with his daughters like he hadn't talked to his daughters in years. Taking the time to have fun instead of working twenty-four hours a day. And laughing—how could she not want to hear him laugh after all his years of grieving?

Kat heaved the potatoes out of the last sack. She'd helped him. She knew she had. There was no crime in caring for Mick. The crime was in the deception she was playing on herself.

Every time he pulled her into his arms, she conveniently forgot her "little problem." Well? She'd loved her ex-fiancé, but she'd never laughed with him like she did with Mick. She'd wanted Todd, but never with this razor-sharp urgency, this wild, winsome surge of yearning. If Mick took her to bed, couldn't it be different? Wasn't there a chance?

Her heart whispered *try*. Her head delivered a flat *don't be stupid, Kathryn*. If she'd only known one man, she'd known Todd well. They'd not only loved each other, but he'd been kind, considerate, understanding, careful. They hadn't tried once; they'd tried a dozen times. And every scene of intimacy had ended in the humiliation and embarrassment of pain.

"Everything okay?"

"Just fine, Mick," she sang out.

She fed a dozen more pop cans into the refrigerator, straightened up and peered into the last grocery sack. Nothing else to unpack; it was empty. Like her head.

A damp strand of hair tickled her cheek. She pushed at it. She had to get smart. She had to get tough. Helping Mick was one thing, but encouraging a real relationship—an intimate relationship—was another. *It's very easy, Kathryn. The next time he tries to kiss you, think stone. Think icebergs. Think rock.*

"Hey, slowpoke. When are you going to get those clothes off?"

Now there was a loaded question. She swiveled on her heel to face the beach bum in the doorway. The derelict had sandy feet, frayed swimming trunks, far too much bare, bronzed skin and a pretzel in his mouth. She tried to think rock, but her pulse was already racing.

Having some sanity left, though, she propped her hands on her hips and looked the big tease up and down with a schoolmarm's frown. "What happened to the chronic workaholic I used to know from Charleston?"

He fed her half his pretzel and steered her toward the "girls" bedroom. "The same thing that's going to happen to you—exposure to a little sun, a little breeze and a little ocean. As soon as you strip off all those extra clothes."

All those extra clothes consisted of a small green tank top and shorts. From the look in his eyes, she should have chosen to wear her most repressive whalebone corset. But good grief; it was 105 degrees in the shade. She made a point of saying: "Don't get your hopes up, Larson. I tend toward conservative bathing suits."

"What, no string bikini?"

"Nope."

"No suit cut so high you get a sunburn in awkward places?"

"Redheads have to worry about sunburn in all places, and it's okay, you don't have to come in. I've been putting on my own bathing suit for several years now."

"You can," he said in amazement four minutes later, and darn it, he made her laugh. Maybe it wasn't so different than shorts, but she'd dreaded his seeing her in a bathing suit. Bathing suits could be taken as an advertisement for what a woman had to physically offer, and Kat, always honest, had taken care not to advertise for years. No matter how demure her white maillot, though, she felt...displayed. She was just too aware that the promise of bare skin was a promise she couldn't keep.

Mick could have been nice. He could have been sweet and sensitive and perceptively ignored her flushed cheeks. Not him.

"I'll be damned!" He circled her faster than a rabid dog, patted her fanny, plucked at her shoulder strap and then wolf whistled. Maybe his eyes had a hint of dangerous blue, but his clowning teenage-boy act still had her laughing.

"I'll be damned," he repeated. "A female who actually wears a suit she can swim in. I thought the only reason a woman went to the beach was to slather on sun lotion and paint her toenails." He glanced at her toes, and touched his hand to her heart. "Good Lord, no paint. What will Noel say?"

"As soon as I find my backup—your daughters," Kat said. "You're going to be sorry you were ever born."

"Oh, yeah?"

"You think you're so big, Larson? You won't weigh patootties under water. If I were you, I'd start praying."

"I am, I am." Before she could blink, he was loading her arms with terry cloth. "You carry the towels. A man can't be expected to pray and carry towels, too."

She chased him out the door, almost as if...she were having a good time. Almost as if it felt as natural to play with Mick as it did to talk to him, and be with him, and to feel this crazy wild surge of laughter and love filling her up every time she was near him.

If she didn't know better, she might even believe she was falling in love with him.

Luckily she knew better than to let that happen.

Five

Most of Hunting Island was made up of state parkland,
and in the heat of the summer its shoreline was packed.
Few, though, wandered as far as Mick's jagged strip of
white beach. There wasn't a soul in sight, which suited him
just fine.

Sea oats and swamp grasses swayed on the dunes. This
late in the afternoon the tide was sneaking in, one bubbling
wave at a time. Gulls soared over the shallows, checking
out dinner but too lazy to work for it yet. The sky was still
a blinding white, but the sun had lost its baking heat. Mick
raised himself on an elbow to lift his shirt from Kat's shoulders. Earlier, her fragile skin would have burned to a crisp
if he hadn't protected it.

She stirred from his touch but didn't really waken, which
gave him a few more minutes to look his fill. The view
would have aroused a saint. Until she woke up, he could
look all he wanted.

One suit strap had slipped off her shoulder, and she was sprawled on her stomach with one leg tucked up. A ribbon of sand had dried on her nape. After their swim, her hair had been dripping in long wet ropes. Now it was fluffed up, a tangled swath of sun-kissed auburn.

He found a light spray of freckles dusting her collarbone, and another cache at the dip of her bathing suit. Her fanny, which he'd become an expert on in the past hour, was too slim, too small, and had to be the most erotic, enticing, sassy slope of rump he'd ever seen. He considered whether he'd developed a recent prejudice.

He decided, humorously, that he had, but he wasn't going to worry about it. If a man was going to go crazy with worry, Kat provided ample possibilities without dwelling on the trivial.

She could outwork and outcompete any man he knew in business, yet fell for a hopelessly frivolous carousel unicorn. She talked common sense to his daughters, then tore through town daring red lights. She was hardheaded and stubborn and she faced trouble head-on. That first night, she'd tackled him about the girls because she simply didn't know how to walk away from something she thought was wrong. Strong? The lady was a brick.

She was also the most sensual woman he'd ever met, not only in looks and temperament but in touch. She drove him damn near crazy with her responsiveness, but she was scared off at the line of any real intimacy. And the operative word, Mick had finally concluded, was *scared*. Hurt scared, gut scared, blind scared.

He didn't understand why. He didn't understand *her*, and it had taken him several weeks to accept that he didn't have to. No other woman had ever made him feel this tug, this draw, this intimate sense of completeness. No other man was going to lie beside Kat—not in the sand, and not in a bed.

Those things he understood just fine.

She hadn't meant to fall asleep, he knew, and he was the one who deserved the nap. Between his daughters and Kat, he'd been dunked, raced and challenged to any water game where it was possible to pit three against one. Kat didn't like things fair. She liked the odds all on her side. She also liked a full quota of chaperons.

Beside him, she stretched sinuously, like a cat, and her lids opened sleepily. Momentarily she was disoriented, not realizing that his shadow covered her as possessively as his gaze. Momentarily her eyes met his and need, raw and honest, charged between them. Momentarily she told him what he needed to know, that she wanted him—that she cared. And the most potent draw of all: that she needed him.

Not surprising him in the least, she abruptly jerked awake, tore her eyes from his and began a frantic search of the beach. "Where are Noel and Angie?"

Poor baby. He hated to tell her that her chaperons had taken a powder. "There's a camp store in the state park, which is Angie's favorite hangout. Ride a bike up there, and she inevitably runs into a group of kids her own age from the campground. And Noel found some teenagers playing volleyball down the beach. She had her eye on one poor unsuspecting boy with freckles. I doubt we'll see either of them until they're starving."

"When did all that action happen?"

"While you were asleep."

"I wasn't asleep," Kat assured him. "I couldn't have been. I never nap during the day."

"While you weren't sleeping," he said mildly, "I covered you up so you wouldn't burn. Except for your nose." He patted the pink nose in question, almost making her smile, but she was clearly distracted.

"Mick?"

"Hmmm?" He couldn't wait any longer to brush away

the bit of sand on her nape. While he was in the vicinity, he let his fingers thread through her hair. Sand was mixed in with the silky strands. Even so, Rumpelstiltskin had never spun gold like this.

"I believe you told me that the girls had 'outgrown' their love of camping. That they didn't want to come because there was nothing to do here. And the reason I had to come with you this weekend was to help entertain them."

"Did I tell you that?"

"You did."

"Ah, well. I lied." Judiciously he adjusted her bathing suit strap. She didn't seem to realize that she was raised on her elbow, exposing him to a view of one small, shadowed breast. Fixing her strap gave him a chance to look like a gentleman.

"Mick?" Possibly she wasn't fooled. She lifted his hand like a mother who was removing a cookie from a toddler. There was so much patience in her expression that he had to grin.

"Hmmm?"

"I will discuss your lying habits with you shortly. For the present, however, there seems to be a bird about six inches from my face."

"Didn't you wonder why we bought ten loaves of bread for one short weekend? Sit up, very slowly, very quietly. He'll eat right out of your hand if you want him to, but be prepared."

"Prepared for what?"

The minute he reached behind him and handed her a loaf of bread, the first grape-winged gull was joined by a friend. Kat hadn't untwisted the wrapper before a dozen gulls squawked up in the air. North, south, east, west, the message traveled that they had a sucker on the hook, and the flocks soared in.

Kat started chuckling and couldn't stop. "For heaven's sake, help me!"

"You're doing fine." He watched her shredding bits of bread at the speed of sound. The sunlight streamed through her hair, caught on her laughter. She rocked on her heels, a sea nymph surrounded by a hundred strutting, fluttering conventioneers.

"The whole loaf's going to be gone in two seconds—stop that, you thief!" One bold gull went straight for the bread wrapper. Another pushed his sister out of the way, and a third hovered in midair, expecting to catch his treat in flight. "I thought the critters on this island were supposed to be wild."

"You call this manners?"

"I call it wonderful." Her eyes softened to a dark, liquid brown when a bird plucked a tidbit right out of her hand.

"Don't fall too hard for the greedy scavengers. We're talking a love 'em and leave 'em mentality. Once the bread's gone, they won't remember your name."

"That's disgustingly cynical, Mick."

"But dead true."

"I don't care. Aren't they beautiful?"

He thought *she* was beautiful. The nap had refreshed her; he knew damn well she worked too hard. He also knew that she was smart. Smart enough to have found an excuse for the weekend if she didn't want to be here, smart enough to avoid his kisses if she didn't want them. And smart enough to know that he wasn't a man who played, not with a woman's emotions or his own.

They were spiraling, dangerously fast, toward intimacy. She had to know it. She may not know that when they were together, he felt as if he'd never been alive before. Not as a man. He touched Kat and it was all there. What was possible, what he'd missed, everything that could and should be between a man and a woman.

Some guy had burned her. Hell, it didn't take a degree in psychology to figure that out. The pain from that burn kicked in every time he crossed a certain sexual line, and Mick would have worried more about that if not for the obvious. He knew who he was as a lover; he knew what would happen when they made love.

Kat had reason to be nervous, all right, but only because he intended to immerse that wary redhead in more satisfaction than she could handle.

Soon. At the moment he was content to watch the sun, wind and sea work its magic on Kat. The island had always been a source of renewal for him. Its spell was sneaking up on her. He shook his head, watching her cavort down the beach, madly throwing bread crumbs and giggling in the sun. Had he once been positive she wouldn't enjoy the simple pleasures?

Even when the bread was long gone, she didn't want to leave the gulls. He had to swing an arm around her shoulder and murmur sexy sweet nothings about steak, baked potatoes, burned marshmallows. "But we can't start dinner without the girls, Mick."

"Trust me. They'll be here." Back at the cabin, he built a teepee of twigs in the fire pit while she showered. When she came back out, she was wearing a French braid and a short yellow jumpsuit that zipped to her throat. He tampered with the zipper until there was a shadow of cleavage to tease him—she let that happen. When he came out of the shower wearing only cutoffs, she obviously still had her mind on zippers because she leveled a stare at his, making him laugh.

"It's buried pretty deep, Red, but I think you just may have an itsy bitsy bawdy streak buried deep in your closet," he drawled.

She flushed to the roots of her hair. "I don't. You obviously misunderstood."

"No, I didn't. For almost a whole afternoon, you forgot to be careful." His voice softened for her. "I like you natural and easy with me. Don't fight it."

It was obviously the wrong thing to say. She tensed up, emotionally retreated as if she'd done something criminally wrong in flirting with him. They still talked, but every few moments her head swiveled toward the woods. "Are you sure I shouldn't try to find the girls?"

"They'll be here," he repeated. The sky turned from white to a deep sea blue as the sun plummeted in the west. By then, foiled potatoes were baking in the coals. He fiddled with the grill and started forking on the marinated steaks.

Two minutes to formal dining time, Kat's chaperons showed up—with reinforcements. A freckle-faced boy was trying to hide behind Noel. Angie had a scrawny sidekick with a wholesome grin.

Kat immediately relaxed. "So that's why you put on so many steaks," she murmured.

"We may not have done this in a long time, but old patterns are hard to break. My daughters are not shy."

Neither was Kat...with his daughters. The extra company took off after dinner, but his three lingered by the fire. By then, the sun had long set on a whistling-still night, and the coals, spitting hot, glittered orange and yellow in the darkness. Kat squeezed in on a log between Noel and Angie, with a long stick in her hand, and burned her tongue on more scorched marshmallows than either of the other two.

Not surprisingly Mick was suckered into the hot seat between knees—Kat's and Angie's—and given the job of marshmallow distribution. Payment was their most pitifully burned offerings. Contentment seeped through him. Because of his workaholic obsession for the past two years, he could have lost this with his girls—their ability to enjoy each other, to just be together as a family. He'd recognized his mistakes before meeting Kat, but it was her hands-on-hips-furious lecture that first night that had spurred him to action.

Whether she knew it or not, she had an equally powerful effect on his girls. He listened, disarmed to hear the three of them talk nonstop. June had mothered his daughters. Kat questioned, argued and challenged them. She had the authority of an age difference, but she also respected them as equal and interesting human beings. He didn't know that Noel had opinions about the homeless, that Angie had been reading about the environment. He also didn't know a whole lot about differences in makeup, but he got an earful.

In due time they ran out of marshmallows, and yawns slowed down the conversation. It was past ten. Mick started banking the fire.

"Noel and I are going to take our sleeping bags to the beach, okay?" Angie bounded over to throw her arms around his neck. Only from his youngest would he have taken that marshmallow-sticky smack on his cheek. "Thanks, Dad."

"Wait a minute. I don't remember saying yes."

"That's okay, you know you're going to let us. We already know all the rules: no swimming, set up high behind the tide line and scat if anybody else shows up on the beach." Angie grinned, the little devil had known for years he was putty for that grin, and then raced for the cabin and the sleeping bags.

Noel's good-night hug was just as exuberant, but then she pointed a finger at him like a schoolmarm. "Don't worry about Angie, you know I'll watch out for her. You two just behave yourselves, take care of Kat and don't stay up too late."

When the two had hiked out of sight, he scratched a

tickle at the back of his neck and gave Kat a rueful look. "Give it to me straight. Have I lost total control?"

Kat chuckled, but she was instantly aware that they were alone. In the dark. And that her bunking companions had just deserted ship. "I think you're paying the price for raising them to be independent."

"Too independent?"

Her gaze darted away from the too dark, too empty cabin, instantly diverted by the uncertain quality in Mick's voice. The only time she had ever heard Mick less than sure was on the subject of his daughters. "You said it yourself, Mick. How can you possibly raise a child to be too independent?" she asked gently. "How can anyone develop character if they haven't had the freedom to try things, to make mistakes, to test out who they are and what they can do?"

"Yeah, that's the principle." Blocking her view of the cabin, Mick reached down to claim her hand. He pulled her up and close, but only for a moment. "The reality's a little different. Every time I see a boy around Noel, I have this instant urge to check out convent tuition costs."

"She's testing her feminine mettle," Kat agreed wryly. "But at least she's busy trying to charm the entire male population. It's when she singles out one boy that you'll undoubtedly need tranquilizers."

"Did you?"

"Did I what?" They seemed to be walking deep under the swaying tropical palmettos. The night was magical. Fireflies danced in the moonlight-speckled path and it was happening to Kat again. She was supposed to be careful and wary around Mick. She was supposed to remember that she wasn't like other women and that she had no business encouraging a relationship with him.

She was supposed to not feel a heart-singing zing when he loped an arm around her shoulder and teasingly repeated the question he obviously thought she was avoiding. "Did you test your feminine mettle at Noel's age?"

"To the limit. Past the limit," she admitted humorously. Maybe it was the cool sand under her toes, the whisper of a summer breeze, the scent of sea and trees. But the personal doors she found so hard to open with people just wouldn't stay closed, not with him. "I dated the wildest boys in school and broke every curfew my parents set. My poor mother! I know darn well she started going gray when I was in high school, and all for nothing."

He dropped his arm and amused her with his leonine scowl. "Doesn't sound like nothing to me."

She laughed, and spilled out a little more. "I was all show and no go. Never missed a Saturday night at the local lovers' lane, but the most active thing I ever did was direct traffic. Hells bells, I stuffed my bras with tissue all through high school. Do you think I'd have let a boy discover that?"

There was a moment's silence, but his eyes glinted at her in the darkness. "You didn't really do that."

"Direct traffic?"

"Stuff your bra."

"Sure, I did. And you can quit choking on that chuckle, Larson. I didn't do anything that wasn't a time-honored ritual. Puritans used to sew in tucks; Victorian teenagers used to stuff their whalebone with batting and I don't see that the girls in this generation have changed so much. Haven't you noticed that Noel is slightly...lopsided from day-to-day?"

"Are you trying to tell me that my daughter—?"

"Isn't and couldn't naturally be that lumpy." She won a throaty chuckle from him, but was more conscious of his palm sliding down her spine. He was steering her toward the left fork in the path, out of the woods and toward the beach. Once over the dune, sand mounded beneath the arch of her feet and the ocean was suddenly there, big and black and endless.

She loved the ocean, but not at night, not alone. Mick took the space between her and that dark abyss. Kat thought fleetingly that Mick would always do that with the woman he cared for—come between her and all those dark abysses in life.

She mentally pulled herself up short when she realized where the direction of that thought and emotion was taking her. "I told you what I was like as a teenager to be honest with you, Mick. I really am probably the last person to give you responsible, respectable advice about your daughters." She added swiftly, "They have to miss June."

Mick heard her but didn't respond. Kat might want to talk about June, but he didn't. She'd given him another puzzle piece that, like her carousel horse, didn't fit. He could far too zealously picture a redhead who'd teased half the boys in the county in the local lovers' lane...but it wouldn't reconcile with a grown woman who'd chosen celibacy for the past five years.

"Mick?"

She was obviously going to worry the subject until he dealt with it. He sighed. Maybe it was time. "I know the girls miss June." He sucked in a lungful of sea air. "On a rare night, I try to convince myself that I'm doing all right as a father. But that's not to say I ever have illusions I could take their mother's place. It's tough on them both."

"And just as tough on you. I'm sure you miss her. June never made any secret about how happy she was." Kat's smile was gentle. "She must have told me a hundred times how you were the only man on earth she could have lived with."

She'd said the last comment to make him smile, yet the moonlight caught his austere profile, the glint of some unexpected emotion in his eyes. Pain? He said, "I hope and believe she was happy with what we had together."

"You can't doubt that? She never made any secret about it. You two were perfect. The whole neighborhood knew." Kat groped through suddenly troubled waters. She hadn't started the subject to probe, but because Mick talked easily about his daughters. She'd just wanted him to know she was there for him if he wanted to discuss June as well. "Weren't you? Happy?" she whispered.

Mick's voice was flat, quiet, blunt. "We were married. And if she hadn't died, we would still be married."

"Which tells me how you feel about loyalty and fidelity and marriage vows, but that wasn't what I asked you. I asked you if you were happy."

"She was. And I have to believe that, or else fourteen years of my life didn't make much sense. Come here, Red." When she didn't immediately move, he reached out and cupped her nape with his big palm. He hauled her against him until their hips bumped as they walked. "Getting pretty brazen these days, asking me personal questions, acting like you have a right to know."

"I don't have any right to know—"

"Yeah, you do. If you want to know if I've forgotten June, the answer is no. I haven't, won't, and don't expect to forget someone who was a part of my life for that many years."

"Of course not."

"But what you really want to know, what you were pretty sure you were going to hear I think, was that I have yet to get over the loss of my wife. I have good memories of June, Red, but nothing that could ever threaten you. I don't see her when I look at you. I don't want her when I touch you. I'm not lonely for what I had. When I'm with you, I'm damned lonely for what could be." His eyes roamed over her face, slow, real slow, and her heart suddenly kicked in like a rocket booster.

"I—" Kat told herself that Mick had completely misunderstood why she'd brought up his wife. Completely. Only his gaze held hers like a magnet. Damn, but his eyes were blue, even in the darkness, and she was afraid he understood too much. Like how deeply and thoroughly a woman could lie to herself, for example.

"You were starting to say something?"

"I forgot whatever it was," she admitted.

"Good, because that's enough of serious subjects. The night's warm and the stars are out, and five bucks says I can beat you to that piece of driftwood high up on the beach. I'll give you a head start to the count of five."

"Mick—"

"One—you still dawdling, Red? I could have sworn you wouldn't turn down a dare. Two..."

He drawled the word "two," staring down at her from his towering height. Maybe he was in the mood for some crazy, silly race, but Kat was feeling stunned. It had never occurred to her that Mick had been privately, painfully unhappy with June. More than that, Kat understood that she'd run into a door that was permanently closed in Mick. The sign on that door was honor. Mick was not a man who would ever say a negative word about his wife, not in this life.

"Three..."

She never made a conscious decision, but simply acted on instinct. The subject was not one he could talk about and he wanted it dropped. He wanted to play. He needed to play, and Kat's response was automatic.

She ran, kicking sand in her wake.

His blond head streaked by her, then slowed down like the hare in the fable, arrogantly sure of his male-dominant win. She caught his grin and suddenly matched it. Adrenaline started pumping and her legs started aching, and running, just running as wild as hell, felt wonderful.

The surf roared next to them and the stars showered light, and she was panting and laughing as freely as Mick when she reached his fallen driftwood. Being no gentleman he'd beat her there, and he wanted his money.

"Forget that, you turkey. I never shook hands on that bet."

He was huffing as hard as she was but his eyes narrowed dangerously. "Don't tell me you're a welsher."

"I'm not a welsher. I never bet!"

"You ran. You lost. You owe."

"Only a man who won would reason that way."

"So you admit I won!" He slugged his fists on his hips. "You have two pockets in that jumpsuit thing you're wearing. I'll bet you have a little cash tucked in one of them. Like maybe my five."

"I don't. Good grief, you keep this up, I'm going to smell your breath. No, Larson." She backed away from the driftwood, edging closer toward the ocean. He stalked. She retreated. He was grinning, and her heart was suddenly beating, beating, beating. "I'm telling you, I *promise* you, I don't have any money in my pockets."

"You don't seriously think I'd trust the word of a welsher?"

"Behave yourself." The Atlantic at her back was hardly a help. She put a hand in front of her as if she thought it would stop a charging bull.

"I just want to see what's in your pockets."

"Don't you touch me, Mick Larson. You come any closer and you're going to be sorry. You're going to be eating sand. You're going to be—"

She'd turned halfway to run when he pounced, his right hand snaking around her waist and his left hand diving into her pocket. She felt his fingers through terrycloth at the intimate crease in her thigh. She was still choking back laughter when her pulse rate suddenly soared off the chart.

"Damn. Nothing in this one," he said innocently, and spun her around to face him.

"You reprobate. You overgrown adolescent. You—"

His kiss cut off her threats. Either that or she forgot them. Her arms seemed to be dangling in midair, her lungs stranded without a breath of air.

It wasn't like being swept away. It wasn't like the rest of the world blurred when he touched her. The crash of surf roared in her ears. She felt the waves sip at her feet, could feel the sting of sticky salt on her flesh. The whole night was flavored with heat. And Mick. She could hear his soughed breath, feel his leather-rough palms sliding up her bare arms. She could taste Coke and marshmallows on his tongue. She could taste him.

Every time she felt his arms around her, she knew she shouldn't, couldn't, risk this. She had no excuse for coming with him this weekend; she had no excuse for inviting a relationship. She knew what Mick wanted—it had nothing to do with "friends" or helping his daughters—and by responding with honest emotion, she had given him every reason to believe she wanted the same thing.

And there was the rub, because she did want exactly what he did. Nothing had ever felt as good as his big warm hands gliding over her skin. She wanted his tongue; she wanted his hips pushed hard and erotically against her, and she wanted the feel of his rough, coarse hair rippling around her fingers.

Unlike the child who'd been burned once, she just didn't learn. She kept coming back for more. She kept coming back for Mick, because it was so powerfully, wonderfully special with him. It wasn't just hard. It was becoming impossible for her to believe that anything could go wrong if the man was Mick.

Mick had fully intended to steal a few kisses. He'd intended to steal more than a few. He already knew the exact point where Kat would be scared off, and he knew exactly what she did to him when she responded wildly. There was a fragile, explosive line where teasing stopped being fun, where desire could become a tortuous, physical need. A man, a lover, who knew what he was doing could ride that line. He wasn't going to push her. He wanted Kat willing, not wary. Free, not unsure. And there was no question in Mick's mind that he had the control to pull back whenever he had to.

Only he hadn't planned on Kat. Always, her kisses had been winsome and sweet and responsive—even wild. But not desperate. Always, she'd let him know in subtle, physical ways when she wanted him to stop.

He shifted his hands to her narrow hips, rubbing her against him. Hard. Deliberately. Carnally.

Kat didn't pull back. She rubbed back.

They sank to their knees in the sand, neither severing an openmouthed kiss involving tongues, tastes, promises. Their first kisses were electric. These could have short-circuited a power plant. She sent him definite physical messages, none involving a "no."

She was scared, he felt it, yet the fragility and femininity in Kat had all the flavor of hunger and a woman coming alive. Her fingers climbed his arms, slid over his shoulders and coiled in the sparse white hair on his chest. Her lips clung to his.

Mick tried to keep control, only he'd wanted, craved, dreamed Kat would touch him like this. Freely. Honestly. Not just with sexual need, but with need. The emotional soul-deep need of a woman who wanted him for completeness.

She would cut it off now, he was sure.

Only she didn't. Her small white hands slid down to the

waistband of his cutoffs. Her mouth latched onto his, an aching kiss, a yearning kiss.

He rubbed a thigh between hers, announcing he was aroused and hot in a way she couldn't possibly misunderstand. Over the roar of surf, the whispered rustle of trees, she had to hear the whisper of a zipper sneaking down. He flipped the bra latch. Her breasts were white in the moonlight. Tiny. Taut. Perfect. His tongue worked the nipples into little stones. She arched for those soft, slow, wet licks.

"Call it off, love." He knew his voice sounded rough, even harsh. "Honey, do it now. Because if you don't do it now—"

She slicked her hands through his hair and reached for a kiss.

"Dammit, Red—"

He kissed her mouth. He kissed her throat. He unzipped her jumpsuit the rest of the way, telling himself that it might have gotten beyond Kat, but he was stronger than that. There was no way he was going to make love to her for the first time on a public beach with sand digging in uncomfortable places and the ocean screaming in the background.

Carefully, shyly, tentatively, her fingers slid down to the bulging hardness in his jeans.

He suddenly didn't give a hoot in hell where they made love.

"Please, Mick…"

Her whisper was a call of need, sweet, low, desperate. He still had control, he promised himself.

"Please…"

He lost it. He totally and completely lost it. She was silky bare before he ended the next kiss. Lord! Her skin against the sand, her eyes against the moonlight and the warmth of her….

He shucked his cutoffs. The way she looked at him, he'd

have shucked his soul if she'd asked him. Willing was just a word. Kat needed him.

He framed her thighs around him. His weight and hardness caressed her softness. She could have been scared off then. She could have changed her mind. Her lashes lifted, her arms swept around his neck and she whispered, "Hurry. Now, Mick. Nothing's ever felt this right, not like this. With you. Please."

He had to take her. He had to, he wanted to, he was positive he would have died if he didn't. The surf roared in the distance, the sand gave for his weight on her weight. He tasted love, as he'd only dreamed of it. He tasted the allure of a woman wanting him, as only Kat had ever wanted him. He tasted need, denied him forever, and it tasted like her mouth, her skin, her fragrance. She was ready.

And at the first probe into her intimate nest, she cried.

He'd hoped, dreamed, anticipated that she would make a sound just like that.

Only her cry was supposed to be of pleasure.

Not pain.

Six

Kat's eyes were closed, acting as a shutter to the tears that were backed up clear to her throat. It wasn't as if she was going to die. It wasn't as if she couldn't handle it. Pain was just...pain.

She wanted Mick inside her. Moments before she'd wanted him inside her like a clawing in her body, mind and soul. That hadn't changed. It was just...pain had a way of dousing even the most powerful sexual desire with a bucket of water. Every muscle in her body had locked and she burned like fire. There. At the precise spot where her sheath and his fullness created the most intimate bond a man and woman could have. Unfortunately it was a heck of a vulnerable spot to have to deal with pain.

And then she didn't have to deal with it. She heard Mick take one hard, shuddering breath. He withdrew. At least that part of his body withdrew. He rolled on his back with one arm coiled around her and clamped her cheek to his chest, not too gently. His heart was beating like a rocky, revved-up engine. She tried to lift her head. He hauled her closer.

"Maybe it'll be easier if we do this together. Breathe out, breathe in, real slow, real long breaths. Blank your mind of anything except the Red Sox's last loss. Hell, Red. If you think the Dodgers would work better, we'll try them." There was humor in his voice, but there was also grit, like he was doing his best to chew sand. His lips ironed her forehead, as hard as a stamped-on label. Again she tried to lift her head. Again, his arms clamped around her. "If you want to haul off and hit me, go ahead," he murmured gruffly.

"Hit you?"

"The sand, for God's sake. And out in the open. And coming at you like some rutting animal. I never lost my head like that when I was a teenager and my whole life was hormones. You do go to my head, Kat—not that that's any excuse for what I did." He heaved one last breath of control, and he almost managed gentleness when he cocked her chin. Blue, blue eyes pinned hers. "That's no excuse for what you did, either."

"Lord, I know…Mick, it was all my fault—"

"For not letting me know I was hurting you? You bet it was. Just when were you going to get around to mentioning you were in trouble?" Her lips moved, but they weren't producing any sound. They didn't have to. The look in her eyes said it all. "You weren't going to tell me, is that it? You were just going to let me go on?"

Guilt slammed at him. He shouldn't have raised his voice. Her lower lip started trembling and her face blanched. "I…didn't expect you to stop. I didn't think you could and I wouldn't have asked you to. Not…by then. And I thought I could handle it without your knowing."

Mick didn't need to hear anymore. His voice lowered to

a murmur in the wind. "What the sam hill kind of lovers have you been to bed with, Red?" He threaded his fingers through her hair. At the tip of one strand was a tiny, tangled rubber band, all that was left of her French braid. "If you didn't know it before, know it now, a man can always stop. Sure, that can get a little touch and go on the timing." Later he would give himself enormous credit for that understatement. "But when one of us has a problem, we both have the problem. Got that? Anytime something isn't right, you say so. And so I know you've got that clear, say 'yes, Mick.'" The order was in his eyes.

"Yes, Mick."

But she wasn't off the hook yet. His gaze, worried, possessive, swept over her face. "I know I hurt you, so don't go all flustered and Victorian on me now. Are you okay? Could I have torn something? Are you still hurting?"

"I'm fine." She could feel the heat of color streaking up her cheeks. Unlike any other man she'd known, Mick naturally discussed feminine intimacies. She didn't. "I'm probably more fine than you are."

"Yeah?" He glanced down his moonlit body. "Don't worry about it. That'll cure real quick after a lap or two across the Atlantic. Besides, now we know for sure."

"For sure?"

"That you can't die from frustration," he said dryly. When she reached for her jumpsuit, he stole it away from her, stood up and then reached for her hands.

She didn't say anything when he pulled her underpants on backwards. She didn't say anything when he threaded her legs in the jumpsuit, pulled it up and started zipping. He didn't dress her like he would dress a child. Naked, the sea breeze rippling through his blond head, he dressed her with the total concentration of a lover. His palms lingered on her hips. He pulled the zipper up its track, but not before his kisses had made a preliminary run up the same track.

He stuffed her bra in her pocket. He didn't like the bra. He liked the mounds of her breasts through terrycloth, and he brushed his thumbs over the tips through the material. When those tips hardened like buttons, he hardened like a rock.

He told her in a hundred ways that nothing had changed. He wanted her. She wanted him. One tiny setback hadn't turned him off, but magnified the feelings that were growing for her. He cared.

So much that she suddenly slid her arms around his waist and hung on. "Mick." Tears stung her eyes. "You weren't listening before but you have to listen now. It really wasn't your fault. At all. It was totally mine."

"I see. You're responsible for my showing the finesse of a Mack truck?"

"That's not the problem." She whispered hopelessly, "I'm frigid."

"Honey, it's tricky to hear you when you're talking to my chest."

She couldn't help that. On a subject this mortifying and painful, she couldn't face eye-to-eye contact. "*Frigid.* At least I don't know what else to call it, but—"

She heard a rumbling in his chest like the beginnings of an earthquake. Startled, she lifted her head. He didn't even try to choke back a chuckle, and for the first time in an hour his eyes were crinkled with devilish humor. "Trust me. One thing you are not and could never be—not in this life, Red—is frigid."

He thought it was funny. Not a little funny. He thought it was real funny that she could even imagine herself frigid. Kat winged her MG down Calhoun, ran a yellow and let out the clutch.

Almost everyone who knew her thought she was a throwback to the Victorian era. She'd never asked a man out, never even called one except for business. She knew she was affectionate and warm with those she loved, but it was a heck of a jolt to her self-image to think Mick saw her as, well, hot. So hot that the idea of her being frigid struck Mick as belly-laughing funny.

She glanced at the rearview mirror. *He didn't get that impression out of a magician's hat, Kathryn Bryant. You've behaved completely different around Mick than you have with any other man.*

She knew that, which was why she had done an exceptional job of avoiding him for the past three days. Impatiently she shifted into third. The entire traffic in Charleston was driving slow this early August lunch hour. It had to be five million degrees and the humidity was worse. Anywhere skin touched skin, it stuck. Anything that could itch, itched.

Two pieces of paper fluttered on the leather seat next to her. One had been tacked to her back door, the other to her front door that morning. The notes held identical information—dinner tonight, five o'clock, wear boat shoes.

She could have ignored one note. Two was tougher. Larson was on to her. Like the coward that she was, she'd been hiding out for three days, not answering the phone, finding excuses to stay away from home and see to renovation projects away from the shop. Teenage girls acted with more maturity, Kat knew, but that hadn't stopped her from plotting all morning on how she could get out of this dinner.

You're real hot, all right, Bryant. Until it comes down to the crunch. Dammit, how could you have done that to him when you know how you are?

She swung into the alley behind the warehouse, killed the engine and grabbed her keys. Clouds hovered in the west, dark and promising. The heat wave hadn't broken in a month. The whole city was praying for rain, and the heaviness and gloom in the air had to be responsible for her mood. She was not just medium low, she felt on a level with a pit.

If it hadn't worked with Mick, it was never going to work. If you loved a man, if you had trust and empathy and respect heaped way up high on top of the passion and it still wasn't right, it was never going to be right.

She knew how she could get out of dinner tonight. She could simply sneak back home and retack his notes on the doors as if she'd never seen them. There were a hundred places she could hide out past five tonight, her office was an obvious choice. Heaven knew she had plenty of work.

Come on, Kat. You live next door to him. You're going to have to face him sometime.

She knew that. She just wanted that sometime to be later. A lot later. 1995, 1996. Not yet. No lectures on maturity or cowardice, okay, God? I'm being as honest as I know how. I can't handle this.

The bell jangled when she strode in. Georgia glanced up from the cash register. "Have a good lunch?"

"Fine. I'll guard the bank. You take a long one. It's too hot to do anything quick today."

"I had my lunch." Georgia lifted one of those dreadful protein diet drinks from under the counter, making Kat grimace. "And in the meantime, you had a phone call. Mick. He wanted to remind you that he was picking you up at five tonight."

Kat briefly considered picking up the priceless lace shawl on the counter and shredding it.

"And don't worry, Kathryn. He sounded concerned that you might get held up late here. I told him for sure you'd be free."

"Thanks so much." She couldn't wring Georgia's neck. She was too good a friend. Still, there was such a somnolent blandness in Georgia's expression that Kat was briefly tempted to offer her a rich, gooey cream puff. "Anything else happen? Tornado, phone call from the IRS? A robbery?''

"Nothing quite that disastrous—''

"Amazing,'' Kat murmured balefully.

"But you do happen to have a couple of visitors waiting for you in your office.''

"Visitors?''

Mutt and Jeff were feasting on tall glasses of lemonade and raspberry tarts. The little blond with the crimped hair was swinging her legs from the corner of the desk, and the mousse-spiked brunette—dressed in red and white!—had taken over her office chair. "Don't you look terrific!'' Kat complimented Noel and gave Angie a quick hug. "But what on earth brings you two downtown, and how'd you even get here?''

Both of them started talking at once.

"We pooled our money on a taxi,'' Angie admitted.

"We've wanted to see your store for forever, Kat, but even more than that we wanted to talk to you.''

"We needed to talk to you,'' Angie corrected her sister. "This is important, and we couldn't talk anywhere where Dad could be around.''

"Sounds serious,'' Kat said gently. It sounded worse than serious, but she'd already had one of the worst weeks of her life. Fate couldn't possibly be so unkind as to give her another kick in the teeth. "Now listen, you two. If this is girl stuff, that's one thing, but if we're talking about something your father should know—''

"We're not in trouble, Kat. We're not even here to talk about us,'' Noel jumped in. "We're here to talk about you. That it's okay with us.'' At Kat's blank look she waved her hands. "You know. You and Dad. It's okay.''

Kat sank into the nearest, and only, spare chair. She just had the definite feeling Fate was going to give her that other kick.

"I wasn't that sure at first," Angie admitted. "I mean, like, you know, we're friends with you now. So why risk messing that up by you being a stepmother? And I worried about being loyal to Mom. Only like Noel says, Mom thought you were terrific, and it's not like Snow White and Cinderella. I mean, you're not going to change into a total different person if you become a stepmother, are you?"

Kat didn't have time to respond before Noel earnestly leaned forward. "And Dad's been completely different since you've been around. He's got a smile on. He isn't so dead serious. It's like he's Dad again, you know?"

"He's talking and yelling and being with us again," Angie affirmed.

Kat tried to interrupt, but again didn't have the chance.

"And we know why." Noel flipped back a curl. "We're not blind; we can both see what's been going on. And we just want you to know that you don't have to worry about us, we're here to help you. We're on your side. Dad's, too, but see…" She shared glances with her sister. "We're not all that sure Dad knows what he's doing."

Angie, too naive to have guile, said, "We're not all that sure you do, either. Maybe you think I'm only a kid, but I've picked up plenty of pointers from TV."

"You don't do half as much with makeup as you could, Kat," Noel said gently.

"And Dad doesn't know what he's supposed to do, like dancing and flowers and stuff. Noel says you're probably going to have to give him a push."

"It's been a long time for him," Noel said meaningfully.

"Whoa."

"We figured we could give you a few ideas, help you arrange some things. I could cook, Angie found some candles."

"Whoa," Kat repeated. She took a long look at the two hopeful, enthusiastic faces and did her best to recover from a galloping heart attack. If she had the time, she'd have raced for the library to devour a book on the raising of precocious teenage girls. Unfortunately there was no time. "First, ladies. You two are coming—totally—from left field. I'm friends with you, and, I hope, friends with your father."

"Yes, Kat."

"Yes, Kat."

"Second. I have had absolutely nothing to do with any change you see in your father. *Nothing.*"

"Yes, Kat."

"Yes, Kat." But the sisters shared a look.

"Third. I may love you two to beat the band, but that doesn't mean certain subjects aren't off-limits, even between friends. What goes on between a man and a woman is between the man and the woman. That goes for me, that goes for your father, that goes for whoever your father is involved with, now, tomorrow, or ten years from now. You do not interfere in what's none of your business. *Capisci?*"

"Yes, Kat."

"Yes, Kat."

"Fourth…" She shook her head in frustration. "You two have totally misread the situation. I'm not marrying your father. I am not going to be your stepmother. Your dad and I enjoy being together as neighbors and casual friends. That's it. Are we clear?"

"Yes, Kat."

"Yes, Kat."

The girls got a tour of the shop, handfuls of meringue cookies, a chance to try on Victorian straw hats with streaming ribbons and to play with the miniatures in the dollhouse. Eventually Kat called and paid for their taxi home. She'd thought she'd done quite well, until Noel patted her hand on the way out.

"If Dad doesn't come home tonight, I'll make Angie

breakfast," she whispered. "Don't you worry about a thing. I'm old enough to understand."

Georgia found her in the office a half hour later, pulling out the hairpins that held up her pompadour and throwing them at the wall like darts. Georgia extended her palm to reveal two pellets of aspirin. Her other hand held a glass of ice water.

Kat slugged down both aspirin. "That's it," she said, and then gulped down three-quarters of the ice water. "I'm going to move. Skip town. I can't handle them and I can't handle him, and that's that."

"You want some advice?"

"Good grief, no. Advice won't help me. A case of flu before five o'clock tonight, now *that* would help me." She automatically scooped up the girls' plates and the lemonade pitcher.

"Kat, I hate to be the one to tell you this—"

"Then don't, please. Nothing good ever follows 'I hate to be the one to tell you this.'"

"But if you don't want to go out this evening, you don't need a case of flu as an excuse. You have an out. You always did. A simple, honest one."

"Heavens, what?"

"You say no," Georgia drawled. "And since you haven't exercised that option all morning, and apparently aren't going to this afternoon, you must, very much, want to be with him."

"Look, Georgia, if you can't offer anything better than insane, irrational and convoluted reasoning, I would appreciate it if you'd get back to work."

Georgia thought that was very funny, but Kat sank in her desk chair once her office was finally empty. Without ever asking a question, Georgia had managed a perceptive grasp of the situation, but not perceptive enough.

Kat hadn't canceled the five o'clock with Mick tonight

because she intended to keep the date, and had known that all day. Face-to-face was the only way she could straighten out the mess she had so selfishly made.

She had told Mick that she was frigid, but she hadn't told him what mattered: that the relationship was hopeless. That she was hopeless, as a woman, mate and lover.

She took the last hairpin from her pompadour and threw it at the wall. After Todd, she'd hurt. But not like this. Todd didn't have two arrogant, pushy daughters who Kat loved like the dickens. And Todd hadn't been Mick.

Whom she loved from the soul.

If she didn't hurt so much, so hard, so fiercely, she would undoubtedly cry. How could she have been so stupid as to let Mick come to mean the whole world to her?

Mick hadn't bought rubbers since he was a teenager. Then, the little packets had been hidden from sight under the pharmacist's counter. The pharmacist was always busy, so to get them you had to face a woman—it was *always* a woman—and she *always* repeated the whispered request to the entire store in a voice louder than a tuba.

He could still remember feeling like an immoral slink, still remember the taste of guilt. Mentally he thanked God that he was an adult and times had changed.

Holding a tube of toothpaste in one hand and a bottle of mouthwash in the other, he was standing near the paper towels. The household was out of paper towels, so he had every reason to be here. It was just accidental that he was tall enough to see over the display into the condom aisle.

Times had definitely changed.

Good Lord, there were millions of them! All he remembered was two different brands. Those companies still existed but they'd expanded their repertoire so to speak. You could buy them by the packet, by the box, by the stack. You could buy them lubricated, nonlubricated, ribbed or rippled. You could buy them scented, and you could buy them colored. You could also mix and match.

He kept looking. He couldn't see a plain old basic model to save his life, and he sure as hell couldn't picture himself rolling on a fluorescent-yellow prophylactic that smelled like bananas.

"Why, Mick Larson! I see your girls all the time, but hardly ever run into you."

Faster than a thief, he clutched a double roll of paper towels before turning to face his neighbor. The last time he'd seen Mrs. Pincher, she'd been herding his two girls along with her three into a station wagon for a school play. Then, she'd had a frizzy head of brown hair turning gray, worn eyes and a maternal smile. She hadn't changed. There was no escaping her kindly meant chitchat, and she didn't begin to wear down until she'd commented on the heat spell, Harv's newest promotion and how fast all the girls were growing up. "So you're stuck shopping?"

"We were completely out of paper towels."

She tch-tched, glancing at the roll in his hands. "Those cost $1.39. Didn't you see the ones on sale up there?"

Mick obediently looked. "No, thanks a lot."

"No problem. Now don't be making yourself such a stranger, hear? One of these nights, you come over and have a beer with Harv."

"I'll do that," he promised her. She smiled and left him. Mick would have completely forgotten her if her squeaky cart hadn't turned down the condom aisle. His eyes narrowed. Ambling casually, as blithe as you please, she plucked a box off the shelf and rolled off with her cart.

So that was how it was done now. The men copped out and sent the women.

And they said women were smarter than men.

You're mentally dawdling, Larson. Move your buns. Juggling towels, mouthwash, and toothpaste, he made a U-turn into the aisle with the limitless display. The embarrassment dragging at him was abruptly shelved. His choice was, after all, a serious business, and one that affected Kat.

He hadn't had protection on the island. He hadn't expected to need it—not with the girls along, not until Kat felt more sure of the relationship—but he'd known the issue was coming. He hadn't asked if she was on the pill. There was no need to. She hadn't been involved, therefore, she wasn't likely to be prepared. That left the responsibility for birth control on him, assuming he wanted to protect her. Which he did. And assuming they were going to be sexually involved.

Which they were.

But not like the last time.

At the checkout counter, he laid down his purchases and fished for his wallet. He frowned vaguely at the checkout boy, his mind now totally focused on Kat and the evening ahead.

All week she'd done a good job of avoiding him. He understood: she'd been upset that night on the beach. So had he. There was nothing strictly wrong with a deserted beach bathed in moonlight as a romantic setting, but rough sand was not ideal for the first time. Not with Kat.

He was amazed that she'd had him fooled all these years. The flashy sports car, the flaunty walk, the hint of just a little female arrogance when she lifted one beautifully arched brow a certain way. Kat was her own woman, and she shouted it with every aspect of her life-style. Mick respected the gutsy streak, but it was the shy, vulnerable, fragile heart that he'd fallen in love with.

She had some definite inhibitions and a foolish Victorian modesty about discussing sex. Mick liked both qualities, because they showed she didn't take intimacy casually. The guy who'd hurt her was undoubtedly part of that. What mattered, though, was that long before the weekend on the island, Mick had known certain elements were critical to their first time making love. Guaranteed privacy. A comfortable setting without distractions. And a man who kept total control, not lost it.

He'd blown all three.

To a point he'd had to forgive himself. It took two to tango, and Kat took a tango with him to limits that endangered a man's central nervous system. Mick couldn't help that.

But he thought he'd known himself as a lover. He had never once doubted that once he had her beneath him, it would be good. He wasn't unselfish in bed and he knew a woman's body. A man couldn't be married fourteen years without being well aware of the uniqueness of the feminine species. A woman, for example, could change moods and become distracted faster than the flip of a dime. A man wooed her back, if he knew what he was doing.

June used to have the embarrassingly annoying habit of telling the whole neighborhood that he knew what he was doing.

He hadn't known what he was doing with Kat. Sand or no sand, he hadn't sensed her change of mood. Surf or no surf, he'd been positive she'd been as wild and willing to make love as he'd been. Her hands had helped shuck his jeans. Her eyes had the fire of impatience. His name had been on her lips, calling, whispering, demanding. Right up until the precise moment he'd slid inside her.

Dammit, what had he done wrong?

And double dammit, a lover worth his salt should know what had gone wrong, and made sure it never happened in the first place.

A blast of heat hit him the moment he strode out of the drugstore. The inside of his truck was like an oven. He threw his packages on the seat and climbed in. Clouds drifting in from the west weren't coming in fast enough. The whole city was praying for a storm to break this merciless heat wave.

Mick felt a similar frustration. Flipping the key, he cranked on his truck engine. Kat was past getting under his skin; she was tucked under his heart. With her and only with her, he'd tasted the promise of a woman who needed him. At a certain level Mick had always lived with loneliness. Kat had made the mistake of showing him it didn't have to be that way.

Tonight. It was the only word in his head. He guessed Kat was already building a mountain of nerves about the evening ahead. She had reason to be nervous.

But not for the reasons she thought.

Seven

Kat heard the rap on the door at ten minutes to five, and took one last quick look in the mirror. Since "boat shoes" had been in the invitation, she'd built an outfit around casual. Real casual. Her white cotton jeans were baggy, her navy tunic voluminous, and her oldest white tennies had floppy laces. She'd braided her hair with a red scarf and scrubbed her face—no makeup. No makeup, no scent, no jewelry.

It wasn't that she wanted to look unattractive, but she knew what she was facing tonight. Cross purposes summed it up. She had to tell him she was hopeless as a lover and make him believe it. Mick clearly hadn't been scared off after the night on the beach. Kat was terribly afraid he had something in mind along the lines of wine, music and a candlelight dinner. Her dreadful appearance had to help deter that kind of mood, and her mirror image promised her that a sex-starved hermit wouldn't look at her twice.

As satisfied as she could be, she tripped down the stairs and pulled open the front door just as Mick was about to rap a second time. Right off, something tilted in her preconceptions of the evening.

Mick wasn't exactly dressed like Mr. Seducer. He was wearing worn jeans and a short-sleeved ragged sweatshirt that flattened against his chest in the wind. His blond head was rumpled and he'd shaved, but not since morning. He took one look at her and wolf whistled. "Don't you look sexy." She didn't have to worry about Mick. He was clearly out of his mind. "Thank heavens you didn't go fancy on me, Red." He dropped a kiss on her mouth that jammed all the air in her lungs, then lifted his head and grinned. "But no more of that. This is a working dinner, and we don't have any time for dawdling."

She could see that. Mr. Chivalrous bounded down the steps ahead of her and headed for—not his sleek, quiet T-bird—but his dusty pickup. He called "Hop in!" in lieu of opening her door, and it was a good thing she was fast, because they were on the road before she'd had the chance to click her seat-belt buckle.

Kat thought fleetingly that if Mick was in a mood to seduce her, she'd eat crickets. How could she not start to relax? "What is this about a working dinner?" she demanded.

"Not all work, just some. We're going to a christening. The baby's a thirty-two footer, just a small-keeled yacht, more for pleasure than racing, but she's beautiful. I put her in the water this afternoon for the first time, but she hasn't been out yet. Her owner's in Maine; he's hoping to hear by tomorrow how she did on this trial run. You and I are about to find out, but I'm afraid I have to make a quick detour to the shop first."

"Shop?" she echoed. "You mean where you build your boats?"

"You don't mind, do you? It'll only take two seconds."

It took more than an hour, during which Kat was both deserted and ignored. Another woman might have felt miffed. Kat was delighted. The tense, traumatic evening she'd envisioned was fast going down the tubes. Yes, sooner or later, she had to talk to him, but it wasn't Mick's fault that he momentarily had his hands full. And it wasn't her fault that she was insatiably curious. What better way to understand a man than through his work?

Hands stuffed into her pockets, Kat poked and prodded, ambled and explored.

His "shop" was really three buildings, all white framed and as big as barns. One building stored wood. In the second, three men and Mick surrounded a huge, half-built boat; they were talking "bulkheads" and something about a "planking process." Although Mick called her over, Kat could immediately see that she was in the way.

She wanted to be in no one's way, and wandered through the third building alone and happily. This was Mick's world. Her nose crinkled because of the unfamiliar smells of acetone, lacquer thinner and varnish, even though two giant exhaust fans constantly moved air through the long, bare center of the room. She recognized power tools like a bench grinder and circular saw. Others were not familiar to her. The whole space under the rafters held templates and one long set of wall brackets provided storage for mast making. She would have known neither if they hadn't been labeled.

The labels didn't mean a thing to her, anyway. Kat couldn't pretend to know beans about boat building, but she knew what it took to run a small, independent business. Everywhere she looked she saw organization, order and control. She understood the long hours it had taken Mick to build this, and in all three buildings she could almost taste the love—the intense, unspoken, private love of a man for his work.

Mick found her just outside, perfectly content exploring his work yard. "That wasn't supposed to take so long." He was obviously upset that it had. He strode toward her with an exasperated frown and a dirt spot on his chin. "We're getting out of here."

"Are you sure you're done? You don't have to worry about me; I'm having a great time."

"I'm sure we're leaving, if we tiptoe out of here before Josh finds me to tell me another problem. When we turn the corner on the building, you race like hell for the truck and don't look back even if someone yells 'fire.'"

She chuckled. "Which one was Josh?"

"The one with the silly looking beard and lovesick eyes who looked you over good and hard when you walked in." Mick helped her into the truck. "As did the other boys." Once installed on his side, he had to lift up to dig the truck key out of his pocket. The movement tightened his jeans over the masculine bulge under the zipper. The grin he shot her was just as male. "You're lucky you snuck out of there when you did. If you had stayed any longer, the boys would've undoubtedly treated you to a five, six-hour discussion on how boats are built—or anything else they could have thought up to keep your attention."

"Everything I saw had my attention. How many boats do you build in a year? What kinds? And I take it you construct them all right inside those buildings?"

"Slow down there, Red. One question at a time."

He didn't drive toward the Charleston Harbor but toward the Ashley River, and he took Broad Street as if he knew she loved the look of the old elegant homes. Kat did, but her attention never strayed from Mick tonight.

A hot breeze vacuumed through the truck, ruffling his hair. Sunshine tipped in, accenting the lifelines and the hard, masculine planes of his face, but his voice was as shy and excited as a boy's. It was the shyness that touched Kat's heart. How long had it been since he'd felt free to share the love of his work?

He built yachts, ketches, sloops, cruisers. "Hell, I've built more than one canoe in my time. Building boats was what I wanted to do from the time I was knee-high, and I never cared what kind." The pleasure boats he specialized in usually took him a full year to build. Customers found him rather than the other way around. "Word gets around for the obvious reason. There aren't that many craftsmen who work only with wood."

He'd never anticipated growing bigger than a one-man show, but he'd doubled his work load after June died. "I thought I could handle it, until I started to realize what was happening with Noel and Angie. So about four months ago I took on Josh, who's from Boston, and Walker, he's from Savannah. A couple of apprentices make up the rest of the team." He gave her a sidelong look. "The whole crew threatens to quit once a week. They claim I'm a fussbudgety perfectionist who's impossible to please."

"They know you pretty well, hmmm?"

"Hey, whose side are you on?"

His, she thought fleetingly. A month ago, his daughters had labeled him a granite-faced sobersides. Now it wasn't animation and purpose that lightened his strong features as much as it was a building joy of life again. *You can't love him,* she told herself fiercely. But by the minute, those sensible voices in her head were growing weaker. "You browbeat your customers as bad as your employees?" she asked teasingly.

"My customers have a lot of money or they couldn't afford me, so that problem's out of the way right up front. Beyond that, my terms are real easy. We do it my way or

we don't do it." He scratched his whiskered chin.
"Whoops. I guess that sounded arrogant."

"A tad," she murmured dryly.

This time he frowned for real. "I've got boats in the
water from the Maine to the Florida coast. They may have
another owner's name on them, but they're still mine. How
can I not care?"

"I understand," she murmured, and did. Mick was incapable of not caring. "You only work with wood?"

"Right."

"So what's the best wood to build a boat out of?"

Mick chuckled. "Now there's a question you could take
through history and never get an answer. The old Romans
would have told you silver fir; the Vikings swore by oak;
ancient Egyptians favored cedar. The Chinese have always
liked a pine known as sha-mu, when they couldn't get
teak."

"No one agrees what's best?"

"Sure, there's agreement. Any practical boat builder
would tell you that there are high-quality, tropical hard-
woods available today: utile, iroko, opepe. It's only your
bullheaded purists who still hold out for teak, oak and mahogany."

"So what do you build with?"

He looked surprised that she'd asked. "Teak, oak and
mahogany. Or I don't build."

She intended to rib him about the "bullheaded purist"
nonsense, until they reached the docks. Late-afternoon sun
glinted with crystal brilliance on the bobbing boats in the
harbor. Kat didn't know a ketch from a sloop but she
guessed, on sight, which one was his—the incomparable
beauty with the blinding white paint, the gleam of var-
nished teak deck, the sleek and elegant lines. *You do realize
how hopelessly biased you've become, Bryant?*

But she was right. Mick headed down the grassy slope,

onto the wooden plank dock, past beautiful boat on beautiful boat, but he stopped at the one that had captured her attention. Not that he loved the thirty-two-foot baby, but he paused to look for a minute with his hands on his hips and his heart in his eyes.

Darn man. Kat had promised herself that she would stay physically out of reach all evening, but Mick just wasn't giving her a choice. She slid an arm around his waist and hugged him, hard. "You love her."

He squeezed back, just as hard. "Yeah."

"So keep her, Mick. Can't you?"

"Sure, I could. I could give the guy back his money or build him another one. The problem with that is that I get this blasted attached to every one I build." His hand slid down her spine to her fanny, and patted hard. "And what's to keep? For all I know she's going to sink on the high seas, assuming we ever get her out there. And you're about to work for your dinner. Your first job is letting go of the lines."

"Okay by me." She immediately and enthusiastically took off.

"Ah, Red?"

"What?"

"You might want to save the last line until we're on board?" He pushed his sunglasses on top of his head and grinned. "Real seasoned sailor, hmmm?"

"Are we going to sail her?"

He leaped on board first, then reached for her hand. "Not on this trial run. I want to check out her engine, see how she feels and responds in the water. You're going to have your hands just as full. I need everything checked out below deck that can be, and not like a boat builder would do it but like a woman would."

"If you're trying to tell me my place is in the kitchen, Larson—"

"Galley." He shoved a mate's cap on her head and grinned. "You're going to have to get this lingo down. The bathroom's called a head; the beds are called berths. Then there's fore…" He tapped his forefinger to the tip of her breasts. "Aft…" He cupped her fanny. "And while I'm on board you're supposed to call me 'captain,' but hey, I'm not fussy. I'll settle for a respectful 'sir.'"

"You'll settle in the deep six if you keep this up. How's that for a nautical term?"

"Impressive." He would have kissed her, but she wouldn't stand still.

As far as Mick could tell, Kat took to sailing like she took to everything else, passionately and with total enthusiasm. Within fifteen minutes he was steering the boat down the Ashley River toward the Charleston Harbor, which was a tricky business, since both were dominated by shallows and sandbar islands. The wind had picked up, intensifying the sea smells, and the current was strong.

Kat was everywhere: hanging over the rail for a glimpse of the huge white mansions on Charleston's shoreline, then nimble footed exploring the foredeck, where the waves splashed in her face and made her laugh. She demanded a thorough explanation of every gauge and meter on the control console, then bounded below deck to explore the cabin. She spent fifteen minutes there before he saw her head peeking through the open hatch. "I just thought I'd better tell you. You're keeping her, Mick. You're just going to have to tell that poor klutz in Maine that he's out of luck."

"Like her, do you?"

"Like? What kind of word is that? I'm talking love; I'm talking grand passion."

She was still crowing when she disappeared from sight. He hauled her back up to see a school of dolphins, then to see a covey of sandhill cranes that had sought sanctuary on one of the mini wild islands that dotted the harbor. It didn't take long for the wind to destroy any semblance of neatness to her braid. Tendrils whipped around her nape and brow. Her cheeks picked up a breeze-whipped coral. He pelted out an occasional order just to see the saucy grin on her face.

All he could think of was that this was what he'd wanted for her, this was what he had planned. When he'd first picked her up, Kat had been so wary, so sure she was being set up for a seduction scene. She'd been right to be nervous...and wrong.

In these hours together, he'd wanted her to see that they were a natural pair. She was happy with him. The differences between them—she was lace and cameos, he was a physical man who would always work with his hands—were superficial. He didn't have to understand Victorian corsets or gridwork to respect what it took her to manage a business. She didn't have to understand the technicalities in building a boat to share his love for what he did.

He'd wanted to tease Kat—all right, he wanted to seduce her—with the kind of life they would have together.

Past the harbor, in a cove where the waves softly swelled and the sun was just starting to set in rainbow prisms over the water, he cut the engine and dropped anchor. His "baby," on her maiden run, had proven responsive and sensitive to his slightest touch on her throttle. Any skipper knew that patience and experience paid off at the helm.

As a man, he'd forgotten those very good rules with Kat. When they got around to making love, Mick was now prepared. Tonight, though, he had in mind loving her well and thoroughly, but not physically. In a dozen ways she'd told him she was wary of sex. Kat needed time, and Mick was a man of patience, control and experience, which he intended to prove to her if it killed him.

He thought of her mouth, the dance of sunlight in her eyes. And mentally groaned just before heading below deck.

Kat was in trouble and knew it when he served dinner. From the moment he'd picked her up, Mick had sabotaged her nervous, careful, cautious mood. She'd tried to stay nervous, but it just wasn't working. She'd tried to stay tense, but he'd made it impossible for her not to relax. And she'd worked up a reasonably healthy head of anxiety about their one-on-one dinner.

That died the moment Mick set down a steaming, messily overflowing platter of crawfish, then a fragrant, spicy dish of red beans and rice. "We're going to need a million napkins, and what do you want to drink? Iced tea? A beer?"

"Beer, please, but I'll get it." She twisted tops off two bottles and carried them back to the table. Her fears of candlelight and seduction scenes seeming sillier by the minute, she swung a leg under her and ravenously dived into the ethnic food. "You're going to have to eat fast to keep up with me," she warned him. "I haven't had crawfish in a hundred years."

Mick didn't feel obligated to mention that his daughters had clued him in to Kat's favorite foods. "Some people wouldn't mind that lag in time."

"Some people don't appreciate Southern coast cooking."

"I think you have your geography a little confused. This food's strictly Louisiana Bayou, hardly South Carolina coast."

"Who's picky? South is South. And how much red pepper did you put in the beans?"

He didn't answer that, just brought the spice container to the table with a grin. "When you burn your tongue, I'll have a second beer handy, and I can't wait to see how the lady tackles the etiquette of eating crawdads.''

"The only etiquette that applies in this case is enthusiasm.'' Manners didn't work. There was nothing messier than digging into a platter of crawfish. She broke off a tail, poked her thumbs in the ridge of the shell to split it, then used her fingers to pull out the succulent white meat. The first taste was bliss. The second was even better.

Mick drawled, "Is this by any chance your first meal in weeks, Red?''

"Go ahead and make fun. You're denting that platter as fast as I am.'' And he was having a wonderful time doing it, she thought fleetingly. When had she ever heard Mick laugh this much? Or forget all his stress and just be happy?

"I was going to ask you how the checklist went on the cabin, but I've changed my mind. It would obviously be too taxing for you to talk and eat at the same time.''

She ignored that insult, since to respond was to encourage more teasing. But her hand waved expansively around the cabin. "I checked out all the appliances and what-alls on your list, which was a total waste of time. You had to know everything's perfect. Beyond perfect.''

"You think so?''

As they continued to eat, Kat's gaze prowled the cabin. Everything was teak and teal-blue, richness and comfort.

The main cabin was luxurious. The open galley was tiny, but more fully equipped than her own kitchen. The U-shaped dinette faced a couch cushioned with thick, fat teal-blue cushions. Above the navigational desk was a compact entertainment system. She couldn't see the head from where she was sitting, but if she craned her neck she could glimpse the edge of the water-blue comforter on the raised double berth in the "bedroom.''

Boats were Mick's world, not hers. Yet because they were Mick's world, it was easy to imagine a honeymoon on a boat like this. Making love, sailing the seas, waking to the rhythm of sleepy waves and making love all over again. Kat's eyes suddenly squeezed closed.

"You're not giving up already?" Mick scolded.

She forced a smile as she pushed aside her plate. "I'm shamefully full now."

"But you only ate enough for three men, Red. I was sure you could do better than that."

She roused the energy to toss a wadded napkin at him. It didn't make it halfway across the table, which was, not surprisingly, a disastrous mess. "All right, Larson, you're all done playing boss. Close your eyes and put your feet up," she ordered him. "I'll take care of this."

"We will," he corrected her.

"There isn't enough room in the galley for two. Besides, I can do it twice as fast alone."

He wouldn't listen. Every time Kat turned around, she was bumping into Mick. Her thigh brushed his when she bent over the silverware drawer. His arm grazed her shoulder when he reached to put away a glass. Desire hummed between them, as unspoken as moonlight, as familiar and potent as the growing love she felt for him.

Outside, starlight filtered in the open portholes. When the moon had come up, the wind had died. The Atlantic was out there, the whole night smelled of a moon-drenched ocean, and Kat kept telling herself to get real, get tough and face up to what she had to say. Loving Mick didn't make any difference. She wasn't normal. She wasn't like other women. No relationship was possible.

Only she couldn't seem to believe that when she was with him. She felt no more, no less and no different than any other woman in love. She didn't want so much. Just the right to other nights like this, nights when she bumped into him in a kitchen, nights when they ate dinner in bare feet, nights when she put up with his teasing and she was so damned happy she forgot that her hair was a tangled mess.

Mick never cared what a woman's hair looked like. All he wanted in this life was someone he could share with. Although he'd never criticized June, Kat understood something had been missing in the relationship, something he'd felt guilty for wanting, something he'd felt badly for needing.

There was no guilt in need, no shame in weakness. He was weakest where he loved most, his daughters, his work. He didn't seem to understand that that didn't make him less, but more, of a man.

She'd tried, by listening and being there, to coax him out of his shell. She knew she'd helped, only it suddenly, painfully occurred to her that she had never had a way to tell Mick how much she thought of him as a man.

When she folded the dish towel, Mick was just turning from where he had been storing a tray in a closet. "Are there still things you need to do on the boat?" she asked him.

"Not really. I have a list to take back to the shop tomorrow morning, but it's just little fix-it things. Nothing I need to handle now." Mick's hand was halfway to an itch on the back of his neck when his heart stopped beating. Kat took a step toward him, which didn't have to mean anything at all except that she was moving away from the galley. There was just something in her eyes. "On the ride back, I have a few things to do. She's well equipped for night runs, but I put an extra safety package on her that I'd like to—"

His heart restarted. But with a pound, not a beat. Kat wasn't walking by him but coming to him. When her arms roped around his neck, blood slushed through his veins in a rush of heat. When her lips lifted to his and connected, he felt a loss of balance.

He tasted good. A little spice, a little beer, a little Mick. He was awkwardly tall to kiss when she wasn't wearing shoes. Leverage was only possible on tiptoe. Leverage didn't concern her. His mouth did. Reaching it, savoring it, exploring it.

She already knew that Mr. Larson liked kissing. She'd had no idea how much he loved being kissed. Amazing, how quiet it suddenly was in the cabin. All she could hear was the distant splash of sleepy waves and the low—wild and low—groan in the back of his throat when she kissed him again.

"Ah, Red?"

"Hmmm?" Her smile was brazen, calm, confident. He'd never know she was more scared than a kitten in a tree. She unwound her arms and let her hands slide down to the bottom of his sweatshirt. The material raveled around her wrist as her palms glided back up. His blond chest hair curled around her fingers, and his flesh was supple and warm. Very warm. Far too warm for him to need the sweatshirt.

"Is this all to tell me you liked the crawfish?"

"No, Mick. This is for you." It's all she had to say for that arrogant smile of his to fade, but he didn't move. She knew what he wanted. She'd known what he wanted all evening—the one thing she couldn't give him—but that need was in his eyes now, flaring hotter than blue fire. He delivered the dare, just not verbally. *If you want it, babe, you're gonna have to come and get it. I'm not going to push you.*

She pulled the sleeve of his sweatshirt off one arm.

Then the other.

When his sweatshirt was in a nice little puddle on the floor, she framed his face between her hands and raised on tiptoe again. Her tongue moved over his bottom lip, lazy and slow. She nipped, whisper light.

And then she took his mouth as though she'd die if she couldn't have it.

He liked that kiss. A lot. Every muscle coiled in his body like a single-loaded spring. She sampled his tongue with her tongue. He liked that, too. He liked the feel of her palms climbing up the warm, smooth skin of his spine; he liked the way her soft pelvis rubbed right where he was hard... and Kat told herself that she was nuts.

Only she didn't feel nuts. She felt a trembling deep inside. It had been her fault he'd felt badly about the night on the beach. He was a beautiful, powerful, virile lover. Putting a definite end to the relationship—Kat had no choice. But it suddenly mattered terribly that she first show him how she felt about him, how she saw him, how much he meant to her.

And there was only one way to do that.

"We can make love, Mick," she whispered. "Just not...regular...love."

"Regular?"

He didn't seem real involved in the conversation so she persevered. "I have to be honest, okay?"

"Sweetheart, you just don't get much more honest than this." Sometime during the last kiss—or the ten before it—he'd loosened her braid and freed the red silk scarf from the tangled plait. His mouth crushed hers, and when his tongue drove inside, a roar filled her ears like the sound of a waterfall.

"I...need you to listen."

He claimed he was, in between stringing a pearl of kisses down the length of her throat. Those kisses were destroying her concentration, but maybe that was just as well. If it were any man but Mick, she'd never have managed this at all.

"This has to be just for you...I..." The words weren't coming out, but she was sure he understood. She wasn't naive. Hey, there were other ways to please a man besides missionary positions and penetration. "...I know of two. Only I've never done one, Mick, and the other...I'm just saying I might need some help, okay?"

Somewhere between kisses and gulped whispers, she seemed to have caught his attention. He raised his head. When had his eyes turned that piercing, fierce blue? With intense concentration, he brushed her kiss-swollen bottom lip with the pad of his thumb. And then he smiled. A slow, sure, man's smile, so wicked they would have banned it in Boston.

Her knees turned to rubber. His mouth dropped back on hers again and his hands shifted, sliding down her spine to cup her bottom. He lifted her, winding her legs around his waist without ever breaking the kiss, and carried her through the carved arch to the back cabin.

She landed on the thick comforter with a whoosh. He landed on her, not with his full weight but enough of it. He was aroused.

The back cabin was dark. Courage came from the darkness, from determination, from the power of her emotions. At least it started out that way. Kat knew exactly what she wanted to do—make him feel loved and desired and beautiful as a man. Bold like she'd never been bold, she spread kisses like confetti on his mouth, throat, shoulders, chest. Brazen like she'd never been brazen, she rubbed her palms down his side, rimmed the waistband of his jeans, splayed her fingers on the hard ridge of his hips.

He liked what she did—his response left her no doubt— only Mick stopped cooperating. She'd done her best to explain that this had to be her ball game, only he wasn't helping at all. Her tunic was loose, making it easy for his callused hand to slip inside. The tip of his thumb traced the lace rim of her bra. She felt a nasty sensation, like falling out of the sky.

"Mick—"

"Sssh." He lifted her as delicately as if she were a spring flower...but he tugged off her navy-blue tunic and hurled it away like unwanted baggage. He didn't seem to think much more of her best lilac, lace-edged bra. A zillion degrees Fahrenheit, the humidity worse, and her bare nipples suddenly puckered as though she was freezing. He ducked his head.

His tongue had a way with a nipple. She arched for the teasing spear of his tongue, then felt his teeth. She was small, and flat on her back she was certainly smaller. His palms cupped both breasts, giving him something to lave, tease, torment, lick. She couldn't catch her breath. She couldn't stop her heart from pounding.

Rolling over him, her hair falling like a curtain around her face, she kissed him. A wet kiss this time. A wet, open-mouthed, wanton kiss, because, dammit, he was asking for it. "Mick..."

"You're unbearably beautiful, love."

The man was not himself. "I wish you wouldn't do that."

"You love it when I do that."

"But this is supposed to be for you." She found the button on his jeans. Her voice dropped an octave when she slid down the zipper, and her voice hadn't been all that high to begin with. Mick didn't wear skintight jeans. It was just now they were fitting that way. "I thought you understood. I want to..." Her fingers slid under the waistband and tugged down. "I need to...I want to...Mick, I—"

"Red, it can't be all that hard to tell me you want my jeans off." He kicked the last of his clothes free, and kissed her mouth with a smile. A smile loaded in the darkness with TNT.

"You don't understand."

"Believe me, I do."

"Mick, I want to please you."

"You do that by breathing."

"I mean just you." Dammit. His tongue was on her neck, melting her collarbone, at the same time his knuckles were pulling at her jeans zipper. "It won't work any other way. And I don't care. I don't need anything for me. I just want—"

He had to lift her up to pull off her jeans, then the bare strip of violet lace panties. He never looked at the clothes, just at her face, her eyes. "This time, just this time," he said softly, "I want you to trust me to know what you want. Stop worrying, Kat. I love you, don't you know that?"

"I—"

"I'd sworn I wouldn't let this happen. Not tonight. I'd sworn I was going to give you all the time you wanted, but the look in your eyes, honey…time is not what you're asking me for."

She tried to say something else. "Sssh," he murmured, and came back down to her, bare skin against bare skin, kisses tangling in a fast unraveling skein. It seemed to have taken him forever to interpret her desperately low mumblings to mean that she had the cockamamy idea of getting him off and not her.

If she thought he'd buy that, he had an island in Iowa he wanted to sell her. Tomorrow.

Not now. Right now there was only one thing on Mick's mind. Kathryn was scared, he knew, but not half as scared as she thought. Her eyes were sleepy with passion, her limbs winding around his, her small white breasts so swollen they had to hurt her. This time Mick was sure. This time there'd be no bungling his precious cargo. Her mouth yielded more than passion under his. The tension building in her lower body sought release from more than the physical.

She wanted to be loved.

His mouth claimed hers as his palm traced her inner thigh, then cupped the soft protective moss between her legs. She was damp, and bucked around his hand, trying to draw him closer at the same time her teeth nipped his lip. He stroked and kissed until her nails dented the skin on his back, but Mick ignored those messages. There was a time for a pell-mell rush into passionate oblivion, and a time for that wicked country ballad about slow hands.

This was a time for slow hands.

She loved the music. She loved the music so much he nearly went out of his mind—but didn't. Nothing was going wrong this time, because he wasn't going to let it. Lord, she was beautiful, all sweetness and silk and scent and need...

"Mick."

Damn tinfoil. He kissed her the whole time he was rolling on the condom. As it happened, she wouldn't have noticed if it were fluorescent yellow or plain. She didn't care. Her eyes were glazed, as lost as a kitten's, and she wasn't playing at brazen now. She wanted, and her feverish kisses were filled with the wonder of that; awkward then sweet, wanton then impatient. It was as if she'd stored up desire for the past ten years, stored up love to shower over him, and he sure as hell wasn't going to disappoint her.

He repositioned his thighs over her thighs, her soft cries driving him as much as the fierce trust in her eyes, the passion in her hands. As if he enjoyed torture, he hesitated at the entrance. Not for long. He wasn't made of steel. Just long enough to savor how good, how right, how erotic he felt. And how much he loved her.

"Please, Mick...."

He intruded that slick, warm velvet, and felt his heart climb out of his chest. He heard her call his name, again, again.

And then again, this time differently.

She'd been as wet as a river. He knew it. He'd felt it.

Only now she was suddenly as dry as a drought in the Sahara, and the moisture in her eyes wasn't a glaze of passion but tears.

Eight

Mick withdrew, clamped his jaws together and fought for control. A triple shot of bourbon might have helped him. There was an alliterative locker-room phrase starting with "blue" that described his immediate physical condition. Desire didn't want to die. Wanting her refused to go away. She didn't help matters when she squirmed.

"Just where do you think you're going, Kathryn?"

"I was—"

"No, you're not."

"I need to—"

"No, you don't." She was trembling, which annoyed him no end. He tucked her back where she belonged, next to him and naked where she could cause him more torture. Her face was as white as ice and her eyes squeezed closed. "Look at me."

Kat didn't want to. She wanted to click her heels three times and end up in Kansas, preferably with an assumed name and under the protection of an Auntie Em.

That choice being impossible, her lips framed an apology, but the words clogged in the lump of guilt in her throat. No apology justified putting him through this twice. Her conscience wouldn't buy the excuse that she'd only wanted to please him and had never intended their lovemaking to take the turn it had. Although that was true, she could have stopped it. There was a moment when she'd known the blind, powerful wave of desire was taking them both. She'd let it happen—for the unforgivable reason that making love with Mick had seemed the most natural thing on earth.

Once more she'd let herself believe that it had to be right with him.

Once more she'd hurt him. Being swallowed by a black hole had a lot of immediate appeal. Anything was better than opening her eyes and facing him. "Blow up if you want to, Mick." Her voice was as low as the scratch of sandpaper. "If I were a man, I'd be spitting mad."

"If I were a woman, I'd probably be spitting mad, too." That made her eyes blink open. He saw her confusion. She obviously expected him to be angry. Maybe he was, but at the situation, not at her. One look at Kat's face and tenderness tore through him. "As far as I can tell, both of us are biting the same bullet," he said quietly. "You got cheated just as badly as I did."

"That's different because it's my fault. Completely." She lurched up. "I should have told you before and I'm ashamed that I didn't. What happened shouldn't have, because I knew. I was engaged to a man named Todd five years ago; we broke up because of this, so I knew. You're talking lynching guilty from the start—I knew I had no right to become involved. Not with anyone, never with you. Please believe that I never wanted to hurt you—"

"Get back here, Red," he said calmly.

She wasn't listening. If it wasn't so dark, if her vision

wasn't blurred by tears, if the boat wasn't rocking, she'd undoubtedly be able to find her tunic somewhere on the floor. She'd have settled for sack cloth. Anything to cover herself.

"There are zillions of normal women out there. You won't have any trouble finding one. The best I can say for me is that I'm a walking advertisement for safe sex. For a long time I've tried to see the humor in that. I mean, hey, I'm the safest date in town. Real funny, isn't it? Dammit, I can't talk about this. I never could, I never will, and I will thoroughly understand if you drop me in the Atlantic on the return ride home. I just—"

She was still searching for her tunic when Mick's hands closed on her waist from behind. She was redeposited flat on the bed with the ease of a sack of potatoes. Naked suddenly had a new dimension. He'd wedged her between the solid cabin wall and him. She wasn't going anywhere. His eyes were steel blue, uncompromisingly patient and inarguably determined. "No one, Kat, is laughing or thinks anything is funny. No one wants to drop you in the Atlantic, and if you ever want to see me really lose my temper, try handing me that garbage about 'not being normal' again."

His leg pinned her as securely as a manacle, but infinitely gentle, his fingers sifted through the auburn strands that clung damply to her temples. "We're going to talk."

"We just did talk." She didn't understand. "I've told you the truth. There's nothing else to say."

"Maybe on your terms. On mine, we haven't even started." His thumb brushed the last drop of moisture from her cheeks. The teardrop was almost as fragile as her mouth. Not quite. Nothing was as fragile as Kat's mouth. "I guessed you were involved with someone. A turkey. He's the one who dropped the label 'frigid' on you, wasn't he? There are no frigid women, honey, only callous lovers.

I don't know whether he physically hurt you or was just damned selfish.''

She shook her head. It didn't dislodge his hand. "Todd wasn't a turkey and it wasn't like that. It was just me. My problem. And I know I should have been more honest with you from the beginning.''

"You are honest with me, every time I touch you, every time you respond. Washington would have given you an award for emotional honesty, sweets, it's just words that get tricky for you. So we'll work on that.'' He tucked a pillow under both their heads. "You told me about the fiancé, but what about before him? Maybe somebody came on to you real strong? Maybe worse than that?''

"Good heavens, no.''

"You told me you were pretty wild as a teenager.''

She rolled her eyes and made her voice deadpan. "I also told you that was fake. A boy named Sammy Rogers copped a feel in the school hallway when I was in seventh grade. I knocked him flat. That's my entire history of sexual scares.''

"We're talking about being honest.'' There was warning in his tone.

"I can't talk at all. Not about this.'' She lifted her head. "Don't you think we should get dressed? Wouldn't you like a beer? How about if we talk about boats?''

He raised one bushy blond brow. "You wouldn't be trying to get out of this bed again, would you, Red?''

"I think a vertical conversation would be wise.''

"I think that certain conversations can only take place prone.''

"I don't do much of anything well when prone. That's what I've been trying to tell you. There's just nothing else to say, except that if I were you, I'd throw me off the boat. Think about it, Mick. It's good advice.''

He fussed like a schoolmaster. When he was done rear-

ranging body parts, his thigh had locked between hers, her
cheek was on his chest, her head was wedged under his
chin, and his arms were tightly, securely wrapped around
her. "Now." There was a wealth of masculine satisfaction
in his voice. She couldn't imagine why. He'd successfully
rearoused yearning, lustfully active hormones that she'd
been praying were dead, dead, dead. "If we can't find a
problem with *you*, Kat, it's pretty obvious we have a problem with *us*."

"Not us. Me."

"Wrong. You don't have a problem, love. We do. Because that's how it is when two people love each other.
You did realize that, didn't you? That you love me like
hell?"

She swallowed hard. His tone was teasing, but Mick
wasn't. His heartbeat thumped right under her cheek. How
could she lie to him? "Yes."

"And maybe you're telling me there was no big emotional trauma that led to *our* little problem. But unless I've
misunderstood one heck of a lot, we have absolutely no
problem with chemistry or desire. To put it as delicately as
I know how—" Mick cleared his throat "—you've kind
of given me reason to believe you want me like hell."

"Lord, Mick, do you think I'd have let it go this far if
I didn't? I know that's no excuse, but every time we..."
She gulped. "You think it's not embarrassing that I turn
on like a light switch every time you..." Her breath caught
again. "For heaven's sake, I'm thirty-three years old and I
haven't dated anyone in five years. Don't you think I know
what control is? It's only with you that..." Her arm sprang
out, trying to express what she couldn't. "That was the
whole problem, why I kept letting it go on without telling
you; it was just so hard for me to accept that anything could
go wrong when it was you."

"Hmmm." His lips skimmed her temple. "I think you

just gave me an enormous ego boost, but it's kind of hard to tell between all those 'it's' and 'anythings' and hesitations." There was a smile in his kiss, but his eyes were serious when he tilted her face to look at her. "I want you, too," he said softly. "In a way that feels out of control, in a way that feels right, so damned right it scares me. And where I come from when a man feels that strongly he doesn't turn tail and run out at the first sign of a glitch."

The emotion in his voice made her throat swell—until his last words. She choked out, "Mick! This is more than a glitch!"

"Yeah, well, we're about to come to that." He sighed, not without humor. "I know blunt and bawdy isn't exactly your style, Red, but we've talked around the problem as far as we can go. Ever had a nice, plain, explicit course in anatomy?"

She was not amused. "Come on, Mick. I mastered the birds and the bees a long time ago."

"And that's good, real good, but this time I have a little more advanced course in mind. In this anatomy course we're going to cover slightly trickier material, starting with what the thigh bone's connected to and moving on to how you work, how I work, what you like, where you like it." He wagged a finger at her. "Only I know you, Red. The rules are no euphemisms, and no fill in the blanks. Think you can manage that?"

If he wanted to know what she thought he wanted to know, that answer was easy. "No."

"Sure, you can. If it's with me. I thought you already knew there was nothing you couldn't talk to me about, and besides that we'll start out real easy." He drawled, "There's a certain whatchamacallit that's pressing real hard against your thigh at the moment. By any chance do we know the proper name for that whatchamacallit?"

"Mick!" Darn him, she was starting to laugh.

"That question too hard? Don't sweat it. This professor's prepared to cater to the class." With his brow furrowed in deep concentration, he traced the shape of her breast with the pad of his thumb. "Now this dohickey here. What do you like to call this, Red?"

There was no controlling the devil. The blunter the question, the more mercilessly he teased. If she dared turn shy, she got a big scolding about Victorian missish modesty...and another explicit question.

It wasn't the use of proper words that embarrassed her. Kat could certainly handle a discussion on basic biology, but there were certain things she'd never imagined sharing with a man. How could she talk about what turned her on, where she was sensitive, what physically happened to her when she made love?

Mick made it very clear that no subject was taboo between lovers. Ever. Always. Embarrassment was okay. Skimpy answers were not. Unfortunately he expected her to know more about her body than she actually did. Good grief, a busy woman had more to do in a day than analyze her bodily functions; how was she supposed to know if PMS affected her sexual responsiveness?

It had to be the most awkward, dreadful, squirmy discussion she'd ever had in her life.

Or it started out that way. Over time, starlight drifted through the porthole skylight. Over time, the boat kept rocking to the lulling, sensual rhythm of the sea. Over time, she understood exactly why she had never been able to stop herself from falling in love with Mick. What she couldn't possibly share with another living soul, she could share with him. The vulnerable part of a woman's soul that she guarded so carefully was safe with him.

Mick Larson was a man to hold, cherish, protect, love. She desperately wanted to do all those things, and at the first lull in the conversation, she lifted her head to look at

him. His blond hair was disheveled. He was still lying naked—it would never occur to Mick to be self-conscious
about nudity—but his face was set in grave lines.

She reached over to smooth the furrow in his brow. "Is
the inquisitor finally done?" she murmured.

"No."

But she knew he'd finally run out of questions. That was
why he was so unhappy. Mick had thought their talk would
yield answers—a reason, a clue, a key to her problem. He'd
counted on that. "I need to tell you something that we
haven't discussed," she said softly. "Something…terribly
personal, terribly private."

She had his full attention and she took advantage of it.
"You are," she said quietly, "the most exciting lover I can
imagine. You're not getting away with thinking that you've
failed me as a lover, because you haven't. All those questions, Mick…but there was never anything you failed to
do, no 'technique' you missed, and you already know more
about a woman's anatomy than I do." She put a finger on
his lips when he tried to talk.

"Every time you've touched me, you've pleased me.
I've loved what you do, everything you do. There's no way
it could have been better, no way you could have been more
alluring as a lover. The problem is strictly mine, not yours,
and so is the answer. I have to stop seeing you."

"No."

But she closed her eyes and took a long breath. "Yes."

Ed's fuzzy white head appeared in the doorway. "Rith-
wald's on the phone, wants to know when you're going to
finish the price on the Bickford renovation."

"1999."

"Ah." Ed cleared his throat. "He was sort of counting
on a week from Tuesday."

"Whatever." Ed disappeared. Kat glared at the recipe

for Princess Cake clothespinned in front of her. She poured an egg, three egg yolks and three-quarters of a cup of sugar in the small mixing bowl. The mixer whined, oblivious to ringing phones, customers and Georgia's quietly hummed "Battle Hymn of the Republic." The batter spattered and swirled for a solid three minutes. When Kat switched it off, Georgia was still humming. "Would you stop it?"

"Stop what?"

"Stop humming that blasted song!"

"It seemed to suit your mood," Georgia said mildly. She glanced at the potato flour and baking soda Kat was mixing in the bowl. "You're supposed to cream the mixture, darlin'. Not beat it to death." She dipped a spoon in the stovetop double boiler. She tasted, then kept stirring. "You suppose it's been the heat affecting your mood for the past two weeks?"

"If you're implying I've been difficult to work with—"

"I think you could've given lessons to the Ayatollah," Georgia said genially.

Kat stopped stirring. "I'm sorry." She lifted her head. "Honestly sorry, Georgia."

"Forget it. You've put up with my low spots for five years; it's kind of nice to have the chance to return the favor."

"I'm not low."

"Of course, you're not."

Exasperated, Kat flipped the mixer back on to beat the egg whites. No one could talk over the sound of the mixer at its highest speed. Ed popped back in, took a wary glance at her, and popped back out. The college girl manning the store wandered through, and when Georgia shook her head, she disappeared again.

Wednesday afternoons were traditionally baking times at the store. That tradition had become possible because the building had originally housed a restaurant. The cooking facilities were ancient but functional, the customers loved the Victorian treats, and cooking was a love of Georgia's—not Kat's. Georgia couldn't remember a single Wednesday in which Kat had ever done more than sample the products.

Eventually the egg whites were peaked and glossy. The moment Kat shut off the mixer, Georgia subtly pounced. "So, are you going to New Orleans with Mick this weekend?"

Kat dropped the spoon. "Isn't anybody's private business sacred around here anymore? How did you even know he asked me?"

"Someone had to clear your schedule if you wanted to be away," Georgia said logically. "I gather he has someone named Uncle Bill to take care of the girls, but your working hours can be a little harder to rearrange."

"There's nothing to rearrange because I won't be going. Which Mick already knows." Kat folded the egg whites into the cake batter, poured the batter into the pan and put the whole thing into the oven. Thirty minutes to bake. If she had thirty minutes with nothing to do, she'd go crazy.

"I think he thinks you're going."

"That's only because he doesn't listen." She could prepare part of the topping ahead of time. Not the powdered sugar, but she could mix the food coloring for the nine-ounce roll of marzipan—assuming she could find the green coloring. Her fingers knocked over a half-dozen spice containers. Good Lord, it was hot and humid. "Mick doesn't listen. He doesn't understand the word no. He's sneaky and unprincipled. And he lies."

"I had no idea," Georgia said mildly. "To look at him, you'd think he had integrity stamped all over his face."

"Quit the humor, Georgia. I'm serious." She jammed the spice containers back in place. "He called me last Thursday morning, all upset because he'd caught Noel kissing some boy. He just wanted to have lunch and talk to me, he said." She glared at Georgia. "What was I supposed to do, ignore him? He was upset. I couldn't just..."

"Of course you couldn't."

"The lunch was a total setup. He'd hired a horse-drawn buggy for a drive around the harbor, set up this picnic lunch in the grass by the water, and dammit, he brought me roses."

"Now there's a loser for you," Georgia murmured obligingly.

"He lied, Georgia. He did not want to talk about Noel."

"Lynch the sucker," Georgia advised.

"You keep laughing, but you don't have the whole picture," Kat said irritably. Finally she found the green food coloring and started shaking it in the bowl. "Last Saturday night, Angie called me. She'd cooked her first dinner, entirely by herself, and she was so proud of herself she was going nuts. I could hardly hurt her feelings."

"Of course not."

"So I went over there, expecting four at the table. The menu was burned coq au vin, tepid champagne and raw broccoli. The table was set with candles and a neighbor's borrowed sterling, and the girls ran giggling out of sight the minute I got there."

"Leaving you alone with Mick?"

"He knew." Kat shook a dripping spoon at Georgia. "He let the girls set that up. He knows damn well they're becoming far too attached to me, and all he keeps saying is how they're thriving under my feminine influence, how they need me. He's deliberately encouraging the girls to believe I could be part of their lives."

"No question, the man is scum. Slime. A man who would use his own daughters—"

Kat was no longer listening to Georgia's nonsense. Her tone had turned wistful, her eyes lost. "And I'll never, never, forgive him the camellias."

"Camellias?"

"You remember Monday how busy we were? I didn't get home until late, so tired I could hardly walk. All I wanted out of life was a long soak in the bath, so I crawled upstairs and there they were. A tubful. An entire tubful of beautiful, fragile, precious white camellias." She looked helplessly at Georgia. "I love camellias."

Georgia nodded. "That man obviously has a real vicious streak. You can't get much more down and dirty than camellias."

"I can't go with him to New Orleans. I've told him no to New Orleans, no to the relationship, no to everything. I said no and I meant it, Georgia. I simply have to stay out of his life." Something was terribly wrong. The few drops of food coloring were supposed to turn the marzipan pale green. The mixture was as dark as an Amazon emerald.

Georgia glanced over. "Don't come within five feet of my cream filling, darlin'."

"I'm not."

"There's one more roll of almond paste in the refrigerator, but only one more. Maybe you'd better let me do the marzipan."

"Don't be silly. I can handle it. I know perfectly well what I have to do...." The words caught in her throat. Kat always had known what she had to do and had always done it. Until lately. Lately she couldn't seem to concentrate on her work, her life, nothing. Nothing made sense.

Blunt, practical, physical Mick had started this crazy romantic courtship when he *knew* her problem.

Camellias.

For a woman who couldn't make love.

She was going to rent that man a straitjacket. The very first day she stopped feeling so weepy.

Georgia said casually, "Wynn was his name."

"Whose name?"

"The man I was in love with. Did I ever tell you about him?"

Kat abruptly turned her head. Georgia knew perfectly well that she'd never mentioned a word about her past.

"Hmmm. He was tall and good-looking, and you can't get much more Yankee than a Vermonter. He was built on the lean side, had a little Newman in the eyes, and you know I'm a little sensitive about my weight?"

Kat nodded, feeling her heart reach out to her friend. She knew.

"Wynn wasn't. Wynn liked plump. He also liked raspberries and mint juleps and books. He had too much money for his own good. He was a Type A all day, prone to worry, didn't know how to relax. I soothed him, he used to say. He didn't soothe me. When I was around him, he stirred me up more than a fox in a hen house." Georgia shot Kat a smile. "I left him."

"Oh, sweetie, why?" Kat asked softly.

"Couldn't have children and he wanted children. He knew, said we'd make a go of it anyway, but I was afraid he'd come to resent me. So I decided to make it easier for him and call it off." Georgia stuck her finger back in the double boiler, burned it, and was satisfied the mixture was finally done. "I've had seven years to live with that decision. Seven years to reap all the rewards of doing the best thing for Wynn."

It didn't look that way to Kat. Georgia moved swiftly and efficiently to the counter with her cream filling, but her eyes were filled with banked despair. "Do you know what happened to him?" Kat asked quietly.

"Yes. He's married now, with a toddler and another on the way." Georgia switched on the taps and put the double boiler in the sink to soak. She said lightly, "I could have had those urchins. We could have adopted, if I hadn't been so busy seven years ago making decisions for Wynn that I had no business making.'' She swiped at a counter. "Don't do it, Kathryn.''

"Don't what?''

"Don't assume you can make choices for the man you love. You're the one with the problem? That's no big shocker. I always guessed you had a problem. Most of us have problems unless we've already been canonized. Don't assume he can't handle it.'' Georgia put her mixture into the refrigerator to cool, then straightened. "Wynn married someone else. I won't. He's there every time I look at another man; he always has been and he always will be, and you are going to New Orleans with Mick.''

"Georgia—''

"Sometimes you only get one shot at the brass ring. I blew mine. Damnation, Kathryn. Mick looks at you the way Rhett looked at Scarlett, and if the man asked you to spend the evening in a mud puddle, you'd find four hundred excuses to do it for him. What else is there to say? You're going to New Orleans with him, and that's that!''

Kat saw the tears in Georgia's eyes and walked over with her arms outstretched. Georgia needed the hug—for Wynn, for sharing the kind of secrets only women kept, for being an irreplaceable friend.

Truthfully, though, Georgia didn't understand about Mick. She also didn't know why Mick had asked her to spend the weekend in New Orleans…and yes, she was going.

Mick was counting on New Orleans for a miracle.

Kat was counting on New Orleans for the only possible way and means to end the relationship cleanly and irrevocably. It had to work. She'd stopped believing in miracles a long time ago, and even a miracle couldn't seem to help her stop loving him.

But for the first time in her life, Kat needed help to be strong. And she was counting on that help in New Orleans.

Nine

Throughout history, men had done a lot of things to prove their love: climbed mountains, crusaded, fought duels, competed, avenged and revenged.

Mick doubted any of those guys had to go this far. Head bent, he leafed the magazines in the gynecologist's office. He found a *Woman's World*, *Woman's Day*, *Woman's Life*, and *Woman*, but not a *Sports Illustrated* in the bunch.

Pink vinyl chairs were lined up against one wall. Mick willed his shoulders to shrink, and he squeezed in between a career woman with a swinging ankle and a red-faced housewife. He was the only man in the packed waiting room. Not that he felt out of place, but he was probably the only human being not wearing perfume and waiting for a Pap smear.

Kat had given him the out. "Didn't I agree to go? But there's no reason on earth for you to come to the doctor's office with me."

Technically she was correct. Just as technically, she could have made a doctor's appointment on her own in Charleston—only everyone and his cousin knew Kat at home. No one at home would guess they had anything but a romantic weekend in mind if their destination was New Orleans. More important was the doctor. Not that Mick was fussy on the subject, but he'd nearly had to scout coast-to-coast for someone to fit his qualifications—a woman with a specialty in sexual dysfunction and credentials ten miles long.

"You're not going alone," he'd insisted.

"I don't see why."

He'd touched her cheek. "You don't see why because you're still thinking of this as *your* problem. It's *ours*, Red, and when we have a problem, we handle it together."

Mick figured he was getting good at pontificating. Kat, thankfully, didn't have enough experience with men to recognize one who was desperate.

Twice he'd taken her to the brink of sexual fulfillment. Twice he'd failed her. Something was his fault. He knew it. He felt it enough to have made an appointment with his own doctor, who'd been amused. "After all those years of marriage?" Samuel had murmured. "Teach her to relax, Mick. That's all there is to it, and while you're at it, consider relaxing yourself."

Relax? The doctor hadn't been with her all those hours on the boat, bare and close, where the moon caught every strand of copper in her hair and danced in those soft, vulnerable eyes.

It had taken her a long time to drop her guard and really talk with him. He'd teased her about being Victorian, a judgment that he'd come to understand wasn't fair. Kat wasn't missish. She was proud—fiercely proud and private about infringing on anyone with her problems. She had the insane idea that this dryness was her fault—as if fault had anything to do with intimacy. If he'd left it alone, he knew she planned on never nearing a man's bed again. Much less his.

He wanted her in his life, not just his bed, but the questions were getting a little tricky. How far did a lover's rights extend? Particularly when the lover involved wasn't, precisely, a lover. Particularly when the lady panicked at the first mention of the future. Not surprisingly, when the problem of intimacy was hanging over her head.

But Mick was coming to understand that he had a problem of intimacy hanging over his own head.

Kat needed him. Not for food or shelter or security, and not even—although she saw it as the problem—for sex. Mick understood her particular brand of loneliness because he'd lived it himself. She needed a man she could be honest with, a man who could help her cross those emotional rivers that were tough going alone, a man who'd be there when she wakened from a dark dream in the middle of the night.

Mick needed those same things in return, but he hadn't recognized what he'd been missing until Kat. She was sunshine and warmth and the click of a smile on a gray day. He touched her, and there was the missing half to the whole.

Only Mick needed to know, for himself as well as Kat, that he could come through for her, fill those needs, be that man she could always turn to.

He wouldn't be worried if the situation were your average hurricane, tornado or avalanche. Mick knew what kind of man he was in a crisis, and maybe he was a late starter in this romancing business but catching up wasn't so hard. Lord, the look on her face after he'd sent those camellias!

Maybe a real hero sent camellias, but on a scale of 1 to 10, Mick was willing to bet there wasn't a woman alive who considered being bullied into a gynecologist's visit even remotely romantic. *And what are you gonna do if the doc doesn't find a problem, Larson?*

He didn't know. At the moment, all he knew was that the office was hot, his palms were perspiring and his stomach pitched acid every time he mentally pictured what was going on in the examining room. Before making the appointment, he'd grilled Dr. Krantz on the telephone for more than an hour. She'd reassured him that the examination didn't hurt.

But she didn't know Kat, and maybe it was irrational, but Mick didn't trust anyone physically near Kat but him. She hurt easily, he knew. She was sensitive and she was scared.

He checked his watch for the eighth time. She'd already been in there ten minutes. *Ten minutes.*

In one sense, he wanted the time to race. In another, he'd rather take this torture in slow motion because he knew the toughest time was yet to come. He was increasingly aware that the minutes she spent in that examination office could affect Kat's whole life. But it was how he handled the moment when she came out—regardless of the doctor's diagnosis—that could affect his. Theirs.

Either he would be the man Kat needed or he would fail her. And as a man, how he wanted to behave and felt he needed to behave for Kat's sake were two entirely different things.

Kat decided that there must be a law regarding doctors' examination rooms. The temperature always seemed to hover around the freezing point. The ceiling tiles always seemed to be pock-marked. And the look of the gloves, glop, and instruments on the counter were designed to make a woman's hands and feet sweat. Copiously.

The door opened, and Kat felt her mouth go dry. The tall woman who strode in had soft gray eyes, flyaway brown hair, and a smile as natural as sunshine. "Kathryn? I'm Maggie Krantz." She extended a hand. "I hope you're as comfortable with first names as I am. Formality never seems to work for me."

"First names are fine," Kat said, and over the next few minutes felt relief gradually slow her hammering pulse. For Mick's sake, she had planned what she was going to say, and whoever stepped through that door didn't make any difference. It helped, though, that the older woman immediately proved easy to talk to. "I know Mick gave you some of my background on the phone, Maggie, but I have to confess that I'm here on false pretenses."

"Oh? I understand you had a problem with dyspareunia." The doctor smiled as she lifted the stethoscope prongs to her ears. When the preliminaries of the exam were finished, she continued, "I know painful intercourse is a touchy subject to talk about, but if you were unaware of this, Kathryn, you're not alone. Very few women escape a bout with the problem at some point during their adult sexual lives. Many times, there's an easily found solution."

Kat shook her head. "I need to be honest with you—"

"That's what I'm here for." Easily and calmly, Maggie started asking questions, each more intimate and personal than the last. Kat was half surprised to find herself unembarrassed—Mick seemed to have chased that quality out of her character—and she probably answered more thoroughly than the doctor wanted. Her mind wasn't on the questions but on getting back to the subject that mattered. And the first moment Maggie paused, Kat jumped back in.

"I knew before I came here that there was nothing physically wrong with me. Mick knows I have a hard time talking about this, so he thinks I haven't pursued it—not totally, not enough. That isn't true. I have a family doctor at home and an annual exam every year. Five years ago I sought a second opinion. There's just nothing physically wrong.''

"No? Scooch down a little, Kathryn."

Kat slid, closed her eyes and kept talking. "Since there was nothing medically wrong, the obvious next stop on the train was psychological. Maybe I haven't taken that far enough, but I went once to a psychologist a long time ago—a total joke. He kept trying to pull some deep fear of sex out of my mental closet, but it just wasn't there. I was never attacked, never abused. My parents are wonderful. I'm not afraid of men. This psychologist said a little hypnosis might help me feel in touch with my real feelings. So we did that.''

"And?"

"And he discovered my darkest secret," Kat said dryly. "I'm scared to death of spiders."

"Spiders?" Maggie lifted her head and met Kat's eyes over the sheet. "Me, too." More gently she added, "You're less tense than you were. This'll be done before you know it. Just keep talking, Kathryn."

Kat took a huge breath and did. "What I'm trying to tell you is that I came here for Mick, not for me. I know there's nothing wrong with me, but he needs to think there is. And maybe it isn't medically proper, Maggie, but I'm asking you to invent something. Anything. Right now he's blaming himself for something that's my problem, but he won't listen to me. If you came up with some fancy sounding diagnosis, he'd believe you and he'd stop feeling responsible, and I…''

Her voice dropped off.

Mick thought he'd talked her into this doctor's appointment. That was never true. The truth was she was incapable of walking away from the relationship, and Mick knew it. Mick was under the disastrous impression that she was in love with him—probably because she behaved like she was winsomely, passionately, wildly in love with him every time she was in the same room.

She'd have walked on water for that man. She'd have leaped tall buildings in a single bound because yes, of course she loved him. How could she not? Mick was a heart stealer. He was warm and funny and real, generous in giving, committed, brick-strong and far too perceptive for a woman's peace of mind.

He was also sexy. As hell.

And only a eunuch could have lived with her problems.

"Just about finished, Kathryn."

"Fine," she murmured, but she wasn't. Her heart had never felt so sad. Mick had been trapped in this limbo of a relationship because of her. She couldn't seem to find the strength of character to let him go, and Mick refused to walk away. This doctor's appointment had presented the only solution she could see.

"Maggie, I would pay you. Double your fee or whatever you asked. I don't care what's medically ethical and I don't care. You *have* to tell him that it's me, nothing he could possibly be responsible for."

"No problem." Maggie leaned back and started pulling off her gloves.

Kat felt relief flood through her. "Thank you."

Maggie's smile was dry. "Don't thank me for lying, because I haven't and I won't."

"Pardon?"

"It is you, Kathryn."

Kat jerked up to a sitting position.

"How often have you had a reason to take a prescription for oral antibiotics?" Maggie asked calmly.

"I don't know. Maybe once a year? But I don't see—"

"Why don't you get your clothes on while I take this slide to the lab? And then we'll talk in my office."

* * *

Mick saw her the moment she came out. She didn't walk right into the waiting room but stopped at the receptionist desk, and his so normally graceful Kat was having a bout of clumsiness. She was fumbling with her purse, checkbook and pen while she was also trying to hold on to a small slip of paper that any five year old could recognize as a prescription form.

The presence of the prescription form told him part of what he needed to know—the doctor had found something, an answer. But the look of Kat told him more. The receptionist was trying to tell her the amount of the bill. She wasn't listening. Her gaze was searching the waiting-room crowd for him.

He wasn't hard to spot. He was the one with the thudding heart, the gray complexion and the slick hands.

Their eyes met and every bone in his body went soft. She looked a little dazed, a little disoriented...like maybe she'd just won the lottery and couldn't believe it yet. Peach tinted her cheeks under his steady, intense perusal. He had no doubt whatsoever that she'd forgotten the receptionist, never saw the other waiting patients. The intimate emotion in her eyes was for him, only for him. *I can love you, Mick!!!*

But Mick also saw what he'd expected—what he'd been afraid he would see. There was more than the celebration of hope in Kat's eyes. There was a new shyness, a crushing sheen of vulnerability and uncertainty, and Mick thought, *Careful, careful, careful, Larson.*

She may have won the lottery, but she hadn't spent the money yet. Obviously that was just occurring to her.

It had already occurred to him, but for now he strode toward her. Someone had to save the receptionist who had given up talking and was waving a hand in Kat's face, trying to get her attention. Kat had dropped her pen, had her checkbook upside down, and the prescription form was about to slip on the floor.

He confiscated the prescription, and within three minutes, neatly steered the bundle of nerves that was Kat out into the New Orleans sunshine.

Nothing was exactly wrong, Kat told herself. At the tail end of August, New Orleans was just as simmering hot as Charleston, but it was cool inside Galatoire's.

The fourth-generation bistro was located on Bourbon Street—their plane didn't leave until morning, so they had the rest of the day and evening to explore Bourbon Street and the French Quarter. Galatoire's couldn't be a better place to start. It was loaded with atmosphere. Mick had already ordered the house specialties: pompano, a jackfish, eggplant stuffed with crabmeat and oysters *en brochette*. He'd backed that up with a liter of bubbling dry champagne. The first glass had already gone straight to her head.

Mick, sitting across from her, had stashed his sport coat. His white shirt complemented his tan and the width of his shoulders. There were other good-looking men in the room. Pip-squeaks. No one had the electrical male charge around him that Mick did; no one else had that slight crook in his lazy grin. He tried to pour her another glass of champagne.

"If I have another one, I'll be weaving instead of walking," she warned him.

"After you eat all that food?"

"I can't possibly eat all this food. You ordered enough for three."

"I've seen your appetite before, Red. You'll have this polished off while I'm still on the first course."

See, she kept telling herself. Nothing was wrong. Mick was teasing her just like he always teased her, smiling like he always smiled, and he was relaxed in a way that usually gave her enormous pleasure that he could relax around her. He just hadn't mentioned the doctor.

Somehow she'd been quite positive that he'd be in a rush to hear the doctor's news.

On the cab drive through the city, she hadn't known quite what to say or how to say it. Now, though, she felt abruptly impatient with herself. If there was a human being alive she could discuss anything with, it was Mick—he'd taught her that, and maybe it was past time she proved that his lessons had gotten through. "The problem," she mentioned casually, "is called *Candida Albicans*."

His gaze was riveted on her face, but only for a moment. His grin was lazy and slow. "Sounds like a Mexican breed of jumping bean."

She ducked her head to spear a bite of jackfish. "Actually it's nothing more than a common yeast infection. Nothing serious, nothing awful. There's no reason to think seven days on medication won't take care of it—although Maggie suggested I follow up with my own doctor, given my own particular history." She was still having trouble believing it. Seven days to erase a problem that she'd spent years building into an unbridgeable emotional trauma. She wasn't inadequate. She wasn't half a woman.

And the man who'd made sure she found that out calmly split a roll in half and handed her the buttered wedge. "If it's all that common—"

"It's common, but Maggie said it can be very hard to diagnose. Many women have clear-cut symptoms; I never did. At least, nothing I understood was a symptom." She shifted restlessly in her seat. Mick was listening, but he wasn't asking any questions. She could have let it go right there, if she hadn't learned to demand real honesty—from herself and for him.

"I never lied to my family doctor, Mick. I just didn't realize that there were certain things I should have told him.

I didn't know there could be a link between broad spectrum antibiotics and yeast infections. I didn't realize that a yeast infection could be a reason why a woman felt pain when she was making love. And the one physical symptom I had…'' Kat hesitated. It's not that she wasn't willing to tell him, but ''itches'' were hardly conversational material around a gourmet lunch. ''I never understood it was a symptom; I just assumed it was a problem that all women had. Being fussy about personal hygiene has always been second nature to me, and other than that I never thought about it.''

Mick lifted a bite of eggplant, silently asking her if she wanted to try it. Kat shook her head, becoming more confused by the minute. Mick was as relaxed as if they were discussing the weather.

''Maggie said that it happens all the time. Women are very good at ignoring physical symptoms, especially if they think their real problem is sexual. Bring in sexuality, and their first impulse is to believe it's their fault, something they're doing wrong, something they're lacking.''

When Mick saw she was finished, he signaled for the waiter. ''Women don't have a corner on that market, Red. Men are just as good at setting that scene themselves. Beds can be an emotional land mine for both sexes.''

''Yes,'' she said vaguely. When he'd set his napkin down, his fingers had brushed hers and immediately withdrawn. Sort of like his hand had come in contact with a hot potato.

He smiled at her when they rose from the table, and he guided her through the restaurant with a hand at the small of her back. His hand, however, never quite touched.

They heard hours of wonderful music that night. The down and gutsy jazz New Orleans was famous for, rock coming out of neon-flashing nightclubs, the ancient and enduring lovesongs from a place with candlelight and dark corners—Bourbon Street had it all. At two in the morning they were still strolling the streets, stuffed on Creole cooking and champagne, high on music and the lights of a city created for lovers. And in smiles, in quietly shared looks, in everything he said, Mick made her feel like the most cherished of all lovers.

But when they reached the hotel, he simply fitted her key into the adjoining door next to his. His knuckles brushed her cheek but he didn't kiss her. Didn't even try. "Sleep well, sweetheart."

Alone in the hotel bedroom, Kat started tugging off clothes. She told herself that it was perfectly natural that he was keeping a physical distance. For one thing she was out of commission, so to speak, for at least the next seven days. And for another, she'd put Mick through some heavy tease and torture from the very beginning of the relationship. He undoubtedly didn't want to start something that couldn't be finished, and she'd commit hara-kiri before putting him through that again.

Only not kissing or touching her was unlike Mick. He was physical, had always been physical. He touched as naturally as he breathed. He'd kissed her a hundred times when it wasn't wise. For that matter Kat couldn't remember a single time when Mick had had her alone that he'd cared chicken scratch for wisdom.

She slipped in between the cool sheets and fluffed the pillow. *Kat, that man has invested one heck of a lot of grief in you. He would hardly be likely to turn cool now, when there's finally a chance of a future.*

Unless, of course, that had hit Mick. They had a chance of a future now, and perhaps that possibility had hit him like a binding noose. He hadn't been that happy with June. He hadn't been that unhappy single, and she'd hardly been God's gift to a man's life. Mick had needs. Their whole relationship had been dominated by hers.

* * *

"Of course we had a good time with Uncle Bill. We always have a good time with Uncle Bill." Noel, sitting in the back seat with Angie, hadn't gotten her father's attention since they were picked up. "Unlike you, Dad, he lets us stay up to all hours and eat anything we want."

"Mmmm."

She tried one more time. "We also saw an R-rated movie. Lots of violence, lots of sex."

"Hmmm."

Noel shared a glance with Angie. Angie shrugged. "You two had a good time in New Orleans, right?"

"Wonderful," Kat murmured.

"Terrific," Mick concurred.

The radio was on. A male tenor was making a tragedy out of "It Had To Be You." The sun had been blinding bright from the moment they'd stepped off the plane; tiredness had seeped into Kat's soul and Mick's thigh was inches from hers. All day, there'd been a thousand chances for that thigh or his hand to touch hers.

Noel suddenly swung over the front seat. "Uh, Dad?"

"Hmmm?"

"Funeral homes probably have a hot line to that radio station. You don't mind if I find something peppier, do you?"

"It Had To Be You" was instantly replaced by an ancient beat about a guy who couldn't get no satisfaction. Mick switched off the radio so fast that Kat felt her cheeks burn.

"You know it's the first of September tomorrow, don't you? That means school," Angie groaned. "It's not fair. It's still too hot to go to school, and besides that it's my birthday next week. Nobody should have to go to school on their birthday, should they, Kat?"

"No way," Kat agreed. Two days ago Mick would have teasingly called her a traitor for siding with his daughters.

Now he gave her a vague smile, like the kind he'd give a wayward sister.

Coming home, Kat had been worried how the girls would take their weekend. Mick argued with her that it was a healthy thing for any kid to understand that adults occasionally needed time alone, and nothing else had to be said. She could see he was right. Maybe the girls were curious, but they were hardly stressed out about it, which meant that being around his daughters was hardly a reason for Mick's increasing distance.

"I invited a few friends to spend the night next Friday rather than have a birthday party this year. That's okay with you, isn't it, Dad?"

Mick stared at his youngest in the rearview mirror. "How many is a few?"

Noel, suspiciously smoother than oil, piped in before Angie had to answer. "I'm going to die if I don't eat soon. How much farther until we get home?"

"Another fifteen minutes."

"What are we going to have for dinner?"

"The first thing I find in the freezer that'll defrost at the speed of sound. I think the larder's down to either liver or meat loaf."

Both girls groaned, but more than that Kat heard the weariness in Mick's voice. Again, she was conscious of how often her needs had dominated their relationship and she automatically responded. "Your dad's tired. Why don't you all come over to my place? I know I have some fries, and it wouldn't take very long to whip up a salad and put some chops on the grill."

"That's a great idea, Kat! Then you can help me decide what to wear to school tomorrow."

"And I want to talk to you about my pajama party."

Mick interjected, "Kat has to unpack and she's just as

tired as I am. The last thing she needs to do is put on a dinner for four.''

"Honestly, I don't mind. I already have everything around, so it's no trouble,'' Kat promised him.

"So let's do it, Dad! It's okay with you, isn't it?''

Stopped at a red light, Mick turned his head. The look in his eyes was as warm as love, as intense as a flame. She didn't belong to him, but with him. The hunger in his gaze was so real she could have reached out and touched it, but then it was gone. As carefully as a man dealing with dynamite, he said quietly, "We'll come, but only if you're sure that's what you want, Kathryn.''

If you're sure that's what you want, Kathryn?

Mick hadn't been that courteous when he'd been married and they'd been mildly acquainted neighbors.

Kat was briefly tempted to shake his big shoulders good and hard. She might have done that if she hadn't been feeling more and more despairing. Mick was emotionally closing off from her and she had no idea why.

Ten

The following Thursday night, Kat walked in her door at nine o'clock after a tennis game with the three Larsons next door. The game had been hilarious. Mick was the only one who could play; the three females had done nothing but chase balls. All four of them had laughed, including Kat, but she wasn't laughing as she headed for the shower.

If Mick was trying to totally destroy her sanity, he was doing an excellent job of it.

Tonight it had been tennis. The night before she'd had to work late, and the whole crew had shown up with fast food so she wouldn't have to cook. Tuesday Mick had asked her to shop for Angie's birthday present, and Monday they'd all piled into the car for a trip to the grocery store.

Nothing was wrong with any of those outings, and certainly none of them were contrived. Each, though, had reminded Kat of how inexorably the two households had been merging for some time. The girls had long had a key to her place. Kat's favorite brand of tea was in Nick's cupboard; his Allen wrench was in her drawer; and the girls' clutter of shoes and tapes and forgotten sweaters was as much in evidence in her house as his.

Such togetherness was perfectly natural when the two adults involved were about to form a permanent alliance. Judging from the amount of togetherness Mick had pushed this week—she hadn't had a free minute to herself—Kat could hardly doubt he had marriage in mind. A dozen times she'd told herself that nothing had changed, but it had. Oh, God, it had.

Suddenly Mick had developed the manners of a knight, the camaraderie of a girl's best friend, and the trustworthy dependability of a Boy Scout.

He just stayed as physically and emotionally far away from her as if she'd recently contracted a lethal case of cooties.

By midnight, she still couldn't seem to sit, settle, or sleep. Carrying a glass of cooking sherry, she opened her bedroom's French doors and settled on the wrought-iron balcony. The household next door was dark, and it was a good night for an insomniac's brood. The air was sultry and still, darker than secrets and redolent with the scents of late roses and honeysuckle. Even a hardened cynic could turn romantic on a night like this.

Miserable, Kat gulped another dreadful swig of sherry.

"Hi, Red."

Startled, she looked up to Mick's third story. With the lights off behind him, she could just make out his shadowed form straddling the windowsill. Heaven knew how long he'd been there.

"Couldn't sleep?"

"No," she murmured, unaware until that moment that he had a clear view into her bedroom, wondering how often she'd undressed with the light on behind sheer lace curtains.

"Often, honey."

"Pardon?"

He talked for a while. About what, she had no idea. What mattered was that he wanted to talk, and the hunger in his voice carried in the darkness like a call to her senses. She was only dressed in a nightgown. There hadn't been any reason to put on a robe. It was hot, it was dark, it was past midnight. He couldn't see her, no one could see her, but she felt the intensity of his eyes on hers. She felt his voice like the touch of skin. She felt Mick. Lonesome and alone in his third-story bedroom.

And chitchat suddenly wasn't going to cut it. "Mick," she said quietly, "if there's something on your mind, I wish you'd say it."

"Something on my mind?"

She took a breath. "If there's something bothering you, something you want to talk to me about…"

He hesitated. "There is something."

She could feel herself bracing for the blow. This was it. The reason he had been withdrawing from her. Mick had changed her whole world, though, and Kat promised herself she would do her best to be understanding and supportive, no matter how much it hurt.

"I'm real confused about putting together this quarter's tax forms. You fill out the same small independent business forms that I do, don't you?"

It took a moment for her vocal chords to function. "Taxes? You want to talk about taxes?"

He did, productively and enlighteningly, until nearly two in the morning. Twice Kat opened her mouth to interject a change of subject, but in the end simply couldn't. How, after all, could a woman possibly ask a man why he'd lost total interest in sending her camellias?

* * *

Exhaustion caught up with her by Friday. She'd fallen asleep on the couch when the phone, most unkindly, jangled at eleven.

"I'm in trouble, Red."

If he'd meant it, she would have jumped. If he'd needed her, she was dying to jump, but the way he rolled "Red" off his tongue lacked any trace of seriousness. Kat couldn't take anymore, not tonight.

"Mick," she said softly, "Don't."

"Don't what?"

"Don't play it like this. If this is your way of letting me down easy by playing it like friends, I'd just rather—"

"I have no idea what you're talking about, but this is no time to dither. I have a crisis situation here."

"Sure, you do."

Aggravation seeped through his voice. "There are thirteen girls downstairs. I was banished to the third floor from the time they all got in pajamas."

"I'm not coming over there," she said firmly.

"I thought they'd go to sleep. They're never going to sleep. You have no idea what my living room looks like. Lord, I just heard a lamp crash."

"Mick—"

"They keep screaming. For God's sake, Red. I can't handle this alone."

It sounded as shaky as a used-car salesman's line, but there was, after all, the thousand to one chance Mick actually had his hands full. Kat pulled on jeans and a blouse and arrived next door within five minutes, only to discover that thirteen girls having a pajama party said it all. She stayed downstairs long enough to share a pop and potato chips and to meet Angie's friends. Then, most reluctantly, she went in search of Mick.

She found him at the top of his third-floor stairs, hunched over with his elbows on his knees, and suddenly the whole situation wasn't as easy to read as she'd assumed. Maybe he'd trumped up a silly excuse to get her over here, but the shadows under his eyes were as dark as hers and the tension in his shoulders was real.

"Could you reason with them?"

"Mick, you don't reason with girls at a pajama party."

"They shriek every time I go downstairs. Even my own daughter."

"Shrieking at pajama parties is the status quo. So is renting horror movies and staying up all night."

"Did you see their faces?"

"They've been experimenting with makeup. That's status quo, too."

"Not for Angie. Angie doesn't like makeup and she can't stand boys, but do you know what they've been talking about nonstop for the past three hours?"

"Boys," Kat said dryly.

"Do you have any idea how much pop thirteen girls can take in?"

"Yes," she said calmly.

"Ten pizzas. Thirteen girls. They're pigs."

"Yes," she said calmly.

"It's no wonder they have to yell. Every appliance is on in the place, TVs, VCR, radios, tape player. Don't try to tell me that's natural."

"Mick, they're having a perfectly wonderful time."

He murmured, "Yeah. I know."

His voice was barely a murmur, but the humor was punctuated by the kneading pressure of his thumbs somewhere in the neighborhood of her left shoulder blade. She remembered sitting on the step below him, but not the precise moment he'd shifted her between the scissor of his legs.

She was either a sucker for a back rub or a sucker for Mick. Probably both. Especially since he hadn't come this close in nearly a week. "You're so tense, so tired, Red. And you think I like those circles under your eyes?"

The stairwell was shadowed and he wasn't making much sense. For a brief time she didn't care. He gently pushed her head down and used his fingertips to give her a scalp rub. She closed her eyes and felt muscle after muscle liquify. His thumbs and palms pummeled and soothed, not a prelude-to-lovemaking kind of back rub but a more intimate kind. He knew her body. He knew where every nerve was strained, every muscle was knotted.

"Talking purely theoretically, you're going to make a rotten stepmother, Kathryn," he murmured absently.

"Hmmm?"

"Not on their terms, just on mine. Your concept of discipline is zip and you're never going to back me up." He sounded amused. "You side with every damn thing they do. You understand every damn thing they do. And I'm telling you right now, Red, I don't want you to change. We'll probably fight, but that's okay. Stay the way you are, and...hey, where're you going?"

Maybe every tendon in her body had turned into noodles, but her weight miraculously held when she stood up. *"Home."* Either his back rub or his "theoretical" discussion of stepmothers had brought on an instant attack of the blues.

"Honey, turn around and look at me."

She didn't. His voice was as smooth as melted butter, and like a fool, she felt dampness coat her lashes. She headed down the stairs. Quickly.

"It's not what you think, Kat. Try to remember we were friends long before we tried to be lovers."

She remembered that for the next week. It didn't help. Mick might want to return their relationship back to friends, but that wasn't the emotion she felt for him and it never would be.

Alone in her house the following Wednesday night, she took a long warm shower guaranteed to relax her. It didn't. Afterward, she paced the house in her towel. She circled her carousel horse, tracked the length of the hall, then stalked upstairs. Pausing by her bedroom window, she saw lightning slash a zigzag of silver against the night sky. She saw...but not really.

Until midday yesterday, she'd clung to the hope that there was an obvious reason for Mick's change in behavior. Although her prescription had run out after seven days, she hadn't been able to schedule the follow-up visit with her doctor until yesterday. Conceivably Mick had deliberately avoided any physical contact until she had the doctor's okay. Last night, though, she'd managed to slip in an "I'm fine" over a tuna noodle casserole dinner with him and the girls, and Mick hadn't blinked an eye. More relevant, lots and lots of hours had passed between last night and tonight.

The hurt was starting to feel as sharp and real as a knife wound.

He cared. Kat couldn't possibly doubt that. He'd pursued her with exhausting single-minded determination. He spent every moment of his free time with her. Kat had always known she wasn't prize stepmom material, but she loved Angie and Noel. The reverse was just as true, and Mick was the one who'd pushed for an even deeper relationship with his daughters.

What mattered even more to Kat was that Mick had changed. Couldn't he see it? Work was no longer his life. He still made a big deal out of every crisis with Noel and Angie but that was nonsense; he was a terrific father—at least he was now that he'd let himself open up and just be with them. He'd just needed someone to tell him that was okay. Someone who could make him laugh, someone he

didn't have to feel on with, someone who accepted him for
the man he was…and wanted to be.

Kat had so fiercely believed she was part of those
changes in Mick. She'd thought he was growing, changing
in ways he wanted to grow and change. She'd thought…
maybe…that he was capturing something with her that really mattered to him.

She'd thought that he loved her.

Kat shoved her shower damp hair back from her scalp.
The ache of loss would tear her apart if she let it. Anger
was the easier emotion to deal with, and she certainly felt
that, too.

Didn't she have a reason? He'd taken her halfway to the
moon and then pitched the mission. He'd made her want,
ravenously, and then shut it off. He'd forced her to talk
about dreadful things, face up to mortifying and embarrassing things, dragged her to that doctor and made the
whole damn thing seem natural between a man and a
woman who loved each other. And then dropped her back
to the status of friends.

Kat would have tried to accept that if it just made sense,
but it didn't. Mick would never deliberately hurt her, would
never leave any woman hanging. He had a mischievous
side, but he was an honest and straightforward man. If he'd
stopped loving her, he would have cut the relationship off
cleanly.

And the only exception that Kat could think of was if
Mick had barreled in something he couldn't be honest
about…couldn't handle…at least not alone.

Heaven knew, Kat understood the dimensions of that
kind of problem, and she had paced halfway to her bedroom
when that particular mental light bulb switched on. The
wattage started at dim and gradually accelerated to illumi-
nating brightness. Damn, she thought.

Abruptly she dropped her towel, shimmied into a robe,

strode into the study and punched the buttons on the telephone on her desk. The phone rang once. Then again and
again. Mick picked it up halfway through the fourth ring.
He'd obviously been asleep, because his voice was groggy
and scratchy.

Hers was belligerent. "I need your help, Larson. I have
a leaky faucet."

There was a brief hesitation. "Now?"

"Now."

"Sweetheart, it's almost midnight."

"The faucet is very leaky."

"We're talking flood?"

"You bet your sweet patooties we're talking flood."

"Okay, honey. I'll be there."

He hung up, and Kat felt her whole body turn shivery.
Would he misunderstand all that drivel? She hoped not.
Mick might have taught her that honest communication was
the key to a relationship...but he'd also taught her that a
light touch worked best when the subject was sticky.

Problems didn't get any stickier than this, and she swiftly
glanced at a clock. It wouldn't take him three minutes to
tug on a pair of jeans. That left her barely enough time to
fix the sash on her robe, take a brush to her hair and race
downstairs to answer his knock.

Thunder growled, close and ominously, as she opened
the back door. Mick stepped into her kitchen wearing a
sweatshirt and jeans and carrying a tool kit. He took one
long look at her and smiled. Slowly. "So...where's the
leak, Red?"

"The upstairs bathroom."

"Ah."

She climbed the stairs ahead of him. He set the tool kit
down on the bathroom floor and surveyed her spotless black
marble sink with a grave expression. "Looks pretty serious."

"I know."

"I'm pretty handy, but I'm afraid this is bad enough for a qualified plumber."

"I was afraid of that."

"You know where the pipes under the sink go?"

"In there."

"In where?"

She motioned vaguely. "In there."

He didn't take the tool kit into her bedroom, just strode in ahead of her and paused, taking in the sleigh bed, the Victorian hatboxes, the bottles of scents on her dresser, the fireplace and stained-glass windows. "Can't see a single pipe," he mentioned.

"You sure?"

"I'm sure. Maybe if you'd turn off that overhead, I could see better."

She turned off the glaring overhead light, which left only the soft-prismed glass lamp burning behind her bed. "Better now?"

He didn't answer the question. His focus honed with hopeless intensity on her short silk robe, her tousled hair, her mouth. Especially her mouth. Lord, was his tongue suddenly dry. "The leaky pipes were fun...but I'm through with that anytime you are. You're obviously on to me, Red."

"Heaven knows why it took me so long, but yes."

"I don't want you scared. I never wanted you scared."

"And that's what these past two weeks have been about, wasn't it?" Gently she closed the bedroom door. "For the first time in my life I could make love—and that was wonderful, Mick, only you knew I'd suddenly realize that was the first time. The first time that mattered." Her fingers unwrapped the sash of her robe. "There's no way on earth I would marry a man I couldn't satisfy in bed. I wouldn't do that to me, and I'd never, never, *never* have done that to you.''

"Honey—"

He stopped talking when she pushed the robe off her right shoulder, then her left. Gravity did the rest; it whooshed to the floor. Mick wasn't seeing anything he hadn't seen before, but the emotion in his eyes was new. Hunger, yearning, desire, need—she'd seen those in him before...but not anxiety. Never before anxiety.

"Given the time to worry about it," she said softly, "I would have built that 'first time' into a test...such a critical test that I'd be tense as a wire—a sure guarantee it would go badly. You knew that, didn't you, Mick? So you made very sure I had no time to worry about it. You told me in a hundred ways over the past two weeks that sex was absolutely no priority for you."

His voice hoarsened, deepened, when he saw her walking toward him. "Sex isn't a priority. Love is, and I mean that from the heart, Kat. We don't have to do this, not tonight, not if you don't—"

She latched her arms around his neck and effectively silenced him with a kiss. Mick was sensitive and perceptive and wonderful, but just this time he was dead wrong. They did have to do this, and there was no way around it being a terribly critical test. Kat had always understood what the stakes might be the first time they consummated their love—she could lose him.

She was physically and emotionally incapable of not being afraid of tonight...but at this precise moment she was less afraid than she could be, might be, probably should be. Mick had walked in the door with a slow smile, but she'd also glimpsed the stark anxiety in his eyes.

Mick was the only man she knew who understood the terribly fragile, mortifyingly private fears in a woman's heart. How could she have failed to realize that he had buried fears of his own? In a few minutes she would undoubtedly remember to be afraid again, but right now she had a man to take care of. With alluring softness, with the power of a woman's soul, she kissed him until his arms swept around her and his hands were clutching her hair.

Still, he tore his mouth free from hers. "Honey, if you're not absolutely sure—"

She pushed. He fell. The sleigh bed had high sloping sides, a feather bed mattress, a dozen pillows. Sprawled, Mick looked as much at home as a lumberjack in a perfumery. Crystal lamplight twinkled on his slow male smile.

"Your whole bedroom's pure woman. No surprise." His thumb rubbed the line of her cheekbone, his gaze never wavering from her face. "I'm getting the feeling that you're in the mood, Red. Like to hell with the tests."

"Larson, I've been waiting thirty-three years. Not for this, but for you. I'm dying and you want to talk?"

"I'm just trying to understand. What happened to the worry? What happened to my Victorian lady of the corsets and cameos? Where are all those inhibitions I know so well?"

His teasing made her smile, but not for long. His pulse was erratic, his heartbeat thudding, and his eyes had the sheen of desire, but the anxiety was still there. Mick didn't want her to know that he'd made his own test out tonight. He was just as afraid as she was. She'd guessed that he was afraid of physically hurting her, and even more of failing her as a lover and a man.

Kat knelt beside him. The only man she would ever love had a problem: a problem so private, so vulnerable, that he assumed he couldn't share it.

Those were the problems that lovers shared best. Mick had taught her that, but if he didn't know it applied to him, he would. Soon. Slower than slow motion she pushed up his sweatshirt and let her palms glide sensually over his warm, bare skin. He eased up to a sitting position only long enough to drag it off, but when he reached for her she shook her head.

"I've worried so much about this," she whispered, "and all for the wrong reasons." Her fingers walked down his ribs to the snap of his jeans. She nudged the snap, then met his eyes as she slid down the zipper. "I built up fear, and for what? We've never failed at anything that mattered, because we've never failed each other. Love's continued to grow—not in spite of, but because of what we've shared together, so how can I be afraid of loving you? I'm not. I'm not even afraid of telling you how desperately and brazenly I want you...."

Her palms slipped inside his waistband. His jeans wanted to stick to him like a jealous woman. Kat wasn't tolerating any rivals, not tonight. She tugged and pulled the denim, well aware that Mick had heard her because slowly his eyes darkened, softened, blurred. He wasn't breathing as well as he had been. His body temperature was rising, and it wasn't anxiety tautening his muscles now.

Kat, though, wasn't through. "I've had dreams about you," she whispered. "All through this heat wave, I've had a recurring dream about you...and the heat...in a storm." She had to get up to pull his jeans off. On the way back, her fingers skimmed against the grain of his hair, over knees, then thighs. When she reached his white cotton underwear, she took a long, wanton look at him. He liked that look. His response was so elemental that she had to continue. "They weren't nice dreams, Mick. They were dark and erotic and wild. I dreamed about making love with you, outside in a storm, with the rain coming down on a hot, windy midnight, and you bare. Just as bare as you are now, and I ache in that dream. Shamelessly. You're so hard and powerful when you move between my thighs and suddenly

you're riding me. The rain keeps coming and your skin is
all hot and wet and slick—''

"I hope you're through talking, Red, because if you
don't cut it out you're going to see a hair-trigger problem
like most boys outgrow by fourteen.''

She heard the end-of-a-tether growl in his voice. She
smiled soothingly…and dropped his briefs off the end of
the bed.

He swore, very low, very softly—maybe softer than
she'd ever heard him swear—and then reached for her.
Somewhere, thunder rumbled. The curtains billowed with
a sudden burst of cool air, but Kat barely noticed. She
found herself abruptly sandwiched between perfume-
scented sheets and Mick—a towering, tense and primitively
male Mick.

She couldn't see a single trace of anxiety. He'd also lost
all interest in talking, and his first kiss singed and sizzled
all the way to her belly. He wreaked further devastation
with the second, and then his tongue claimed hers, sweeping the dark warmth of her mouth, sipping the moisture
from her. He raised himself to cup one pearl-white breast,
rubbing the tip until it swelled, then letting his tongue cool
the surface until it throbbed.

Kat had wanted him to feel so wanted and desired that
he would forget any fears that it wouldn't go well. She'd
forgotten that he was a master of the same game. Lamplight
washed his features golden and hard. He kissed her everywhere, anywhere, until her flesh shimmered and her bones
turned liquid. His hands were magical, his mouth dangerous, and he played on the one fear she hadn't known existed. She was going to die soon, if he didn't take her.

Lord, she loved him.

Outside, lightning lit up the black sky. A giant roar of
thunder made the bedside lamp blink, then grow dark. With
the darkness came rain, but Mick didn't care. Kat was com-

ing apart, for him...with him. She'd come to him in passion before, but never with a need so seeped in love that the two were inseparable.

Her legs twisted around him when he stroked her soft core. The deeper he probed, the more ember-hot her kisses became...and the more satiny moisture he found. He clawed the air on the side of the bed for his jeans.

"No," she whispered fiercely. "We don't need it." She gently bit his shoulder, skimmed her hands down his sides to his hips. "Wouldn't you like a son, Mick?"

Love rushed through him to the beat and spatter of rain.

"I love you," she whispered.

He'd known, but she'd never said it. He couldn't seem to breathe. He couldn't seem to stop his heart from swelling.

And then she whispered, "Come to me."

Kat opened her arms, beckoning. She kissed his face, his throat, his mouth—dozens of impatient kisses—as he shifted over her and wrapped her legs around him. He lifted her hips and it began, the slow snug intrusion, the sensation of being impaled and a part of—irreversibly a part of—the man she loved. Mick didn't move then, didn't dare breathe.

In the darkness he saw her lashes lift and her luminous eyes meet his. Her arms and thighs tightened at the same time. "Don't you dare ask me how good this feels," she murmured.

He didn't have to. He could see. He could feel, and he gave her a fantasy ride of making love in a midnight wind with the rain pouring down, hurling toward ecstasy in a heat wave created solely by two. He gave her pleasure, as she'd only dreamed of it...but she made him love, as he hadn't known was possible.

"I'm back!"

"So I see," Mick murmured humorously. She had stayed

cuddled in his arms for a long, languid and loving half hour. Knowing Kat, he should have known that peacefulness wouldn't last. She'd sprung up with the electric excitement of a new millionairess. The storm was still raging. She'd jumped up to close the windows and then raced downstairs to bring up candles.

Finally she was back where he wanted her, straddling him with her long white limbs, stroking close. The flickering candles illuminated the indefatigably sassy glint in her eyes. Her shoulders had a provocative tilt. Her mouth had a saucy curve. Conceivably, just conceivably, the lady had just discovered that without a doubt she could make love—real love, wonderful, unforgettable love.

Mick had never seen her higher, but he planned to. Over the next sixty years, he had a lot of plans for Kat.

"Am I cutting off your circulation?"

"Only when you squirm." Which, he was well aware, she was doing deliberately. He couldn't seem to stop smiling. He pushed a strand of hair behind her ear.

"Mick?"

"Hmmm?"

"I'm unbearably happy."

"You just think you are. You still have miles to go before you ever catch up with me." Her brow needed a kiss. "The girls are going to think I'm going to marry you. Particularly if I call them at six in the morning for the express purpose of telling them that."

"Good heavens. Was that a proposal?"

He shook his head. "No way. Tonight we'll order some moonlight and maybe a gremlin will pop for camellias. We'll have a little dinner, a little champagne. Then, maybe you'll get a proposal. I'm not promising. You'll just have to worry until then whether my intentions are honorable."

She shifted her legs in a way that made him groan, and

her smile. Honorable intentions were not on her mind. "You liked that idea of a son."

"Our son? Yes, love."

"It'll undoubtedly be a daughter."

"I'm prepared for that. The odds are already against me. One more female couldn't possibly make my life more difficult."

"Mick..." She brushed his eyebrows with the pads of her thumbs, but she was suddenly serious. "From the moment I walked into your backyard, you've made my life terribly difficult. So difficult that I don't know what would have happened to me...if it hadn't been you. Just you. Have you ever tasted despair?"

He said gently, "Oh, sweetheart. I definitely tasted yours."

"I thought it was me and I thought it was hopeless and I'd given up."

He combed both hands through her hair, making a tangled mess, but at least it held her head still. Blue eyes met tobacco brown. Neither even tried to look away. "You'd only given up, honey, because you hadn't been in love before. Not in love the right way. If it's the right way, honesty becomes second nature. If it's the right way, being vulnerable isn't scary because both people are looking to protect each other's needs. And Kat?"

"Hmmm?"

He said softly, "You weren't the only one who needed that lesson. I needed to know—as much as you did—that I could tell you when I was afraid. Afraid as a man. Afraid as a lover."

She kissed him. A reward for owning up that he'd been afraid. She had some work to do with Mick before he really believed he could equally come to her with a need, any need. She'd be there. He knew that now, but he'd know it even better after fifty or sixty years together. She kissed him again. Hard and thoroughly.

"Lord, you're in the mood again," he murmured.

"Yes."

"How much can a man be expected to handle?"

"I don't know about most men." She kissed him again. "I just know about you. There isn't anything you can't handle, Mick. There also isn't anything you haven't. Not where I'm concerned."

"It's past two..."

"Poor baby," she said sympathetically.

"Minute by minute," he said delicately, "you're getting more brazen, more bold, more wanton."

"Yes."

"Your hands are in the cookie jar again, Red. You like trouble."

"Yes."

What could he do? He twisted her around and slowly down, and before her spine reached the sheets her arms were around him.

* * * * *

Don't miss these next exciting
titles from Jennifer Greene:

You Belong To Me, part of
MONTANA MAVERICKS:
WED IN WHITEHORN,
on sale August 2000

Rock Solid, part of BODY & SOUL,
Silhouette Desire #1316, on sale September 2000

Silhouette ROMANCE™

Escape to a place where a kiss is still a kiss...

Feel the breathless connection...

Fall in love as though it were
the very first time...

Experience the power of love!

Come to where favorite authors——such as
Diana Palmer, Stella Bagwell,
Marie Ferrarella and many more——
deliver heart-warming romance and genuine
emotion, time after time after time....

Silhouette Romance——
stories straight from the heart!